Under
the Tequila Sun

by

Sam Saladino

© Copyright 2017
Sam Saladino

Library of Congress Cataloging-in-Publication Data

Names: Saladino, Sam, author.
Title: Under the tequila sun / by Sam Saladino.
Description: Wellesley MA : Branden Books, [2017]
Identifiers: LCCN 2016052671 (print) | LCCN 2016059484
(ebook) | ISBN
   9780828326469 (pbk. : alk. paper) | ISBN 9780828326469 (E-
Book)
Classification: LCC PS3569.A457 U53 2017 (print) | LCC
PS3569.A457 (ebook) |
   DDC 813/.54--dc23
LC record available at https://lccn.loc.gov/2016052671

ISBN 9780828326469 Paperback
ISBN 9780828326476 E-Book

Branden Books
PO Box 812094
Wellesley MA .2482

Book orders:
www.brandenbooks.com
branden@brandenbooks.com
Amazon.com

Dedication

I dedicate this book to:

Debbie, Sammy, and Heather

Disclaimer

There may be persons alive who took part in events similar to those described in this book. It is possible; therefore, that some may be mistaken for characters in this book.

All the characters in *Under the Tequila Sun* are the complete creation of the author, and although fictional, the people are a vehicle to the real world that I have experienced during my life. The exceptions, of course, are those public figures mentioned by name. Events that I drew upon took place while working at a children's home as a residential counselor and supervisor. My crisis intervention and investigative experiences were also vital to the creation of this account. Many facets of this story happened as described; consequently, there is a fine line between fact and fiction.

A Note of Thanks

Patrick Monson and Mary (Tootsie) Saladino Hamburg for their assistance.

"In order to write about life, first you must live it." **Ernest Hemingway**

"Whoever battles with monsters had better see that it does not turn him into a monster." **Fredrick Nietzsche**

"We gain strength, and courage, and confidence by each experience in which we really stop to look fear in the face ... we must do that which we think we cannot." **Eleanor Roosevelt**

"Courage is resistance to fear, mastery of fear, not absence of fear." **Mark Twain**

Chapter 1

In a quaint Chicago suburban neighborhood, Big Jake's index fingers performed a drum roll on the stirring wheel of a Mercedes-Benz sedan as though preparing for an execution. Moon rays illuminated the forty-two-year old man's hollow eyes peeking back and forth between a church and a rectory. Abruptly, he throttled the stirring wheel on seeing an image through the rectory window. Gasping, sweat trickled down his forehead despite the air-conditioning blasting against his face. The image disappeared and he wiped the salty flow from his eyes with an unsteady hand. Taking a deep breath, he held it for a moment before exhaling and then an uncontrollable lip twitching erupted. He rolled down the window, spat on the ground with a scowling expression, and gagged as if a brigade of gnats had flown into his mouth. Regaining control, he covered his mouth with praying hands and gazed at the church's steeple cross. This was not the first time he sat mesmerized in front of this rectory and church. Reaching into the inner pocket of a Giorgio Armani suit jacket, Big Jake pulled out a letter he had written, opened it and eyed each word with contempt: *I am a disgrace. I am a pervert. I like little boys. I do not deserve to live. I've done terrible things throughout my life. If there is a heaven, I will never find it. If there is a hell, I am on my way there now. I confess my sins before I leave this world.*

Big Jake knew the words by heart. This was the seventh time in five years that he went through an identical ritual. After a fiery outburst of swearing and maledictions, tears merged with runny streaks of sweat, causing him to loosen the strangling tie and undo the choke hold button of a tightening shirt. Exasperated, he crushed the paper, put the car into gear and floored the gas pedal. "*I'm not the bad* guy," he yelled at himself. "*Jesus Christ almighty I've failed again.* Next time I'll do it. What the hell's wrong with you? You're *Big Jake. Act like it.*"

In another *Land of Lincoln* city, halfway down the state, Rosetta Meady, a college student, sat in the comfort of her home, listening to music, while stroking the canvas of a new creation. In the painting, Rosetta's own image was amidst munchkins and a wizard who was attempting to guard her against the creeping hand of an ogre. The hand, erupting out of the ground, was reaching for the unaware, innocent image of the girl. Anxious, Rosetta paused, stood up, backed away and cried, "*Enough is enough. The fiend got me in the past. I won't allow it to happen again.*" Sitting back down, eyes focused on the creeping hand, she dabbed the brush in paint and like magic the hand disappeared as the final strokes completed the painting. Beaming, eyes closed and hands clasping together, she nodded and giggled causing her puppy, Leonardo, to paw her leg and whimper. "Okay baby," Rosetta said, picking him up and comforting him on her lap. "Mommy's just happy because I am finally in control. Do you hear me? *I'm in control.* That's one monster out of my life. I didn't think I had it in me to do it. You know baby, there's a time when I wouldn't have got rid of the monster 'cause I felt like a helpless prey unable to defend myself. But I did it. I really did it with my own hand and brush. I refuse to be a victim again. Do you hear me, Leonardo?" In deep thought, looking at the wizard in her painting, made her think of the movie, *The Wizard of Oz*, which was the inspiration for the painting. Rubbing Leonardo's belly, she said, "I should have named you Toto." Then she blurted, "Now I can tell the world the ogre is dead. Yes, yes, it's kind of like Dorothy saying that old wicked hag is dead. Do you get it, Leonardo? I stood up to that monster like I only dreamt of doing all those years ago. I was a terrified kid back then. Now I'm a fighter." Leaning down, she kissed and hugged Leonardo, saying, "And I'm a lover too. Aren't I baby? Yes, yes, you're my sweetie, aren't you? Do you hear that song you little stinker? It's "Jack and Diane." Sing it John Cougar Mellencamp. I love that tune," she said, singing along with the song.

With the moment of joy passing, Rosetta looked about the bedroom, converted into an art studio, reflecting upon what she had just done to the painting, but knew the real ogre's in her life where still out there. "It's time to bury the past," she told herself. Nodding, bold-faced, she scoped all of the accomplishments, hanging and sitting on the floor against the walls, and then eyed a painting that she had done of her baby boy. There were dozens of creations, but when she stood and stepped away, following her movement, were the eyes from the painting of the five-day old child she had given up for adoption. Unable to take another step, she trembled as she turned toward the painting. Creeping to it, she carefully took it off the wall and placed it on another wall in a dark corner of the room. "I'm in control," she told herself. Walking away, she stopped, lost in thought, turned around, grabbed the painting and placed it back where she had got it from. "I'm in control," she assured herself. "I can handle it, but my baby boy you have got to understand I wanted to keep you, but I was very young...." Staring at the baby's image, she stood in a trance and once again she grabbed the painting, took it down, placing it on the wall in the dark corner of the room. "I love you, baby," she mumbled, and continued in thought, "but I can't have you looking at me all of the time because I need to be in control. Don't you understand how my life has been so out of control? That's why we're not together. Your father was an ogre, my dad's a monster too, and you are a beautiful baby, but you have no idea what I had to go through...."

Wanting to regain the moment of joy, she had experienced moments earlier, Rosetta pressed a button to replay the song, "Jack and Diane." Smiling, she looked at the painting she had just completed and pranced about to the music that could be heard in the background. "Can you hear that song baby?" she said to Leonardo. "Yes, I hear you, John Cougar Mellencamp. Baby, he sings about life going on. I feel strong for the first time in my life Leonardo...."

It was a warm September evening and all was not well on the other side of town. Rosetta's best friends and mentors were eying each other with contempt. When their looks intensified, a trigger happy Amy Paradisio, hissed, *"Listen here Mr. Smartass,"* and then shot off a double barrel of insults at her husband Tom. Cringing, Tom uttered a sly remark, followed by a smug smile, which vanished when she snapped right back at him. With perked ears, he flinched, casting stoic eyes, but the way they gleamed she expected him to blow at any second. Refusing to be intimidated, she stood firm, hands clenched and clammy, studying his changing expression. As a smirk erupted, he nodded with a squint, let out a sigh, turned away and walked to the stairway. Once there, he hurried up to their bedroom, let go of the facade, and paced like a caged hyena, but wasn't amused as he grabbed shorts and a tee-shirt hanging from a closet hook.

After slipping into the weathered jogging clothes, Tom rushed down the stairs, passed Amy without a look, and out the front door. Whenever she said, 'Listen here Mr. Smartass,' Tom knew he needed to take a stand or retreat. The last time he stood his ground, an argument escalated, resulting in the first physical clash of their relationship – Amy's claw-like hand reared back to strike, but halted on seeing him puckered-up and egging her on with hand gestures to do it. Infuriated, she flipped him the finger. When his eyes dilated in defiance, she lost control and backed handed him across the face, causing his pucker to deflate and eyes to wince. She was as shocked as he was by the hit and ran sulking to the bedroom. Not wishing a repeat of their last argument was reason enough for Tom to flee.

Although stress at the children's home where they worked at was a factor for their troubled relationship, some of it was anxiety over a below the surface issue, which created ongoing friction and tended to transfer to mundane problems. Even though he didn't want to admit it, Tom knew deep down what Amy's anger was all about. Amy didn't enjoy arguing and tearing up every time Tom squirmed when she brought up her desired needs. In addition, she thought Tom needed to grow up and take responsibility for his behavior, which she saw as self-centered. With him gone, she stared out the window, mumbling and nail biting, and then headed to the kitchen where she pulled out a baking pan. Leaving the way he did set her fingers tapping as if typing poison pen thoughts.

While Amy connived, Tom, who was accustomed to jogging five miles a day to keep in shape and to ease his anxiety, strayed from his normal route. Fired up, replaying the argument in his mind, he grumbled, as running strides increased, head pounded and blood pressure climbed. It was dark out as he raced through neighborhood after neighborhood. Trying to gain control of his anger, he pushed himself hard, but was bombarded by thoughts and grabbed hold of an old kids saying – 'sticks and stones may break my bones but words will never hurt me.' Sometimes words did hurt he reasoned, pondering over each derisive words that Amy had jabbed him with.

"So she thinks I'm a dumbass," he told himself. "An idiotic one even. Guess I shouldn't think about it. All I get is pissed off. Just keep your butt moving ... She says we're drifting apart. I need to feel some real emotions from her. I mean feelings for me. She's so cold. I feel like I've been shut out from her world. Why? What's happened to us?"

While Tom stormed ahead, Amy smiled as she sprinkled mint, the final ingredient, into a bowl and turned the handheld beater on. Once finished, she placed it into the oven, and pranced around jabbering, "Thank you, thank you, thank you. A chocolate yummy, yummy, for Brenda and me." With cell phone in hand, Amy's fingers sprang into action, texting her good friend Brenda:

Hey there. It's almost that time. I just stuck my chocolate ecstasy into the oven. Tom took off for a jog. The way he left, I don't expect him back for an hour or two. He was a little teed off. He can be such an ass. He love's chocolate more than any man I know. They say it's a sign of being sexually frustrated. And if he isn't, he's going to be. Why don't you come over early? We can talk while he's out. Oh, I added mint to the ecstasy. Tom hates mint. Ha, ha. See you soon.

Amy

Well into his jog, Tom slowed down to a trot. "Got to be three miles from the house by now," he thought. "This isn't the best neighborhood I've been in. What's that I hear?" he asked himself, seeing a front porch light on up ahead. "Sounds like laughter. It looks like a group of people carrying on. I can't tell how old they are. Kind of looks like teens. Considering the neighborhood, it could be a gang. Keep your distance."

Crossing to the other side of the street didn't help Tom as the laughter got louder, but he tried putting it out of his mind, fearing they were making fun of him. Then someone waved with their middle finger. "For Christ sakes," he hissed. "Is he giving me the finger?" he asked himself. "Don't look. Don't look. He's going to set you off. He better not say anything. Just keep running."

"Dumbass jock!" a male shouted out, followed by hysterical laughter by the group.

"*Dumbass my butt,*" Tom blurted, igniting a fuse, causing his head to burst like an overinflated helium balloon. Without thought, blasting towards the porch, he saw smiling faces become fretful, laughter wavering and cocky eyes bugged-out in fright. One person panicked and ran inside. With emotions set free, Tom followed him into the house and dashed down a hall in pursuit. He was only feet away from grabbing him when the person escaped into a room, slamming the door in Tom's face. Tom, unsure of what to do, stood trembling. "What the hell are you doing?" he scolded himself. "Get your butt out of here. This is *insane.*" He turned about, crept toward the group of big-eyed, freaked-out teens and gazed at them as sweat trickled down his face. "Want to make something of it?" he snapped.

"No," they pleaded, heads shook and bodies fluttered.

After a couple more seconds of evil eyeing the group, he sped off in a daze. "What did you just do?" he asked himself. "Get control of yourself. This wasn't some out of control kid at the children's home you were dealing with. What the hell were you going to do if you caught him? Are you out of your mind? You're acting like a *dumbass. Holy shit.* Maybe Amy is right? Think of something else. Yeah, like how you could have got your ass

10

whipped running into a group of misfits like that. Get away from here. Calm down. Take that busy street up ahead. Think of something pleasant ... You're almost there. Yeah, great. This is better – lights, traffic, and spectators. I feel like I'm under a spotlight. Sort of out of place, but it's kind of a neat feeling. Good thing I'm in shape but wish I was in better shape with so many eyes on me. There's a cute chick up ahead? I think she's smiling at me. Smile back. There you go. That was pleasant. Check out that car with the hot looking babes. One of them is waving. Is she waving at me? What is she yelling?"

"Nice ass baby," a female shouted.

Looking at the girls, he smiled and thought the ass remark sounded very different than the one from the kid he had chased. When they whistled at him, he felt like his head was on a cloud. Unexpectedly, he stumbled out of the cloud, plummeting into a crash landing.

"*Aw shit. Damn it,*" he moaned, falling forward, face saved by quick hands that cushioned the fall and sprang him back up. "*Damn rock,*" he raved in pain.

He kept running like nothing had happened but turned down the first side street he came to. Embarrassed, he imagined that the entire world had just witnessed his fall. There was no way he was returning to center stage to make a fool of himself again. All he needed was for someone to make a wisecrack. Stopping to check out the damage, he sat on a curbside and was relieved that no one was around as he rubbed his scraped and aching knees. He chuckled in pain, collapsed on the lawn, closed his eyes and let his mind wander. Tripping on the rock rattled his senses. Rock equated with stone and he started thinking of that sticks and stones saying again.

"I don't know if I ever believed in such childish wisdom," he told himself, "but that was a long time ago. Kids were pretty cruel to each other back then. Some goofballs thought it was cool to cuss. I didn't. Sure I'm not a kid anymore, but I don't cuss or swear like that constipated shit-faced turd in the stall next to me at the Red Lion last week. Man oh man, what a drunken whiner he was. Yet when teed-off or in pain four-letter words just shoot out. Darn just doesn't cut it after falling on your face. Jesus, I felt like such an idiot falling. And those girls saw it. Damn that pisses me off. Then there's the tongue lashing I took from Amy. I still can't believe I walked away from her. By God, shit and damn has its place. Sure darn and heck's my choice in front of a preacher, but I haven't seen one in ages unless you count a co-worker preaching to me that I needed to become a born again Christian. What exactly does that mean anyway? Holy shit. What to do? I'm not all that anxious to get home. Lately, every little thing becomes a big deal between us. We'll bark and growl with an occasional temper tantrum, but I've never touched her in anger. She's only slapped me once. A onetime great relationship sure has turned pissy. I guess it's kind of like grabbing a bottle of booze for comfort; you take a swig and discover someone filled it with urine. If that doesn't open your eyes and cause you to gag, nothing will. Well, that's the way things have been going – you try to reason with her only to become the urinal for her pissy mood ..."

While Tom's mind churned away, Amy went to Tom's desk, sat down and called her mom. "Mom how are you doing? ... Well, I've been better. Nothing seems to be going right. I don't think Tom will ever grow up. You know what's been on my mind for a long, long time... I know, I know. Sometimes I think nothing will change. But it's going to have to ..." As she conversed, eyes focused on a computer printout sitting on the desk, which she began reading, causing her to lose concentration and to stand up seething. "Mom, I'm going to have to go now. Something else has come up right now. My friend Brenda is on her way over too, so I need to get ready. Yes, yes. I'll talk to you next week. I'm fine. Okay. Goodbye. I love you too." With the print out in hand, Amy paced and continued reading the three pages:

When she walked in the house, I eyed her up and down; noticing how the tight knit top showed an outline of what turned me on. My wife smiled at our friend and had her sit down next to her. I got up, went to the kitchen, and then returned with our guest's favorite drink, a Singapore Sling..."

"*He wanted me to read this*," Amy hissed, fidgeting with her golden brown shoulder length hair, and then thought, "that's why he left it out. I just know he wanted me to read it. This is the way he gets back at me. I can only imagine who the girl in the tight knit top is ..."

Not having moved, still lying on the ground, Tom continued to reflect, "This month's been the worst. I should get up, but I ache. Oh yeah. Just try to relax. No one's around. It's an empty lot and our friend, Brenda, is probably over at the house by now visiting. So there's no rush. Try thinking of something pleasant. It's easier said than done. Let's see, there was that weird book I just read. For having a degree in history and master's in lit, you sure read some of the craziest shit. Oh well, just chalk it up to your work at the children's home. Sometimes you go that extra mile for a funny, crazy kid like Tommy Wizel. He was just diagnosed as bipolar and told me I should read this book of his because I seemed depressed. I don't know why he thought I was depressed, but you did the right thing taking it. It put a smile on his face. It was a good way to connect with him. But when I saw the title, I laughed thinking it was a joke. Then I noticed who published it. You just notice things like that when you're struggling to get your first novel published. It was a subsidy publisher. I just can't afford to pay someone to publish my book right now. Amy would kill me if I did. But like I said, I laughed. I mean really– '*The Mumble Jumble Schizophrenic Chronicles*' by Professor Frantic. I took the book and I can't believe I actually got into it. Sure the Professor doesn't have a P.H.D., but what he brings to the table is his understanding of insanity. He admits to being an honest to goodness, bonafide schizoid. If that isn't credential enough, I don't know what the hell is? You got to love him. There is actually some sanity in his insanity. The book is a confusion of mumble jumble at times, but I really think I learned something. I mean right now my world bites, but since reading the book, he gave me hope that this roller coaster ride with Amy will all come together. At least he ended his masterpiece with kind of an optimistic note: 'There is hope. There is always hope. I hope.'"

Was there hope? Or was it seven years down the drain? They had been married for five years, but with living and going together it was seven years. Stretching out and reflecting, Tom asked himself, "Is it possible that the seven-year itch is creeping up on us? I don't know what to think. Where do we go from here?"

As Tom continued psychoanalyzing their relationship, Amy was at home entertaining Brenda, a co-worker friend, who was invited over for a drink, music, and snacks. Being a Saturday evening, the work week over, Brenda, who was single and not in a relationship enjoyed Amy and Tom's company. In fact, Amy and Brenda did a lot together with and without Tom. Although Amy was Brenda's supervisor at the children's home, where the three of them worked together, Amy considered her an equal and never came across as a superior while at work. As they curled up on each side of the sofa, beer in hand, enjoying the music and laughing, Brenda reached over to a table and turned the music down.

"Alright," Brenda said, "what's going on between you and Tom now?"

"Just the usual B.S.," Amy replied. "I spent the entire morning cleaning and he was on the computer the whole time. I even said, boy it would be nice to have some help. And do you know what he said?"

"What?" Brenda said, smiling.

"I got all the garbage together last night and took it out to the street. You know how long that took him? *Oh.* He's going to mow the lawn this weekend. I cook, clean, pick up after him ... He really pissed me off and I let him have it. Then he said he would help out later by going to the store to get a brownie mix so I could make brownies. That's when I called him a smartass. He actually held his tongue and took off jogging. I wanted to kick him in the butt."

"You know what I think, don't you?"

"I know, lighten up. It's just that he acts like an idiot sometimes. I don't think he'll ever grow up. He works out and writes all the time. And he really pushes my button with some of the shit he writes about us. I didn't ask to be in his book."

"He shows you what he's writing about?"

"Shows me? *He drives me insane.* Does this sentence sound okay, how do you spell this or that or do I need a semi-colon here. But that really isn't what bothers me. It's when he writes about our arguments and he has me come across as a royal bitch. Then there are bizarre things he'll write that just tee me off."

"Like what?" Brenda said intrigued.

"Don't say anything," Amy said getting up. "Okay?"

"My lips are sealed."

Amy returned with a page from his manuscript. "Take a look at this crap."

Brenda's eyes lit up as she read. "Spicy," she said. "Who is this character? Who's he talking about? A Singapore Sling is one of my favorite drinks. He's not talking about me is he?"

"*It's Tom,*" she hissed. "I don't think so, but *I'd* like to know who he's talking about too. He'll laugh and say he's just being creative. That's just the half of it. You know how I want to have kids …"

Still lying back, gazing at the sky, Tom continued thinking: "Maybe working side by side has poisoned our relationship. I don't know. I don't know much anymore. I guess our real problems started at Prism – working as foster parents with messed up kids. That took its toll on us. Rosetta was worth it, though. She made the whole nightmare worth it. Yeah, sweet Rosetta. She knows Amy and me are having problems. Now at the children's home, I think the stress is tearing our marriage apart. We're both residential counselors and supervisors, but we can't counsel ourselves to solve our own damn problems. Tomorrow we're having a get-together over at our house. It's the end of summer celebration. Being a holiday weekend is as good of an excuse as any to raise a little hell. People at work love to party. It doesn't feel like fall is almost here with the way I'm sweating. We've got to at least act as if everything is peachy between us tomorrow night. Maybe tomorrow we can start the day off with a better attitude and commit to solving our problems. Let's see? Should be close to a dozen coming over. I imagine we'll get pretty loaded. Guess I had better get up." Sitting up, Tom's knees were sore, but he was ready to jog the rest of the way home. He took a deep breath and pushed his aching body up.

"Damn it! Shit almighty!" he yelled, hobbling around as his leg cramped up. Limping on one leg, he tried stretching, but all he got was more pain. Then he rubbed his thigh for a minute and took a step as if fearing to step on a landmine. Once the leg felt better, he started a light jog, taking his time and trying to block out the pain. He smiled realizing Amy and he had talked about a ski trip to Colorado in December. They loved to ski. The last time his leg cramped up like this was last year when they went skiing. Shaking his head in thought, his phone rang causing him to slow down as he answered it.

"Hello," he said.

"Tom. How are you guys doing?" Rosetta asked with her dog, Leonardo, on her lap.

"I was just thinking about you. I'm out jogging right now. Just getting over a leg cramp. Amy's at home. But how are you doing? What's it been a month since we saw you for your birthday?"

"Yeah, too long, but I'm doing great. Can you believe I've started my last year in school? I'm almost a college graduate. I just wanted to remind you guys to come to my art exhibit tomorrow."

"Of course we will. We were just talking about it yesterday. It's on our calendar..."

While listening, she opened up an old letter, and said, "A surprise guest will be at the exhibit."

"Who's that?"

"Think back a few years. Someone you worked with."

"I don't know. My mind's kind of foggy tonight."

"How about this," she said. "You handed me a letter on my eighteenth birthday from this person. You would know if I read it, but I can't. It was personal..." As she talked, she looked at the letter in her hand:

Dear Rosetta,

You will finally get to drive that car you loved so much. You don't know how much I regretted driving you away from your home that insane night. I was a different person then and yet I knew that was not who I wanted to be. The whole situation ate away at me and that's why I made the choice to help you escape. I am just sorry I put you through that hell. I should have sent Da Chang away rather than giving you a plan on how to escape him. I was gutless because of that maniac Big Jake – you know the guy who killed Gomez. He had me in a stranglehold and I didn't know how to get out of it. It doesn't matter. It's no excuse. I can never repay you for what you went through, but this is my attempt to try. It will not compensate, it will not let me off the hook but please accept it with my sincere apology for my past mistakes. I will be in touch with Tom and Amy to see how you are doing. I've included my cell number if you need or wish to talk. Do not hesitate to ask for help in the future … The house, the car and the bank account I have given you is not really a gift as you have earned everything with all the pain you have gone through. I am just sorry that I had anything to do with it. Phone: 800-222-0123.

Happy Birthday!

Andre and Windy

" … I give up. I don't remember giving you a letter," he told her. "So who's coming?"

"Well then it'll be a surprise," she said, giggling.

"*Be that way.*"

"I will. We'll see you guys tomorrow …"

"It's great that Rosetta is doing well," he thought. "The hell she went through makes my marriage problem seem minor. To think she was our foster daughter when we worked at Prism. I guess we were actually house parents, but our working title was specialized foster parents. I really felt for her with the pain she suffered at the hands of her dad. Then there was the terror Gomez put her though and that whole nightmare of her giving birth to his son and giving him up for adoption. Those were totally insane days. What's it been now? A little over three years ago, I guess. She's a survivor. It's hard to believe she's twenty-one. I can't believe I'll be thirty this year." Jogging again, he continued in thought, "Is your life supposed to fall apart when you turn thirty? It's a lot easier to see someone else's mistakes and to tell them what they should do than to see your own mistakes and to know what to do. For now, the do is to get home. My leg's feeling better so I better get my butt moving. I'm going to try to go home with a positive attitude. I guess reminded about Rosetta's personal hell makes me want to try harder. She looks up to us and we're acting like nitwits. Yeah, Rosetta is a reality check … Now get your butt moving."

Upon arriving at the house, Tom saw Brenda's car in the drive. Hesitating at the front door, he wondered what Amy had told their friend and co-worker. He was sure she told her they had been arguing. Gripping the key, he took a deep breath, stuck it in the lock, opened the door and walked in. Amy and Brenda were laughing and carrying on. Each held a can of beer and the music was blaring. Looking up, Brenda smiled at Tom and Amy smirked.

"Hey, Brenda," he said, smiling, talking above the music.

"How's it going, Tom?" Brenda responded. "Get a good run in?"

"Definitely, but my leg has been cramping giving me a lot of pain. I need to soak in the tub."

Amy said, "Should I put you out of your misery like a lame horse? And don't use all the hot water."

"Aren't you the humanitarian," Brenda said to Amy with a half-smile.

Tom frowned. "Now I wouldn't use all your precious hot water would I?"

"It depends," said Amy, his twenty-six-year-old wife. "You still in a *pissy* mood?"

Tom swallowed hard, thinking before he replied. "I ran it out of me."

"Glad to hear it."

"Oh, by the way, Rosetta called while I was running and reminded us about the art exhibition tomorrow. I told her we would be there. That okay?"

"Of course, we already planned on it."

"Great. I'll save you some hot water."

Hobbling up the stairs, he paused at the top trying to listen to the voices below. With the music blasting, he couldn't make anything out. He wondered what they were saying, but assumed they were talking about him. Ears perking, he thought he heard the word Tom, but gave up out of frustration. Going into the bathroom, he squeezed the faucet handle and the water stormed out into the tub while he kicked the door shut, which caused a radiating leg pain. After one foot dove into the hot water, he flinched remembering why he preferred taking a shower. Inching downward, he splashed a little water on himself trying to adjust to the temperature before taking the final plunge. Once engulfed in the soothing water, he relaxed and fell asleep.

The next morning, Amy and Tom entered the art gallery. Rosetta gleamed, hurrying to them and gave both a big hug.

"We're proud of you," Amy said.

"You bet we are," Tom added.

"Come on over and look at all my painting," Rosetta said excitedly.

There were a handful of people wandering and admiring the paintings. Amazed by her ability, Tom studied all the works she had created, focusing on a painting she did when she lived with them.

"I remember this one," he said with enthusiasm.

"Really," Rosetta said, tossing her long, silky, dark hair back and smiling. "If I remember right, you wanted to use it for a book cover if you ever wrote one. So are you ready to use it?"

"I wish. So far all I've gotten is rejection slips."

Casting sympathetic, large crystal blue eyes at him, she replied, "Don't ever give up on it. Besides, you took my advice and called it *Child of Chaos*. With a title like that, someone's going to publish it. Right?"

"I guess," Tom said sliding his fingers through his dark wavy locks.

"He's become obsessed with writing," Amy interjected. "Writing and working out. Enough of him. Oh, look at this painting. I love it. What a beautiful fairytale painting. It has a magical effect to it. Like out of the *Wizard of Oz*. It's even got you in it. I just love it. In fact," she said, picking it up. "I'm buying it."

"You don't have to," she said. "You can have it. In fact, this is the painting I took a stand on determined not to let the past dictate my life. This is the only painting I have ever done with my image in it. Originally, I had the hand of an ogre in it trying to grab me. I fought back and got rid of the hand. There was a time when I couldn't fight back. You know what I'm talking about. And I think I might have told you about this painting before."

"I do remember you telling me about it. You told me you felt liberated. I am very proud of you. It is definitely settled – I'm buying it. It's settled," Amy insisted.

"And I'm buying my book cover painting," Tom said, "whether it ever gets published or not. But I'm proud of you too. You have come a long way. The bad guys better watch out if you become a cop."

"I love you guys," she said, glancing out the window and then smiling. "You won't believe who's coming here today."

"Oh yeah," said Amy, "who's that?"

"Must be that surprise guest," Tom beamed.

"Turn around and see for yourself," she responded.

Walking up the front steps were Andre and Windy. It had been over three years since they left Springfield, Illinois and moved to California. They had fled town in a hurry and had given Rosetta their fully paid off house and sports car. "It was bizarre," Tom thought, "but wonderful what they did for her. I guess I'll never know why they did it, but all that matters is that they did it. Poor Rosetta finally got a chance to turn her wretched life around. I never did understand where Andre got all his money. It definitely wasn't being my supervisor at the group home we worked at together. I just know them leaving town had something to do with that guy who owns the strip joint in town. I think his name was Big Jack or Jake. Yeah, that's right it was Big Jake I think and he put a bullet in Gomez's chest after Rosetta gave birth to their son. Sure Gomez was a sick kid and tormented the hell out of her, but he didn't need to leave this world like that ... And then there's Andre's wife Windy. She's a real looker. A natural blond I believe. Rumor has it that she had been a stripper. But what do I know? Rosetta's giving each of them a hug. It's my turn to greet them. I think a firm handshake will do."

"Andre," Tom said, gripping his hand and patting his shoulder.

"Great seeing you guys," Andre carried on.

Amy, Windy and all of them shook hands and gave small hugs.

"Aren't you proud of her?" Andre nodded, looking at all of the paintings. "How many can I take back on the plane with me? What a talent. *I am impressed.*"

"She's my favorite artist," Windy interjected.

"Knock it off guys," Rosetta said blushing.

"It's amazing," Tom thought. "The five of us here together after all these years. The last time we were all together wasn't so pleasant. Oh yeah, what a night. Rosetta had given birth out in the woods because of Gomez's crazy imagined Indian ceremony he forced on her. What a horrid night. I can still see the nooses around Rosetta's and Gomez's necks. We stopped Gomez from carrying out his hanging insanity, but we just couldn't keep him from getting blown away by Big Jake ..."

With a gasp, Rosetta stared off into the distance. She trembled while the others glanced in the same direction out the window looking at a face pressed against it, which rapidly vanished. Rosetta continued to shake, staring out the window. Amy grabbed Rosetta's arm and tried to comfort her.

"*Oh God,*" Rosetta screeched.

"What's wrong?" Tom said. "You look like you just saw a ghost."

"Worse," she raved. "*My dad.*"

"But he's in jail," Tom insisted.

"I don't know," Rosetta pleaded. "He's supposed to be. I must be hallucinating. Didn't you see him?"

"Well," Tom said quizzically. "I saw a face looking in for a split second."

"*Andre*," Rosetta cried. "You saw him didn't you?"

"I saw someone that kind of looked familiar," Andre fretted. "I guess it could have been your dad. It's been a long time since I saw him."

"Definitely someone was looking in," Windy added. "The face looked distorted against the glass."

Grabbing Rosetta's arm, Amy said, "It's okay. It wasn't him. With the distortion you just imagined it."

"Could he be out of jail?" Rosetta said swallowing hard, teetering. "Please, someone go out and see."

Tom looked at Andre. They nodded at one another, dashed to and out the door, looking for the mysterious man who was nowhere in sight. Checking around each side of the building turned up no one. On returning, entering through the front door, Tom shrugged his shoulders and Andre flipped his hands up.

As they walked to the group, Tom could see the terror in Rosetta's eyes. All knew what Rosetta was dealing with and Tom squinted drifting into thought, "I have to wonder about Andre's comment about having not seen him in a long time. When would he have ever seen Rosetta's dad? It was Amy and me who took her to court to testify against him. Andre was never involved. I guess it all goes back to why Andre had such a passionate desire to help Rosetta? All that matters right now is whether that was her dad or not? Or is she still so terrified that she can't rid herself of the nightmares of him that we dealt with when she lived with us? Maybe the nightmares never stop? Maybe every stranger resembles her dad? Everything was going so well. We need to calm her down. We've got to. This is her day."

"Rosetta," Amy said, "on Monday we'll find out if your dad's still in jail. Everything will be okay. Believe me. It wasn't him."

"I guess," she said flustered.

"It'll be alright," Tom assured. "We'll find out when he's going to get out."

"Come on, let's celebrate your exhibit," Andre insisted. "We're just here for the weekend. It's been close to a year since we've been able to get away to come see you. Let's see a smile. Why don't you tell me about this painting? It looks like something that should be in the Sistine Chapel in the Vatican."

"That is interesting," Windy added. "Heaven and Hell in one painting."

"Let me guess," Tom said pondering. "Yeah, I see a baby kicking away from the Hellish scene you've created trying to reach Heaven's gate. He's saying, *hell no.* I'm not going down there. So, am I right? "

"I don't know," she responded with a smile.

"No," Amy asserted, "I see an angel being cast out of Heaven into Hell."

"You're both wrong," Andre insisted, causing Rosetta to giggle. "What we have here is a baby caught in a quandary trying to choose between Heaven and Hell. Don't you see? Look into his eyes. The *pain.* The *desperation.* He's trapped not knowing right from wrong."

Rosetta's face exploded with a grin and she said, "And you Windy, what do you see?"

"Of course they're all wrong," Windy responded. "What we have is a baby representing mankind who is obviously in Purgatory waiting to know his fate."

"So tell us," Tom insisted. "Who's right?"

"You're all right," Rosetta said. "It is what you see it to be. Nothing is black and white. I painted it after the adoption of my baby was finalized. That's what was on my mind then. I guess it still is. I guess you never forget. Remember the last time we were all together. That is the baby and all of us. Gomez was on the ground bleeding to death. We all gathered around him. I held the baby in my arms ... You know he turned four recently."

"Four," Tom said, amazed. "I can't believe it's been that long."

"I always wonder how he's doing. Can't you see it in all of my paintings – the mystery, the pain, the search for the unreachable?"

"When I look at all your paintings," Tom reflected, "I see a brave new world in the making. You're Aldous Huxley with a paint brush."

"You're on to something Tom," Andre added. "But I see an unleashed Nietzsche in that paint brush."

"I hope you guys know," Rosetta said, smile blossoming, "that I don't have a clue about what you're talking about. I mean, I remember reading Huxley's *Brave New World* for a class once, but – you got me."

"What it all comes down to," Amy added, "you're just a damn good artist."

"Amen to that," from Andre. "It's hard to believe with all your artistic talent that you're majoring in both art and criminal justice."

"I learned a lot on the streets you know. Especially about who needs to be taken off of them. Besides, it's hard to earn a living as an artist I've been told. It doesn't hurt to have a backup plan now, does it?"

"You're a very smart girl," Andre said. "You are capable of doing a lot of things. But I just know you'll make it as an artist."

"You guys are all just great," Rosetta said. "I don't know how to thank you. But this I do know. If it wasn't for all of you I could still be going through a living hell with no future ahead of me. You know I was at the bottom of the barrel. I'm lucky to be alive. Just maybe I can help someone someday. Art is my life, but there could be another calling. I'm a fighter and my head's together the best it's ever been. Yeah, I still have issues, but who doesn't …"

Rosetta's exhibition went well, ending late in the afternoon, giving the group time for dinner together and enough time for Tom and Amy to prepare for their company that evening.

Chapter 2

Everyone that worked at the Springfield Children's Home loved to unwind after a week of dealing with delinquents and emotionally disturbed residents that the home provided for. Sometimes it was difficult to distinguish between the groupings, as some of the kid's motivation for their behaviors factored into the equation. Since Tom and Amy owned their own house, as the majority of the young co-workers lived in apartments, it was routine for them to host a party for their friends. There was a time when Tom and Amy refrained from drinking any type of alcohol, but with years passing and the memory of a drinking binge that almost destroyed their marriage fading away; weekend boozing crept back into their lives. For the staff dealing with the restless juveniles whose nature was to act out, a pounding headache resulted for most by the end of the work week. Being that it was a three-day holiday weekend, it was a perfect time for Tom and Amy to host a party. As the guest arrived, they shed their inhabitations once through the festive doorway. Chatter and laughter greeted them and music, alcohol and the scent of a lit joint was the green light for all to chill out.

Word had spread around at the home about the party, and a dozen guests came and went throughout the evening. Marty Lain, a co-worker, and close friend arrived with his fiancée, Pattie Harris. Burt Crebo, a former co-worker, showed up half out of his mind, having started celebrating at the bars prior to arriving. Burt continued binge drinking, pranced about, slurring words and stomping on people's feet, but everyone was happy to see him as he had left the children's home for another job over six months earlier. There was only one bathroom in the house and that was upstairs. Standing, Burt announced that he needed to use the commode and carried his brewery scented body with him. Moving up the stairway, Burt made it to the top and then let out a big moan of relief that caught everyone's attention with all eyes looking up at the open stairway. Tom's jaw dropped, seeing Burt's fly open, as urine trickling down the stairs, spraying the carpet like a feline marking its territory. People laughed, but Tom stared with blood rushing to his face.

"*Come on Burt*," Tom yelled, "use the bathroom for God's sake."

Burt smiled and blurted, "I am." Closing his eyes, the urine exploded out like a fire hose for two minutes.

"*Oh shit*," Tom said as the rest laughed encouraging Burt's behavior. "For Christ sake, he's making the stairway a commode," Tom grumbled drowned out by laughter. "Oh God," he thought, "I'm going to have to clean it up."

Teetering, Tom looked at Amy who smiled, head shaking as Burt staggered down the stairway and plopped down on the sofa. With a long frowning face, Tom left the party to gather towels. Returning, he gagged, trying to soak up the pee, then fled to the basement and dumped the soaked towels into the washer. The evening of partying continued, but the lingering stench continued to aggravate Tom while the others ignored it.

As the evening wore into the morning hours, all but Burt had left. Tranquilized by the alcohol, the clock chimed at 5:00 AM and the last of the fireplace flames faded into ash. With only a dim light on and the music off, Tom stretched out on the sofa fighting to keep his eyes open. Across from him, Amy and Burt sat on a sofa with a coffee table separating them. Eyes closing did not keep Tom from listening, as for some time he had become suspicious of Burt's complimentary intentions. He had even read Tom's unpublished novel giving it great praise, comparing it to a recent best seller. Tom hadn't read the book but soon did after Burt's comment. Before long, Tom's ears perked on hearing a whispering voice.

"I want to go to bed with you," Burt said.

As Amy giggled, Tom's blood pressure erupted. With eyes cracking and ears amplifying, he listened for a response but heard none. Both looked at Tom whose impulse was to spring up in rage but controlled the urge pushing his tired body up into a seated position.

"Hey," Tom mumbled, gawking at them. "I'm really beat. I need to get to bed."

There was total silence as Tom stretched with Burt and Amy staring and smiling at him.

Standing, Tom said, "It's bedtime."

"Well, I better go then," Burt said.

"You're not driving," Amy insisted.

"Oh, no, no," he babbled. "I'm okay."

"*No*," she said. "You can sleep in our spare bedroom."

"Alright then," Burt said. "I'll just sleep here. Right here on the sofa."

"I don't believe it," Tom told himself, wondering if he should confront them. While he and Amy walked up the stairs to their bedroom, Burt crashed out on the sofa. With each step taken upward, the stench below caused him to grumble Burt's name and to swear in an undertone.

After going to bed, Amy curled up and passed out. Tom tossed and turned, glancing back and forth between Amy and the window. He couldn't get the words, 'I want to go to bed with you,' out of his mind. Like a scratched 'Ground Hogs Day' DVD, he replayed the words. Then he remembered Amy smiling when he looked at them. "I should have waited," he told himself. "I don't know what would have happened, but at least I would maybe know something. Christ almighty," he scolded himself. "What was Amy's reaction to that disgusting whisper? She was smiling at me when I opened my eyes. *Damn it anyhow.* Is she going down to him after I fall asleep?" Agonizing thoughts went on for hours when a loud noise came from below. Tom looked at Amy who was sound asleep. A door shut and Tom slid out of bed and froze listening. A moment later, a car engine started and he looked out the window to see Burt backing out of the drive. Creeping down the stairs, trying to avoid stepping on the urine wet carpet; he imagined what Burt had knocked over, praying that it wasn't their antique family heirloom lamp. On entering the living room, he saw the lamp intact but did find a bottle on the floor oozing out beer. After cleaning up the mess, he crept upstairs and passed out on contact with the bed.

Late the next afternoon when Tom woke up to an empty bed, he rolled off of it, crawled to the window, pulled himself up and saw that Amy's car was gone. Lying back down, he replayed the previous evening through his mind and debated a course of action – confront Amy or lay back and observe. Once Amy returned, she began making dinner. In slow motion, Tom made it to the kitchen still uncertain of what to say or what to do.

"Finally up," Amy said with a smirk. "You hungry?"

"Yeah," he replied, holding back the urge to confront her.

"You got really loaded last night."

"You did too." Trying to hold back, he said, "I couldn't sleep."

"Why's that?"

Those words ignited him and he blasted out, "*What the hell's going on with Burt?*"

"What do you mean?"

"You know what I mean," he growled.

"No, I don't."

"What did he say to you last night right before I got up to go to bed?"

"Heck if I know. *What's your problem?*"

"I don't know. Never mind," he said, flustered.

"*Good,*" she snapped, "cause I don't like your tone."

With a flare in his eyes, Tom said, "He said, '*I want to go to bed with you.*'"

"What?" she said wide-eyed. "You're crazy."

"*I heard it.*"

"You were drunk. He was drunk out of his mind. Now that you mention it – I do seem to remember him saying something like I need to or I want to go to bed. Yeah, I think it was right before you got up."

Looking down, hands on temples, unsure of himself, he said, "I don't know. Are you sure?"

"Yes, I'm sure! Just knock the crap off. So are you hungry or not?"

"No," he said, "I need to take a shower."

"Take your shower and eat when you want."

Tom walked away and Amy sat down to eat.

It was a Monday afternoon when Rosetta entered the college art studio carrying a new painting. The latest class assignment was to make a creation that encompassed conflict. On this day, Rosetta was scheduled to present a work of art for a class discussion. Taking the two by three foot canvas out of a cloth bag, she set it up on an easel for the class to view. The painting revisited Rosetta's wizard theme, but with the conflict twist required, which is exactly what she had boldly taken out of the last wizard themed work. As the class stood around examining the painting, Rosetta nibbled on a fingernail for a moment until the professor made a comment.

"Yes indeed Rosetta," said Professor Sanchez. "You never seize to amaze me. Alright, class, comments."

A young man said, "It kind of reminds me of "*The Wizard of Oz*." However, the girl who looks like Rosetta," the student said, smiling at Rosetta, "is showing a strength that Dorothy didn't have in the movie. I mean my gosh look at how the girl is holding up her fist to the witch who looks like she's ready to melt in fright."

"I like it," a female student said. "First of all, Rosetta always has a master touch to her works and this is no exception. "I see this as girl power defying evil. The girl's image just seems so strong."

Another female student chimed in, "Well I think Dorothy was very strong in the movie, but I have got to admit this girl figure rocks with strength. It's a great painting. I like the way the colors overlap and blend pulling you into the scene...."

Professor Sanchez smiled at Rosetta and said, "Do you have any comments, Rosetta?"

"I appreciate all the remarks. I believe in sending a strong message in my paintings," she replied. "Sometimes you're at the mercy of what fate might dictate to you, but with a brush and paint, you can make a statement that can contradict fates hand. And by the way, I like wide colorful strokes in fantasy art."

"Well," said Professor Sanchez, "you definitely have the wide and colorful in this painting. However, the girl and the witch are dead on photographic images with invisible strokes."

"Sometimes," said Rosetta, "you make a point using a different stroke. Of course, my point here is that the ugly in the world can be stopped and must be stopped. Maybe through art, you can create your own *"Brave New World"* like Aldous Huxley wrote about. Or maybe as an artist, you can become an unleashed Nietzsche. At any rate, I guess that's why I'm majoring in art and criminal justice. If I fail to kick a little booty on the streets," she said, smiling as classmates half-chuckled. "I guess I can always get justice with my paint brush."

"Very interesting analogy," said the professor. "I like your approach and thinking, but I suggest that you stick with your paint brush. You're too gifted not to devote all your time to the canvas."

Rosetta blushed and said, "I wish I could, but I don't know. It's complicated, but I appreciate the confidence you have in me."

When the class was over, Rosetta headed to a criminal justice class, head held high, walking with strong strides. With a half-smile, she giggled thinking about having brought up Huxley and Nietzsche – remembering Tom and Andre's comments about them. "Did it even make sense what I said about them?" she asked herself. "I mean Jesus," she continued in thought, "I hope I didn't sound stupid or something." With a slight chuckle, she shook her head and thought, "Oh well, I think I actually kicked a little booty. I think I did good…. That's right – think positive."

On this same afternoon, Amy slid out of the car seat while Tom toiled, inching his way out. Hating that it was the start of a new work week, he moved toward the old brick fortress constructed in the early part of the twentieth century which housed between fifty and sixty boys and girls on any given day. The second shift was when most the action took place as the kids were about to return to the building from school, which was on grounds and staffed with special education teachers. Most residents were in special education due to behavior and learning disorders with some hard-core delinquents mixed in the group. Many admitted to the emergency unit, were abused, neglected or runaways, but it was undetermined if they fit in with the others. The majority were placed in the home by the state with an occasional one by the family despite the large cost involved. There were four units; the adolescent boys, the juvenile girls, the emergency floor taking in five to seventeen-year-olds, and the young boys who were in a building behind the main one. Those in emergency placement on the first floor were waiting to get into one of the other units, a foster home or to return home. Amy was in charge of the girls and staff on the third floor while Tom took charge of the boys and staff on the second floor. Being hands on supervisors, they were right in the mix of things like the residential counselor whose job was to interact and keep control of the residents. On the surface, it didn't seem like a lot of responsibility, but with troubled teens, ten to twelve or more on a unit, they never knew when all hell would break out – fights, restraints, runaways returning drunk or high, threats and pranks such as fire alarms going off at all hours bringing the fire department out as often as twice a day. Then dealing with the fallout of an ignited fire chief threatening to see the home closed down. Those were the predictable problems. The unpredictable ones often required emergency action creating a circus atmosphere at times. Sometimes the police or an ambulance needed to come to the home. Dull moments were the exception as the kids were like raccoons getting into things they shouldn't. On most weekends there were planned activities, to movies, skating, or a host of other adventures. Being out in public had its risks as the boys and girls were mischievous and if there was a way to get into trouble they would find it. Going shopping with them meant keeping a watchful eye, as they tended to have sticky hands and no conscience about theft.

As the day turned into evening, the residents were winding down. Amy sat at a desk, which was in an open area at the entrance to the third floor. Most of the dozen girls were in the recreation room down the hall, listening to music, on computers, playing ping-pong and conversing. The queen-bee of the unit, Chastity Holycross, had two girls distract Amy while sneaking by hoping she wasn't noticed going into the large, aged, restroom. A boy named Ralph, from the second floor, had climbed out the boys' bathroom window, and up the fire escape, which connected all the restrooms of the three-story structure. Once in the restroom, believing she was not seen by Amy, Chastity unlocked the bathroom window letting Ralph in. Going into a stall, their clothes fell to the ground. Out of control passion followed as they, like all the romantic teen couples at the home, took advantage of every opportunity to connect with each other. Five minutes passed when Amy, still cornered by two girls, stood and smiled.

"Alright," Amy said, "what's going on?"

"Whataya mean?" the girls blurted.

"You're not pulling anything over on me. I saw Chastity sneak by. If she's in their smoking," Amy said, looking at the restroom, "you'll all be grounded."

"*What do you mean*?" one of the girls exploded.

"*That's it*," Amy spat, hurrying toward the restroom. "You're trying to warn her." Storming through the door, Amy found no lingering smoke, but Ralph on top of Chastity lying on the floor with feet sticking out from under the stall. "Get your butts up now!"

Scrambling, the kids dressed and came out to face a frowning Amy who felt as if she was always a step behind them, but being young understood their smiling faces. Escorting them out, she phoned Tom while Ralph frowned looking down, mumbling, "Tom's gonna be pissed."

"Come on," Chastity begged, "let him go."

"Just go to your room," Amy commanded. "I'll deal with you later."

"*No*," she said standing firm.

When Tom picked up the phone, Amy roared, "*You need to get up here right now.*"

"Sure," Tom responded, not asking questions knowing something was wrong.

Alerting the other two staff, Tom took off rushing up the stairway. On seeing Ralph standing by Amy, he shook his head saying, "*Now what*? What did he do this time?"

"Just the usual," Amy said. "Ralph was trying to get Chastity pregnant again."

"Let's go," Tom said nonchalant and they left.

Amy and the three girls stood eyeing one another when snickering erupted from the girls.

"It's not funny," Amy scolded them.

"You're right, it isn't," Chastity smirked.

"All three of you are in trouble." Amy stood boldly. "Of course you are all going to lose points from your behavior chart, which means no skating activity for you this weekend. And Chastity you are going to be really grounded…"

"*Just screw off you bitch,*" Chastity exploded, giving her the finger.

"You better be careful with your mouth," Amy fired back, "because it'll only get you in more trouble."

"What ya going to do sic your hubby on me?"

"Why don't you give her a break?" one of the other girls blurted.

Chastity roared, "She's too much of a *fuckin' bitch.*"

"If you don't settle down –"

"*What*?" flared Chastity. "What ya going to do?"

"I've had it," Amy said, picking up the phone, asking a staff in the recreation room for assistance. When the female staff arrived so did a group of girls who followed, despite being told to stay put, which was an open invitation for them to be defiant.

"I didn't want all of them with you," Amy blasted the female staff.

"I told them to stay," she countered, then eyed the girls. "Go back to the rec room now."

"Don't listen to *the bitch*," Chastity yelled.

"What's going on?" the excited girls grumbled.

"That's all we need," Amy sighed, "a bunch of girls climbing the walls around here."

"I'll climb the walls for you," Chastity jubilated, running across the room, grabbing a steel support pole stretching twelve feet from floor to ceiling and climbed to the top, tossing a middle finger down at the group. The girls beamed at the spectacle, winding them up and flicking on their out-of-control button.

Panicking, Amy scooted to the desk yelling for everybody to calm down while alerting Tom with a phone call. Slamming the phone down, she rushed to Chastity swirling halfway down the pole like a stripper on speed. Amy shouted, "Get your butt down now."

"Whoopeedo to you," she chirped and laughed.

"I mean it," she sneered, "you're not funny."

With a gleeful smile, she let her body drop, hanging upside down staring Amy in the face. "Whoopeedo, screw you."

"*Get down*," Amy insisted. "Please, I'm begging you before you get into serious trouble."

"I'm already in trouble so I don't give a shit," she said, staring upside-down.

Walking away frustrated, Amy pleaded for the other girls to return to the recreation room. Just when it appeared that they were going to do as asked, Tom hurried through the doorway. All the kids were now determined to stay not wanting to miss the action. Amy grabbed Tom by the arm, pulling him into the hallway and unleashed her anxiety on him before returning to confront Chastity.

Chastity climbed to the top of the pull as Tom approached.

"Chastity," Tom beseeched her. "Please listen to me before things get out of hand."

"What did you do to Ralph?" she snapped.

"Ralph is in control which is what you need to be right now."

"You people make me sick."

"Just get down for starts. Okay?"

"So you can chew my butt out? I don't think so."

"Now you don't want to end up in the time-out room do you?"

"You're not putting me in that shitty little lockup room. You hear me ass-wipe? *Can everyone hear me?*" she screamed at the top of her lungs. *"Don't let them take me to the torture chamber."* The onlookers became rowdy and Tom stood back from Chastity who gave him the finger, which caused the girls to whine for him to leave. Fearing that things were about to get out-of-hand, Tom moved to Amy and told her to call for backup.

"Who's with me?" Chastity shouted. "I say let's all leave this hole." Sliding down the pull, she stormed toward the exit where Tom sped blocking her way. Trying to push him away, with the other girls standing back, he didn't back off. Amy and the other female staff moved in front of the girls to stop them. *"Let me go through,"* Chastity screamed pushing at Tom and Amy.

"Please calm down," Tom begged to no avail.

While Chastity kicked and yelled, two more male staff arrived to help take control. Grabbing legs and arms, all four carried Chastity down the hallway. She screamed and laughed at the same time as if enjoying being carried to the padded time-out room. However, when the room door closed, she pounded on it, cursing and swearing at the top of her lungs.

Chapter 3

After a visit to their favorite restaurant, Andre started up the rental car with Windy next to him and Rosetta in the backseat. Being the first time back in a year, Andre wanted to cruise around Springfield to view the old sites. Remembering how Andre and Windy vanished from the town over four years earlier, Rosetta had always wanted to ask them about it and decided this was a good time to do it.

"You know," Rosetta queried, "I remember Tom saying when you moved away that you guys needed to leave town in a real hurry. I recently reread that letter you left me back then. It might not be any of my business." She paused and then continued uneasy. "But, a, you know, since you left your house, sports car, bank account and all the other stuff to me – I feel so indebted to you. I mean, I can't help think my good fortune came at some high cost to you guys. I just feel a little guilty."

"You feel guilty?" Andre half-chuckled. "What I put you through I can never repay you back. I'm the one who feels guilty."

"You took me away from my home, but you weren't behind selling me. You were preyed upon like me weren't ya? And you did help me escape from that Chinese fiend Da Chang. You ended up doing the right thing."

"Well, yeah," he said with a squint. "But I should have never been involved in the first place. I mean –"

"*That's alright,*" she said. "It's past. You don't have to explain. At least we found out my dad is still in jail. I don't know who was looking in the window the other day. But my dad, well, he's supposed to get out in six months. I can't believe it."

"Try not to worry," Windy added.

"I know," she muttered, "I'm just uptight I guess."

"Can you tell me," Andre asked, "is that strip club still open where Gomez got shot at?"

"I don't know. I've never had reason to go back down to that area of town."

"Keep it that way, but I'm curious to find out," Andre said, heading toward the club.

As they neared the club, Andre came to a halt at the same stop sign he had four years earlier on that tragic night of terror for Rosetta. A large lit neon flashing light said *The Lost Souls Club*. Creeping by with all eyes focused on the entrance, Andre sighed, and said, "Guess Big Jake's still in business."

"Scumball," Windy blurted.

"I remember," Rosetta thought, drifting back in time, remembering what she had seen and what she was told happened during the incident from four years earlier at the club:

Gomez held a knife in one hand and used the other to open the door. Blasting music blared at him, a roaring crowd could be heard and Big Jake walked from the bar to the doorway eying Gomez, and then lit up a cigar while stared him down. Seeing the wicked knife ready for action caused Big Jake to pull out a pistol and to point it at Gomez's forehead, pushing him backward out the door into the parking lot. At the same time, Andre's car came to the stop sign in front of the club.

"Look!" Rosetta shouted, pointing at Gomez, which caused Andre to pull into the lot.

"Get the hell out of here punk," Big Jake growled, cigar glowed and then he kicked Gomez in the groin who fell to his knees doubled over. Big Jake turned away walking back into the doorway and Gomez, sweat rolling down his face, sprang to his feet running at him.

"Behind you, boss," yelled the door attendant.

Big Jake turned; saw the knife coming at him, pulled the gun's trigger which exploded sending Gomez back, plummeting to the ground. Gomez collapsed in a pool of blood, stared up at the glowing cigar and then focused on the neon flashing light. Big Jake turned away talking to the other man and stomped his cigar out as everyone in Andre's car ran to Gomez, even Rosetta carefully hurried holding the newborn baby. All gathered around Gomez, who was conscious. When Rosetta arrived, she showed Gomez the baby.

"Do you know who this is?" Rosetta said, showing the baby to Gomez. "This is your son."

"He's alive?" he said brightening.

"Yes, I lied to you. I hid him nearby in the woods when I heard you coming back for me. He didn't die when he came out like I said. I was afraid you would hurt him as crazy as you were acting."

"I've called an ambulance," Andre said, "hang in there."

"Help me up," he demanded.

"No stay down," Tom said.

"You're right Tom," Gomez said, standing on his own with blood oozing out of his gut. "Now I can go like a warrior. I live in my son. My spirit will live in him." Bending to pick up his knife, he moved to the doorway and before anyone knew it, Gomez grabbed Big Jake by the back of the hair and with a wild slash scalped him, taking hair, a chunk of skin and tissue. Big Jake fell to the floor doubled over bleeding profusely from the head. Gomez stumbled back out the doorway and landed on his back, looking up; he smiled with glowing, eerie eyes at the neon-lit sign, *The Lost Souls Club*.

Tears streaked Rosetta's face as she returned to the present, stomach churning after remembering what had happened to Gomez.

Once the club was out-of-sight, Andre began a sermon. "Alright, Rosetta you need to know the whole truth about your dad selling you and my involvement."

"Really you don't have to. It's okay. It's past history."

"I want you to know," he paused. "I mean, especially since Big Jake appears to still be around. It's just that I need to tell you."

"The scumball," Rosetta interjected, and then smiled, looking at Windy.

"A very dangerous scumball," Andre said, pausing. "Maybe I should let dead dogs lie?"

"Just tell her," Windy interjected. "You need to get it off your chest."

"Go ahead," Rosetta said, "I can handle it."

"For your own safety and my peace of mind you need to know. Don't go near Big Jake. He was behind the whole mess of your dad selling you. I sadly got suckered into it. I, a, I," he stammered. "Shit almighty," he said looking down. "Don't know how to say this, but I chloroform you and drove off with you from your dads. I'm so sorry. Then Da Chang came to my place and took you."

"*He was a rapist*," Rosetta roared.

"You're right. I'm sorry again. That's another reason I owe you so much."

"But you let me escape from the fiend and that knife you gave me saved me from being raped. I stuck it right in his leg and did just like you told me to do to get away."

"I got dragged into the whole mess because Big Jake scared the hell out of me. He's a *blood sucking leech*. Your dad owed him big bucks and you were the payment. He was threatening to kill your dad."

"You're saying Big Jake was behind all the terror I went through."

"Oh yeah, he was. Don't ever get involved with him. That's why I'm telling you. You see him. You run. I was involved because I was weak. I owned a club like his and he baited me, dragging me into the whole mess. I'm just sorry I was so *gutless* back then."

"But why did you leave town?"

"I sold Big Jake my nightclub in another town years earlier and he felt like he could manipulate me to get him teen girls from Prism when he knew I was working with kids. He wouldn't take no for an answer. I was a different person before I started working with kids. He wouldn't believe I had really changed. I had reasons to change. You didn't know I was a seminarian. I really did have a conscience, but booze clouded my head. It ate away at me along with other garbage. I had to get away from him and that nasty world."

"Especially after your granny died," Windy stressed. "She laid one heavy guilt trip on you."

"That's why you helped me escape?" Rosetta rationalized. "You knew it was wrong?"

"*Yes, absolutely*. Once we left town we were of no use to him. I couldn't give him what he wanted anymore. That's it in a nutshell. I feel *so, so* ashamed. Can you understand any of this?"

"Yeah, I think so."

"Bottom line is *don't* go near Big Jake."

"It's too bad Gomez didn't kill him," Windy said.

"He hurt him real bad," Rosetta said. "But I guess he survived. Talking about Gomez, I can't help thinking about him and my baby that I gave up. You know how insane Gomez was. I mean he drugged me, got me pregnant and yet I wonder where my boy is at. I wonder a lot. Ironic. Big Jake killed Gomez and it turns out he was responsible for so much of the *hell* I went through. But what my dad did to me – only he is responsible for all the other misery I went through. You know," she hesitated, "I know you know – *Jesus*. You guys know about my dad," she stammered, "you know what he did to me besides sell me. I had threatened to turn him into the cops right before he sold me. That's why I think he really did it. Don't ever want to see him again. Can't believe he'll be let out in six months."

"It'll be okay," Windy said.

"He has no reason to bother you," Andre added. "Does he know you live in Springfield?"

"No. He shouldn't at least."

"You did say," Andre said, "that you were going to do an internship with the police. Right?"

"Yeah," she uttered.

"You'll have an in for keeping tabs on him," Andre assured her.

"I guess so. Too bad you guys have to leave tomorrow."

"We're a phone call, text or e-mail away," Andre said.

Windy added, "And he means it. Call us anytime you like."

"I'll just keep painting and studying like I've been doing. And it's all because of you guys paying my tuition and everything. You've given me a chance to do something with my life."

"You're doing great," Andre said. "I can't wait to come back to see some new paintings and buy some of course."

"You've bought enough," Rosetta said blushing.

"Believe me," Andre said, "there is never enough of a good thing. Your art is great."

"You're just being nice," she said. "You probably don't know anything about art."

"This I know," Andre stressed. "Reality explodes at the tip of your paint brush. Those strokes scream with passion, imagination and radiate a reality that the world needs to see."

"I don't know about that," she smiled. "All I know is I don't know where I'd be without your help. I don't understand how you could afford to pay for my college and everything you've given me? The bank account and house."

"I wasn't always a social worker. Big inheritance, good investments, selling my business and that's how. Don't worry about it."

"I just didn't want to be a financial burden to you guys."

"Well, you're not," Andre assured, driving toward the brick home they had left her before moving to California. Rosetta had insisted that they stay at the house while visiting, which they had accepted.

Tom hobbled back from an evening jog, feeling the effects from stumbling a week earlier. While nearing the house, consumed in thought, his mind had a way of working against him with so much time to think. Still on edge about what he thought Burt had said to Amy caused him to grumble to himself. Walking through the doorway, Amy and Brenda were smoking a joint on this Saturday evening; a habit that Tom didn't partake in anymore believing that pot made him feel paranoid, which is how he felt, as he sniffed, seeing the swirling smoke in the distance. Glancing at his desk, he had an unpleasant reminder setting on it – two rejection slips he had received in the mail that day. One was a publisher and the other was a literary agent, who had asked to see his novel months earlier, but lost it when relocating and had asked for another copy.

Being used to rejection slips, most of which were through e-mails did not make it any easier to bear. Saying hello to Brenda, he headed upstairs to take a shower and returned downstairs after getting dressed.

"Here you go Tom," Brenda said, holding out the joint for him to grab.

Cringing, he grabbed the joint not wanting to appear unsociable. Once between his lips, he nibbled on it until it glowed. He then handed it back and headed to the kitchen where he blew the smoke out of his mouth never having let it go down to his lungs. Returning with beer, he handed Brenda and Amy each a can, hoping he could avoid another passing of the joint.

"I hear," Brenda said, "I missed out on all the action with Chastity the other night."

"Oh, yeah," Tom said, "we had a hell of a time. You missed all the fun."

"That's what I hear," she said, passing Tom the joint again.

Smiling, Amy said, "Tom especially loved it when she kicked him between the legs while we were trying to carry her to detention."

"Yeah that made my day," he replied, putting the joint to his mouth, covering the lit end with his hand and pretended he was inhaling while Amy continued talking.

"Isn't Burt coming over?" Brenda asked.

Tom's eyes brightened looking at Amy.

"I saw him earlier and he said he might stop by," Brenda added. "I told him I was coming over."

"Tom's still pissed," Amy hissed.

"You still mad about him pissing all over the place?" Brenda asked, smiling.

Looking away, shaking his head, he blurted, "I don't know."

"Get over it," Brenda insisted. "He was drunk. He was being Burt."

"I know," he replied, looking at the stairway, and then making a face, sniffing, still smelling the urine.

"The smell's gone," Amy said, frowning at Tom.

"I don't smell a thing," said Brenda, still smiling. "Don't be a party pooper, Tom."

"I'm over it," Tom said, half-agitated.

"Good," Brenda snickered. "Do you care if I give him a call to come over?"

"Call him," Tom said, looking dejected. "I don't care."

"Okay I will," she said pulling out her cell phone and calling.

A half-hour later, Burt arrived, big grin and carrying a bottle of tequila. "Don't worry Tom," he assured. "I know where the urinal is now. Really, man, I'm sorry about it. I mean, I didn't even know I did it until someone told me about it the next day."

"Just forget it," Tom said.

"You can't smell a thing," Amy said coming to his rescue, bright-eyed and walking to the kitchen. "I'll get some shot glasses."

"Don't get me one," Tom blurted. "I don't need any."

"Come on," Burt insisted. "Bring him one."

Smirking, Tom shook his head as Amy returned and handed everyone a shot glass. Brenda handed Burt a one-hitter pot pipe, which he lit and sucked on as if he was taking his last breath. Amy poured tequila into everyone's shot glass.

"A toast," Burt said teetering, "to Tom and Amy. "Great friends who put up with my shit."

"Cheers," from Brenda.

Everyone drank their shot and the party continued. Tom couldn't help but to keep a close eye on Burt and did all he could to stay sober – sipping on a beer, faking taking a hit of pot as the rest unwound not paying any attention to Tom who on occasion would put on an act as if he were drunk. As the night wore on, the party fizzled out and Burt and Brenda left. Once in bed, Tom cuddled up to Amy, kissing and caressing, but she pulled away saying she was tired.

"Come on," he pleaded.

"Go to sleep."

Grabbing her breast, she rolled over. "I mean it knock it off!"

Frustrated, Tom turned over and went to sleep.

Rosetta had persuaded Andre and Windy to stay in town longer than planned. On the last day, Andre took off saying he wanted to take a drive to Sandtown, twenty minutes away, where he had started up an experimental group home for teen's years earlier. Andre discovered that the house was no longer a group home and on his way back, decided that his curiosity about Big Jake and The Lost Souls Club needed to be resolved. Going to the club in the late afternoon, he wore a baseball cap, jeans and sported a mustache and a goatee that gave him a different look than when he lived there. Clean shaven and casual slacks rather than jeans had been his typical appearance when he worked and lived in Springfield before. Sitting in his car observing, he battled the urge to go in but decided he needed to find out if Big Jake still owned the club. Putting on a pair of reading glasses, which he recently started wearing, he felt his disguise was solid and knew the lighting would be dim in the club. Besides, he rationalized that four years of being away would make the likelihood of being recognized slim. In addition, he knew Big Jake had clubs in Chicago and his old club ninety miles away in Saplecreek, near Danville in central Illinois. Big Jake could be at any of them, he reasoned. Then he got out of his car, strolled through the front door, head down with the glasses on the end of his nose so he could see above them scouting the place out. Being that it was late afternoon, there was only one striptease act going on for the handful of deadbeat patrons. Sitting, a waitress came up to his table.

"What can I get you?" the youthful-looking girl asked.

"A light mug," Andre replied, having given up the hard liquor that he had been so fond of for so many years. When she returned, he nonchalantly asked, "Who owns this great club?"

"Big Jake does."

"Oh, so is he around?"

"Haven't seen him much around lately 'cause he just opened a club in Vegas."

"*Really*. Las Vegas, huh?"

"But I heard he's at his club in LA."

"*LA*," he said with concern. "He really gets around. He's big time."

"You bet he is."

"You look awfully young."

"I'm old enough. You ought to visit our backroom. It's the V.I.P. area. That's where the girl's hangout if you're looking to relax, get a body massage and have a good old time."

"Thanks, I'm fine."

"Okay, I'll be back later to check on you."

"Sure thing," he nodded.

Satisfied with the information he had received; he stood to leave but reseated himself as he spotted Lee, a former nemesis from years past. Once Lee was distracted, he made his move and slipped out of the club undetected. Returning to Rosetta's, he told them what he had done and found out. Rosetta stood by listening.

"I can't believe it," Windy stressed. "He's in LA where we're at. Heaven forbid he ever found out we're there and that we operate a runaway shelter for teens."

"LA is huge," Andre assured. "Unlikely we'll ever reconnect there."

"Unless he starts looking for teen girls or say one of our girls should go to work for him, then come back to us with him following her to the shelter."

"There are a lot of ifs," Andre said, wrapping his arm around Windy. "We'll be okay. When we get back I'll see if I can find out where his club is located – I mean if he calls it The Lost Souls Club."

"If he doesn't," Windy said, "you can call around to the different clubs and maybe get the info that way."

"Don't worry, I'll find out."

Rosetta interjected, "I wish I could put him behind bars like my dad. No one should have to go through what I had to. I wish Gomez had finished the job."

"I have an idea," Andre said, changing the subject. "Why don't we give Tom and Amy a call to go out to eat with us since this is our last day in town? It's a Sunday, they're probably not working. Right?"

"Probably not," Rosetta smiled, "I'll give them a call."

"Something doesn't seem quite right between those two," Andre said. "Does it?"

"I've been noticing that," Rosetta said, "for the past year. It really upsets me."

"Sorry to hear that," Windy said. "But they can work it out. They're a good couple."

"Go ahead call them," said Andre

As Rosetta phoned, she said, "I don't know what's up with them?"

Chapter 4

With a new workweek started, Tom and Amy waited for the onslaught of youngsters to come storming in from school. Slouched back in a office chair, Tom daydreamed, debating who the biggest thorn in his side was; Chastity, who berated him whenever she could for placing her in the lockup room; or Dick Muster, another supervisor at the home, whose antagonism toward Tom stemmed from Tom's popularity among the staff and residents. The debate soon ended, when stomping feet up the stairway snapped Tom back to reality. Although Tom had his own office, he preferred to be out with the boys to interact with them. The exceptions would be if he needed to deal with them or staff away from the others. The workers liked his approach since it took some of the burdens off them as they were with the boys around the clock. Dick Muster, on the other hand, preferred to stay in his office. He was the supervisor of the emergency unit, which accommodated new males and females. He preferred to have individual sessions with the kids rather than to mingle with them. Although his supervisory status was the same as other supervisors, he acted as if he had more authority than anyone else. Leaving his office, Tom went to the recreation room where most of the boys would congregate after school. Regardless of his good nature and the fact that he enjoyed working with young people, Tom's patience was wearing thin as he had been dealing for years with troubled teens that had been chipping away at his sanity. He realized something had to change, but just didn't know what or how. Despite the grind of dealing with incorrigible youth, he didn't know another line of work to pursue. In fact, his only outlet from all the everyday hassles was to work on a new novel, even though all he had to show for the first one was rejection slips. Writing away frustrations, working out at the health club and jogging were his escapes. He rationalized that it was healthier than an old habit of eating away his frustrations, which caused him to have a yo-yo weight problem. The weight now under control did not solve the ongoing troubles with Amy. However, as he glanced up, sitting at the recreation area desk, he saw a new concern headed towards him. Thirteen-year-old Tommy Wizel had problems at school throughout the day and stomped into the room frowning, complaining and arguing with another boy.

"Tommy, knock it off," Tom said, standing and moving away from the desk.

"I'm sick of this place. I'm sick of that ignorant school and all the screwed-up kids around here."

"Come on," Tom insisted, "let's go talk in my office."

"I don't feel like talking," he whined.

"Then settle your butt down," Tom said as two more boys came over towards them.

A fifteen-year-old boy chirped, "He's been like this all day at school."

"*Shut up Bobby*," Tommy screamed.

"Make me," he growled.

"*Alright*," Tom said moving between the boys trying to grab one another. "*Knock it off.*"

"No," Tommy flared, shoving Bobby. Tom pushed Tommy and Bobby away from each other.

Snorting like a wild boar, Tommy yelled, "*Bobby's a dumbass.*" When he saw a can of soda on the staff desk, he grabbed and threw it at Bobby, but hit Tom's chest, splattering on him and Bobby.

Grumbling, touching the wet shirt, Tom grabbed Tommy, forcing him to the floor putting a restraint on him. "Go get some staff," Tom commanded, looking at the other boys gathered around him.

Tommy laughed, making a face at Tom who tightened the restraint. Tommy cursed and swore, causing Tom to want to spank his butt, but held back remembering that he had once been suspended for three days for spanking an out of control boy. Tommy continued laughing, trying to egg Tom on who exploded, "I mean it. Don't push me. I've had it with you." A group of boys gathered around Tom whose face contorted while Tommy held a tight grin that vanished when Tom lost control saying, "Get that shit eating grin off your face you little ass."

"Ooo," the group of boys sang in choral, gathering around, never having heard Tom cuss at anyone before.

Tom looked up not seeing any help coming and felt bad about cussing but still held onto Tommy.

"Alright, alright," Tommy whined. "I'll stop. We can talk, okay?"

With a grunt, Tom said, "If I let you up do you promise to calm down?"

"Yes, Yes," he pleaded. "I promise."

"Alright then," Tom said. "Let's go to my office." Letting loose, he was leading him away when two workers rushed to the scene. Tom told them he was dealing with Tommy and asked them to stay with the other boys.

Once in the office, Tom flopped in his chair and told Tommy to sit. Elbow's resting on the desk; chin held up by the palms of his hands, Tom shook his head. "What in the heck is going on with you?" Tom said, looking down at his wet clothing.

"I hate that school," he said clenching his teeth.

"So you throw a can of soda on me?"

"I was upset. I was aiming for Bobby."

"I gathered that," Tom said, sitting up straight.

"I didn't mean to get you."

Pausing, Tom sat back shaking his head. "So now what?"

"I don't know, I guess I owe you an apology."

"Well, that's a start."

"It's just that I'm sick of everything."

"What was the problem at school?"

"That stupid asshole teacher made me feel like an idiot in class."

"You don't have to cuss."

"*Well, you did.* Get that shit eating grin off your face you little *ass*," he said smiling.

"I don't know what got into me. I'm sorry about that."

"Did you read my book by Professor Frantic?"

"Well, yeah, but that's not what we're talking about."

"What did you think of it?"

"I don't know, but what happened at school?"

"Mr. Butt Face made fun of me in class. He said I was sitting on my brain …"

"What did you do to aggravate him?"

"He kept asking me stupid questions I didn't know."

"And?" from Tom.

"Well," Tommy smiled, "when he asked me if I was sitting on my brain I just rubbed my forehead."

"Then what?"

"He got all *pissy*."

"Why?"

"Because all the kids laughed."

"Why did they laugh?"

Grinning like a chimp, he said, "I guess 'cause I was rubbing my forehead with my middle finger."

"You were giving him the finger."

"Can't a person rub their head with any finger they want?"

"No, they can't. Have you been taking your meds?"

"You know," Tommy said, "Professor Frantic said meds were an excuse to legally push drugs. I don't want to be no druggie. He said meds were an excuse to create bipolar people. If I don't take the drug, I won't be bipolar anymore. It's all a conspiracy he said."

"Tommy, Tommy you're not taking your medication. What are you doing spitting it out after they give it to you at school?"

"You read what he said. You said you read the book didn't you?"

"Professor Frantic admitted to being a bonafide schizophrenic."

"No, he didn't."

"The book's title is 'The Mumble Jumble Chronicles of a Schizophrenic."

"No, it's not. It's the 'The Mumble Jumble Schizophrenic Chronicles."

"That's what I meant."

"Are you sure you read it?"

"Dead sure."

"Okay, prove it. Why did Professor Frantic say we were all bipolar?"

"He rants about how everyone has an alter ego and there is good and evil in all of us. And we all have our ups and downs."

"And it just manifests itself more in some people," Tommy stressed, "and they call those people bipolar. He said bipolar people use to be manic-depressives until the drug companies came out with a new super drug that needed a more clinical term for the gifted people like us. He said manic-depressive was too emotional and carried a stigma with it ..."

"Yes, yes that's what he said. And you are a very intelligent boy. So did I or did I not read the book?"

"Well, I guess you did."

"But you got to admit there was a lot of mumble jumble off the wall psycho babble that left you confused at times."

"It all made perfect sense to me."

"*Alright*. Enough of the book. Getting back to you. If you were taking your meds, we wouldn't be sitting here right now. Right?"

"When I don't take them I feel alive."

"A live wire," Tom said, smiling.

"You're real funny Tom. Professor Frantic would call you a Pooper Scooper."

"What?"

"I thought you read his book?"

"I can't remember every detail of all his labeling and constant outbursts at the establishment. I mean he dissects everyone from politicians to media stars as being behind a vast conspiracy to brand the people they don't like and agree with as being bipolar kooks."

"It is all a conspiracy," Tommy raved, "to make us take their drugs so we don't think for ourselves. That's why I won't take them."

"Alright, I can see this conversation is going into never-never land. What are we going to do with you? You know I've got to tell the school you're not taking your meds."

"Traitor. Pooper scooper. I never said I wasn't taking them."

"Please, Tommy just give me a break. It's just the beginning of the week."

"You give me a break and I give you a break."

"And how do I do that?"

"If I can prove I can control myself without," he paused with a whimsical smile, "that is control how I act – then you don't have to tell them what you think that I'm doing."

"That would mean," Tom stressed, "no problems at *school or here.*"

"We got a deal then? I can do it."

"One screw-up and I'll alert the school about what I think you're doing."

Tommy stuck out his hand for Tom to shake. After a moment of deep thought, Tom shook his hand.

About to arrive at LAX international airport, Andre and Windy's flight sailed over the mountains surrounding the greater Los Angeles area. Looking down out the window, Andre wondered where Big Jake's snake pit lied below. After all, they had fled Illinois four years earlier to get away from his smothering grip. Now the reality of him being in their backyard ate away at Andre. After landing, they returned to the runaway shelter that they ran and made sure all was fine there. It was located in the heart of the cities nightlife that drew runaways like bees to a hive. Having been in touch with a phone, texts, and e-mails throughout their entire trip, there were no surprises for them upon returning to the shelter. Taking care of immediate business was the priority; however, once back into the routine of dealing with the multiple issues of the runaways and an ongoing intake of new kids; Andre opened the phone book to nightclubs. As if fate were staring him in the eye, the first page shot at him with a big ad saying *The Lost Souls Club*. Half-delighted that there was no longer a mystery, but disheartened at the fear of a cancer returning overwhelmed him. Showing Windy the ad, only gave comfort in knowing he had someone to share his anxiety. What neither of them knew was the location of the club from the address. Windy got on the computer and located the club, which was twelve miles away. The distance was tolerable, but twenty or thirty miles would have made them feel more secure.

"What ya looking at?" one of the runaway boys asked, peeking between Andre and Windy staring at the computer screen.

"Ever hear of The Lost Souls Club?" Andre asked.

"No," he responded.

"*I have*," a voice said. A girl sitting, using a computer ten feet away, smirked, looking at the group.

"You have?" Andre queried, jaw dropping.

"Sure. When I first got to LA this guy I met on the street promised he could make me a star and took me down to the club."

Andre and Windy went to her. "What happened?" Andre asked in awe.

"They wanted me to become a stripper. I told them that I was an actress. They told me they made movies and I could be a star. Of course, I was smart enough to realize they were in the porno business. As soon as I had a chance I ran my tail out of there."

"He's in the porn business now?" Windy said, looking at Andre.

"It's legal, well, unless they use underage kids," he hissed. "And we know what he's capable of."

Windy nodded her head.

"Whataya mean?" asked the girl.

"You stay far away from that place," Windy growled. "That's what he means."

"What they going to do?" the girl asked. "Whore you out?"

"Or worse," Andre added. "Bad, bad people so you did real good running from them."

"I knew it," she nodded.

"We need to have a meeting tonight with all the kids and warn them," Windy said.

"You got that right," Andre replied.

Returning from classes, Rosetta went to the spare bedroom used as an art studio. An easel sat with a four by three foot canvas, which she struggled putting the brush to it. An outline of two figures emerged as she thought about the tragic past stimulated by Andre and Windy's visit. Feeling a mental block, she stopped unsure of where to place the next stroke. Setting everything aside, she grabbed the car keys and rushed away to the hellish past, the subject of the painting. She had a mission and nothing else mattered at that moment. Arriving at The Lost Souls Club, she parked away from the overhead lights, but in view of the front door entrance where the horrid shooting of Gomez and the wild scalping of Big Jake took place. Reliving the horror, she believed was needed to complete the painting. As their faces came into focus, Rosetta knew she was on the right track. Sitting in deep thought, eyes closing, she shuddered, recalling what happened and then moments after reopening them; a man, wearing a brimmed hat, puffing on a cigar, stepped out of the nightclub's front door. Hypnotized, she carefully watched in awe, believing the man to be Big Jake and when he moved into the light it was confirmed. Curious at what grossness lied under the hat, she visualized the gore as she remembered it. The hat hid all signs of Gomez's scalping, which made her imagine some grotesque scarring being covered up. Fearful to move, she observed, face flush, realizing all the pain he was responsible for. He and her father had opened up a world of misery that she feared she would never get over. Although her dad was behind bars, for now, this monster stood, puffing away on a cigar, standing a free man. The least she could do was send him into permanent agony by locking his torment in a painting. Satisfied with what she saw and that Big Jake had reentered the club; she put the Alfa Romeo sports coupe, that Andre had given her, into gear and sped off returning home. Captivated in the moment, not stopping to eat dinner, she stroked the canvas beyond midnight until she was finished. An enraged Gomez, oozing blood from his gut, slicing Big Jake's head open, captured and imprisoned their agony on canvas forever while giving Rosetta a new sense of satisfaction. At last, she could go to bed relieved that she had some feeling of control, even though every time she looked at the painting, she knew it wasn't enough.

The next morning, Tom and Amy took care of routine business before having to go to work. Tom had already gone to the health club, hit the weights hard, but saved his cardiovascular workout for the evening with the boys. He had started up a jogging activity which had gone over well, but for now, he and Amy sat in the kitchen eating lunch discussing work.

"… and Chastity hasn't learned a thing from the incident," Amy said. "I think it's all a big joke to her."

"She gives me a face every time I see her," Tom commented.

"How's Ralph been doing?" Amy asked.

"Better than expected considering he's on restriction. But yesterday I had a problem with Tommy."

With a smug smile, Amy said, "It's because of his name. Being a pain goes with the name."

"Ha, ha," from Tom. "At any rate, I had to restrain him."

"Oh yeah. For what?"

"Fighting with another kid, throwing an open soda at him, and hitting me with it instead. I hated doing it. We usually get along."

"Did you put him in the detention room?"

"No, we got it resolved before it came to that. You know, he's really a smart kid. If he could only channel and control all that energy."

"I guess being bipolar is an obstacle."

"Sometimes I wonder if he really is. We'll be finding out."

"What do you mean?"

"He had a rough day at school before he showed up on the unit yesterday. He stopped taking his meds at school. He's spitting them out. At any rate, we made a deal that I wouldn't tell on him if he had no more problems at school or at the home."

"You can't do that," Amy hissed. "You could get in trouble."

"What do you mean? I didn't do anything."

"*Well*, you're not telling the school."

"They'll figure it out if his bad behavior continues."

"You need to tell them," Amy said frowning.

"But I made a deal with him. Plus I don't know for sure what he's doing. I mean I just guessed and he didn't deny it. If he stops his bad behavior without the drug, then the problem is solved."

"You're really an idiot sometimes. I hope you don't get in trouble."

"Why? Are you going to say something?"

"Just grow up."

With a sigh, Tom left the table and went upstairs to the bedroom where he plopped on the bed in deep thought until it was time to go to work.

After driving off to work, Amy texted away arousing Tom's curiosity, but he kept it to himself. Once there, they waited for school to get out. Amy dealt with a sick girl while Tom worked on behavior reports that the home's director received at the end of each week at a meeting for supervisors and therapists. The resident's progress and digressions were the focus of these meetings. Amy like Tom mingled with the kids rather than staying put in her office. Brenda and another female staff worked on the floor with the teenage girls, but Amy's presence made it three staff on the front line. Chastity and two of her friends went up to Amy after arriving from school.

"You know," Chastity, blurted, "I think you guys could get in trouble for locking us in that *hell hole*."

"Why is that?" Amy asked.

"Because it's *inhuman*. They lock dogs and animals up. That's how you treat us around here."

The other girls nodded their heads in agreement.

"If you act like a wild animal, you'll get treated like one."

"*Who was acting like a wild animal?*" Chastity raved.

"I've seen monkey's at the zoo behave like you did that night."

"Monkey's!" she shouted and then started scratching under her arms and making strange faces at the other girls who laughed while Amy cracked a grin. "They treat monkey's better than me. And that husband of yours is a big beast. Next time he touches me I will seriously kick him where it hurts again. If you don't let him know, *I will*."

"I'm sure you will anyway," Amy said.

"So you think I should do it, huh?"

"You heard me."

"*Gotcha*. Kick him where it hurts. Then grab the family jewels and squeeze until he turns blue."

"Way to go," the other girls carried on while Chastity made a monkey face.

Standing, Amy said, "Just leave me alone. I'm not in the mood. *I mean it*. Do something constructive or else each of you can have an individual session with me in my office. We can work on your behavior charts or –"

"Bye," the girls said in unison and walked away.

Back on the boys' unit, Tom just got beat at a game of ping-pong by the floor champ. Walking away disappointed, he headed up the hall and saw Tommy who gave him a high-five slap on the hand.

"Are we celebrating?" Tom asked.

"Mission accomplished," Tommy bragged, grinning.

"Slow down buddy. Take it easy on the hand slapping. No problems at school? Am I right?"

"You got it."

"Good going. That's what I like to hear, but it's only one day."

"I told you I could do it and I'll do it tomorrow and the next day."

"Well, we'll see."

"I'm good I'm telling you."

"Well, if we're still giving high-five's at the end of the week we might be onto something."

"We will be," Tommy insisted. "You know what Professor Frantic said in his book?"

"Go 'head tell me 'cause I know you're going to anyway."

"He said with every pill down the drain, a new soul is born and every drain will scream in pain. Now if that isn't inspirational I don't know what is."

"Oh, yeah. I seem to recall that line. The verdict is still out, though. Prove him right. I will be checking with your teacher every day. So we'll see."

"Every drain will scream in pain," he chirped, walking away with a big grin.

That evening, after dinner and all the homework was done; Tom gathered the group of seven joggers from his unit and they scampered off, heading to the large park about a mile away. The jog took place almost every evening as Tom believed a tired out kid was a kid drained of mischief. On this chilly fall evening, Tom made sure everyone was dressed in warm clothes. Making it to the park, they jogged down the middle of the narrow, paved, lit road as no one was in sight. Tom took the lead with the boys, ranging from fourteen through seventeen, following behind as if in a procession. Determined to get a good workout, Tom drove them hard but knew their limitations having done the activity for months. Some of the showoffs would prod Tom to move faster at times to the displeasure of the stragglers, but he knew how to keep a good balance for all.

"Hey Tom," shouted a boy. "I'll race you to that light up ahead."

"That's got to be two hundred yards away," Tom stressed.

"*Chicken,*" he spouted. "You know I can beat you. In fact, I'm faster than anyone here. You know it and I know it."

After taking enough egging on, Tom started to run backward. "I'll tell you what Jimmy boy. You think you're so fast let's see how you do racing me backward."

Jimmy, never refusing a challenge, turned around, joining Tom in his backward antics. "*You're on.*"

"On the count of three," Tom said, smiling at all the boys behind him.

"*Burn him up Tom,*" one of the stragglers yelled.

"No one's burning me up," Jimmy shouted.

"Alright!" Tom exclaimed. "One, two, three."

Speeding off, they wobbled along the path to the delight of the amused boys who ran as a group right behind them. Struggling to keep their balance, they moved like drunken ducks at times. Two steps behind Tom, Jimmy fell on his butt to the delight of the others but sprung back up moving all the faster to catch up. Twenty yards from the finish, Jimmy was ten steps behind Tom and tumbled once again. Slower to get up this time, he ran forward acknowledging defeat.

"You look like a spastic," Jimmy yelled, trying to save face.

Crossing the finish line, Tom came to a halt breathing heavily, seeing his breath in the cool air. "Hold on guys," he said. "Let me catch my breath."

"Can't take it?" Jimmy said.

"Yeah, you got me," Tom responded, panting.

"How about we all race backwards?" a boy shouted.

"Oh no," from Tom. "I've had enough. Everyone take a break."

Tom moved to a park bench under a tree hiding him in its shadow while the others stayed on the street, horsing around until they saw headlights coming their way. As the car approached, they got off the road, but it came to a halt and a window rolled down.

"How's it hanging?" a gangbanger said, holding out a bag of pills. "Looking to trip out?"

The boys gathered around the window as Tom stood up. "Hey man our staff's over there," Jimmy said.

"Staff?"

"Yeah. We're from the children's home."

"We're not scared of the man," he replied, looking at the driver.

"You better be," another boy said.

"What's going on?" Tom demanded, walking toward the car.

"Punks," the passenger said to the boys.

One of the boys gave the passenger the finger.

The big gangbanger pushed the door open into them and stepped out, grabbing Jimmy by the throat, putting a gun to his head. The others backed away while Tom stepped up into the guys face showing a lit up cell phone.

"The *cops* are on their way now," Tom ranted. "They said they're thirty seconds away. You don't have a *helluva* lot of time to get away."

"*Hey man let's split,*" the driver shouted.

Eye to eye with Tom, the gangbanger shoved him away and hopped in the car which sped off.

"That was quick thinking calling the cops," a boy said to Tom.

"You mean a good bluff," Tom said, punching 911 on his phone. Talking to the dispatcher, he asked for immediate assistance just in case the car was to return. In all the months of jogging, this was the first problem encountered. The park's safety had never been in question due to being in a decent neighborhood. Moving to the park's entrance, the group met up with the police. Tom told the officer what had happened and gave a description of the car and the man with the gun. The excited boys told all that they knew and bragged how Tom outsmarted them. The officer took names, made a report and suggested they jog back to the home, indicating he would follow in the distance until they got back.

Chapter 5

While hurrying through the quad, arms full of books, Rosetta was running late to meet with an academic advisor. When a book dropped, she swept it up and then moved through a glass door entrance where her reflection came and went in a flash. For a split second, Rosetta shuddered, reminded of the sprite face in the window at the art exhibit coming and going. Although satisfied that her father was locked up, his presence was still felt, motivating her to pursue a criminal justice degree as well as an art degree. Rushing along, long shiny dark hair flowing, centerfold body in stride and blue eyes gleaming, many heads turned as she had a way of lighting up onlookers eyes. Despite being the desire of many male glances, with all that she had been through, she shied away from relationships being content with classes for now. On reaching the office, she stopped, took a deep breath, made eye contact with the advisor, entered and sat while the woman looked through a file. When the advisor glanced up smiling, Rosetta was looking at the wall clock and said, "Gee, I don't believe it, I made it on time."

"Believe this. You're in great shape for graduating. Let's concentrate on your criminal justice degree."

"Sure," Rosetta replied. "I'm pretty sure I'm squared away with my art degree."

"You sure are. I don't see any problems."

"Fantastic. I just can't believe half the semester is almost over."

"It'll move even faster with the good news I have for you. Your internship request at the police department is all set up. You will be working with Detective Palermo."

"*Great*," she said, eyes bright.

"It's for half this semester and half of next semester. I have all the paperwork you will need to read before you start in two weeks. So are you ready for it?"

"I'm excited about it."

"Good."

"Do you know anything about this detective?" Rosetta asked.

"Only that this is his first time taking on an intern."

"Is he young, old, fat, cute?"

"If you must know," the advisor smiled. "I would guess the late twenties and very pleasant to look at."

"You said, Detective Palermo?"

"That's right, Detective Mike Palermo."

"Sounds Italian," Rosetta said with a sparkle in her eye.

"He looks very Italian."

Rosetta brightened thinking of Tom who was Italian and whom she had a long time crush on despite having been her foster parent.

Back in Los Angeles, Andre couldn't help himself one late afternoon. While out on an errand, he drove by Big Jake's club. Thoughts overwhelmed him as he parked across from the club and watched people enter and leave. "Why is this happening?" he asked himself. "I put that piece of crap behind me years ago. I guess you never get rid of your past. You can run, but it eventually catches up to you." Stroking his goatee, his eyes closed, remembering Big Jake and his thugs grabbing Windy and taking her away. The pain of watching, at gun point, caused him to quiver at the memory. "Just stop thinking," he told himself. "The past is past. He doesn't know you're here. Stop worrying. LA is huge. It's just that I can't believe I'm sitting here. Just stop thinking. You're working yourself up for nothing. How many times have you beaten yourself up expecting the worst? Then the worst never happened." Looking at his watch, he realized that he needed to return to the shelter to pick Windy up as it was time for them to go home. After returning, Windy told him that Sandy, one of the girls whose time limit to stay at the shelter was running out, left saying she was going to The Lost Souls Club to get a job.

"*What?*" Andre flared. "I can't believe it after I warned everyone here to stay away from there. Did she think I was joking about it being a snake pit?"

"She was upset that her parents refused to take her back. Her time is running out here and —"

"I know, I know," he said with open hands. "We could have given her and extension while a foster home was sought out. I just can't believe she went there. How's she getting there? When did she leave?"

"She headed for the metro rail about a half-hour ago. It'll take her a few blocks from the club."

"What do you say we try to catch up to her? She doesn't know what she's getting herself into."

"Let's go," Windy said.

Andre hurried away in his midsize car, which was part of a new image of the average citizen rather than flaunting his wealth that no one was aware of other than him and Windy. Upon arriving at the club, Andre found the same parking space he had left earlier. Uncertain if they had beaten Sandy, they sat waiting, eyes shifting from the clock to the club door. An hour had passed when Andre decided he needed to check inside the club.

"Do you think it's a good idea?" Windy asked.

"No, but I can't just sit here. Where is she?"

"Maybe she decided not to come."

"Or maybe she's being swallowed in the pit right now."

"What if Big Jake is there and he sees you?"

"What if there's no tomorrow for her?"

"Let's go," Windy said.

"*Oh no*, you wait here."

"But –"

"But nothing and I mean it."

"You afraid he's going to put me back to work stripping?"

"I'm afraid we double the chances of being spotted together. I will inconspicuously go in, look around and be right back."

"Hurry," she said.

Grabbing a baseball cap from the back seat, Andre put it on and crept into the glimmering club looking down, and then peered about at the crowd entertained by strippers, music, and alcohol. Relieved that there was no sign of Big Jake or the girl, he sat observing, saw a waitress approaching, stood and returned to the car shaking his head and gasped.

"Well?" Windy said.

"Not there that I could see. And no big asshole either."

"I'm sure we would have beaten her here. Maybe she just had to cool off and she's back at the shelter?"

"Maybe? Maybe we'll never see her again. You know how things go in this crazy business. Here one day gone the next."

Driving away, Andre glanced at the flashing sign through his rearview mirror – *The Lost Souls Club*. Half-sick to his stomach, he couldn't help feeling somewhat responsible for Sandy's fate. Just the fact that he brought up the existence of the club ate away at him, thinking he somehow caused her to want to give up and accept Hell.

A ray of moonlight brightened Tom and Amy's dark bedroom, as each curled up on their side of the king-size bed. Tom turned over and looked at Amy who appeared to be asleep. Wanting to make amends, he slid to her side, cuddling and smothering her neck with kisses.

"No," she moaned, but Tom continued. "Knock it off."

"Come on," Tom pleaded.

"You don't want to have a baby then don't touch me."

"A baby isn't going to make things better between us."

"How do you know?" she snapped.

"Working with so many screwed up kids, I mean, come on. I don't think I could handle it right now."

"Well, I can."

"I don't know. I just don't know."

"Well, I do so just stay away from me."

"Fine," he snarled.

The next day at work, Tom and Tommy were engrossed in a checker match when Dick Muster, supervisor of the emergency unit, interrupted them.

"Have you seen Joey Nance around?" Dick asked. "He ran off after fighting with another kid and I saw him run up the stairway."

"I haven't seen him, but I've been sitting right here. Go look around if you want. Check the bedrooms out."

"Alrighty."

Leaving the recreation room, Dick started looking through the many bedrooms and entered one where a kid was lying on a bed playing a handheld video game.

"Have you seen Joey Nance?" Dick asked.

"No Dick," the boy said, "I haven't seen that twerp."

"You don't mind if I look around then?"

"Yeah I do *Dick*."

"Don't mess with me *jerk off*."

"You just have a poetic name. Dick Muster," he chuckled. "By the way, you like mustard on your wiener Dick?"

"Kiss my ass."

"Screw you," the boy said, standing.

Going to the closet door, Dick pulled it open. "If you're in here get your butt out."

"Just get the hell out of here dickhead."

Going up to the boy, Dick grumbled, bumping into the boy knocking him back onto the bed. "Oh sorry, didn't see you."

"*Come on*, leave me alone."

"Bye," Dick said, wide-eyed.

Returning to the recreation room, Dick told Tom that he hadn't found Joey and that he was going upstairs to look for him. Eyes peering around a hallway corner, Joey watched Dick ascend the stairway. Once there, a number of girls congregated around him. Putting his arms around two of them, he smiled and whispered while a female staff walked up the hall in their direction. Letting loose of the girls, he moved toward the staff.

"What's up?" the female staff asked.

"Aw, Joey's raising hell and is on the loose somewhere in the building."

"I haven't seen him."

"If you do, let me know."

"Sure thing."

Heading down the two flights of stairs, Dick caught sight of Joey down the hallway. "*Get back here now,*" he yelled. Joey took off running to another stairway. "The little jerk," he said, returning to the unit, knowing he would have the final word with him before the end of the day. Joey made it up to the girls' floor and peeked around the corner. Chastity, in her room, saw Joey peeking from the unit entrance and motioned for him to come over, which he did without being seen. Before long, the bedroom door shut and Joey was sitting on the bed with Chastity, enthused and excited. Chastity felt Joey's undressing eyes all over her and decided to take advantage of it.

"Could you massage my back?" she asked, lying on her stomach.

"Oh, yeah," he said getting aroused.

"You know dickhead was up here looking for you?"

"Yeah," he chuckled.

"Would you like to do me a favor?"

"*Sure,*" he said.

"Well, I have an idea," she said, sitting up, putting an arm around him and resting her head on his shoulder.

"Anything you want," he said, grin intact.

"I have a plan. I'll get one of the girls to help us. This is the deal ..."

Fifteen minutes later, Joey sneaked down the stairs to Tom's floor. Moving up the hallway to the boys' recreation room, Joey spotted Tom talking to two boys. Making sure Tom saw him, he gave him the finger. Tom took the bait and hurried toward Joey who moved to the exit with Tom chasing him up the stairway to the girls' unit. Joey scrambled to Chastity's room with Tom in pursuit. When Tom entered the bedroom, Joey was nowhere in sight. Noticing someone under the bed covers, Tom snickered while bending down. He placed his hand on the cover and jerked it off expecting to see Joey, but what he found was Chastity in bra and panties. Throwing her arms around his waist, she pulled him down onto the bed unaware of a girl shooting a video of them from the hallway.

"Let go of me," Tom said struggling to break loose. "Knock it off."

"That feels good," she raved. "I'm glad you came to see me."

"Stop it!"

The girl in the doorway rushed off so she wouldn't be spotted, but got on video what Chastity had wanted. Chastity let go of Tom who scrambled away to Amy's office at the end of a long hallway. Amy was in conference with a girl when Tom barged in.

"*What?*" Amy said.

"I was chasing Joey," he said frazzled. "I ran up here and he ran into a bedroom and I followed him. I didn't see him anywhere, but someone was under the bed covers so I pull the cover off and Chastity was there in bra and panties and grabbed me and was all over me."

Amy sprang up, gripped Tom's arm and led him away. "What the *hell's* wrong with you? Are you an idiot? You don't go into the damn girl's room without a female staff."

"I know. I know. I'm an idiot. But he ran in there and then I didn't see him."

Leading the way, Amy headed to Chastity's room. When they got there, no one was in the room.

"Well I don't know what to think," Amy said as she opened a closet. After looking around, they went to the recreation room where Chastity was playing a game of pool. A huge grin erupted on her face on seeing Tom and Amy approaching.

"Did Joey come up here?" Amy snapped.

"No, but Tom did," she said, moving to him with enticing eyes. "Why don't you play me a game of pool Tom?"

"Oh no, oh no," he stammered unsure of himself. "I've got to get back. Yeah, gotta get back," he said, walking away. "I need to find Joey."

"Bye Tommy," she said, smiling at Amy who sneered.

Steaming off, Tom thoughts were ignited. "What the hell was she trying to prove? She was almost naked. *Holy shit* if someone had seen that? Oh God, she's going to try to mess with me, I just know it. This is not good," he told himself, visualizing Chastity's cleavage in his face. "She's going to play this to the hilt if I know her. How could I be so stupid? ..."

Late one evening, homework completed, Rosetta sat back in a recliner, holding and petting a cat while watching a crime drama on television. With the show over, she flicked the screen off with the remote control. Eyes closed, mind wandering from internship issues to the completed painting of Big Jake, to the imagined face of her dad in the window; she then fell into a deep sleep. Once again, the thousandth rerun of her dad on top of her played out:

Young Rosetta shivered in bed, afraid to fall asleep fearing daddy would be in any minute. Then he was there kissing all over, fondling under pajamas and sweat clothes over the pajamas. She tried wearing as many clothes as possible, but it didn't stop him. Nothing would stop him. Then the nightmare shifted to when she was a young teenager clasping her stomach in terrible pain: "No dad! Please," she begged, and then screamed as he kicked her in the stomach. Turning, she ran up the stairs to the bedroom with him storming after her. "Why did you kick me? I'm having terrible pains in my stomach. Susie says her mom has pains like mine and she's pregnant. Could I be pregnant?" she asked, causing her father to land another blow to her stomach.

"Come here! You ain't pregnant," he insisted, but fearing she was as she hadn't started menstruating since the last time he forced himself on her.

"Stay away from me. I mean it. Please don't touch me. Ow! Ow!" Rosetta screamed being kicked in the stomach; tumbling down the short flight of steps, blood filling the crotch of her pants. "What's happening?" she whined.

"You have to stay in bed," he said, lifting and carrying her to her bedroom. "Everything will be okay."

"Why did you kick me?" she sobbed. "You hurt me. I'm going to tell Lynn. I won't take it anymore. You belong in jail. I mean it. I'll see you behind bars."

Tossing and turning, awakening from the night terror, "You made me miscarriage," she sulked, stomach churning at the thought that he had impregnated her. Eyes opening, she sighed in relief that it was only a nightmare, but began to weep believing the distress would never end. Sitting up, she went to the computer and typed in, 'How to end ongoing nightmares?' A number of sites came up offering advice, which she carefully read. One site suggested relieving tension through facing your fears by writing them out or drawing them, and then burning the paper in a safe container every night before bedtime. Although deviating from the suggestion, Rosetta drew a monstrous image of her dad; photocopied it and printed out a dozen copies. Taking one, she put it in a tall metal container she had found in the garage and torched the image with a lighter, watching the swirling smoke fill up the room, setting off the fire alarm. "Oh no," she screamed, rushing to open a window and holding the smoldering can out it. "What an idiot," she scolded herself waiting for the alarm to go off. Realizing a new nightmare needed to be dealt with, she left the bedroom to the art studio, took a photo of the agonizing painting of Gomez and Big Jake she created and made several copies of it. Once again, she continued the ritual by burning the photo, but this time lit it in the container outside on the concrete patio. Uncertain if relieved, she went to bed, visualizing the burning images of the past horror as if she were counting sheep.

Mind exhausted, sitting at his office desk at the shelter, Andre drifted off believing the worst for the girl who left in anger and despair. He imagined Big Jake getting his grubby hands on Sandy and forcing her into prostitution or trafficking her to a wealthy Arabian sheik for his harem; or to Hong Kong's Wan Chai's red light district, which had been Rosetta's designation when Big Jake tried to traffic her years earlier. Now Sandy's parents were willing to take her back after he had extensive phone conversations with them. He realized all of his efforts might have been in vain. All those memories of dealing with Big Jake and the past were put to ease when a bright-faced Windy hurried to him with the runaway girl. A sigh of relief radiated on Andre's face. Standing, he moved to them, nodding his head saying, "Pardon the cliché, but you are a sight for sore eyes."

"I had to let off some steam," Sandy replied.

"For two days?"

"Was it really two days? I must of lost track of time."

"Hey, I got good news for you," Andre said. "I've been talking to your parents. They're very concerned and they want you back. In fact, they're flying out here."

"That's hard to believe."

"It's true."

"Well, I don't know what to say or think. I can't stand them and yet –"

"Come on now. Try to work things out. This is your life were talking about. Don't be sorry someday that you didn't try. I can tell you from personal experience –"

"Please," she blurted. "Don't preach to me. I can't take it."

"Alright," he said with hands flipping up. "No preaching. Just give them a chance. That's it."

"Being on my own has been fun," she sighed, "but scary at times. I guess I should give them a chance. You did say they're coming here? Didn't you?"

"That's right. Give them a chance and give yourself a chance. Every second that ticks by is a second less to redeem yourself."

"*Redeem*?" she snapped. "You preaching to me again?"

"Sorry. I'm delusional. I plead insanity. Just talking about myself. When you get older, the clock ticks faster and there's less time to put your demons to rest. At any rate, this is your time so make it count."

Late in the evening, two hours before Tom and Amy's shifts were to end, Tommy returned from the girls' floor having delivered a book upstairs to Amy. While there, one of the girls, who despised Chastity, told Tommy to tell Tom that there was a video of him and Chastity and that he wouldn't like it. She told him that Tom better hurry upstairs because the girls were trying to put it on You Tube. Tommy wasted no time in telling Tom.

"Thanks for letting me know," Tom said to Tommy. Staring off in deep thought, face reddening, mind churning, he shot up as if zapped and moved in desperation to get upstairs. Upon arrival, he saw Amy in a bedroom talking to a girl. Seeing the frantic look in Tom's eyes, she went to him.

"Are you okay?" Amy asked.

"Where's Chastity?" Tom said, looking pale.

"What's wrong?"

"That thing I told you that happened."

"Yeah, what about it?"

"I just heard that someone videotaped it and the girls are trying to put it on YouTube right now."

Jaw dropping, she said, "They're in the rec room on the computer."

Tom stormed off with Amy following behind. On nearing the girls, Tom roared causing the group of girls to split apart like a tree hit by lightning. Without hesitation, Tom grabbed a hold of the memory card in the computer while seeing half-naked Chastity and himself on the screen and then yanked it out. Turning about, he looked at Amy shaking his head and walked away while the girls snickered.

"Jerk!" Chastity spat. "Hey dork, that's my memory card you just stole. You can't do that. You'll get yours. I won't forget ..."

After work, Tom and Amy got on their home computer and looked at the video on the memory card.

"You look like you're enjoying it," Amy said.

"Yeah, right," Tom said, smirk contained.

"She's got her big boobs right in your face. You look like you're sucking on 'em."

"Just make a joke of it. It's not funny."

"You've done some stupid things before at work, but letting them sucker you into this tops the list."

"What should I do about it? Do I let it go? Should I tell the boss what happened?"

"Don't you think you better tell him? In fact, you should write up an incident report."

"I don't know. Let me sleep on it. If I can sleep."

"Well I'm going to bed now," Amy said, half-enticing. "You coming?"

"I guess," he said, trying to sort things out about Amy's eagerness to go to bed.

Soon Tom found out when Amy came from the bathroom, wearing a scanty nightgown and a seductive smile which he hadn't seen for months. Getting on top of him in bed, she smothered his face with cleavage.

"This must be your lucky day," she said, "boobs in your face twice in one day."

"Oh yeah," Tom said, uncertain of what had gotten into Amy. "Yours is all I need."

"It better be."

After a passionate hour, they cuddled, exhausted and sweaty while thoughts showered their brains.

With a deep sigh, Tom said, "Isn't this much better than all the bickering that's been going on between us?"

"Of course. Don't you want to keep it like this?"

"Oh, yeah. Believe me, I do."

"Good because starting tomorrow I'm off the pill."

"What do you mean?"

"What do you think I mean?"

"Come on," he pleaded. "I'm not ready yet."

"I've heard it all before. You'll never be ready."

"It's just all these messed up kids we deal with. I want to come home to get away from kids."

"Then let's get out of this business."

"Easier said than done," Tom said.

"You know what?" she said scooting away. "Just don't touch me anymore."

"Come on," Tom said, reaching for her.

"*Stay away*. I mean it."

"You know having a baby under these circumstances couldn't be good. We both need to be on the same page don't you think? I really want kids, but it needs to be the right time for both of us. You don't want to have a baby and have me resent it do you?"

"I think you're scared to have kids. Aren't you?"

"Under these circumstances, yes."

"Just screw off."

Not wishing to argue anymore, Tom turned over facing away from Amy who did likewise. Feeling as if their moment of ecstasy had just turned into agony, Tom and Amy tormented the rest of the evening tossing and turning right into the break of dawn.

Chapter 6

A week of quarreling with sniper aimed eyes, Tom and Amy put on their armor to deflect the onslaught of words. Several attempts at making up were made, but when someone's glance seemed too shifty or a deep breath was too intense to tolerate, a blowup would follow. During the next week, they found a way to resolve the bickering – normal routines were carried on, but what was missing was communication other than a smirk, frown, sigh, yeah, yes, no and the like. The skirmish carried over at work, which was noticed by staff and residents. At bedtime, an invisible line stretched down the center of the bed. During the day, they cooked, ate and avoided one another as much as possible. Other than an occasional sly remark, their behavior became a silent war. The rift had been building and their reaction had created a thick wall bonded with mortar rather than icing as in past disagreements. There were no signs of either of them giving in until one evening; Tom realized that Christmas was approaching and that they would be visiting both their parents. As he looked out the window, the season's first snowfall had begun which delighted and motivated him to end the ongoing agony, wanting to recapture the passion of better times. While Amy was in a cushy chair in front of the fireplace reading a novel, Tom pushed away from the computer and inched his way towards her.

"I've been thinking," he said as she sneered.

Agitated by the response, he walked away and returned to writing. After pounding away on the computer keyboard for another hour, Tom stopped dead, stood up and repeated, "Alright we can have a baby. I'm okay with it. We can have a baby. I'm really okay with it. Besides, I told you before that after I completed my last novel that we could have a baby. It's not published, but it's been completed for awhile."

"Well, I've changed my mind for now."

"What?" he said, unsure of himself.

"It's not a good idea right now."

"Oh? Well –" He was speechless. "Aw, okay. Why?"

"Because I think you need to grow up. And I know you're still writing about us in your new novel and I don't like how you're portraying my character."

"You've been reading it?"

"Well, you're always asking me questions day and night about whether this or that should or shouldn't be in it. Then you print it out leaving it in plain sight inviting me to look at it. You know I'm right."

"Well yeah, I don't know, but –"

"*But nothing.* I don't like what you're writing."

"Come on," he pleaded, touching her shoulder.

Pushing his hand away, she said, "Leave me alone. Besides, I'm on my period and you usually don't want to touch me when I'm on it. You treat me like shit like I got a disease or something." She cast defiant eyes waiting for him to fire back, but he stood looking down.

Frustrated, knowing where this was headed, Tom retreated upstairs and put jogging clothes on. Returning downstairs, he slid into a winter coat, struggled with the zipper; yanked a pair of gloves on, slipped on a stocking cap, and exited into a sea of blinding snow relieving his burden of thoughts for the moment. An hour later, he returned, only to concentrate on warming up in front of the fireplace. Amy wasn't sitting by the fire as when he left but could be heard upstairs talking on the phone. After warming up, he headed upstairs to take a hot shower. Hearing Amy say goodbye made him wonder whom she had been talking to. While in the shower that wonderment became speculation, thinking about Burt Crebo on the night of their party and what he thought he had said to Amy. Asking himself if she could have been talking to Burt played on his mind. After turning the shower off, he heard Amy go down the steps in a hurry. Exhausted from thinking, he went into the bedroom, got under the bed covers and turned the television on. Flipping through channels, unable to find anything to watch; he blurted, "Damn it, a thousand stations and nothing's on." Eyes closing, he drifted off and had a thought that prompted him to get up and look out the window. Intrigued by the beauty of the snowstorm and winter's sudden appearance gave him an idea. Going to the computer, he looked up ski resorts in Colorado. Printing off some package deals, he headed downstairs, went to Amy who was watching a reality television show and handed her the printouts. Amy, whose passion for skiing was as great as Tom's, gleamed with interest as she read.

"What do you think?" Tom asked. "Don't you think we could use a vacation?"

"Yeah, I was thinking the same thing with it snowing out."

"What do you say we do it before Christmas?"

"Are you trying to make up?" she said.

"Well, yes."

"I'm for skiing."

"Good," he said, uncertain if that meant she wanted to make up. "I'll make arrangements for us to fly out there. Okay?"

"Yeah, sure," she replied with a half-smile.

"I can't wait. The thought is like seventh heaven."

"We'll have to put a vacation request in on Monday."

"There shouldn't be any problem getting off. Well, I guess I'll work on my novel."

"Just be kind. Don't make me look like a bitch. You hear me?"

"Okay," he said, squeezing her shoulder, happy that she did not flinch or complain. Walking away, he went into the other room and resumed working on his novel at the computer.

Rosetta found out she needed to deal with new fears, facing the world as a student intern at the police department. Detective Mike Palermo, the intern supervisor, had her observing and following him around on cases. He was single, handsome and couldn't help being attracted to her beauty, perkiness and desire to learn. She was determined to overcome the past in order to move forward. Being a part of the criminal justice system was a way of trying to deal with it. Completing the paperwork trail was fundamental to the learning experience, but being out on cases was exciting and horrifying at times. She got to observe and participate in the investigation of a robbery, a shooting, and even a murder. Dealing with tough situations was nothing new to Rosetta. As a juvenile, she fell into the pit of drug and alcohol abuse, coerced prostitution and suicidal thoughts. On this day, Rosetta followed the detective into a house. Everyone sat around a table as the victim of a home break-in described what took place.

"Well," said a middle-aged man, "I told the officer last night the whole story."

"I know," Detective Palermo said, "but your break-in was one of three last night in the area. I wanted to see if you could give a detailed description of the guy. There has been a rash of break-ins lately and we think they are all connected. First tell me what happened."

"Well," the victim said. "It must have been around 2:30 in the morning. I thought I was waking up from a dream. I was in bed. It was dark in the bedroom because the door was shut. I had the door shut so the cat wouldn't mess with the parrot. I had a nightlight on in the other room. I don't really know what woke me up. Maybe I heard something. I'm not sure. But it was like a nightmare where someone is standing over you and you wake up to stop the nightmare. But in this case, there really was someone standing over me. It's like I could feel his presence. I could even smell him. I couldn't believe it. Can you imagine waking up and seeing someone standing over you? I mean, I live here alone. I flicked the light on and there he was."

"Why was he standing over you?"

"I don't know. I don't think he even saw me until I turned the nightstand light on. He walked into a pitch black room."

"Then what happened?"

"I said to him what are you doing here. And he said I thought this was Joe's crib. And I said well it's not and you're leaving. I jumped up and chased him out."

"So he ran?" Detective Palermo asked.

"Not really. I just ushered him out the front door."

"What did he look like?"

"I couldn't really tell I was in such shock. I think he had a jacket and a stocking cap on. He was white and thin. That's all I can tell you now. If I can remember more about him, I'll let you know."

"You told the officer last night that you didn't see anything missing. Is that still the case?"

"He moved the stereo but apparently couldn't get the speaker wires undone. And he messed with my camera but the batteries fell out so he must have set it back down. But I couldn't find anything missing."

Rosetta attentively listened, but could not resist asking, "How did he get in?"

"Well," said the victim shaking his head. "This is a good neighborhood. I usually lock my doors, but I just forgot to lock the backdoor last night. As I walked around after getting him out of here, I could just smell his presence. I could tell where he had been in the house from the smell."

"You probably smelled drugs," said the detective. "Possibly crack-cocaine."

"You said there were other break-ins around here?"

"Just up the street."

"The officer last night told you not to touch anything because we would want to dust for fingerprints."

"I didn't touch anything after he said that."

"Good," said the detective. "Show me what you know that he touched."

"Sure, just follow me."

After the detective dusted for fingerprints, he and Rosetta walked out the front door. Before they got to the car the detective said, "I'll put my dustings in the car then we can talk to neighbors to see if they saw or heard anything."

"Can I do one on my own?" Rosetta asked.

"Well, I guess I could let you have some hands on experience. You take the house next door and I'll go to the house across the street. You know the routine. Get people's names and take their statements. If there's anything big come and get me. Does that sound like a plan?"

"Got you," she replied. "Anything worthwhile come and get you."

"Alright, I'll meet you back at the car."

Rosetta cased out the house as she had been taught and then went up to the front door. After knocking, a man opened the door and had an uneasiness about him that caught Rosetta's attention.

"Yeah," said the man, looking Rosetta over, and then taking note of the unmarked police car in front of the house.

"I'm with the police department and we are investigating a break-in next door. I need to ask you some questions."

"Well, I guess come on in," he said, leading the way to a kitchen table.

Rosetta followed, paying close attention to her surroundings as she had been taught. She made sure that she knew where all the exits were in the case of an unexpected attack.

"Sit down," the man ordered as he sat at the kitchen table.

Taking a seat, she noticed empty beer can's on the counter and kitchen table. In another room, she saw a woman and a teenage girl who were preoccupied, but who became almost silent when they saw her.

"A burglary next door?" the man asked concerned, hands in pockets.

"Yes, and I was wondering if you saw or heard anything last night?"

"What in the hell happened there?"

"Someone broke in and was trying to rob the place during the middle of the night. Did you hear or see anything?"

"Didn't see or hear a damn thing."

"Well," she said, smelling the scent of alcohol on him. "Do you think they heard or saw anything?" she said looking into the other room.

"*Oh no,*" he said, fists forming inside of his pants pockets. "They didn't see nothing."

"Do you care if I talk to them?"

"For what?" he said agitated.

"I just told you why."

"And I just told you they don't know shit."

"What's your name sir?"

"Why you want my name?" Mr. Engel asked.

"This is just routine."

With their voices getting louder, Mrs. Engel and the teenage daughter, Brittany, walked into the kitchen.

"What's going on?" Mrs. Engel said.

"There was a break-in next door," Rosetta said, "and I was wondering if either of you saw or heard anything?"

Mr. Engel was uneasy, but let them talk.

"I had no idea," Mrs. Engel said.

Brittany hesitated, and then spoke up. "I saw him run out of the house and down the street."

"*You did?*" Rosetta said, sensing fear from the girl.

"All I could make out," she said, "was an orange hood sticking out the back of his coat. Must have had an orange hooded sweatshirt on. I saw the neighbor step outside and the man run up the street."

"So it was a man?"

"I'm pretty sure," she said.

"Alright," Rosetta said, "I need to write down your statement and I want everyone's names."

After collecting the names, she took Brittany's statement who spoke with a slight tremble, no eye contact and an empty look, which caused Rosetta to wince; hands opened pleading for her to open up.

Brittany licked her lips, paused and then said, "You know, I wish I could tell you more."

"Is there something else on your mind?" Rosetta said, observing the girl jitter, glancing at her dad.

"No," she replied looking down. "No, no, that's it."

"Okay, if you think of anything else contact me," Rosetta said writing down her and Detective Palermo's name and office phone number.

On meeting up with the detective who was waiting in the car, Rosetta told him about the interviews and that she was suspicious that something bad was going on in the house.

"You need more than a suspicion," Detective Palermo said.

"It's just a gut feeling that I have."

"And what is it?"

"I think she's being sexually abused by her dad."

"Why?"

"The way she acted. The way she looked at him. And he reeked of booze. Beer cans were all over the place. You could tell they were both scared of him."

"We need more than that. Did she say anything?"

"Nothing specific," Rosetta sighed.

"There's nothing we can do based on what you've told me."

"I just know," she said, and then told herself, "I know because I've been there. I've lived it. I saw my life in that girl." As she held her thoughts in, the detective drove off and spoke about the break-in.

"Hey," he said changing the subject, "we'll be getting off in an hour. How about going down to Rosie's Tap with me. It's a regular hangout for cops."

"I've told you I don't drink."

"Come on loosen up a bit. This job will drive you nuts if you don't."

"I really can't."

"They have good food there. I'll buy."

"You asking me out?"

"Oh no," he said, "a – I mean, that might not look right while you're still an intern. Let's call it a friendly appreciation for your assistance – you know like you're my partner right now."

"We'll if you put it that way," she said looking into his bright eyes. "Yeah, sure. Why not."

Nodding he said, "Alright then. I thought you might be allergic to my cologne."

"Well, I might be. Don't plan on me getting that close to finding out."

"Have it your way."

"I will," she said, smiling.

On returning to the station, there was a message on the office phone for Rosetta from Brittany. Mike handed her the phone and said he would be back in awhile. Listening to the message, Rosetta detected a wavering tone in Brittany's voice which said there was something else she had thought of and that she would call back soon.

"I knew it," Rosetta blurted, and thought it better to wait for the call than calling back fearing the dad would answer it. Before long, the phone rang, and Rosetta picked it up saying, "Springfield PD, Rosetta speaking." There was silence. "Is this Brittany?" she asked.

"Yes," she said in a low, secretive voice.

"You called?"

"Well, a, well yeah."

"There's something you didn't tell me isn't there?"

"Well," she hesitated.

"Believe me you can tell me," Rosetta said.

"I just wanted to tell you that I thought the burglar was drunk or high on something."

"Oh?"

"Yeah, he wobbled and fell once while he was running. You know, I don't know, if that helps or not?"

"You never know. There's something else on your mind isn't there?"

"Well," she hesitated, "not really."

"You sure?"

"That's all I wanted to say."

"It's okay. You can tell me."

"I better not, there's nothing else to tell."

"Alright Brittany, I'm here if you need anything. I mean it."

"Okay, thanks."

Rosetta sighed and paced, thinking about how she had told Brittany that it was okay for her to tell and how she responded, 'I better not.' This was all needed to be convinced Brittany needed help. When it was time to quit for the day, Rosetta tried changing her mind about going out, but the detective wouldn't hear of it. Leading the way in his car, she followed behind. Once at the club and seated, Detective Palermo insisted on being called Mike. Trying to humor him, she called him Michael. After ordering food, Rosetta headed to the restroom and received a pat on the butt by a drunk who tried wrapping his arm around her until she jerked her elbow back cracking him right in the snout.

"Oh shit, damn it, damn it," the man moaned wiping the blood from his nose. "You stupid bitch."

As he reached to grab her, Mike grabbed the man's arm, "Take it easy buster."

"Who the *hell* are you?"

"The man who's going to arrest you if you don't settle your butt down."

"I don't think so," he growled, cocking his arm throwing a punch. Mike backed away catching the man's arm and twisted it behind his back.

"You think I'm kidding ass wipe?" Mike said, pushing the man up against the bar.

"*Hey, Lou,*" the bartender shouted at the trouble maker; "this guy is a cop. I want you out of here now or he can take you to jail."

"You heard him," Mike whispered in his ear. "You have one chance to walk out of here. Take it."

After letting go of the man's arm, the man turned around, eyeing Mike, and then looked at Rosetta who stood nearby. "You ain't no fuckin' cop," he said, tottering.

"*Yes, he is,*" the bartender yelled.

"Oh really?" Lou's face cringed while he moved his head from side to side, trying to analyze if Mike was a cop. When Mike pulled his coat open revealing a holstered sidearm, Lou nodded. "Okay, I'm out of here."

After he was gone, Rosetta and Mike sat to eat. "You know why I didn't arrest him don't you?" Mike said.

"Because he was just a stupid drunk."

"Yeah, he was, but I didn't want him messing up our dinner. You know, paperwork, calling for help to haul him away."

Smirking, she said, "I got him good in the face."

"You sure did. Hey, I'm really sorry about this. Generally, there are a bunch of cops here after work and this guy wouldn't have shown his ass."

"Forget it. It's not your fault."

With dinner finished each went their own way. Instead of heading right home, Rosetta drove to Brittany's house, parked across the street, and observed as her fingers gripped the steering wheel. Hoping to catch the girl leaving the house, she wanted to find out the truth and planned to use the next door break-in as an excuse to confront her. At one point, she saw the girl walk by an upstairs window and thought it was Brittany's bedroom. When the dad walked by the same window; Rosetta's heart sped up and mind raced back to the horror of her dad sneaking in her room at night. Then the room light went out. Rosetta wanted to scream. Fighting the urge to storm the house, she shook agonizing over what to do. Moments later, she saw the girl through a window on the main floor and sighed in relief. A half-hour later, Rosetta turned the engine key, took a deep breath with foot tapping the accelerator and the car crept by the house.

Chapter 7

Andre and Windy arrived at the back door of the runaway shelter to relieve the third shift staff. The female worker rambled about a new arrival and stressed that Sandy, who was meeting with her parents at the shelter on this day, was pacing the floor and had threatened to leave. Andre attended to the new arrival while Windy went to Sandy who stood by the front window.

"Sandy," Windy said. "Try to calm down. Everything will work out."

"You don't know my parents."

"They're flying in from Indiana and they wouldn't be coming if they didn't care about you."

"I need a smoke. Come on," she said leading the way out the door. "But they're mean to me."

"How's that?" Windy asked shutting the door while Sandy lit up a cigarette.

"They treat me like a baby," she said pacing. "They're always making rules. I had enough of their restrictions. That's why I'm in LA. *Freedom.*"

"Freedom? Come on wise up. There's always a price for freedom."

"Whataya mean?"

"Sleeping in a shelter or maybe on the streets for one. Wondering where your next meal's coming from or who's going to do you harm. The streets are rough, I've been there. You're not free. You're prey for the slime ball creeps waiting to use you. Believe me, I know."

"You really think they want me back?"

"I know it."

"So help me if they get in my face I'm out of here."

"Go home before the streets eat you alive. Don't fight them. Work it out. Your life isn't freedom. You're a step away from slavery. You want to be some pimps whore?"

"Not me."

"Be smart. Don't be sorry. Earn your freedom ..."

In another room, Andre spoke to the new boy. "Looking at the paperwork completed on you Michael, I see that you are seventeen, from Iowa and hope to become a star."

"I act, I sing, I play the guitar," he said.

"So do half the kids that come here. The only stars I see are falling stars. You don't even have to go outside to see them. They're on the evening entertainment news every night."

"But everyone back home said I was bound for stardom. I had the leads in high school and community productions ..."

"I know this is a cliché, but many are called and few are chosen. Half the kids coming here are California dreaming about stardom or a better life. Don't you know the unemployment line for actors is out of sight? If you're so talented why didn't you continue your education in the arts before coming out here? Or at least come out here for school to prepare for your dream?"

"I got kicked out of the house. It's cold in Iowa. I'm ready now. They say I'm a natural."

"But how's your luck? Can you beat a fixed slot machine or dodge a bullet aimed for your head? Do you feel real lucky? Do you know anyone out here that can make your dream come true? Are you more talented than a thousand other kids auditioning for one available role? If the answer is yes to all those questions then I say go for it. You're ready because being faster than a speeding bullet puts you in a class of your own ..."

Later in the day, Sandy sat in an office while Andre and Windy led the parents to her. Half-shaky, half-relieved to see them, Sandy's chin dropped unable to speak as they approached with extended arms. Standing up, Sandy and the parents hugged with tears of joy.

"I'm sorry," Sandy said.

"We've been worried sick," the dad said.

The mother wept saying, "Oh baby, thank God you are okay."

The parents and daughter returned to Indiana, but Andre and Windy's resolve, in this case, was a small victory as they knew that a runaway or homeless child was headed to their doorway in need of shelter. Later that evening, at their home, Andre and Windy relieved the stress of the day between the sheets. Kicking the covers off the bed; they moved as one together, bodies intertwined until exhausted. Spread out on the bed, silence prevailed for minutes as they collected their thoughts.

"What got into you tonight?" Windy said.

"You still know how to flick my switch."

"You sure it wasn't that hot new girl that came in at the end of the day dressed like a whore that got you all hot and bothered?"

"Of course not, but you know she did make me start thinking about the past and how Big Jake is too close for my liking. I would like to see someone shove him back in that rat hole he crawled out of and end his preying, scheming existence. I can remember talking to Tom when we worked at the group home together about a poem he wrote called Erebus and it being a long dark passage to Hell. I thought he got sent down that dark hole once but it looks like he crawled back out."

"Maybe he's changed," Windy said. "I mean you did."

"He hasn't. You have to have a heart and soul to change. He's darkness personified."

"Personified?" Windy said with a quizzical look.

"You know – darkness in flesh and blood, alive and kicking. He can be a person's worst nightmare. He was mine at one time sucking the life out of me. Some things are too agonizing to bury."

"You're right, he's scum and to close for comfort."

"If he knew we were here and what we are doing I would absolutely go nuts. We fled to get away from that cancer. He can't ever find out we are here."

"It's a big city," she said, grabbing his hand.

"Just not big enough. You know cancers have a way of creeping up on you when you least expect it."

"Just screw him. We can't live fearing the past."

"True, but it's the present that worries me."

"Come here," she said, rolling her warm inviting body against his.

"Oh yeah, again? Trying to drown me in ecstasy?"

"Yeah, a little ecstasy to free your agony," she said, smothering his face as if he were a nursing baby.

In winter's grasp, Tom and Amy sought to break through the glacier dividing them. That break landed them in the heart of Colorado ski country, hoping that their desire to escape would thaw their disposition. The powdery snow in Vail brought smiles to their faces while coasting along a pleasant, smooth-sailing run. With a black diamond slope in sight, the daredevil in Tom blossomed and they slowed down and stopped to evaluate it. Both smiled at one another and Tom swooshed away. Amy, who thought she was as good of a skier as Tom, followed his lead, staying close behind. When the slope took a diving plunge, Tom lost control tumbling and sliding on his butt. Amy slowed down to avoid the same mistake and snowplowed to the snow covered Tom who was struggling to get up. Coming to a near stop, Amy smiled and then sped off down the hill. Once up, Tom hurried to try to catch up but failed to do so until he reached the chairlift line. While alone on the two seated lift, Tom broke the silence.

"Why didn't you stop and wait for me. I could have been hurt."

"You weren't," she said.

"You didn't know that."

"I could tell. You smiled at me."

"See if I check on you when you take a spill."

After skiing for the day, Tom wanted to stay in and order pizza, but Amy wanted to go out to eat and to take in Vail's nightclubs.

"But I want to hit the slopes early," Tom whined. "We'll get up late if we go out. Plus I thought we could spend some time in bed together. You know?"

"The only thing I know is that it's always got to be your way."

"Let's compromise. We'll go out to eat, but we won't go to the bars."

"Whatever," she grumbled. "Oh, by the way, I'm off the pill. How does that grab you?"

By the fourth day, Tom and Amy's bliss of powdered ski runs was taking an agonizing tumble off the slopes. They hoped to renew their passion for one another, only to find themselves arguing about whom took better photos of the other skiing or about one thing or the other. Since Tom had suggested skiing, he thought he should try to break the ice. They hadn't made love the entire trip and while Amy got under the bed covers, Tom did likewise and turned the light out.

"Good night," Amy said.

"Can we talk?"

"Yeah," she muttered.

"I really don't know what's happened to us but I'm tired of bitching at each other. I'm tired of being miserable. Listen to me. We're both counselors. We can work this out if we try. We're not really trying. We feed into each other's quirks and pet peeves. It just seems like you don't know when to let up."

"*Me*? It's you who won't let up."

"Here we go again."

"What do you suggest?" she asked.

"Let's just put an *end* to it right now."

"The end," she blurted.

"Don't do this," he pleaded.

"Do what?"

"I'm trying to be sincere. In fact, I've done a lot of thinking."

"Come here," she said, pulling him close enticing his passions. Embracing, kissing and out of control lovemaking followed. Sweaty bodies collapsed after ten minutes. Skiing had worn them down but their aroused passions had thawed the iceberg between them for the moment.

Eyes closed, Tom's fading voice said, "Like I said I've been doing a lot of thinking and I guess this was my answer."

"What do you mean?" she whispered.

"Well, you're off the pill so I guess a baby is okay."

"I don't think so."

"What do you mean?" he stressed.

"I'm back on the pill."

"But you said you were off of it and I thought –"

"I changed my mind. I was only off of it for that one day."

"What?" he said, unsure whether he should be relieved or upset. "I don't understand?"

"You're not really ready and I decided I'm not ready."

"But this is what you've wanted for the past five years."

"Go to sleep. We gotta get up early. Tomorrow's our last day."

"Yeah," he said resigned. As he tried to sleep, he tossed and turned thinking of what Amy said. "She doesn't want a baby," he told himself. "What does it mean? Maybe something is going on between –" he hesitated. "Just shut up. Maybe it's too late for us. You've screwed up man. What to think? And I thought I surprised her by having sex thinking she was off the pill. What the hell's going on? I just felt like I was in seventh heaven and now feel like shit. How ironic. Ecstasy turned to agony. Is this what I'm going to be writing about when we get home? She's already pissed at what you've written …"

Past demons kept Rosetta from getting close to any male. Horrifying experiences, beginning with her father, to boyfriends, culminating with Gomez's obsession, and making her a part of it, contributed to distrusting males. She liked Mike and could tell that he had feelings for her, but for now, all she could concentrate on was completing the internship and dealing with the anxiety it was producing. Every evening after work, Rosetta found herself observing Brittany's house, hoping to find the opportunity to talk to her again. This evening was no different. Having seen Brittany through upstairs and downstairs windows, she feared seeing more than she could handle. An ongoing nightmare of what she imagined was taking place drew her back to the house. Believing Mr. Engel was a monster that needed to be stopped, she was there to do it. On this evening, observing the girl through the upstairs bedroom window, peering out at the light snowfall, she noticed Mrs. Engel walk out the front door and drive away. Seeing Mr. Engel seated in the living room was reassuring, but when he stood up, she jumped watching like a cat eyeing a mouse. When he went up the stairway, panic crept up her throat. Then Brittany looked away from the window and Mr. Engel appeared in the room. Grip tightening on the steering wheel, Rosetta saw what looked like an argument. Then they disappeared from sight. When the bedroom light went out, Rosetta stepped out of the car and rushed to the house. Walking back and forth in front of it, she didn't see anyone. Panicky, she looked all around to make sure no neighbors were watching and then crept along the side of the house looking through window's, but still saw no one. Unable to stand it, she scrambled back to the car and called Mike on his cell phone.

"Hello," Mike said.

"It's me," she said.

"So did you change your mind about going out tonight?" he asked.

"Listen to me," she said. "You know the house next to the break-in I told you about?"

"Break-in? Oh yeah."

"You know I told you about my suspicions. Right?"

"I remember."

"It's happening right now!"

"What?"

"He's doing it to her right now."

"*What*? How do you know?"

"Because I'm outside their house watching."

"You can see it happening?"

"No, but the light went out in the bedroom. They were both in there. I didn't see anyone come out."

"Start from the beginning and explain every detail including why you are there?"

"I've just been watching from my car once in awhile. That's not illegal, is it? At any rate, the mom left and he went up to the room ..."

"Alright, calm down. Sit tight and I'll come over. Maybe we can do dinner later. Okay?"

"*Okay*. Just get over here now."

Fifteen minutes later, Mike pulled up parking behind Rosetta's car. Stepping out, he went to the passenger side of the car and got in. "This is a small car. It's nice. Looks expensive. Okay, calm down. So what's happened?"

"I don't know," she said fidgeting, "but dad's downstairs in the kitchen now."

"So you didn't see anything. Right?"

"But I just know," she whined.

"Maybe you're right, but there's got to be more to go on. Now he's downstairs. What can you prove?"

"I can just sense it," she said, tears in her eyes.

"You know I shouldn't be saying this, but if you want to make an excuse to talk to her again then do it. However, for now, you have nothing but a feeling. It may be right, but you need more."

"Alright, I'll find a way to talk to Brittany."

"So where do you want to eat?"

"I don't know. I don't care."

"Calm down. Okay. The dad's sitting in the kitchen. Oh, and look. Is that mom pulling in the drive?"

"Yeah it is."

"So where will it be?"

"You decide and I'll follow."

"Good. Just follow me." Leading the way to the police station parking lot, he got out while she stayed in the car. Going up to her window, she rolled it down and he said, "Come on, ride with me."

"You're making it more complicated."

"Not me. We're just carpooling to save gas."

"Yeah, right."

"Come on."

"Can you think of any reason for both of us to go back to that house on business?"

"I've got a plan, come on get in."

Hesitant, but eager to hear his idea, she got in the car and said, "So what's the plan?"

"Well, you know a sketch was drawn of the perpetrator based on the break-in victim's description."

"Right."

"We can go back there and show the sketch to the dad, mom, and girl and see if they recognize the image. Oh, by the way, the fingerprints for the break-in didn't turn up anything."

"That's too bad. But getting back to Brittany – can I talk to her alone?"

"We can try to think of something."

"Can we go there right now?"

"*Now?*"

"Then I'll let you take me out to eat."

"What?"

"We're right here at the station. Go get the drawing. Besides, if something just happened, she might say something."

"You drive a hard bargain, but I'll be right back."

Fifteen minutes later, they were knocking on the front door at Brittany's house.

"Get back," the dad told his daughter, "I've got it."

Opening the door, Mr. Engel's jaw tightened and hands slid into his pockets. "Now what?" he blurted.

"Mr. Engel," Detective Palermo said, "could we come in and talk for a moment?"

"What's this about?"

"It's about the break-in next door."

"I told you all I know."

"We got a sketch of the intruder."

"Go 'head show it to me."

"It's better if we come in. We want everyone to look at it."

"Alright then," he said with apprehension.

Rosetta caught sight of Brittany and the mom seated in the living room while she and Mike were led to the kitchen. All took a seat and Mr. Engel looked at the sketch.

"Don't know him."

"Let me show it to your daughter," Rosetta said, grabbing the sketch.

"Hold on," Mr. Engel said. "*Brittany*," he shouted. "Come here. And bring the old lady with you."

Rosetta glanced at Mike with harsh eyes and then saw Brittany walk in, eyes cast down, followed by her mom who squinted at her husband as she mumbled, "The old lady." Rosetta stood and showed them the sketch, but neither of them recognized the image.

"Is everything okay?" Rosetta asked the girl.

Pausing for a moment, the girl's eyes flashed to the dad's in awe and Rosetta took notice. "Well yeah," she said, rubbing her hands together. "I mean, I kind of have an upset stomach, but I'm okay."

"You sure?" Rosetta prodded, glancing back and forth between them.

"*You heard her*," the dad snapped. "So are you done 'cause we're busy?"

"No!" from Rosetta, noticing a frown from Mike. "I mean –"

"Yes we're done," Mike said. "Thanks for looking."

"Brittany," said Rosetta, "you said you saw the man running watching from your bedroom. Could you take me up there and show me."

"Why you need to go up there?" Mr. Engel asked.

"I just need to verify that you could tell a specific color looking down from the room. Brittany had said he had an orange hood. In fact, do you have any orange clothing in the house?"

"*No*," Mr. Engel said.

"I have an orange scarf in the closet," Brittany said.

"Good, get it," Rosetta insisted.

Brittany hurried to the closet and back and handed Rosetta the heavy winter scarf.

"Here Detective," Rosetta said handing it to him. "Put it around your neck and go walk on the street."

"Sure thing," he responded.

As he went out the door, Rosetta told Brittany to lead the way. Mr. Engel stood, casting hard eyes at his daughter who proceeded to lead the way upstairs.

Entering the bedroom, Rosetta took note of the entire layout of the room, and then went to the window and looked out. "Yes, you can definitely see the orange scarf. You never know what information might become useful."

"I'm glad I could help," Brittany said.

"One other thing," Rosetta said low-keyed. "If there was something bad going on here you would tell me wouldn't you?"

"What do you mean?"

"Like if you were being mistreated or something like that."

Brittany's mouth dropped, eyes looked down as she said, "Everything's okay I guess."

"Something's wrong isn't it?"

"I don't know – I mean nothing's wrong."

"Look me in the eye and say that."

Brittany's empty eyes stared through Rosetta as she said, "Nothing's wrong."

"Okay, but if there is something wrong and you don't want to tell me, promise me one thing. Tell your mom. Do you hear me?"

"Yes," she said teetering back and forth.

Footsteps could be heard coming up the steps to the distress of Brittany who said, "Let's go back down."

"Sure," Rosetta said, leading the way and meeting Mr. Engel halfway up the stairway.

"I was wondering," said Mr. Engel, "what was taking so long?"

"Well we're done now," Rosetta said restraining herself from further comment.

Mike came back in and handed Brittany the scarf. "Could you see it?" he asked.

"Definitely," Rosetta said as Brittany gazed off without saying a word.

"Thanks again," Mike said.

Walking toward the door, Rosetta and Brittany's eyes connected. Rosetta was certain that she was hiding something, but had no choice but to leave.

While driving away, Mike said, "You were pretty bold there. That was quick thinking about the orange hood. So what happened upstairs?"

"I was right all along," Rosetta said.

"She told you?"

"*Yes.*"

"You're kidding," Mike said stunned. "What did she say?"

"It's not what she said. It's what she didn't say."

"What are you saying? Did she tell you or not?"

"Not in words, but her behavior was right on. She couldn't look me in the eye. Everything was there but the words. I got her to commit to telling her mom."

"She said she would tell her?"

"Basically yes."

"You need to explain yourself better."

"You had to be there to know what I mean. She promised me that if there were something going on she would tell her mom. Let's see if we get a phone call from her or her mom."

"Maybe you're on to something, but right now it's still not enough."

"When I look at her I see my –" she paused. "I mean, I see the anxiety in her eyes."

"Step back and give it time. But for now, let's get a bite to eat."

"No, I'm not hungry now. I'm too uptight about all of this."

"You can't back out now. Come on we'll talk more about it at dinner."

"I guess," she conceded.

Chapter 8

In the hub of Chicago's nightclub district sat The Lost Souls Club. On entering, dim ruby floodlights created a dark, but an intriguing atmosphere as the lights moved in all directions. The packed club had people standing to watch Sister Barbie, a headline striptease act, direct from Las Vegas with young girlish looks, packing a pair of 38 D silicone perfections. Waiting for her introduction, the crowd chanted *Barbie, Barbie*. In a large soundproof room with thick panel glass separating them from the crowd sat a large round table, seating eight well-dressed men. They drank, watching the white and blue floodlights beaming down on the stage while the patron's shouted and clapped their hands. Wearing a brimmed hat, front turned down, a broad-shouldered, stout man spoke while the others listened.

"They say the economy sucks," Big Jake said. "But lucky for us sex sells in good and bad times. So let's watch Sister Barbie do her thing and then we'll carry on with business."

The show went on to the delight of the audience. Big Jake who owned a half a dozen nightclubs, two in Chicago, two in the heart of Illinois, one in Vegas and the other in LA, had his hand in sex, gambling, drugs and human trafficking. Other than the nightclubs, he tried to keep his operations low-key and off the radar from the authorities. But like all power hungry individuals, he grew more daring and confident believing that he was untouchable. This was due to large contributions he made too many elected candidates. Some of those political figures were also patrons who frequented his prostitutes. He had a leash on many affluent people who wanted to keep their skeletons locked in a closet. Having come up through the ranks of major corruption, he never dirtied his hands as a petty criminal. His connections crossed borders and seas. The orient was an area he was trying to expand to for human trafficking of teenage girls. He was developing a strong relationship with the Chinese mob after opening a nightclub in Chicago's Chinatown.

After Sister Barbie's performance, the backroom group got down to business.

"You know," said Big Jake, "my favorite gal is the gal making me a buck. Unfortunately, I don't have time to squeeze every new fine ass you bring in. We need fresh, clean, young and beautiful girls."

"I say we just seek and snatch off the streets," said a cohort.

"Johnny, Johnny boy," said Big Jake. "Your brains are in your ass, you knucklehead. We're not maniacs, we're businessmen. We arrange for our girls to come to us. We groom them. We gain their confidence. And of course," he said with a smile, "we drug them if all else fails, but we don't snatch the *snatch* off the streets. I better never hear of you doing such foolish bullshit."

"But you complain," Johnny said, "that the demand is greater than the supply. In fact, the supply has really been sucking lately."

"We've tried different approaches," Big Jake said, standing and pacing. "We've gotten teens as payment for gambling debts, but that rarely works out. Runaways' coming to work for us has been our money tree. Runaways can disappear forever? Right? What happens when we send them to rich sheiks? What happens when we send them to the red light district in Hong Kong or down across the border to our bordellos. I'll tell you what it means. *Big bucks.* If we act like buffoons, we risk getting caught. I want to pursue an old idea that never developed. I've got a girl working for me that came out of a children's home and she thinks that's our gold mine. Those kids there have a big runaway history and we need to connect with these sweeties. We need someone on the inside to pick out the right girls – one's that don't have a family or at least a family that don't give a shit. Kids that won't be missed by someone. We don't want some parent all over the news raising cane. Low-key is our new policy. Is that understood?"

The group of men nodded in agreement. "How do you get someone on the inside?" said a man.

"I'll work on that," Big Jake stressed. "I've had dealings with this in the past and have ideas. I will deal with it …"

A Chinese associate spoke up. "I don't care how you get these honeys, but get them. We only get one girl from you for every ten we bring in from China."

"That's because," said another man half-chuckling, "one American ass is worth ten Chinese ones. It translates to that in money terms. Our sweeties command five times as much as your whores. But I'm with you. More is always better. But prime beef commands more."

At Big Jake's request, an attractive, scantily dressed waitress entered the room with a round of drinks. All grabbed a drink with a few grabbing the waitresses lower assets, which caused her to giggle and smile on receiving tips stuffed in the cleavage of her low cut top.

Johnny spoke up, "Why don't we deal in young males? There's a market for them ..."

While Johnny spoke, Big Jake fumed inside thinking of how as a young kid he had been repeatedly molested, which no one but him and the molester new about. Moving to Johnny, Big Jake snorted setting his hands on his shoulders. *"I don't like dealing with perverts,"* he roared, grabbing Johnny's hair and yanking his head back. "You're getting real stupid Johnny. I don't like stupid people around me. If I hear any more crap out of your mouth, you won't be opening it again." With a sudden jerk on the back of his chair, he sent Johnny to the floor.

Johnny looked up in fear and then said, "You're right boss, you're right. I hate queers. I'm a moron."

"Well, you better not be one of those cock suckers that like little boys," Big Jake growled. "So help me if I thought –"

"Not me! I'm no pervert boss."

"You better not be," he said lighting up a cigar-puffing away, placing a foot on Johnny's shoulder, and then shouted, "pull down the shades." Two men stood and did as commanded. "Now we got some privacy." Pulling out his pistol, he placed the barrel in Johnny's mouth. "If you like to suck on things, suck on this." Johnny froze, barrel pushed deep into his mouth, eyes protruding ready to explode. "I said *suck*." Sucking is what he did while saturating his pants until Big Jake pulled the gun out of his mouth.

"I'm sorry," Johnny pleaded, trembling.

"Shut the fuck up and get up. You smell like piss. Get the hell out of here now." Big Jake took his brimmed hat off, revealing a full head of hair, and held up a shot glass, "A toast," he said, "to a great new year of business for us. I will be flying to our club in LA tomorrow. So keep things rolling here."

Back in the City of Angeles, Andre and Windy heard from Sandy's parent's two weeks after their return to Indiana. Sandy had taken off from home again and they feared she might return to California. Although disheartened and concerned, Andre and Windy knew there was little they could do unless she returned to them. What no one knew was that the girl had met a twenty-five-year old man while in Los Angeles whom she lived with for a few weeks before their break-up. That's when Sandy ended up at the refuge. She still had feelings for the man and after a number of phone calls; he convinced her to return to Los Angeles and purchased a train ticket for her. A week after their reunion, a blow-up occurred when she caught him in bed with a girl who lived across the hall, which sent Sandy fleeing to the streets. With duffle bag over the shoulder, she caught several buses that dropped her off two blocks away from the shelter. Once near it, she paused, trying to decide what to do fearing her parents wouldn't take her back. Creeping by the front door, she glanced in but went by too ashamed to enter. Only going ten feet past the door, she stopped, knowing there was nowhere else to go. Windy, who saw her peek in, hurried to the front door and out the building. Before Sandy knew it, Windy caught-up and insisted that she return to the shelter. Once inside, they walked to the back of the room, where Andre was consulting with a worker preparing meals in the kitchen. Upon seeing Sandy, he beamed and went to them.

"You're back," he said, nodding his head. "Your parents are worried sick about you."

"I had a boyfriend here," she replied, looking down. "That's why I'm back, but it didn't work out."

"All that matters is that you're back. You're really too young to be on your own. I hope you're planning on going back home?"

"Well, I guess if they'll take me."

"Oh, I think they will," Windy sighed, "as concerned as they sounded."

"*Yeah*," Sandy wailed, "but ya didn't hear the riot act I got from my dad if I were ever to leave again."

Andre squinted and said, "Well, we'll be calling them and try to work things out for you."

"Good luck," she said, frowning.

"Dinner's almost ready," Andre added, "and you know the routine if you're staying."

Nodding her head, she went with Windy to an office to complete the paperwork for admission to the shelter. After dinner, when things were quiet, Windy took Sandy back to the office to make the phone call to her parents.

Sandy shook saying, "I'm scared to talk to them. They gave me a cell phone, but I threw it at my boyfriend and he smashed it with his foot."

"Do you want me to leave while you talk to them?"

"Why don't you talk to them first?"

"Well, I'll tell you what. I'll have Andre call since he's better at smoothing things over."

"Sure."

Moments later, Andre made the call and all seemed to be going well, and then Sandy got on the phone and was left alone to talk to them. Ten minutes later, she stormed out of the office crying.

"What happened?" Andre said concerned.

"I'm not going back there," she sobbed. "*I hate him.*"

"Calm down, just give them some time. We'll work it out."

"Not with him, you won't!"

"Please calm down."

"I'll be back," she said, storming to the front door.

"Let's talk," Andre insisted following her.

"*Give me some space,*" she flared.

"Okay, just promise you'll come back."

Head down, steaming off, she fled out the door, walking aimlessly with Andre watching from the window shaking his head. Talking to himself, he went to Windy asking her if he should call Sandy's parents.

"I'd back off for awhile to give everyone time to cool off."

"Yeah, you're right."

An hour later, Sandy returned but kept to herself for the evening.

Back from their vacation, Tom and Amy worked at being civil to one another as a New Years Eve party had been planned for a month. On this last day of the year, everybody wanted to unwind to kick off the New Year. At Tom and Amy's home, the usual guests of Brenda, Marty Lain, and his fiancée Patsy, Burt and a half dozen more co-workers came to celebrate. Burt tried to be on his best behavior sensing Tom's uneasiness about him, but the true alcoholic that he was; he could not help but show his rear-end after slobbering talk and many shots of whiskey. The inebriated Marty Lain confronted Burt, telling him that he was making an ass of himself. That was just enough prodding for Burt to pull down his pants and to moon Marty. When others saw his smiling butt, they were amused and egged him on, including Amy who grabbed a camera off the fireplace mantel and snapped shots of his glowing ass. Tom let out a sigh but then smiled, as everyone seemed to enjoy the spectacle and broke out into hysteric laughter. Amy showed everyone the photo shots on the screen of her camera. Burt sat back grinning while everyone, but Tom, gathered around to look at the photos.

"I want a print," Brenda said, gleaming. "Print them now."

"Should I?" Amy said, seeing several heads nodding.

Tom smirked and said, "Hey! If you've seen one asshole, you've seen them all. Let's *party.*"

"*No, no,*" Amy ranted, "I'll print them now. Party those buns off. I'll be back." She left and then returned with enough copies of

Burt's ass for everyone. All gathered around to look at the prints and to grab a copy. This delighted Burt, who stood, arms spread open, and took a bow.

"*A toast*," Brenda yelled holding up a beer, "to Burt's smiling ass."

As the fireplace flames faded, all had left but Burt who slouched in a chair and Marty and Patsy who had been trying to leave for the past hour.

"When you come into work on Monday," Marty slurred, "remind me I need to tell you something about something I heard going on in Dick Muster's unit."

"Sure," Tom said. "Just remind me to remind you."

Marty smiled, nodding his head. "Hey, what we going to do with asshole here?" he whispered, looking at Burt.

"He can sleep here," Amy interjected overhearing the comment.

"Oh no," Burt grumbled coming out of his stupor. "I'm fine."

"No you're not," Amy said.

"I'm fine," he retorted, standing on rubbery legs.

Tom grabbed his arm saying, "Take it easy before you knock something over."

"I'm fine. I'm fine," Burt repeated.

"Don't be a jerk," Tom whispered in his ear.

"I want a copy of my ass," he blurted. "Amy you got a copy for me to take don't you?"

"Sure, but you're not going anywhere like this."

"Like what?"

Grabbing Burt's arm, she led him to the sofa, helped him down and threw a cover over him. Tom's jaw tightened as he paced while Marty and Patsy stood saying they needed to leave. Tom insisted on them spending the night in the spare bedroom. Declining to stay, Patsy, who was half-sober, said she could drive safely. Tom continued to insist, and they agreed to spend the night. Once everyone was settled. Tom and Amy went to bed.

"Why in the hell is he down there?" Tom mumbled.

"What?" Amy said.

"I don't like him being down there. He'll probably piss all over the sofa."

"He'll be fine."

Swearing in an undertone, Tom stretched out and fell into a restless sleep.

Christmas break was over and Rosetta put the final touches to a painting she had been working on for some time. With a sigh of relief, she stood back examining the large painting, a project due for an art class the next day. Rosetta's heart and soul struggled with the surrealistic image that echoed a likeness to Marc Chagall's earlier twentieth-century painting, *Young Girl in Pursuit*. Rosetta portrayed Brittany pulling apart at the seam trying to flee the house, stopped at the front and back door by two images of her father blocking the escape. Putting the brush down, she was satisfied. The next morning, Rosetta carried the covered artwork into the classroom. When it was time to display the creation, she stood in front of the class and uncovered it. A discussion followed.

"No one has noticed an interesting feature of the girl," said Professor Sanchez. "When she pulls apart, look at the eye of each image and see if you notice anything?"

Students gathered around the painting. "I see it," an enthusiastic voice said. "The eye of the split girl is brown on one side and blue on the other."

"Precisely," said Professor Sanchez. "So does this change anyone's interpretation?"

Rosetta stood back, dumbfounded as though she was unaware of the two different colored eyes.

"I think," a student said, "this is a split personality unraveling. You know, like unable to escape."

"Or maybe," said another student, "it is actually two different girls ..."

As the discussion continued, Rosetta asked herself, "How did that happen? It's Brittany on one side and yes, it must be me on the other side. That blue-eyed image is me. I try and try but can't bury the past. Why did I paint two different eyes and not realize it?"

After class, the young, handsome Professor Sanchez asked Rosetta to stay for a moment. "You are very talented Rosetta. I just can't help to wonder what direction you are going in. It's hard to believe with as much talent as you have that you're interning at the police department. It doesn't make sense to me. There's no correlation between the two fields. You need to focus on an art career."

"You think so?"

"My lord yes. With your gift, you must."

"I think this painting defines me. I have two worlds tearing me apart."

"I would like to take you under my wing as a graduate intern."

"Me?" she said. "Really?"

Setting his hand on her shoulder, "You have exceptional ability."

"I'll consider it," she said, "but can we talk about it at another time? I need to leave now ..."

Rosetta spent the rest of the day at the police department, reading different case files while Mike worked on overdue paperwork. When the shift ended, Rosetta drove by Brittany's hoping she had spoken to her mom but doubted it. Unsure of what else to do, she kept driving toward Tom and Amy's to have dinner with them. Rosetta loved to visit and felt the need to unload on them. Tom and Amy had taken a day off from work to add to their New Year holiday to make for a four-day weekend. Rosetta's favorite dish was served for dinner, and when done, they caught up on each other's lives other than the rift Tom and Amy were going through. Rosetta, aware of the rift, did her best to keep them focused on her, as she couldn't stand to see them argue or even make sly comments to each other.

"So what direction will you choose?" Tom asked. "It's great to have options. What a dilemma having so much talent."

"Yeah right," she half-laughed. "I love art, but I think I can be of help to people with my criminal justice degree. Maybe I'll become a social worker cop. Like a child abuse investigator. I don't know which way I'm going."

"Just do both," Amy said. "Social work's your calling, but art is in your blood."

"That's probably where I'm headed. The idea of a master's in art wasn't in my plan, but I guess I should consider the offer."

"I think you made your decision with a double major," said Tom, "so you could do both."

"Yeah you're right but do you know what bothers me about criminal justice?"

"What's that?" from Amy.

"*Getting justice.* I've told you about the girl that I just know is being abused. I feel so helpless. What else can I do?"

"I think you've done everything possible," said Tom.

"There's gotta be something else," Rosetta stressed.

"Try catching her," Amy said, "when school lets out. Talk to her before she gets home."

"Sure, before she gets home," she replied. "It couldn't hurt. Right?"

"Sure go for it," Tom said. "If your gut feeling is right you'll be sorry if you don't."

"It's settled then. I'll find her after school."

After an enjoyable evening of talk and playing a game of scrabble, Rosetta parted, hugging and kissing Tom and Amy before leaving. Once on the road, she couldn't resist driving by Brittany's. On seeing her through the bedroom window, she slowed down, then stopped, parking across the street and watched for ten minutes. Noticing the garage door open, the family car gone, she thought Brittany was home alone as no one else seemed to be around. Sitting back, eyes closing, thinking about what to do, she drifted off in agonizing thought unaware that Mr. Engel had pulled into the drive. Being observant, he noticed someone sitting in the car and pulled into the garage. Creeping out of the car, he slithered like a snake to the side of her car, pounded on the driver side window, causing Rosetta to scream with eyes shooting open and body trembling. Staring down was Mr. Engel. Frozen in fear, unable to breathe, she gazed up at him imagining her father's face. Banging on the window again, Rosetta swallowed hard, regaining her composure enough to roll it down.

"*What do you want?*" he roared.

"Nothing," she said, shaking.

"I saw your little sporty car parked here before. What the hell's going on? Hey, ain't you the cop that was here?"

"We have a lead, a lead on a, a possible suspect in the neighborhood burglaries."

"Who is it?" he demanded.

"I'm not at liberty to say."

"Well, I just couldn't figure out why you were here."

"Well, that's why," she shuddered, and then mumbled under her breath, "you feeling guilty?"

"*What?*" he snapped.

"I'm feeling guilty that we haven't caught the guy."

"Yeah, right. I'll leave you be then. I just didn't know who you were. That's all."

"I'm done for tonight, but we'll get him."

"Let me know now if you get 'em so I don't worry about someone breaking in."

"Of course we will," she said starting the car and then looked up noticing Brittany looking out the window.

Walking to the front porch, he turned to see if she had left and watched her pull away. Once inside the house, Brittany came halfway down the stairs, hesitated, but then continued down.

"Who were you talking to across the street?" Brittany asked.

"Whataya doing spying on me?"

"I wasn't. I was just in my room looking out the window."

"Aw, it was that pesty girl cop who came here about the break-in. I went over to see what was up."

"Oh? I think she's nice and just trying to catch the bad guy. I don't think she's pesky. You know pesky with a k."

"Don't get smart with me. I said pesty. You know, like a *pest*. I've seen her car there before."

"And?"

107

"Bullshit if you ask me. She said they have a burglary suspect living around here that they're watching."

"I wonder who that could be?"

The mother entered the room carrying laundry from the basement. "I bet," said Mrs. Engel, "it's that no good Collin's kid up the street. You know how we had trouble with him last year snooping around the neighborhood. People complained that he was a weirdo."

"Yeah," Mr. Engel said. "He's a punk ..."

Brittany had heard enough, returned to her room, and cuddled with a large stuffed bear on the bed. Looking out the window at the bright stars, she imagined one falling and was quick to make a wish.

Chapter 9

The next day, as Tom and Amy dressed for work, Rosetta got the okay from Mike to talk to Brittany after school. Mike did not have a lot of confidence in Rosetta's gut feeling but figured it would keep her busy and out of trouble to pursue it. Believing that she could catch the girl walking the three blocks from the high school to her home, Rosetta sat parked on the street. With students passing by her car, Rosetta perked up, waiting and watching until Brittany's face came into view. Walking alone, carrying an armful of books; Rosetta sensed hopelessness in the girl's features and went over in her mind what she was going to say. Getting out of the car, feet shuffling, she waited, noticing Brittany's eyes connecting with hers. When they were feet apart, Brittany slowed down, eyes to the ground and then stopped.

"Brittany," Rosetta said. "Can we talk?"

"My dad said you've been watching someone," she said, avoiding eye contact.

"That's right."

"You going to get him?"

"I hope so. It's going to take your help."

"What do you mean?"

"Have you told your mom?"

"Told her what?"

"You promised you would tell her. I've been where you've been. You've got to speak up and put an end to it." She looked at Rosetta nodding in awe. "*I mean it.* If you won't tell me tell your mom."

"You don't understand."

"Oh yes, I do."

"What do you want me to tell her?"

"The truth. It's the only way. Would you please talk to her?"

"The truth?"

"Tell her tonight."

"Well," she paused, "tonight?"

"You can do it. So I'll be talking to you tomorrow. Okay?"

"I guess so."

"Look at me in the eye and take this," she said handing over a card with her cell phone number.

At last, Brittany and Rosetta made eye contact. Rosetta nodded her head and Brittany did likewise.

Entering the children's home, Tom and Amy parted going to their respective floors. Marty Lain, the first shift supervisor for the boys, met Tom at the front desk. "You're looking real sober there Tom," Marty said big-eyed and grinning.

"Damn, I was really hung over the next day."

"What happened with Burt?"

"He threw-up all over the floor, then high-tailed it out before we got up."

"You're kidding me."

"At least he didn't piss all over the place."

"Who cleaned it up?" he asked frowning.

Tom smirked, shaking his head. "It wasn't me."

After speaking about how the day went at the home, Marty reminded Tom that he was supposed to ask him a question when he got to work. "Come on think," he told Tom.

Pondering, Tom replied, "You got me, I don't remember."

"I'll give you a hint," Marty said. "Dick Muster. Do you remember now?"

"Oh yeah. So what's the deal?"

"Kids have been talking about a log book Dick and his team have been writing in that's supposed to be sick, perverted shit about kids and female staff."

"You're kidding?" Tom said.

"That's the gossip by the kids."

"You haven't seen it then?"

"Nope."

"You mean those idiots have shown it to the kids?"

"No, the book is supposedly locked up at the front desk. Apparently, they were carrying on and laughing after the kids were in bed, which prompted the boys to snoop around. You know it doesn't take anything to pry open the desk drawer."

"And?"

"I heard they pried it open when staff wasn't around and read the book. There's no reason for them to make it up."

"Have you asked anyone?"

"No."

"I can see your point. I think I might just have to investigate this myself."

"Go for it."

"Yeah, I will."

"Let me know what you find out."

"If it's true, Muster needs to get his ass busted with all the crap he pulls around here."

With the shift exchange completed, Marty gone, Tom decided on a plan of action while waiting for the boys to return from school. Once they were back and settled down, Tom asked Tommy to follow him to his office.

"Am I in trouble?" Tommy said, fidgeting.

"Calm down," said Tom. "You're not in trouble. There's a rumor going around about a staff book on the emergency unit. Have you heard about it?"

A grin, finger antics, and tap dancing eyes said it all, and then he chuckled and blurted, "*Bingo*. Heard about it. You kidding me, I've read it."

Eyes brightening, Tom said, "Oh yeah," and walked into his office and shut the door.

"It's wild stuff about the girls and female staff mostly. Dickhead even mentions me in it."

"I heard it's a bunch of perverted stuff."

"It's funny," he laughed.

"So would the girls and female staff think it's funny?"

"No way," he laughed.

"So where's the book kept?"

"Top right drawer of the staff admissions desk. It's locked, but easier than shit to pry open."

"Hmm, interesting. How's everything else going? I haven't heard any complaints from the school."

"I told you I could control myself without meds."

"That you did."

After they finished, Tom and the other staff gathered all the residents and herded them down to the cafeteria for dinner. When everyone in the building was in line or seated eating, Tom slipped away unnoticed and scrambled to the emergency unit. Once he was sure that no one was around, he pulled a flat edge screwdriver out of his pocket and pried open the staff desk drawer. Sure enough, he found the staff book, glanced through it to make sure the rumors were true, shut the drawer and sped off with it. After entering his office, Tom hid the staff book in a briefcase, locked it up, rushed down to the cafeteria and got in the serving line. No one had missed him for the ten minutes he was gone. Relieved that he accomplished getting the book, he couldn't help but gloat while waiting in line. When the shift was over and Tom and Amy returned home; he pulled the book out of a briefcase, sat at his desk with Amy looking over his shoulder and both began reading:

12/28   This is a book to be used for messages, notes, bitches, and general bullshit between shifts and individuals ... Keep it non-clinical and friendly. It's staff therapy. Who's first??? Just let it all out.

Your supervisor, Dick Muster

12/29   Non-clinical you said. I suggest that the next time Delbert threatens suicide that we put him out of his misery. I'll even volunteer to drill a hole into that brainless skull of his so all the shit can drain out. B.A.

12/30
Remember boys! A book of this nature could be subpoenaed if residents are to be spoken about in it.   Larry

"At least Larry has some sense," Amy said.

"Yeah," from Tom, "but look at the next lines."

12/30   This is your supervisor and I want to know who the stupid prick is that gave Tommy Wizel my home phone number? He called to say he was going to kill Ames. Watch it Mike, that fucker's crazy enough to do it.

D. Muster

1/02   Now let's get down to important business like sex and girls. My nomination for female staff of the year has got to be Connie. Every time I go over to the girls unit, I get this thriving pulsation in my pants that makes me want to attack that heavenly crotch of hers and dangle from those two huge orbs of joy... Hold me down.

D.M.

1/02   Alright! It's time for nominating the resident of the year. Nancy Gordon's got my tongue – I mean vote, for reasons known by all staff. Shit! I mean you know as well as I do that I'm the only one Nancy will allow to counsel her after she returns from runaway.

Yours truly

"This is disgusting," Amy grumbled. "And Muster's a supervisor. He should be *fired*."

"I don't care if this is supposed to be just between staff," Tom said. "They're idiots. Plus the kids have seen it. Tommy thought it was hilarious." Continuing to read, he said, "What other shit is in here?"

1/02   If the above statement doesn't verify what we all knew all along about Thornhill then I'm not your supervisor. Thornhill you're a depraved, sex-starved fiend. I'd be all the more pissed off if it wasn't for the fact that I'm banging sweet Jackie Kane ...

D.M

1/03   All I can say is that it takes great courage and intestinal fortitude for both Muster and Thornhill to bare their souls in this diary of lust and perversion. It's easy to see why they're the leaders of this motley bunch of Croatians. Besides Muster's so damn good looking, charming, witty, handsome, talented, and humble!

1/03   Muster, we all know you wrote the above paragraph. You don't have to pat yourself on the back for having a sick depraved mind. It's common knowledge in the ghetto world of the Home.

1/03   Jesus almighty! Steve can write.

1/04   Holy boom boom kaboom. Have you seen that new chick on the admissions unit? Imagine her ...

"I've read enough of this crap," Amy said, seeing several more pages of entries.
"Yeah me too," Tom replied, slamming the book shut. "This is a bunch of bullshit. So what do we do with it?"
"I would like to shove it up Muster's ass."
"Should I turn it over to the director?"
"You damn well better or I will."
"Tomorrow before work I'll make a copy of it. I want Marty to see it before I do anything. This might need some thought and planning. I mean, I did take it."

Before midnight, Rosetta received a phone call, but the person calling wouldn't speak. The caller ID showed that it came from the Engel's home.
"Hello," Rosetta said. "Brittany, is that you?"

The phone clicked. Rosetta hung up and paced trying to decide what to do. Certain it was Brittany, she couldn't return the call. Emotions bubbling, she got dressed and drove off in a hurry. Ten minutes later, she slowed down passing by Brittany's. The upstairs bedroom light was on. Turning around, she went back, parking two houses down on the opposite side of the street. Despite the dim light, Mr. Engel was seen seated in the living room. Brittany's bedroom light was on, but no one was seen in the room. With bated breath, Rosetta crept out of the car and walked by the house. Continuing for fifty yards, she stopped to regain her composure and headed back. Glancing up, Brittany and her mom were upstairs standing by the bedroom door. They hugged and it looked like Brittany was crying. Mrs. Engel left and Brittany entered the room and disappeared from sight. A minute later, the room light went out. "Must have gone to bed," Rosetta thought. "I think she told her mom. I really do. Where did her mom go? Just go back to the car. There's nothing you can do. Why did she call me and not say anything?" Rosetta returned to the car, sat feeling helpless for minutes before starting the engine. Once in gear, foot creeping to the gas pedal, she froze on seeing Mr. Engel stand up; looking like judgment day had arrived. Rosetta pulled away, parking right in front of the house to get a better look at what was going on. Shaking his head, hands spread open, he appeared to be pleading. No one else was visible. Then he backed up toward the large living room window, continuing to shake his head while arguing with someone. Rosetta noticed Brittany's light go on, and then an explosive sound and another followed with the living room lighting up like the Fourth of July. Mr. Engel's body jerked back, spattering against the window with blood and broken glass all over. Shaking, Rosetta jumped out of the car and moved close enough to see Mrs. Engel in the background standing holding a shotgun. In a flash, Brittany appeared at the top of the stairway, ran down screaming as the gun dropped from the mom's hands allowing them to embrace and weep together. Rosetta trembled searching for the phone and called Mike, telling him what had happened. He told her to get back in the car and that he was on his way over as soon as he contacted the station to respond. A few minutes afterward, Rosetta spotted flashing red lights headed to the scene. A police car arrived and then an ambulance came a minute later. Remaining in the car, she let the responders take care of business. When Mike arrived five minutes later, Rosetta hurried out of the car and rushed to him. Together, they entered the residence and when Rosetta saw the body, she turned away in a flash. The sickening scene of the bloody torso made Rosetta's stomach turn, but in her mind was relieved for Brittany and herself, as she observed the girl and mother weeping and holding one another. When Rosetta's and Brittany's eyes met, a torn feeling of freedom could be sensed – released from Hell, but in a state of limbo. Rosetta new that she helped to pull the trigger, imagining that the bloody mess was her father blown to Hell. Brittany gazed off while Rosetta studied her trembling body – uncertain if she were the liberator or the persecutor. Before the evening was over, Mrs. Engel left in handcuffs arrested for murder. Mike and Rosetta took Brittany to the emergency unit of the Springfield Children's Home after dropping off Rosetta's car at the police department. Brittany cried begging to be with her mom.

"*Why was she arrested?*" Brittany wailed.

Rosetta seated with her in the back seat said, "I don't know, but they'll let her out I'm sure."

"*How did you know?*" Brittany whined.

"Because I was you," she said, oblivious to the fact that Mike could hear them.

"I killed him!" Brittany shouted.

"He got what he deserved."

"*I want my mom.* Where are we going?"

"Everything will be okay," she said doubting her own words.

Once they arrived at the home, walking up the steps to the front door sent chills through Rosetta, causing her to remember all the misery she experienced at such places as a teenager.

"Why can't she be with her mom?" Rosetta asked Mike.

"I want my mom," Brittany wept.

"We got to get her admitted here," Mike stressed. "She'll see her mom soon."

After all the paperwork was completed, Mike and Rosetta left. Mike told Rosetta she didn't need to come in for work the next day and she nodded as if in a trance and stared off all the way back to the station. She wondered if this was real or just another nightmare that she would wake up from.

After getting out of the car, Mike wrapped his arm around her and said, "Are you going to be okay?"

"I guess. I'm not dreaming am I?"

"Do you want to go somewhere and talk for awhile? For Christ sake, you were dead-on about this whole thing. Maybe you better not drive."

"Thanks, but I think I need to be alone and I can drive."

"All right, I'll give you a call tomorrow. Okay?"

"Yeah," she said and both got in their cars.

Each drove off in different directions deep in thought while back at the children's home, Brittany was taken to a large room where five other girls were in beds sleeping. Given a nightgown and settled in bed, she stared at the ceiling, trembling wondering if she was leaving one hell for another. Nothing made sense. "I did what Rosetta wanted," she told herself. "I just knew how my mom would react. That's why I didn't want to say anything. I don't understand why she was in handcuffs. I should have been pulling the trigger not her. This is all insane." Heart pounding, she sprung up shaking, beads of sweat forming as she burst out weeping, awakening the girl in the bed next to her.

"Who are you?" the girl asked concerned. "What's wrong?"

"I just killed my dad and *mom*," she murmured.

"You what?"

"I feel like dying," she said, covering her head with a pillow and whimpering the remainder of the evening.

In Los Angeles, at the runaway shelter, Sandy stomped out of the office having spoken to her parents. "I told you," she yelled. "He's an asshole."

"What happened?" Windy asked.

"I can't go back."

"That's what he said?"

"He may as well have. He knew I wouldn't go for his bullshit restrictions."

"You think the streets are better?"

"Yeah."

"You know you're wrong. You can work it out."

"My mom's almost as bad. They don't understand me."

"You can fight all you want, but deep down you know they're just trying to protect you from yourself."

"What do you mean?"

"Be honest. Have you made good decisions?"

Looking down, she said, "I need to go out for a smoke." Walking by Andre without a word, she went outside, lit up, and paced back and forth in front of the building. One of the other girls from the shelter went out and joined Sandy in a smoke. Together they talked while Andre and Windy did likewise inside, trying to decide on a course of action. When the girls came in, Sandy went to her room, gathered belongings and with a backpack strapped on, she walked toward the front door.

"What are you doing?" said Andre with Windy standing nearby.

"I'll teach them," she said with sarcasm. "Since they want me to go back to their hell, I want you to tell them I'll find my own hell. What's that club called again? The Lost Souls Club I think. That sounds like my kind of place."

"Didn't you hear anything I told you about that place?" Andre said, frowning.

"Oh, I heard you alright. You can tell my parents they sent me to the snake pit."

"*Don't do it*," Windy interjected.

"*I'll teach them*," she raved, ignoring Windy's comment.

"You need to cool off," Andre said, "please don't leave. I'll call and talk to your parents."

"There's been enough talk," she roared, storming out the door.

"These kids are going to start me drinking again," Andre said, only hoping he wasn't serious about his comment.

"Don't even go there," Windy said. "You've done this long enough to know we can't save everyone from their own stupidity."

"It just feels like the Big Jake fiasco is coming back to haunt us. And she flaunted it in my face after warning her and all of them to stay clear of there. I mean, a drink don't sound all that bad right now. But you know what, it's more than stupidity. It's revenge. She wants to suffer so her parents will suffer. I know. I've been there."

"Yeah, you're right, I've been there too. If it wasn't Big Jake it would be someone else. Right?"

"I guess," he said, flustered, retreating to his office. "I'm spineless and gutless," he told himself.

Chapter 10

Sitting back, drink in hand, Big Jake spoke on the phone to Chung, a man who had establishments in Hong Kong's Wan-Chai – it's red light district, and whom he had done a business deal with years earlier. The deal proved to be a disaster for Chung after he paid a large amount of money for a young Rosetta to be smuggled to him. This was Big Jake's first experience with human trafficking. At the time, he had Andre in his clasp, using him as a pawn in the deal with Big Jake pulling all the strings. Andre, who hated his ties to the gangster, undermined Big Jake by helping Rosetta escape. Big Jake had received his money for the deal while Chung's middleman took the blame for her escape. Chung was the big loser with the money gone and no girl to show for it. With over seven years passing, Big Jake wanted to reconnect with Chung who had established himself as a key figure in the Orients human trafficking. Chung, remembering his prior dealing with Big Jake, insisted that he make amends for his previous loss if they were to do business. Although Big Jake never took the blame for the mess-up, he believed it was in his interest to appease the man and promised to send Chung a gift before commencing business. Squeezing the cell phone firm, he left the backroom of his Los Angeles nightclub and went out to the main part of the club, which had three customers waiting to be entertained. The first show didn't start until 11:00 AM to correlate with the lunch time crowd, as lunch specials were served daily.

Outside of the club, Sandy paced, sucking on a cigarette, wanting to enter but hesitated. "My parents don't care," she told herself, "so why should I? I won't go back and be a prisoner. At least here, I'll be free. So you take your clothes off. You make big bucks. Everyone knows that. What's the big deal? I'd feel better if I lost a few pounds. It's easy, right. Why are you hesitating? Just go in. I'll teach my parents to be assholes. If they don't give a shit why should I?" Battling her emotions, pacing, she stopped in front of the door. "You won't have a life if you enter the snake pit," she remembered Andre saying about The Lost Souls Club. "But I have a lost soul," she thought, looking at the bright lit up club name. "Maybe I'll find it here. What does Andre know? He's just a religious nut. He called it the snake pit to scare me. I'm not scared. I have nothing to lose." Gripping the door handle, she panicked and backed away. Coming up from behind, a young man grabbed Sandy's shoulders, causing her to jump as if touched by a live wire.

"What!" she screamed.

"Don't freak," said the man.

"Who are you?" she said, trembling.

"I work here. You going in?"

"I don't know. Why?"

"Because you were standing there with your hand on the doorknob."

"Yeah, I was thinking about going in."

"I don't recognize you. You looking for a job?"

"I don't know, maybe."

"Come on in and talk to the boss."

After nibbling on a nail, she took one last drag on the cigarette, stomped it out and said, "Okay, you lead the way."

Following the man into the dark atmosphere, Sandy was in a different world. In awe, she peered about at the long bar, the stages, tables and the few patrons' with drinks in front of them. She could feel their eyes as she walked toward Big Jake, wearing a brimmed hat, conversing with the bartender.

"Hey, Big Jake," said the man. "I got a hottie here wanting to work."

"Hey baby," said Big Jake, "aren't you sweet looking. Oh yeah, I'd say you're around a 36 C-cup. Let's see, I'd say you're a 36-23-38. Am I close?"

"I don't know," she trembled. "Does my butt look big?"

"It's perfect. Come on, follow me we'll talk." Leading the way, she followed him into a large back room with sofas, a bar and the walls made of mirrors. Turning the lighting up, he said, "I want to get a good look at you." He led the way taking a seat on the sofa as she stood in front of him, looking down and licking her lips. "Yes, I like what I see so far. Go 'head show me the rest."

Turing in a circle like a model, she quivered believing she would wake up any moment.

"Yeah I like, but I want to see more. Take your clothes off sweetie."

"I don't know if I can do that," she said.

"What kind of job were you looking for?"

"I don't know."

"Don't you know what this place is?"

"Yes, I mean, I think I do."

"How old are you?"

"Old enough."

Standing up, he put his hands on her trembling shoulders. "Relax."

In the main part of the nightclub, a loud voice blasted in the background, which caused Big Jake to pause, trying to make out what was going on. Moving to the door with Sandy following like a lost puppy, Big Jake entered the club, heading to the ruckus at the bar.

"You can tell it to the boss," the bartender said, watching Big Jake and Sandy head toward them. Andre turned, relieved to see Sandy, but unhappy to see the man he fled Illinois from over four years earlier.

"What the hell's going on?" Big Jake roared.

"This son-of-a-bitch is raising hell about some girl," said the bartender.

"What's your problem buddy?" Big Jake thundered, staring down at the shorter man with Sandy expressing a sigh of relief on seeing Andre.

"You know you have an underage girl there don't you?"

Big Jake glanced at Sandy saying, "Did you lie to me, girl?"

"Well, a, a," she stuttered.

Looking back at Andre, he paused, studying his face, mouth dropping. "I don't believe my fuckin' eyes. You! I ought to put a bullet," he said, pulling out a pistol, "between those disgusting, deceitful eyes of yours." Putting the gun to Andre's forehead, he cocked the hammer.

"Don't," Sandy cried.

Glancing at her, he said, "And you're next you little bitch."

"I have people," Andre said, "waiting to see me and the girl leave the building or they will have the cops all over the place."

"I don't know where in God's name you came from," he said lowering the gun, "but we're not through. But for now get the *hell* out. You can count on me seeing you again."

Grabbing Sandy's arm, he started to lead her away but then turned to Big Jake saying, "You're right about Hell. This won't be over until I see you there."

Together they hurried out of the club while Big Jake returned to the backroom where he slammed his fist against the bar swearing, cursing and remembering the last time he saw Andre. All he could think of was Gomez at the club in Springfield, grabbing his hair, taking a big Bowie knife to his scalp and slicing away as if his head were butter. Remembering the agonizing pain caused him to shutter, and then he recalled falling to his knees, seeing Andre and other faces standing in the background before he blacked out. Just the thought of it caused him to double over, putting his pounding forehead against the bar, wondering how and why Andre showed up at the club. "That son-of-a-bitch," he said to himself, "must be working at some kid's home again. He disappeared from Springfield and now he's here. I gotta find where that bastard has been hiding." Grabbing a phone book, unsure where to search; he looked under the heading, *Child*, finding pages of listings for child care. "Screw him," he growled, tossing the book against the bar.

Andre and Sandy hurried up the street and got in the car with Windy behind the driver's seat. Once on their way all breathed a sigh of relief. Sandy still shaky, remained silent while Andre looked back to make sure no one was following them.

"You okay?" Windy asked, glancing back at Sandy.

"I think so," she said.

"I've talked to your dad and mom," Andre said, "everything has been worked out for you to return home."

"And the restrictions?" she asked.

"Just family counseling, okay?"

Pausing a moment, she said, "Okay."

"What just happened," said Andre, "is nothing compared to what could have happened. You hear me?"

"Yeah," she replied.

"Good."

After Tom and Amy arrived for work, Tom went into Marty's office, shut the door and handed him the staff log. Marty read it, shaking his head in disbelief.

"Unbelievable," said Marty, looking at a list entitled, *A Must for the Girl in Your Future.* "I can't believe the shit they put down here. What are we going to do?"

"That was my next question. Should we turn it over to the director?"

"You may not have heard this yet, but the kids are saying they have gotten blamed for taking the book and are in big trouble with Muster."

"Great, so how does that fit into everything? Do I turn it over to the director and admit to taking it?"

"I don't know," he said with a slight chuckle.

"I mean will I get in trouble?"

"I don't see how considering what's in the book."

"Yeah, I guess so."

"Come on," Marty said. "Let's do it together."

"Alright, let's go."

Together they marched down to the director's office and knocked on the door.

"Yes," said the director. "Come in."

Walking in, Tom set the book down on the desk in front of him, and said, "You need to read this."

"This isn't the missing book from Dick's unit is it?" asked the director.

"Well, yeah," said Tom.

"Did you get this from the kids?"

"Well, no," Tom said. "I heard about the book from the boys and confiscated it."

"From who?"

"From the staff desk."

"So you're the one who stole it?"

"I took it because of what's in it and the fact that the kids had been reading it. I don't believe you would approve of the kids passing this around. Take a look at it."

The director opened the book and spent several minutes reading. "I see your point. I will deal with this. You did the right thing in giving it to me."

"What are you going to do?" Marty asked.

"I will talk to Dick about it and that is all you need to know. You are not to talk to anyone about this book. Do you understand me? And I mean *no one*. Staff included. You know you could get in trouble for taking the book in the first place, don't you? So are we on the same page?"

Both nodded their heads saying yes, uncertain what his little speech meant, but assumed that Dick Muster was in trouble. After leaving the director's office, Tom escorted Marty outside who was finished with his shift, giving them a chance to talk for awhile.

Back in the building, Brittany was half-asleep and cuddled with a stuffed animal. Dick, the only staff present, went into the girls' bedroom; eyes searching the room and then focused on Brittany. She could feel his presence as he inched closer to the bed. This was déjà vu reliving the nightmare of an incestuous father's repeated attacks over the years. With eyes cracked open, she imagined him licking his chops, causing her to stop breathing. Terrified, she moved as though waking, which caused him to pause and leave the room?

When done talking to Marty, Tom hurried inside knowing the boys would be arriving from school in minutes. In the distance, the phone rang, and rang, and rang not letting up. Rushing to the screaming sound, Tom picked up the phone to Rosetta's grating voice spelling out all the details of what had happened the night before, including Brittany's admission to the home.

"Unbelievable," Tom said, "Try to calm down. It'll be okay."

"Promise me," Rosetta pleaded, "you'll make sure she's okay. I'm a wreck over it. I can't believe her mom's in jail ..."

Looking down at the newspaper headline on his desk, Tom was well aware of the shooting but had not realized the girl was at the home. He promised to look in on Brittany but was sad that she was on Dick Muster's unit, causing him to hope that he would get the ax over the logbook. Not wishing to upset Rosetta, he couldn't tell her about the situation. Once the kids returned from school and staff attended to them, Tom went downstairs and spoke to Dick.

"I hear you have a new girl named Brittany," said Tom, gazing with disgust at him.

"That's right, that's her over there."

"She's a friend of a close friend of mine so I'll be watching over her. Make sure you take very good care of her. I'm very serious about this."

"We take good care of all of them."

Squinting, he said, "Have you talked to the director today?"

"Just a bit ago," he said smirking. "Why?"

Looking at him with suspicion, Tom said, "Nothing, he just had some B.S. to talk to me about earlier."

"So," he said smugly, "do you want to meet the girl?"

"Yeah."

"Come on," he said, leading the way, eyes full of anger. "Hey, Brittany I got someone here that wants to speak to you."

Brittany looked up at Tom who introduced himself. The two walked to the other side of the room to talk alone. "Rosetta told me about you. I'm glad to see you."

"Rosetta's a great girl. Have you been treated okay here?"

"That Dick guy's weird. He was snooping about the bedroom while I was taking a nap. I felt him standing over me, and when I cracked an eye open he was there. I moved and he left. I don't know what he was doing, but the really big problem is my mom's in jail," she whimpered. "She was just trying to protect me. I want her back."

"I will find out what is going on with her. Okay?" he said squinting. "If you have any problems with kids or staff – come to me. I mean it?"

"Okay."

Tom returned upstairs just in time to greet the boys returning from school. Tommy Wizel stormed in agitated and cursing under his breath.

"What's wrong?" Tom said.

"That Chastity makes me sick."

"What else is new?" Tom said half-smiling.

"*I mean it*. She's going to get my fist down her throat."

"What did she do this time?"

Clasping his head, he turned away and fled to his room. Tom went to a boy named Mark and asked him what had happened between Tommy and Chastity?

Smiling, he said, "She pulled his shorts down in PE class and he had a poop stain on his underwear. Everyone made fun of him. He was pissed."

"I bet he was," said Tom.

Mark shouted, knowing Tommy could hear him, "*Tommy was really pissed off 'cause of the poop stain.*"

"*That's enough*," said Tom.

A moment later, Tommy ran out of his room and out the door.

"*Tommy*," Tom shouted, following him into the hallway.

Running, Tommy made it to the stairwell and vanished from sight, which caused Tom to hurry up to the girls' floor. When he arrived, Tommy was all over Chastity yanking on her jeans, getting them pulled halfway off. Amy and another female staff were trying to pull the two apart. When Tom arrived, he grabbed hold of Tommy separating him from Chastity.

"*Whoopee*," Chastity screamed. "You like what you see Tom? You want to kiss my butt?" she said, aiming it at him covered by scanty, thong underwear.

Holding onto Tommy, Tom said, "Pull your pants up."

"*She's a bitch*," Tommy yelled.

"I heard what you did to Tommy at school Chastity," said Tom. "*Both of you settle down*. This better be the end of it. *Understood?*"

Pulling up her pants, Chastity stood, giving Tommy the finger.

"Knock it off," Amy said to Chastity.

Tom escorted Tommy away and both returned to the smiling faces of the boys.

"What you going to do about her?" Tommy demanded to know.

"You know her wrong behavior doesn't justify your behavior. Two wrongs don't make a right."

"*It's not just me*," Tommy screamed, looking at a group of boys who gathered around him. "*Tell Tom how she is.*"

"Yeah," the group chattered. "What a bitch," they all complained.

Back upstairs, Amy and Chastity were arguing about Tommy.

"You did start this at school you know," Amy said.

"Everyone sticks up for him. You guys are just always against me. That's why I want out of here. I want to be on my own ..."

"I've heard it all before. Besides, you're going to court to try to get your way. You an emancipated minor, at fifteen, would be unbelievable. Be careful what you wish for it might just happen."

"It better or you won't see the end of the havoc I'll raise."

"Let's hope the judge has more sense than you."

"*Just screw off,*" she growled and walked away.

The next day, Tom found out that Brittany's mom made bail, which was set low due to public outrage and sympathy for the mother. To Tom's satisfaction, he learned from Rosetta that Brittany would return home the next day. In the meantime, Tom couldn't help but wonder what had gone on between the director and Dick, as he was still working and there were no visible signs that anything at all had happened. Dick was at work every day and no one mentioned the logbook again, but as time passed, many staff had run-ins with him for one reason or another. Others complained to the director who seemed to have a deaf ear. Then there were rumors' circulating that he was harboring a runaway girl from the home. One resident started it, but no kids would say where the rumor originated which left staff wondering if there was any truth to it. There was no sign of the runaway girl, Nancy Gordon, who had a history of being gone for days and even a week at a time. Having been on Dick's unit, before transferring to the girls' floor, the two seemed to have a chummy relationship. Tom and Marty's blood pressure rose whenever they talked about him. After Tom and Amy returned home from work one evening, Tom pulled out the copy of the logbook he had made. Reading the log repeatedly made him suspicious about one entry:

1/02   Alright! It's time for nominating the resident of the year. Nancy Gordon's got my tongue – I mean vote, for reason's known by all staff. Shit! I mean you know as well as I do that I'm the only one Nancy will allow to counsel her after she returns from runaway.

Yours truly

"Amy, come here," Tom said.

"Yeah," she replied looking over his shoulder.

"Read these lines signed 'Yours truly.'"

After reading it she said, "Our runaway girl. What are you getting at?"

"The next line signed by Muster insinuates that Thornhill wrote that passage, but compare the writing."

"Muster's and the 'Yours truly' writing look the same," she said.

"That's what I thought."

"Are you thinking what I'm thinking?"

"Thornhill didn't write the comment about Nancy, but Muster did. Look at the only entry by Thornhill towards the end of the log," he said turning the page.

"It doesn't look like the same writing Muster said Thornhill wrote."

"If he actually wrote that about Nancy, then maybe there's something to the rumor."

"What are you going to do?"

"I've got to show it to Marty to see if he comes up with the same conclusion."

"It's a good thing you made a copy."

"I can't wait to show it to Marty. Unbelievable, huh?"

The next day, before shift change, Tom called Marty from his cell phone while seated in his car in the home's parking lot. Marty agreed to come out to the car. With Tom and Amy in the front seats, he got in the back. Tom handed him the log and had him read the page telling him to pay attention to the writing.

After pondering, Marty exclaimed, "Well, I don't know. Let me read it again." Mouth dropping, he sighed, *"Oh my God. I think I get it.* Did Muster actually write the entry about Nancy? *Hot damn almighty he did.* That's it. Right?"

"That's what we think," Amy said.

"I guess," Marty said, "we better show it to the boss now before he leaves this mad house. You know next week's his last week."

"Yeah," Tom said, "we don't want to have to start off with this crap for the new guy."

"Just do it," Amy said. "I have to get up to my girls, but it needs to be done."

Tom and Marty looked at one another, nodding. "By the way," Tom said, "I've got another copy of this at home."

"Good thinking."

All left the car with Tom and Marty heading straight to the director's office. After showing him the entries, he said. "I don't believe it."

"You see it too?" Tom said.

"I don't believe you made a copy of the log. I told you this was a dead issue."

"Dead issue," Tom said, hands opening, pleading to be understood. "You don't get it, do you? Muster wrote the unsigned log about Nancy. Look at the writing."

"You really want to bury this guy don't you?" he said.

"We think he's harboring Nancy at his place. Rumors are running rampant from the kids that he is."

"You guys are full of it. Rumors from the kids," he said shaking his head. "Give me a break. I don't want to hear this bullshit about Muster. Do you understand me? Do you have any more copies of this?"

"No," Tom sneered, looking away.

"You better not. Get the hell out of here. It's a good thing I'm leaving. You two have really pissed me off. Give me the rest of the log."

After handing it to him, they both left with the director watching Tom go upstairs and Marty leave the building.

Chapter 11

On edge after a long workday at the runaway shelter they operated; Andre and Windy stepped out the front door and could not resist the allure of the flashing leprechaun sign up the street. Talk of dinner led them to the Irish pub, but the fighting spirit of the sign reflected their mood. Although the food was the lure, stress dictated that tequila would do wonders for their bundled up nerves. Putting the shot glass to their lips, the liquor was vacuumed down causing a tingling sensation. A pleasant dinner and conversation followed. On one hand, they were relieved that they had gotten Sandy to return home to her parents, but it was not enough to compensate for the anxiety created by their old adversary Big Jake. Their demeanor had changed and it showed in Andre's sweltering face as anxiety seeped out of his pores like a bubbling volcano spitting out an overload of pressure. Drinking was a rarity, as alcohol had played a major part in their past indiscretions and volatile lifestyle. Big Jake's emergence near their sanctuary was an unwelcome reminder of that life.

"Now he knows we're here," Andre flared. "Why is this happening?"

"Don't you think," Windy pleaded, "that we're still like a needle in the haystack for him to find us? This is LA, not Farmersville Illinois."

"I don't know," he said downing a shot of tequila. "I think I need another one."

"Slow down and calm down. You hear me?"

After a few tequilas, Andre stared out the restaurant window daydreaming, when a man wearing a brimmed hat walked by glancing in. Andre looked down; hands shielded his face, as sweat trickled down his forehead. "Don't turn around," he muttered. "I think it's him."

"Who?"

"Big Jake," he whispered, peeking through fingers not seeing anyone now. Hands dropping, he looked all around, stood and went to the door, stepped out and saw an old man hobbling up the street wearing a brimmed hat. Returning, he sat with a sigh of relief catching a bead of sweat on the tip of his tongue.

"It wasn't him was it?" Windy said cocksure. "And why are you sweating so much?"

"Tequila sweat, I guess. Seeing that brimmed hat just freaked me out. He wore a similar one the other day when I had to confront him. If looks could've killed that day, I'd be dead right now."

"Don't let that big jerk get to you. You did what you had to. You saved Sandy from his snake pit."

"You know I had to get her out of there. But now he knows we're in LA, and you know he's –"

"Listen," she interrupted, "we fled Illinois to get away from him. We can't let him ruin our life again."

"He's going to try to hunt us down. There's only one way to deal with the devil. Send him to Hell!"

"Take it easy. I don't like the sound of that."

"Survival. That's all. I feel like going back to his *damn* club and putting a stake right through that *bastard's* heart. He's a blood sucking scum ball and needs to be stopped."

"I knew we shouldn't have drunk tonight. You're talking stupid."

"Stupid? No way. I'm just – just – hell, fantasizing what I'd like to do to that scum before he sticks his fangs in us again. You got that *look* in your eye. I'm not *crazy*. Just frustrated. I don't have any stakes."

"I hope not."

"You ready to get out of here?"

"Yeah, but let me drive. You've had a lot more to drink than me."

Handing over the keys, he said, "It's all yours. You know what? Give 'um back. I'll drive."

"Oh, no," she said, putting the keys in her pocket.

"Alright, but we gotta keep our eyes open. He's slithering around looking for us. You know he is."

"I know," she said leading the way out of the restaurant.

Stepping outside, Andre stopped, peered about and said, "It's a big city, but I feel like the spotlight is on us. You know what I mean? I don't like having to look over my shoulder."

"I've got your back," Windy said, placing an arm around him.

"Thank God for you. Otherwise, I'd start worrying about him. Worrying is for warts, right?"

"You getting goofy on me? Or is that the tequila talking? Huh, Mr. Paranoid?"

"Well, you know what Ralph Waldo Emerson said about fear don't you?"

"Of course. Let me see. It's right on the tip of my tongue."

"Can't take the suspense, huh? What he said was, do the thing you fear if you want the *damn fear* to die."

"Those exact words?"

"Maybe not *damn*, but I guess we're back to getting a stake if we go by that philosophy. Right?"

"I'm sorry I asked. Come on," she said dragging him to the car. "Don't argue with me. Get your butt in there. The only *steak* you're getting is the kind you eat."

"Alright, alright," he said, getting in. "Take me home, I'm beat. You're the boss."

"Can I hear that again? I'm the boss. It's about time you saw the light."

"Must be the tequila talking," he said, eyes roaming, shirt absorbing the sweat trickling down his neck with the sun beaming down blinding him. "Damn," he mumbled, "is it the tequila or the sun making me sweat like a hog?"

Rosetta and Mike sat in his office conversing about different pending investigations when Rosetta brought up The Lost Souls Club.

"Did you want me to take you there?" Mike asked, smiling.

"I'm being serious. Do you know anything about the owner?"

"I heard he goes by Big Jake."

"And why would you know that?"

"It's my business to know."

"Does he have a record?"

"I don't believe so. I mean he's no angel."

"You can say that again. What's his story?"

"An old friend of mine got fired by Big Jake and told me I should check the guy out. He was pissed. I blew it off. But I've heard rumblings of him being dirty. So what's the deal? Are you thinking about becoming a stripper at his club, if you are –"

"Yeah right," she interrupted. "I'm being serious now. Were you around when a kid got shot there a few years ago?"

"That's what I meant, he's no angel. Yeah, I remember the case. I was a street cop then and wasn't involved with it. How did you know about that?"

Pausing, licking lips, she strained to say, "Well, it's a long story, but the kid he killed was a friend."

"So that's why you're interested in him?"

"Yeah," she said reflecting, eyes cast down, "that's why."

"Is there something else?" he asked.

"No, not really."

"Come on, spit it out."

"It's just that I think the guy should be locked away."

"Is this another one of your feelings? You trying to tell me you're psychic. If I recall, your friend that he killed had a pretty rough background. What's a girl like you having a friend like that?"

Swallowing hard, she said, "A friend wasn't the right word. Let's just say I knew him."

"Now promise me you're not going to snoop around this guy's business like you did Brittany. Believe me, he's no one to mess around with. You're still an intern. Under my guidance. *Do you hear me?*"

"Yeah, I guess."

"I'm serious now."

"I heard you."

"Good because I don't want you being some Nancy Drew."

"Well, I liked Nancy Drew as a kid. Did you read her mysteries too?"

"Of course not. I read the Hardy Boy mysteries."

"You said that like there was something wrong reading about a female investigator."

"Oh no, I'm not a male chauvinist. I just liked the good old Hardy Boy's."

"*Chauvinist*," she spat.

"Honestly, I'm not."

"Prove it."

"Alright, if you must know, I did read some Nancy Drew books."

"I didn't think you had it in you."

"Does that mean you'll go out with me tonight?"

"You know –" she paused, slight smile and chin up, "I'm still a college intern. But I am twenty-one."

"I don't mean like a date. Just come with me like one of the boys."

"I guess I can hang out like one of the boys."

"*Good.* It's a date then. Right after work."

"Prove to me you read a Nancy Drew mystery. Name one book you read."

Reflecting, Mike smiled and said, "*The Mystery at the Crystal Palace.*"

"Really. I'm impressed. I read that one too. I guess I can hang out with you then."

Big Jake had returned to Chicago, the home base and the center of his operations. Although Andre was on his mind, he had bigger issues to deal with. On this Sunday morning, he, his wife Gail and their three teenage boys exited the front doors of a church where a priest greeted them.

"Jake and Gail it's good to see you," the priest said pulling Big Jake to the side. "I really want to thank you for your generous donation to the school. With our budget problems, it was a big help."

"Father I am glad to help. Hey, Gail and me went and saw that new big movie about that secret mafia priest group in the Vatican. Those boys are pretty ruthless."

Smiling, he said, "That's what I heard, but you do know that is not real don't you?"

"I don't know, it was believable. Hey, just good business the way I see it."

"At any rate, thank you again," he said patting his shoulder, squeezing his bicep with a chuckle.

"My pleasure," Big Jake said, lip twitching, feeling like the priest's grip was an eternity, remembering Father Murphy's hands all over him as a kid. The unpleasant thought refueled his desire to confront the childhood priest whom he had kept tabs on for many years, including where he was located.

On the drive to their Chicago suburban home in Evanston, Big Jake said to his youngest son David, "What's wrong with you boy? You don't talk anymore."

"Nothing's wrong," David responded.

"Then stop looking like you got a corn cob stuck up your ass."

"David's a weirdo," the oldest son said.

Once they were home, Gail took Big Jake into the bedroom. "You don't think the kids will bother us," Big Jake said, grabbing her butt.

"Knock it off," she said, pushing away.

"What then?"

"It's about David."

"What about him?"

"He has a problem."

"Oh yeah? What?"

"I don't want you to get upset."

"What the hell's going on?"

"Do you promise not to be upset?"

"Don't screw with me. Just spare me the bullshit."

"David has a friend."

"Yeah, and what's that mean? I had a lot of friends growing up."

"I mean, he has a boyfriend."

"I had a lot of guy friends."

"I mean, Jesus, you're making this hard. He likes boys. Not girls. Boys!"

"*What?*" he roared, mind-shifting visualizing Father Murphy pulling his pants down.

"Please don't say anything. That's why he's been acting different lately."

Fuming, Big Jake said, "Who's the punk? The son-of-a-bitch has messed with the wrong kid. What's the turds name?"

"Please, this is why he couldn't tell you."

"My kid's no fag. He needs to be taught a lesson." He stormed out of the room toward the stairway.

"*Don't,*" she pleaded. "Get back here."

Big Jake cursed all the way up the stairs. Sitting in front of the computer, chatting and typing, David abruptly turned, staring at his dad who looked like he had just been jabbed by a thorn.

"What's up dad?" David asked, jaw dropping, trying to block the computer screen.

"What the hell you doing there?"

"Just chatting with a friend."

"What friend?"

"A friend."

Pulling David's chair on rollers away from the computer, he looked down reading and then screamed, "*Alright you little pecker head.* Touch my damn son and you won't touch anyone ever again."

"No dad," David cried. "Stop it. Please don't do this."

Pushing the computer monitor over, Big Jake went on a tirade. "*Who is this pervert? Do you hear me?*"

"He's not a pervert dad. You don't understand."

"I understand everything. Do you understand me?" he said, face livid, pointing a finger at David. "You're not to see this *screwball, pecker head, numb nut, pansy ass, pervert again? Understood?*"

Terrified, David nodded his head.

"Say it!"

"I won't see him again."

"And you're no faggot, right?"

"Right," he said, teary-eyed, but under his breath, he said, "but he makes me feel good."

"*What did you say?*" Big Jake snapped.

"Nothing."

"No, I heard you mumble something."

"He makes me," he paused, "feel good."

Grabbing David by the mouth, "I don't ever want to hear shit like that come out of your mouth again. Don't you understand the little pecker head has picked the wrong pecker to mess with? And he won't get away with it. End of discussion. *Now do you understand?*"

"Yes," he struggled to talk, "but –"

Squeezing his mouth tighter, he said, "Not another word."

It was apparent to Tom and Marty that Dick must have had an alliance with the former director now replaced by a new man. Frustrated and uncertain whether to take their concerns about him to Rob, the new director, they decided on a wait and see policy. Many staff feared Dick due to his conniving nature and outbursts at the mention of Tom and Marty's names, creating paranoia among the staff. On this Friday evening, Tom thought he caught a whiff of booze from Dick who was suspected of being an alcoholic. They were paired to head a cheap activity of spooky story telling in the huge attic of the old building. Close to twenty kids signed up for the experience, which included the younger boys from another building on grounds. There was a bell tower opening in the center of the attic, casting moonlight on the wood floor beneath it. An electric lantern set on the floor in the middle of the group. The dim lighting set the mood causing the residents to nest together, eyes scrambling, seeking out lurking creatures as sounds amplified and nerves intensified. Tom started off reading an Edgar Allen Poe tale by flashlight. The kids cringed at every heart throbbing word Tom spoke, holding their breath, whining, fidgeting, teetering and clinging as they sat on the hardwood floor.

On completing the story, Tom made a crackling sound causing the kids to jump certain that a fiend was amongst them. With the tone being set, Dick took center stage. He paced back and forth, garbling in an undertone, staring through the group, taunting them with a snicker as eyes followed, watching him seethe like a maniac. Creeping around the kids, he snorted while moving in and out of the moonlight from the bell tower. When a mounting growl exploded from his throat, the kids screamed in fright, squirming closer together.

"As you all know," Dick said, "from time to time, we have runaways from the home. Sometimes we never hear from them again. Do you have any ideas of what happens to them? *Do yooou?*" he murmured, hovering over their seated bodies. "I'll tell you what happens to them. The pervert gets them. *Every last one of them*. Ha, ha, ha, ha. And do you know where the pervert is?"

"No," the kids trembled in fear.

"He's here in the attic, waiting to *grab you* right now," he said moving in between the kids with a hideous laugh.

The whimpering voices created a sense of panic in all when Dick stuck his face down inches away from their faces. "Do you know who the pervert is? Don't you want to know? Well, how about if I tell you what he does. He takes out a *knife,*" said Dick, pulling out a long shiny object and sliced it through the air causing the kids and even Tom to squirm. "He likes to stick the knife in their guts. Especially the ones he doesn't like." Tom felt his stomach tighten as chills rushed up and down his spine. "And he might just kill someone right now."

Dick walked in Tom's direction with the kids backing up shaking and screaming. Tom stood watching, shuddering, and seeing the shiny object reflecting from the moonlight held above Dick's head barreling downward toward him. Heart leaping to his throat, Tom's arms shot up to protect himself from the blow, but it was not enough to stop it from crashing against his chest. Dick moved on to the next person, stabbing away and then to the next person. Agonizing over what had just happened, touching his intact chest, Tom breathed a sigh of relief, realizing that he didn't really have a knife and this was all part of his act.

"I'm okay," Tom said to himself quivering. "He sure had me going. I thought it was real. I thought he was trying to kill me. Crap almighty. I can't take it. I've got to do something about this maniac."

After recovering from the attic fright night, and the work week over, Tom and Amy met Marty and his fiancée Patsy at a bar. While the band rested, the talk was all about Dick as they drank, unwinding from a stressful week.

"I say," Tom said, "we write a letter to the newspaper about all the bullshit going on."

"Hot damn yes," Marty said. "But what do we say?"

"Everything that's happened."

"Him harboring a runaway and all of it."

"Yeah," Tom blurted.

"You don't know it for a fact," Amy said.

"You don't want to get fired," Patsy added.

"We do know," Tom said, "about the log and what looks like a cover-up to me."

"*Damn right*," Marty said.

"*We'll do it then*," Tom shouted.

"A toast to doing it," Marty said holding his beer up and banging it against Tom's glass. Both downed the remainder of their beer while the girls shook their heads.

"The band is coming back," Patsy said, grabbing Marty's hand and pulling him up to dance.

Tom and Amy looked at one another unsure what to say or what to do.

"Do you want to dance?" Tom asked.

"I don't care," Amy replied. "It's up to you."

"Do you or don't you?" he said, and then stood. "Come on."

"Alright," she said.

Amy followed him to the dance floor, half-reluctant, but got in step with the music. While shaking it up and letting loose, Marty, who loved to unwind, deliberately moved away from Patsy and danced his way between Tom and Amy and backward between them again. All laughed as Marty reunited with Patsy who shook her head at Tom and Amy. With the music roaring, the dancing in stride and the carrying on continuing, the evening allowed all to unwind with worries placed on the back burner for the evening.

Days later, Tom completed writing a detailed article with Marty's input and mailed it to the newspaper. Delighted and frustrated, Tom knew that what they had done could backfire on them. As things turned out, the newspaper called Tom saying that they preferred a more objective article written by their staff and asked to interview him and Marty. They complied with the request on the condition they remained anonymous. Once the article came out, it talked about all sorts of problems at the home, including the claim of a pornographic log and accusations of a supervisor harboring a female runaway. Although their names were not mentioned, everyone at the home assumed Tom and Marty had been the counselors interviewed. The result was bittersweet, they were victorious on one hand as Dick Muster ended up being fired when further investigation of the harboring a runaway proved to be true. The rumors were flying about concerning the firing, but nothing officially came out about it. The article created an upheaval at the home, resulting in Tom and Marty meeting with Rob, the new director, at his request.

"I know you two," said the director, "were responsible for that newspaper article." Tom and Marty looked at one another but did not respond as Rob kept speaking. "The agency administrator wanted me to fire both of you. I don't know either of you that well, but I persuaded her not to. But I want you to know and I'm *dead serious*. One *mistake* and you will be fired. Do you understand me?"

"But –" from Marty.

"But nothing," he blasted back. "One screw-up and *you are gone*. There better not be another newspaper article. You guys are walking on egg shells. That's all I have to say about this matter.

Remember, you are only here because I persuaded the boss not to fire you. She was *pissed*. Do you understand me?"

"Yes," Marty responded.

The director eyed Tom who then said, "Yes."

"Alright, get out of my sight. And I mean it – one screw up and you are done."

Swallowing hard Marty turned to leave and Tom glanced at the director for a split second, lip tightened and then turned to leave.

Chapter 12

Tom and Amy, eager to break free from the grasp of the childcare industry, took a real estate course to become licensed realtors. The economy was bad, but speculation of a turnaround motivated them to pursue this new career. Tom believed his head was scheduled for the guillotine and was waiting for the blade to drop at the home, but prayed the new endeavor would save him from the Marie Antoinette dismemberment fate. After passing the required state exam, they went to work part-time for a realtor. The market had turned for the worse, which made the prospects of making a living at it bleak. They were happy to have their full-time jobs, but a month after Tom and Marty's encounter with the director, Marty made an emotional mistake that sent his head rolling right out the door. With Marty's firing, Tom felt the screws tightening but assured himself that he would not do anything stupid to suffer the same fate. Tom knew that his influence with staff had been compromised due to the article and could tell that all but good friends were afraid to be associated with him. One evening, after their shift was over, Tom walked the grounds waiting for Amy to come out of the building. Reflecting back, over the years, brought a smile to his face. The quiet calm seemed unnatural after all the battles that had taken place with kids and staff. Looking up at the old fortress, he wondered if this was the calm before the storm. He came to the realization that if you are willing to buck the system, you had better be prepared to suffer the consequences. Closing his eyes, Tom's incensed mind drifted off. "I just can't beat them," he thought. "The director dropped a heavy one on me today. He said my days were numbered and there was no future for me here. He said I should move on to something better. It's all like a bad dream. You win the battle against Muster, but you lose the war. I feel too numb to move on. Amy seems so distant that I don't know whose side she is on. Everything seems to be coming unraveled. I need stability and I don't see it anywhere. I feel doomed. Over the years, I've seen may people come and go. I just never imagined seeing myself walking out those doors and never returning. Things will get better," he told himself as Amy stepped out the front door of the children's home.

Approaching Tom, Amy let off some steam, saying, "Chastity is trying to push me over the edge. I should be happy she's leaving. I still can't believe she was made an emancipated minor today in court."

"Unreal," Tom replied. "She's only fifteen."

"And she's legally on her own. Can you believe it?"

"Oh, yeah right. She's such a pillar of maturity. How will she live?"

"She can take care of herself," Amy said. "Just ask her."

"She's definitely a fighter, but she's so stubborn and rebellious."

"Kind of sounds like you, huh?"

"Ha, ha," from Tom. "Who was the judge?"

"Judge nitwit."

"Oh well, she'll be out of our hair. I mean she did push everybody to their limits."

Getting into their Chevy Camaro, Amy added, "She will become someone else's problem. You know I'm right."

"Ditto."

"Let's get going," said Amy, "I've got to prepare for a closing."

"I wish I was getting ready for one. All I've got is a couple of listings."

"They said it takes time."

"I don't have time. You know what? I need to run my butt off when we get home. Did you know Rob met with me today? I feel the noose tightening. I don't know what to do."

"You got to make the real estate work out."

"You know people that have been doing it for years are looking for other jobs. They say business is the worse they've seen it. Rob just has me uptight."

"They're not going to fire you without good reason."

"Look at Marty. He's gone."

"He did something *really stupid*. I mean getting caught pouring skunk oil in Rob's office."

"Sure Rob chewed him out for roughhousing with the kids, but can you believe he did that. I can't believe he spilled it on himself. Otherwise, he might have gotten away with it. I won't give them a reason, but they'll find one."

"You're right. You need to run some of your frustration off when we get home."

"That's the plan."

In Los Angeles, Andre paid an early morning visit to a church within walking distance from his home. The church was empty. Kneeling down, he reflected on the past. After talking to his deceased granny, he asked God to give him the strength to deal with Big Jake and not to return to drowning his anxiety in booze, the culprit that had jeopardized his past sanity. "What do I do granny?" he asked himself. "I could do nothing and hope for the best or I could face fear right in the eye. But you already did that. Didn't you? But I know him and he won't let it rest. I'll always be running from him. Face your fear head on or it will eat away at you until it consumes you. Just go back there and tell him to get the hell out of Dodge and return to his snake pit in Illinois." Face flush, breathing heavy, Andre stood and walked out of the church. Returning home, he and Windy got ready to head to the shelter for the day.

"Where did you go?" Windy asked.

"Just needed to walk and think."

"And?"

"Let's go pay Big Jake a visit. You know face fear right in the eye."

"Are you nuts?"

"Probably, but I have to do something."

"We fled to get the hell away from him."

"I don't want to be looking over my shoulder. Do you?"

"You can't talk reason to a maniac."

"Maniac? Shit. He's a loose cannon ready to go off. I'm fed up with his crap. He wants to take away our life, liberty, and happiness. This is still the good old USA," Andre said, pacing. "Isn't it?"

"Do you think he cares?"

"*Hell no*, but I do."

"Please leave it be. He won't find us."

"He's a cancer creeping up on us and I'm the chemotherapy he needs."

"Settle down," Windy said shaking. "Please think about it. Don't do anything ignorant. Promise me. Do you hear me?"

"I'm just blowing off some steam. Don't worry."

After hugging one another, they finished getting ready for work and left. Andre drove and Windy perked up, realizing he was taking a different route.

"Why are you going this way?"

Smiling, Andre said, "Just a change of scenery."

Windy gripped the dashboard as Andre made a sharp turn. "You're going by there. Aren't you?"

"You know I just can't control myself. The car has a mind of its own."

"Did you forget what happened the last time we were face to face with Big Jake in Springfield? He put a gun to your head and dragged me away. Are you getting senile on me?"

"Some things you just don't want to remember."

"Well *damn it* remember. And didn't you say he put a gun to your head when you rescued Sandy?"

"And I walked out, didn't I? Look what we have here," he said slowing down and coming to a stop in front of the club. "Imagine that. I'll be back."

"No," she blurted.

Stepping out of the car, he hurried to the entrance while Windy covered her face. After gripping the doorknob, Andre turned it to no avail and made a fist, ranting, "Go to hell you big jerk." Returning to the car, he smiled, slid in and drove away.

"Are you crazy?" Windy blasted.

"*Damn right I am,*" he said grinning. "I knew it would be closed. It was just a practice run."

"Practice run," she sighed. "Don't do that to me. You're freaking me out."

"Calm down. Believe me, I'll pull it together."

"You better," she said, squeezing his bicep.

"Just had to get it out of my system."

"I think you're full of it. That was no practice run. You hoped to find him there."

"Calm down. We'll talk about it later. Maybe I'm being too impulsive."

"Have you been drinking?"

"Absolutely not. I'm not going down that route again."

"You swear?" she said, sniffing his breath.

Exhaling in her face, Andre said, "Proof enough?"

"Yeah, you haven't been drinking. I'm relieved. I really thought you had."

"I won't let him do that to me. He might put me six feet under, but I'm not going down drunk."

"Don't talk like that."

"Like what?"

"Six feet under you jerk."

"Oh, don't pay any attention to my blabbering."

"Can we please change the subject? We have a bunch of kids to deal with."

"Yeah, you're right. We have important things to deal with."

"Okay, that's better. So what are we going to do about Jimmy's behavior? Others are scared of him."

"I'm going to have to lay down the law hard on him. He'll have to straighten up if he wants to stay. That's all there is to it. I think he's doing drugs."

On arrival at the shelter, two police cars were in front. Parking behind the building, they hurried inside to find Jimmy irate in hand-cuffs bad mouthing the cops as they led him out the door.

"What happened?" Andre asked the female staff.

"I had to call the police. He was drunk, on drugs or something and acting aggressive with the other kids. Everybody is okay."

"I should have done something about him yesterday when he got cocky with me."

"Police said he lied about his age. He's twenty-four and has a record. He was just let out of jail a week ago."

"Are you okay?" Windy asked.

"Yeah," she said.

Rosetta, on the last day of her internship, sat at the police department across from Mike who was filling out the paperwork needed for the university.

"So did I pass?" she asked.

"I don't know. What are you doing tonight?"

"Celebrating being done and only nine weeks left before graduation."

"So do you think you passed?"

"If I didn't you wouldn't be asking me out tonight would you?"

"Is it a date?"

"Sure, why not?"

"I'll pick you up at seven for dinner."

"So how well did I pass?"

"Best intern I ever had."

Grinning, she said, "The only one you ever had *detective*."

"You really are perceptive you know. You have what it takes."

"I had a good teacher."

Gloating, Mike said, "Thank you."

"I was talking about Tom Paradisio my former foster dad. He taught me to be perceptive."

"Oh, well –"

"But you were real good teaching me about the cop business. I can even shoot a gun now."

"I'm glad to hear that and you are a pretty good shot."

"So," she said, looking at the clock saying 5:01 PM. "I am officially no longer an intern."

"That's right," he said standing, setting his hand on her shoulder, squeezing it. "Congratulations."

"It doesn't give you the green light you know."

"Oh?"

"I'm still a student."

"Of course you are."

Standing, she said, "I'll see you at seven."

"Looking forward to it Miss graduate. Hold on, I'm leaving too. I'll walk you down to the car."

"I'm ready."

"Are you now?"

"To be walked down to the car," she said with a slight smile.

"That's what I meant."

"Your slick cop talk doesn't work on a girl like me."

"Two points for the intern," a passing voice said, causing Mike to look at the back of the officer.

"That's right," Mike said, "hit and run. Get back to your street duty Joey."

"Got it covered," he responded.

"He's a smart cop," Rosetta said.

"Smart-aleck you mean."

"Settle down, let's get out of here."

Pulling up to a curbside on a secluded street, two men got out of a large sedan to the surprise of the young man who froze as they grabbed his arms and escorted him to the car.

"What do you want?" the boy asked terrified. "Don't hurt me."

"You need to talk to the boss," one man said.

Big Jake rolled down the car window, eyeing the boy with disgust. Face to face with each other, Big Jake said, "So you're the prick messing with my son."

"Not me," the boy said.

"You know my son David, right?"

"Well, a, well, I do," he stammered.

Big Jake grabbed the back of the boy's shirt and yanked his squirming body right through the car window. "You little turd," Big Jake growled.

"I haven't done nothing," he whined.

Rolling up the dark tinted window, Big Jake pushed the boy's head against the seat. "If you had we wouldn't be talking. You're not going near my son again are you?"

"Oh no, never."

"I don't mess around punk. We understand each other?"

"Yes!"

"Good because I don't like making personal calls," he said grabbing his hair. "I won't have to see you again. *Right?*"

"You won't see me again," he whined.

Opening the car door, Big Jake said, "*Scram before I get angry.*"

The boy scooted out and ran off never turning to look back.

After dinner, Mike and Rosetta debated where to go. "Well," Mike said, "I think you ought to invite me over to your place. Unless you would sooner see my place?"

"I think I would feel safer at my place."

"Oh yeah?"

"I've got my tiger and ferocious dog to protect me there."

"Protection? Why you got me to protect you."

"Who's going to protect me from you?"

"Me, myself and my handcuffs. Just cuff me now."

"Hand them over. You do seem a little too assured all of the sudden."

"No, not me."

"We'll see."

On arriving at Rosetta's attractive brick house in a nice neighborhood, Mike was very impressed. "So this is how the other half lives? I mean the sports car. This house. Do you own this place?"

"Well yeah, but it was left to me."

"Oh, your parents are deceased?"

"It's a long story. My mom is. My – my dad may as well be dead. He's in prison. Wish he would never get out."

"Oh, well –"

"See my tiger," she said changing the subject as the cat rubbed up against her leg.

"Definitely a tiger with stripes."

"And here's my pooch," she said petting the young cocker spaniel. "Aren't you Buddy?"

"Buddy's ferocious."

Grabbing hold of Rosetta's leg, Buddy started humping her. "Stop it," Rosetta giggled.

"You're a smart boy," Mike said.

Shaking Buddy off her leg, "Knock it off," she commanded and Buddy moved away. "You want a tour?"

"Definitely."

When they entered the art room, Mike's eyes lit up. "You did all of these paintings?"

"Every one of them."

"Wow, what is this one?" he said, looking at the scene of Gomez scalping Big Jake. "That's the person we talked about who got killed by Big Jake."

"Why did you paint it?"

"I thought Big Jake needed to get his due."

"Well, I guess you gave it to him alright."

"It really happened you know."

"Yeah, I remember hearing about it. And you saw it.

"Oh yeah."

"Why," he asked, frowning, "would you want to remember it?"

"I don't know. I mean, I guess it just made such an impact on me I couldn't get it out of my head."

"I really like this one," he said looking at an abstract painting of a fairytale world."

"I call it wonderland."

"Definitely a wonderland. Is that you in the background?"

"It could be, I guess."

"I love it. Rosetta in wonderland."

"Thanks. But you don't like my Big Jake."

"Oh, it's striking alright. In fact, it fits right in with the cop business. It's a masterpiece of suspense and horror. You are multi-talented. I can see you doing this rather than being a cop."

"Really?"

"Oh yeah. Honest to God. You are good."

"Thanks."

"What's this?" he said picking up a photo of the Big Jake horror painting. "Can't get enough of looking at it – you got to take a photo of it?"

"Oh," she stammered, "I, a, you know keep a record of all my paintings."

"Yeah, sure."

"Let's move onto the rest of the house."

"Lead the way."

On passing a room with the door open, Mike said, "What's that room?"

"Oh, that's just my bedroom."

"Looks neat. Can I see?"

With a slight smile, she said, "Now, why would you want to see it?"

Setting his hands on her shoulder, he bent down and kissed her. She returned the kiss. "Just want the full tour. Don't want to miss out on anything you know."

Leading the way into the dimly lit room, she stopped, "I better turn the overhead light on so you get a good look."

"This view is just fine."

"In that case this is it."

Caressing and kissing her, she responded and then backed away. "I think I better call my tiger for help."

"You don't need tiger."

"You need to cool down. I'm not ready. There's a lot you don't know about me."

"I want to know all," he sighed, sniffing the sensual fragrance she emitted.

"We'll see, but not now."

Trying to kiss her, she pecked his lips and pushed away. "Alright, you're the hostess."

"Good," she said, squeezing his hand, leading the way out of the bedroom.

"I think you need an icy cold drink."

"A cold beer would settle me down."

"Only cold soda or juice in this house."

"That's right you don't drink."

"Soda on ice. Okay?"

"That's fine," he said following her into the kitchen. "We can talk for awhile then you better leave. I have an early class."

"Sure thing. Like I said you're the hostess."

After Mike left, Rosetta returned to the studio with a camera and took several photos of the Gomez and Big Jake painting. Having downloaded them on her computer, she proceeded to print several large copies. Mike questioning about the photo motivated her to do what she had wanted to do for months. Taking out an envelope and phone book, she addressed it to Big Jake at his club, placed the large paper copy of the photo in it and stuck it in a purse to be mailed the next day. "Maybe I can torment him," she thought, "even if just a little. It's payback time. It should freak him out. That's the least I can do." Continuing in thought, the reminder of the horrible incident brought back memories of the baby she gave up for adoption. "Little Crow," she thought. "That was your daddy's name for you. You were in my arms when he was almost dead thanks to Big Jake. He did scalp that no good creep. At least he did something good that night. Where are you, baby? I couldn't care for you then. I'm sorry I gave you up..." Going outside to the patio, she took one of the large prints of the scalping, placed it in a metal container, and lit it watching it burn, but it couldn't put out the fire within her. Thinking about the baby brought back the events of that horrifying night when she was kidnapped by Gomez from the hospital and dumped in secluded woods to give birth to their baby. As smoke swirled around rising from the container, she relived what happened that night:

The ride was bouncy, causing Rosetta great pain as she cried, moaned and screamed with every bump. Stopping the car, which was out of sight, Gomez scooted out, grabbed Rosetta and two blankets, and then carried her into the woods, swallowed up by its darkness. Finding a clear area, he set a blanket down, placing her on it and covering her with the other.

"What are you doing?" she begged to know, doubled over in pain.

"The book tells me everything I need to know."

"Please stop this," she pleaded.

"You give birth under the open sky like squaws did in the past. You bite the umbilical cord off."

"What!" she screamed. "Your book's crazy!"

"You can do it. Now give birth to a healthy baby and we'll be free at last."

"I hurt!"

"Have our baby. I'll be back for you. You're to be left alone for this. I know what I'm doing."

"This is insane!"

"This is right," he said walking away. "The Indian way. First animal you see, we name baby after it."

"Don't leave me!" she cried.

Grabbing hold of a tree trunk, Rosetta pulled herself up only to collapse to the ground, sweating and moaning in a semiconscious state. A sharp pain erupted causing her back to arch. She let out a vicious scream. Before long, total darkness set in and Rosetta heard sounds of creatures roaming and eyes appearing nearby, but the pain was so great the fear of the creatures vanished. Unable to leave, she accepted her fate, hoping for a miracle. Wild screams went unheard, but for the critters around her. With head pounding and fingers clawing the ground; she cried, and pulled the white gown over her head feeling kicks inside of her. Grabbing a branch, she put it between her teeth and bit down on it as the pain radiated from front to back. Profusely sweating, she spread her legs apart. A large black bird came down flapping its wings and landed on a branch ten feet above. Her mind drifted for a second thinking of what Gomez said about the first animal she saw. It would be the name of the baby. "Bird," she thought, "for a child's name." Then she thought, "No it's a crow. Gomez will name the baby Crow," she told herself. "*This is insane*," she cried out. "*Someone help me*," she screamed. Trying to deliver, she pushed but the baby stayed in. The pain unbearable, she tried standing but fell back to the ground. Moving from one position to the next, she could not comfort herself.

Opening her eyes, Rosetta returned to the present, panting and blurted out, "For Christ sake. He finally came out. How did I take the pain? I thought I was dying," she said, wiping away a tear streaking her cheek. Returning inside the house, she walked in a daze deep in thought. "He was bloody. But he was my beautiful baby. But, but," she repeatedly thought. "He was his baby. My baby, but his baby. Is that why you gave him up? I guess, but he was yours too. You should have never given him up. You can't undo it. What's done is done." Entering the bedroom, she dropped on the bed, curling up into a ball with a teddy bear. "God, what a nightmare that was," she thought. "Gomez drugged me with LSD and then *raped me*. He was *insane* and all that Indian heritage bullshit," she told herself before breaking down into tears.

Chapter 13

On business, a hundred and twenty miles from Chicago, Big Jake visited his central Illinois club in Saplecreek for a few days before heading to Springfield. Seated at his desk alone, in the Springfield club, Big Jake went through the mail and opened the envelope that Rosetta had sent him. Pulling out the photo, he stared, hypnotized by the image, and then placed a hand on the back of his head where he had extensive plastic surgery. The photo brought back the razor cutting pain he went through from the scalping. Wondering who had sent it and who had painted the image caused him to hyperventilate. Taking deep controlled breaths, he regained control and looked at the front of the envelope. There was no return address, but he saw that it was postmarked, Springfield. Crumbling up the photo, tossing it in a wastebasket, he swore and cursed, but nothing he did stopped the agony. Reaching for a bottle of whiskey on a shelf, he chugged it twice, closed his eyes trying to drown his thoughts. Five minutes passed when a knock at the door brought him back to the present.

"Yeah," he grunted.

"Hey boss," said Lee.

"What?"

"Got a real hottie for you. Wants to work for us."

"So, they all think they're hotties."

"Yeah, but you need to check this babe out."

"Why's that?"

"She's fifteen."

"*What's wrong with you*? She can't work here."

"Get this. She's got legal papers with her."

"What the hell you talking about?"

"She's an emancipated minor."

"What the hell's that mean? Did she get rid of her bra or what?"

"It means a judge has made her legal to be on her own."

"They can do that?"

"I guess they can because it all looks legit."

"So she can legally take her bra off for us?"

"I don't know."

"Bring her in."

Leaving, he returned with the girl who was all smiles. "This is Chastity," Lee said.

Studying the curves of her body, Big Jake said, "Turn your butt toward me. Yeah, you have a nice ass. You're built real good. So what's your story girl? First of all, you're no fuckin' cop are you?"

"Fuck no," she said cocksure.

"Prove it."

"I said I wasn't."

"Pull your shirt up and show me what you got if you're not a cop."

Hesitant, she complied.

"Undo your bra."

"Well, I don't know."

"What did you want to do here? Wash dishes. Are you a cop?"

"No. I heard strippers made big bucks."

"Well let's see the twin peaks," Big Jake said gloating. "If you're a cop you can't show 'um to me. Right? So let's see them."

"*I'm not.*"

"Show me then."

Shaking, she started to pull her bra up.

"Stop," Big Jake said concerned about her legal status. "I guess you're not a cop."

"I'm not."

"What's this about you being legally on your own?"

"The judge made me legal."

"Why?"

"Because I couldn't handle being locked up in a children's home. I rebelled until they set me free."

"I never heard of it before."

"Well, here's my papers."

Grabbing the papers, he looked them over. "They look real."

"They are."

"Where do you live?"

"With a boyfriend on South Street."

"What's he do?"

"Odd jobs until he finds a full-time job."

Pondering, he paced and nodded his head. When he looked down, he saw the wastebasket with the crumbled up photo. "What's going on?" he asked himself. "Is this a setup? I don't know what to believe. And that damn photo. Just be careful. Don't rush into anything." Sighing, lip twitching, he said, "I'll tell you what. Come back tomorrow and we'll talk about it. Okay?"

"Yeah, sure."

"Escort her out then come back in," Big Jake said to Lee. "Oh, make a copy of those papers."

After Lee returned, Big Jake said, "I want to put her to work, but I'm uneasy about it. We got a big operation and I don't want to jeopardize it with uncertain legalities. I can't have the cops coming down on me by doing something stupid."

"Yeah, I agree," Lee said.

"She might be perfect for our China connection."

"Good thinking."

"Let's see if we can persuade her to go voluntarily. She just might go for it. You know, see the world, a big adventure. What do you think?"

"It's worth a try. It would be safer than our usual tactics if she agreed to it."

"But she'll do more than strip over there if I know those boys. Let's play her along for awhile. Give her some dough. Gain her confidence and then drop it on her. Besides, I don't want to rush this. Let things play out for a month or so. I want to know who we're dealing with."

Lee nodded and said, "You seem a little paranoid boss."

"Something happened earlier that's bothering me. I feel like I'm a target. I don't want to be an easy hit for the cops or anyone else."

"I hear you."

"Good. Now leave me alone."

Lee left and Big Jake stared down at the wastebasket, shaking his head.

On a Saturday afternoon, Brenda stopped by to pick Amy up to go shopping. "We're going to have dinner together," Amy told Tom as she was leaving. "Hey, think about what Rob said to you yesterday."

"How could I forget? I'll be working on my book for awhile and then I'm going to the health club."

"Later," she said.

"Yeah, later," he said irritated.

Sitting at a desk, Tom typed away on the computer working out his anger. Frustrated that he had no publisher for the other novel did not discourage him from writing, as writing was more than being published – it was a way to let off steam like a tea kettle whistles away pressure. This novel was a first-person account and close to autobiographical. "Alright, Amy I'll think about what he said," he grumbled. Pounding away on the keyboard, he unleashed the rage building since meeting with the home's director the day before:

The director requested my presence in his office. What now I wondered, feeling extremely anxious as I neared the door. Turning the doorknob, I felt my hands moisten. The secretary told me to go on in, which I did and shut the door behind me. The director's eyes focused on some papers, but then shifted, glancing up at me.

"Sit down," he said.

I complied feeling fidgety but tried to appear calm. He continued to concentrate on the papers, moving his lips in silence and then would pause as if in awe. He did this a couple of times. Setting the papers aside, a frown erupted and then his mouth began to churn.

"I've heard you're unhappy about not getting a raise? You know," he said coldly, "everyone but you is getting a raise or bonus or both in some cases. There's no way you are going to get a raise 'now or ever.' Betsy won't permit it," he said referring to the head of the social service agency. "Let's face it, there's no future for you here. Don't ever expect to get a raise. I don't know

why you have stayed here this long? I really think you need to find another job ..."

All I saw was a vast emptiness staring out the window. ...

"... your performance hasn't been up to par. Your last evaluation was bad. Let's face it, you're burnt out ... You've been here too long. What? Over three years?"

I nodded.

"I think you're going to need to find another job real soon."

"I've been trying to make the real estate work out, but the market's bad."

"You need to find 'something.' I don't know what you're going to say or do after you are gone. I don't know if you are going to the newspaper again or what. In fact, I should just fire you so whatever you might say won't be as credible."

I couldn't believe he said that to me. His face reddened. I stared off.

"You're going to 'fuck up' and I'm going to have to fire you. Sure, you've been shit on in a lot of ways. If I was you I don't think I could handle staying here. I would hate to have to fire you but I will."

Go ahead I told myself. Fire me and see what I'll do. I forced a stare at him.

"Well?" he whined. "What do you have to say for yourself?"

"I went into real estate so I could leave here. It's just not working out like I hoped. I need some time. I, a, need time to work things out."

"Well, I'm not saying you have to be gone tomorrow or even in two weeks or a month. But you know you're not happy here and I think you're burnt out."

I nodded.

"All I can say is while you are here do the best job that you can. Alright?"

"Alright." I stood, paused then weakly left in a daze.

Pushing himself away from the computer, Tom stood frustrated after reliving what he had typed. Stretching, twisting the anxiety from his neck, he paced for a couple of minutes, returned to the computer and clicked on file and the save button. That was enough anguish for one day he reasoned and gathered his workout clothes to go to the health club.

Once at the health club, he worked out harder than he had in years. Pounding his body was the alternative to writing to relieve stress. It had worked in the past. Worried about getting the ax at work and his and Amy's relationship was putting him over the edge. While drifting off, legs pumping away on an elliptical machine, he was approached by a very attractive girl.

"Can I make a suggestion," the girl said, looking up at him.

"Sure," he responded, taken by her comment.

"If you lean forward while you're doing that, you'll burn more calories. You look a little tense the way you're doing it now. Try it, it'll loosen you up."

Leaning forward, Tom said, "Yeah, I'll try it."

She smiled and walked away.

Watching her from the corner of his eye, she went down the stairway to the lower half of the club. Tom continued to lean forward, believing that it was better but wondered who she was and why she had spoken to him. "I've seen her here before," he said to himself. "She's really hot looking. Was that a come on?" he thought. "I don't know. Maybe she's an instructor. I've seen her here a lot. That's probably it. Don't act like a dope. She didn't come on to you. Pull it together. Why is she concerned about me burning more calories? Do I look fat? Is that what she is saying? Then she said I looked tense. What's that about? Well, you are tense. Maybe it really shows. Shit, I don't know what to think. Not thinking is the best thing right now. Just keep on truckin'."

Amy and Brenda, sat eating dinner and sipping beers, carrying on about work and what the director had said to Tom.

"What's he going to do?" Brenda asked.

"I don't know, but he needs to get off his butt and look for another job. The real estate isn't working out."

"It's not his fault the economy sucks."

"No it's not, but it's almost like he doesn't believe they'll fire him. I mean look at Marty."

"It's not fair what they're doing to him."

"Fair or not he needs to find something soon."

"Has he applied anywhere?"

"No, he wants the real estate to work out. People doing it for years are looking for other work. That's how bad it is."

"It's just not right how they're treating him. I hate working at that place. I'd like to get my butt out of there. I'm tired of all the B.S., but at least there will be less of it with Chastity gone."

"Do you believe they emancipated her?"

"She'll probably start turning tricks," Brenda said, smiling. "I mean what is she going to do? She's a terror to deal with. Can you imagine a boss telling her what to do?"

"Heaven forbid."

"That judge is nuts. I sure won't miss her, but it is insanity if you ask me."

"Crazy."

"Hey," said Brenda, "how are you and Tom getting along?"

"Good and bad, but more bad I guess."

"Is he still pissed at Burt for peeing down the stairs?"

"Hell yes."

"I haven't seen him in awhile. Have you?"

"Don't say anything, okay?"

"My lips are sealed. What?"

"Burt came buy one day when Tom was working out and stayed for a beer. I didn't and won't say anything to Tom."

"Would he be pissed?"

"Yes."

"I miss Burt working at the home. How does he like his new job?"

"He does."

"I think Burt has a crush on you."

"Oh, no," she said, looking away. "Don't you ever say that in front of Tom."

"I'm not an idiot."

"Well, you ready for another beer?"

"I'll get them," she replied, standing and going to the bar.

Andre and Windy came to the realization that they could not live their lives based on a fear that they had no control over. With that agreed to, they kept their anxiety about Big Jake to themselves and were determined to act as if it didn't bother them. Late one evening, they sprawled out on the bed sound asleep when their dog Duke jumped up whining and scrambled to the closed bedroom door. Windy woke and nudged Andre who cracked open his eyes trying to gather his bearings hearing the noise.

"Oh shit," Windy blurted, eyes froze on the door.

"What?" Andre said, sitting up, glancing at Windy, and then at the dog. "*What?*"

"I think," she whispered, "I saw something flash under the door. I think a light went on."

Jumping up, Andre went to the door, listening but heard nothing. Duke continued to whine. Windy called 911 while Andre cracked open the door, allowing Duke's nose to wedge it open and for him to burst out of the room growling. Andre followed Duke and noticed the hallway light was on. Running down the hallway barking, Duke entered the living room and grabbed a hold of a man's leg with a crushing chomp. Andre turned an overhead light on, revealing a dark clad person wearing a ski mask. Seeing a knife in his hand, Andre leaped at the man, grabbing his hand to prevent him from stabbing Duke. Struggling with him came to a stop when Windy rushed into the room with a pistol, standing five feet away, she pulled the trigger aiming at the wall, and then the intruder dropped the knife.

"Should I shoot him?" Windy said trembling. "Do you think it's *him?*"

"*Don't shoot, don't shoot,*" the intruder shouted.

"Do you think it's him?" Windy repeated.

Andre backed up grabbing the gun from Windy. "Lay on the floor," Andre ordered. "Who are you?"

"Get the dog off me," he pleaded.

"*Duke*," Andre said. "Who the hell are you? You're not Big Jake. You must be some other maniac."

Duke backed off, but continued growling while Windy grabbed a hold of his collar saying, "The police are on their way."

"Don't move and I won't shoot," Andre said.

"I won't," the man said, and then ran to the door with Duke chasing and chomping down once again. "Aw," the man screamed.

Continuing to aim the gun at the man, Andre was relieved to see flashing red lights pull up.

"*Get him off me*," screamed the intruder.

"The cops are here, don't move," Andre said, rushing to open the door.

With drawn guns, two officers enter and another police car pulled up.

"He broke in," Andre said, grabbing Duke's collar.

The officers handcuffed the man while Windy looked on wanting to see the person's face.

"Who are you?" Andre said imagining it was Big Jake, but knew it was a ludicrous thought.

"We'll find out," said an officer, pulling the ski mask off.

"What?" Windy said, recognizing the man.

"I know you," Andre said, trying to remember.

"He's stayed at the shelter before," said Windy. "It's Jimmy."

"That's right. You were the druggie trouble maker that got arrested at the shelter. I remember you. Why? How did you find us? You had to know we lived here."

"I'm sorry," he pleaded, eyes bugged out and shaking. "I just needed money. I'm sorry."

"What are you on?" said the cop. "You're definitely on something."

"*How did you know we lived here?*" Andre flared, moving toward him.

"I followed you from the shelter."

"You didn't have a car before."

"I was with a friend who did."

"Is someone else here?" Windy said concerned, looking around.

"No," Jimmy said, glancing back. "I'm by myself."

Andre and the other officer started looking around the house and hiding in a closet was another young man.

"Get out of there," said the officer pointing the gun at him. "Turn around and put your hands behind your back." The officer handcuffed the man and led him out of the house to the squad car where Jimmy had been taken too.

After the police left, Andre and Windy examined the cut open glass door panel. A suction cup against the glass kept it from dropping to the ground. "Do you believe how they got in?" Windy said.

"Cut open a square hole just enough to stick their hand in it to unlock the door. That's unbelievable."

"It's scary," she said.

"One of our own kids. Do you believe it?"

"You know who I thought it was don't you?"

Andre nodded his head, "I know."

"It's not so easy to get him out of our heads. Is it?"

"You fear one thing only to be blindsided by another. It's crazy. What's the point in fearing the unknown?"

"Got to chalk it up to, what, bad luck?"

"Fate I guess? I don't know."

"I hope not," she said.

Done with the internship, Rosetta concentrated on artwork, but could not put Big Jake behind her. Waiting at home one evening for Mike to pick her up to go to a movie, she sat on the sofa, petting the cat thinking about the baby she had given up for adoption. On one hand, she gave birth to the child but was bitter about being drugged and forced into sex while out of her mind. "The baby is Gomez's too," she told herself. "He was crazy and I hate remembering what he put me through. Wanting my baby is so complicated. My baby, but his baby. It's better not to think sometimes. So much to bury, but it's hard to. Things are so much better now. You can't forget that," she thought, but could not help remembering the last day she set eyes on the baby.

The doorbell rang causing Rosetta to jump. Setting the cat down, she answered the door.

"Are you ready?" Mike asked. "Or would you prefer to stay in tonight?"

"I don't think that's the plan. Besides, we both want to see this movie, especially since it's in 3-D."

"I know, you just looked tired."

"I kind of dozed off on the sofa."

With the weather turning nice, Rosetta grabbed a light jacket.

Driving to the movie, Mike debated whether to bring up what he learned about Rosetta's past abuse. She had opened up the door by mentioning that her dad was in prison. Sad about what she had gone through, having read about the dad's sexual charges and conviction, he decided to take things slow. "I did some checking about your dad. He's due to be released in about a month."

"That's what I thought."

"You didn't mind that I looked it up did you?"

"I guess I should have expected it since I told you about him."

"Hey," he hesitated. "You know, heck, I don't know, it's just that I feel really bad, I mean –"

"You don't have to go there."

"You know," he paused, "I know what happened?"

"Well, yeah, I mean I don't know. Guess I'm not so desirable anymore."

"That's ridiculous. I just feel for you. I don't know what to say."

"You don't have to say anything. It's okay."

"If there's anything I can do let me know?"

Smiling, she grabbed his leg and squeezed. "How about taking me to a movie and having a good time. I'm okay. It happened a long time ago. You hear?"

"Yeah, I hear."

"Good. If something comes up, we can talk about it. This movie should be good in 3-D."

"They're calling it spectacular. I hope it lives up to its billing."

"I didn't eat so I could fill up on popcorn," she said licking her lips.

"Me either."

"I am hungry. I want a lot of butter on the popcorn."

"Of course, but just one more thing about your dad?"

Fidgety, she said, "Just say it."

"There was an issue about him selling you that you didn't want to pursue."

"It's funny you should mention that. I know more now than I did then."

"Oh?"

"I had my reasons for not wanting to pursue it. Besides, it was enough just dealing with the other stuff. But I've found out something," she said, hesitating. "It's just, just been eating away at me." As he listened, Mike's eyes saddened, empathizing with Rosetta jitteriness. "I know, I mean I know who was behind buying me from my dad."

"Oh, yeah?"

"That guy I was asking you about before. You know, Big Jake. I'd like to see his butt fry for what he put me through."

"How did you find that out?"

"Someone close to me knew the truth."

"Would they testify?"

"I don't want them involved."

"Then you don't have anywhere to go with it."

"*I know he's got to be doing other terrible things,*" she said enraged.

"You're probably right."

"You did say if there's anything you can do? Right? Will you help me nail this creepy scumball?"

"Now you're sounding like a cop. I'll do some checking."

"You said a friend of yours worked at his club?"

"He hasn't for a few years. In fact, I've heard he's hitting the bottle heavy and doesn't have a job."

"Maybe he knows *something*?"

"Yeah, sure I can check with him. I just don't know how reliable he will be."

"Good, but we're here now," she said, seeing the theater. "We'll talk more about it later, okay?"

"For sure. If he's dirty, we'll try to dig something up. Okay?"

"Thanks," she said, kissing his cheek.

Chapter 14

On one hand, Big Jake was pleased to learn from his attorney that Chastity's 'emancipated minor' court papers were legal, but was troubled to find out that there could be legal issues having a fifteen-year-old be a stripper. The solution, he decided, was to persuade her to go to China. To gain Chastity's confidence; Big Jake created a behind the scenes job at the club that he thought would serve everyone's purpose – getting the strippers ready for each performance and attending to their needs. The girls liked having someone backstage helping and were told to butter her up to the China idea. Wanting to become like the strippers, getting high and boozing with them was how she chose to do it. On this night, like every night, the music was loud, the crowds were captivated and Chastity loved the new found freedom.

"Can you fasten my bra?" Candy asked, preparing for the next striptease performance.

"Sure," Chastity said, fastening it. "But why fasten it if you're just going to take it right off?"

"It's the way you take it off that matters."

"Really, what do you mean?"

"Do you want me to show you?"

"Yeah, sure."

After slipping into a cowgirl outfit, Candy turned around and swayed to the background music blaring through the club. Rubbing up against Chastity, she moved to the rhythm of the music, saying, "You want to drive them crazy. Make them beg for you to take it off." Candy reached behind her back, bent forward and unfastened the glittery bra that Chastity had just fastened. Keeping arms under the bra to hold it up, she moved her hips back and forth. Chastity smiled thinking she could do the same thing. In slow motion, Candy let her arms spring out like wings, letting the top drop revealing her peaking breast for a split second and then cupped them, hiding their short-lived unveiling. Moving to Chastity, grabbing the back of her head, pulling it down between the jiggling breasts, she teetered moaning as if in ecstasy. "That's how you get them going."

"You didn't have to pull my head down."

"Just a demonstration. Don't you like them?"

"They're really great. I mean so perfect looking."

"You got to make the guys beg for more. Then they might pay for a lap dance. You get it?"

"I think so, but do you really have to do the lap dances?"

"That's where the money is. That's what you do out there. You got to get comfortable with your body. I'm so comfortable I'd let you squeeze them if you wanted."

"That's okay."

"They're implants. That's why they're so perfect looking. You'll catch on. You with me so far?"

"Yeah, I think so. Hey, is Candy your real name?"

"Everyone has a stage name. You don't want some goofball finding out your real name. Now fasten me backup, I'm about due to go out. Would you get me a double shot of whiskey real quick?"

As Candy looked herself over in the mirror, Chastity went to the backstage bar and poured a glass of whiskey. Returning with the glass, Candy grabbed it and downed it. "Yes, yes," she sighed. "I think that was more like three shots. Just what I needed. They're ready and I'm the star of the show." Slamming the glass down, she rushed off through the curtain to the delight of the audience eager to see the scanty outfit come off. Chastity peeked through the curtain to watch the show.

Returning from a late dinner, Big Jake walked through the club, chatting with people and stopped for a drink before heading to his office. While watching the show and the customers, a man came up to him.

"Hey," Big Jake said recognizing the man. "What's up?"

"I could sure use a job."

"Hey, you screwed up when you worked for me before."

"I know."

"Don't be asking me stupid shit like that."

"I have some information you're going to want to know about."

"What's that?"

"Well,' he paused, looking around. "You know, maybe we should talk in the back room."

"Come on," he said, leading the way. Entering his office, Big Jake started to sit at the desk chair but stopped noticing mail placed on it. Grabbing the mail, he sat glancing at the two letters. The small envelope he recognized as a bill, but the larger one was a mystery and had no return address. The other man took a seat while Big Jake opened the large envelope and pulled out an unfolded 11x14 print of the painting of him being scalped he had received before. Breaking out in a sweat, eyes bulging, he stared at it.

"Big Jake," the man said, "I really need some bucks. You know, maybe you could –"

"Shut the fuck up for a minute!" he exploded.

"Yeah, sure."

Standing, hands clammy, he wanted to crumble the paper, but sat back down putting it in a drawer, and then eyed the man with scorn.

"Bad news?" asked the man.

"What the hell do you want?"

"Like I said I need some money and I thought I could sell you some information."

Pushing away from the desk, he leaped toward the man, grabbing his throat. *Don't screw with me,* he roared. "Tell me and then I'll decide if it's worth paying you, you *son-of-a-bitch.*"

"O-okay," the man trembled, struggling to speak until Big Jake let loose. "A cop friend of mine – a detective asked me questions about you."

"Like what?" he sneered.

"Like if I noticed any illegal activities while I worked here."

"You haven't worked here for a few years. Why the hell would he be asking about me now?"

"I don't know."

Pacing, Big Jake ran his hands through his hair. "What did you tell him?"

"Nothing."

"What the shit do you know?" Big Jake said, grabbing the man by the shirt.

"I don't know *shit*."

Pushing the man away, he continued to pace. "What in the hell's going on?"

"I don't know. I just thought you might want to know about it."

"Who is he?"

"Detective Mike Palermo. He's with the city police."

"How well do you know him?"

"We were buds in grade school."

Opening his wallet, Big Jake pulled out some cash and handed it to the man. "Alright numskull, you keep me informed if you hear anything else."

"My name's Jack if you forgot."

"Alright, Jackass why don't you talk to him and see if you can find out why he's asking questions?"

"We're not buds anymore."

"Well, go fuck him and get back together."

"I'll talk to him sometime. Okay?"

"Do it soon."

"Yeah sure, soon."

"Now get out of my sight."

"Could I get a free drink?" Jack said, looking at a bottle of whiskey.

Gawking at the man, Big Jake boiled, but grabbed the bottle of whiskey off the shelf and poured the man a glassful. "Here," he said handing it to him.

"Thanks," he said downing it, closing his eyes in euphoria.

"If I like the information you bring me, just maybe I'll hire you back."

"I'll work on him," he said, walking away.

Big Jake sat down at his desk and pulled out the large print of his agonizing scalping. Gazing at it, breathing erratic, he stressed trying to figure out who sent the photo. Looking at the local postmark, he shook his head unable to sort it out. Once again, he put it in the drawer, grabbed the bottle of whiskey, downed a glassful and then slammed the glass against the floor watching the shattered pieces disperse. *"When I find whoever you are,"* he yelled, *"you're fucking dead."* Slouching back in the chair, eyes closed, he thought of enemies who were many, but none had a connection to the scalping. After reflecting, he recalled the recent encounter with Andre at his club in L A. "I remember seeing him in the parking lot," he told himself, "the night that crazy kid sliced my head. That's right, he saw it. Why was he there that night? Shit almighty. I don't know, but I remember seeing him standing there. Did he put that kid up to try to kill me? Why did he show up at my club in L A? Maybe he's the connection to all this bullshit? Who in the hell does he think he is messing with me? I got to find his ass. But the postmark is right here in town. I don't think it could be him, but who and why?" Clasping his forehead, shaking his head, he reached for the bottle of whiskey strangling its neck, and then took a swig. "Where is that asshole?" he asked himself. "Who does he think he is getting in my face? Threatening me at my own club. What were his words? 'You know you have an underage girl there.' Then he said he would have the cops down on me if he didn't walk out of there. It doesn't make sense that Andre was connected to this photo. All I know is I need to find his butt for getting in my face. Is he in LA? He must be. He must be working with kids like he was here. I'll get the boys to check out every kid joint in the LA area. Maybe he's connected to this photo in some way. But it's a photo of a painting. Who the hell painted it? It don't matter. His ass needs to fry regardless ..." Picking up the phone, he called his LA club and made it clear that he wanted Andre King found. "You turn over every damn rock in the city until you find him," Big Jake shouted. "Do you understand me? Start by calling different places that take kids in, throw his name out there, and see if someone recognizes it. He's there and you find the bastard ..."

After arriving at the children's home one day, Tom was told to work with the young boys for his shift due to the supervisor and another one of his staff being sick. On previous occasions, he filled in on this unit, which was in a smaller building behind the main one. After dinner, Tom received a planned placement from a foster home. A state worker brought a boy going on five-years-old named Aaron and the needed paperwork to make the transition. Once it took place, Tom and Aaron sat chatting in an office.

"So what's your favorite thing to do?" Tom asked the boy.

"Beat off," he yapped. "I like to beat off," he continued as he moved from one side of the room to the other. "A witch put a curse on my penis to try to stop me from beating off."

"What?" Tom said, thinking he misunderstood him.

"Beat off beat off, I like to beat off since they did an exorcism on my penis. What is this place?"

"It's a children's home," Tom said flabbergasted, "and you're going to be living here. What is this exorcism and curse stuff?"

"Why?" he said, moving next to Tom, opening a desk drawer.

"Please, don't do that."

"I'm hungry."

"I brought a plate of food from the cafeteria since I knew you would be coming."

"I like to come. Beat off. Beat off."

"Where did you get that beat off stuff from?"

"A foster brother did the exorcism. He liked to beat off. He taught me …"

"Slow down buddy. I'll get your food. Wait here a minute." Tom walked out of the room with Aaron following. "Alright come with me." As soon as they passed the recreation room where a group of five boys, ranging from seven through eleven years old were playing games, he charged into the room and grabbed a ball off the pool table creating havoc.

"Don't do that," a ten-year-old shouted. Aaron kept moving ignoring the boy who ran after him. Before, he could catch him; Aaron turned and threw the ball at him. "*Aw*," screamed the boy.

"*Aaron*," Tom shouted, hurrying to grab the child. "What's wrong with you?"

"Don't want to be here."

Taking a hold of his wrist, Tom turned to the other boy. "Are you okay?"

"No," he whined, running at Aaron trying to hit him.

"Enough," Tom commanded. "I'll take care of this." Leading Aaron back to the office, he sat him down and closed the door. "You can't act like that."

"Yes, I can. Don't want to be here."

The rest of the evening, Aaron did everything possible to nettle Tom whose head pounded from chasing and dealing with him.

"I have to poop," Aaron announced in the recreation room.

"The bathroom's across the hall," Tom replied.

Aaron took off and stormed into the restroom.

"He must of really had to go," a boy said.

Five minutes passed, and then ten minutes went by. One of the boys noticed Tom looking at the restroom concerned.

"I'll check on him," a boy said, "I've got to use the John."

"Sure, go ahead," Tom said.

As soon as the boy entered the restroom, "*Oh, shit,*" he screamed.

Tom rushed into the room, face cringed and nose closed to avoid the stench. "Oh, my God," he said.

The boy made strange noises holding his nose, yelling, "Yuck," as he fled the restroom.

"Aaron," Tom said, feeling as if he had to vomit.

"You like my artwork?" Aaron said, streaking the walls with fresh poop. "This is a clown," he said, making a happy face.

"Stop it!" Tom exploded. "Get in the shower. *Holy shit.* This is sickening." Knowing he was going to have to clean the grotesqueness, his head inflated, and eyes rolled while stepping out the door for a moment to try to clear his mind.

"Gross, gross," the kids roared, hearing what was going on.

Tom churned waving his hands for the kids to stop as they approached to peek. "Just stay back guys. Believe me, you don't want to see it."

"Yuk," the boys squirmed when Aaron opened the door.

"Get in there and take a shower now," Tom exploded at Aaron. *"Then you are going to bed."*

After getting all the boys settled for bed, he peeked into the bedroom several times to make sure Aaron went to sleep. Dreading cleaning the bathroom, he toiled to clean the walls and was eventually able to relax before the third shift arrived. Tom knew he needed to read Aaron's case history, even though he hoped he didn't need to be back the next day. Opening the file, he read:

Admission Report: The Springfield Children's Home
Aaron Stuckey
Caucasian/Hispanic Male
Age – 4

Failed Adoption at 1.5 years
Seven failed foster home placements

Psychological Evaluation:

Aaron is an aggressive Attention Deficit Disorder – Hyperactive Disorder child with signs of detachment, impulsivity, and anxiety. He was born in Springfield by a teen mother who gave him up shortly after birth. His teen father died from a gunshot wound he received on the day of Aaron's birth. The adoptive parents, after a year and a half, gave the child back to the courts – claiming that he was unmanageable, screaming constantly, and causing the adoptive father to drink who claimed the child was a wild Indian. Since the failed adoption, he has been in seven foster homes with the longest placement lasting nine months. Every foster home placement has complained of bizarre attention-getting behaviors, including; foul-language, destruction of property, sexual exploration, feces obsession, confrontation with other children and impulsive, uncontrollable behaviors. He is sexually aggressive towards other children and needs more supervision than a foster home can provide. His last two placements were in specialized foster care homes, but concerns for the other children in the homes resulted in the child's removal. The last home he was in believed that Aaron was bi-polar, but due to his young age, such a diagnosis cannot be determined. Due to the many placements in his young life, a lack of attachment and a feeling of abandonment have created a great deal of anxiety in Aaron, which may account for his behavior.

Recommendation:

A structured home with a behavior modification program and ongoing counseling.

Medication:

Ritalin – will be started once he starts school in the fall.

Family History:

Aaron's teen mother, forced into a sexual relationship with his father, gave him up for adoption when he was five days old. Aaron entered the Jones's adoptive home that had the child for one and a half years before turning him over to the courts. The adoptive parents described the child as uncontrollable, screaming constantly and causing their marriage great stress. The child was taken to doctors, including specialist, social workers, and even to a priest, as the parents believed the child was possessed. No one was able to help the adoptive parents resolve the issues with little Aaron.

After the failed adoption, Aaron entered the Thompson's foster home. They kept the child for nine months, the longest stay for Aaron since leaving his adoptive home. This family had the same complaints as the adoptive parents, and after unsuccessful medical treatment and unanswered prayers, they returned the child to social services . . .

Continuing to read, Tom shook his head in disbelief hoping that he would come to his senses at any moment. Sitting back in the desk chair, he closed his eyes, sorting out the past. "It's been over four years ago," he told himself. "Is it possible? It can't be." Rereading parts to make sure he read the words correctly, and then after a third reread he stood, looking dumbfounded saying to himself, "This is too weird. I mean Jesus Christ Almighty. Do you hear me? This sounds like Rosetta's son from all the history. Gomez died over four years ago. The baby was around five days old when Rosetta gave him up for adoption." Looking at the clock, he knew the third shift would be arriving soon. Hurrying to the copy machine, he made a copy of the report and stuck it in his briefcase, despite knowing it was against policy to do so. When the third shift arrived, he gave a detailed description of the evening's events and hurried off to meet Amy.

While they drove home, Tom told Amy every detail about the wild and disturbing evening and then aroused her curiosity about what he had to show her.

"Just tell me," Amy insisted.

"I can't, you have got to read what I want to show you. Besides, we're only two minutes away."

After arriving home, Tom pulled out the report on Aaron and handed it to her. "This is a copy of the report I received about the boy I told you about. Read it closely."

Taking the report, she read as Tom watched in eager anticipation. "What," Amy squealed with eyes flicking from dim to bright. Tom knew she suspected the same thing as he. "This is very, very strange. It's like déjà-vu. I can hardly believe what I'm reading."

Nodding his head, Tom said, "You're thinking the same thing I thought. *Right?*"

"Of course. It's too strange to be a coincidence. Caucasian, Hispanic even. Father died of a gunshot he got on the day the child was born. It's got to be him. Don't you think?"

"That's what I think. You know how Rosetta anguishes over giving her son up. Should we tell her?"

179

"I don't think we should rush into anything. If this is her child, we really need to think about what's in her best interest."

"You're right. This needs serious thought. Is this really her child? We can't be guessing. If it is then his bizarre behavior has to be considered if we told her. How would it affect her? Maybe she shouldn't know."

"First let's see," said Amy, "if we can one-hundred percent nail down who he is."

"There should be more records coming in on him. We'll see what turns up. I wonder if Rosetta new the name of the adoptive family? A name was mentioned in the report."

"When we see her, maybe we could ease into the subject and ask her... But then again, it might not be a good idea to ask her."

"You're right. It would only get her asking question. We need to be very careful with this...."

Andre stayed home from work one morning to meet with a plumber at the house due to a clogged drain. Windy left and Andre was to come in as soon as he was done. While dealing with routine issues at the shelter on this morning, a man entered the building and Windy greeted him with a smile. "You must be the person to pick up Nancy?" she asked.

"No, not me," he said, peering about as if he was searching someone out.

"Oh," she smiled, "what can I do for you?"

"Well, I was looking for a guy, but I don't see any here. At any rate, I heard a guy named Andre might work here."

Smile curtailed, she noticed the man's demeanor and said, "What was the name again?"

"Well the person wasn't real sure, but they thought an Andre worked here."

The longer she looked at the man, the more uneasy she became. "No, not here. I hope it's not urgent," she said, wondering if she should have said that.

"Well it is, but you said there's no Andre here, right?"

"Sorry, don't know anyone by that name."

"Any guys work here?"

"Well yeah, but no one by that name."

"They say he's around forty, dark wavy hair, around six feet. Does that ring a bell?"

"No, not at all. There's no guy's working today."

"Okay then," he nodded. "Like I said they weren't real sure which child place he worked at. This is a kids place, right?"

"It's a shelter."

"Yeah?" he said puzzled.

"For runaways."

"Kids, right?"

"Usually," she said, teetering.

"Well then, I'll leave you be."

Glancing around once again, he nodded and walked away. Before exiting, he turned around and said, "You don't know of anyone named Andre or that description I gave you working at any kid place do you?"

"No, not at all."

"Okay," he said and left.

With breath held, Windy glanced out the window, put on a pretense like nothing had happened, went back to where the kids were eating breakfast and spoke to them until she saw the stranger leave the street corner. Scooting to the office, she called Andre and explained to him what had happened. He didn't like the sound of what took place and said he needed to think things over, but that he would be in later.

"No," she said, "you need to stay away. I told him no male was working here today. I can handle everything. You hear me?"

"I hear you, but –"

"No buts. I mean it. We can sort it out after I get home."

"Well, there are a lot of things I could get done."

"Good. Do them."

"Alright. We'll see you after work."

After work, Andre and Windy anguished going over the visit by the man, as Andre was not expecting anyone at the shelter for him. Both believed that Big Jake was on their trail, even though they tried to rationalize some other plausible explanation. Despite the concern, Andre was determined not to let the incident interfere with him going to the shelter the next day or any day.

Chapter 15

With an Italian candle light dinner enjoyed and a movie seen, Mike and Rosetta left the theater, hand in hand, when her cell phone rang. Struggling to find it in her purse, in a panic, she pressed the send key twice.

"Hello, hello," Rosetta said.

"Rosetta, this is Brittany."

"How you holding up sweetie?"

"I'm scared. I have to testify tomorrow."

"You can do it."

"I don't know if I can. I'm also afraid for my mom. She can't go to jail because of him."

"That's why you have to testify."

"I'm a nervous wreck."

"You want me to come over?"

"Yeah. Can you come now?"

"Sure I can come over now," she said, looking at Mike who was frowning.

"Thanks. It means a lot. You've been a big help."

"I'll see you in awhile," she said hanging up.

"Now what?" Mike whined.

"That was Brittany. She's uptight about testifying tomorrow. I need to go see her to give her support. You okay with that?"

"I understand. I mean it's usually me being called away from one of our dates."

"You're sure now?"

"Well –"

"Come on."

"Of course. I'm just giving you a hard time. Go see her."

Once Rosetta was dropped off, she went into the house and then left in a hurry. After arriving at Brittany's, the two sat alone talking.

"Alright girl, I'm going to tell you something that I never talk about." Brittany looked on dejected but curious as Rosetta said, "I want you to know," she paused, "I was sexually abused by my dad and he's in prison right now. At least for a couple more weeks. I testified against him and it was hard. You at least don't have to look at him or feel him watching you while you testify. Your whole testimony can help your mom. Don't ever forget that. You just tell all of them how it was. The agony and all the fear he put you through. Don't hold back. I mean it …"

By the time Rosetta was done, Brittany had gained the self-confidence that she needed and was assured that she could do it.

The next day in court, Rosetta sat in the courtroom giving Brittany moral support. Once Brittany was on the stand, the prosecution concentrated on the mother's act of killing her father.

"… You didn't see your mother pull the trigger, but you were in the house when you heard the blast from the shotgun. Is that correct?"

"Yes," Brittany responded. "And," she trembled and murmured, "he deserved it."

"How long had your mother been aware of what you claim your father had done to you?"

"*Claim*," she exploded. "He messed with me for *five* years. He got what he deserved," she said, glancing at Rosetta whose eyes encouraged her on. "I mean he – that is he raped me while I'd be in bed asleep …"

"Did you tell your mother about it?"

"Yes!"

"When?"

"The evening he got shot. I wanted to tell for years but was afraid. I finally had to. *Do you hear me*? I had to."

"I see. How soon did the shooting happen after you told your mother?"

"Soon," she whimpered. "Ten or twenty minutes, I guess."

"Why do you remember that?"

"Because she confronted him after I told her and they argued for awhile."

"And then what?"

"He slapped her around. She was crying."

"Where were you and where were they?"

"I was upstairs in my room and they were downstairs."

"So you didn't actually see him slap your mother?"

"He did. My door was open. I heard it all."

"You did not see it. Correct?"

"I guess," she snapped.

"Then what happened?"

"I heard my mom come up the stairs and she was crying. She went by my bedroom into their bedroom."

"Did you see her come out?"

"No. I started crying and put the pillow over my head."

"Then what?"

"I heard the shotgun blast …"

Next, the defense cross-examined Brittany.

"The prosecution established that you are sixteen years old. How old were you when your father first sexually abused you?"

"Objection," said the prosecution. "Guilt was never established for the deceased."

"Objection sustained."

"Can you tell me what your father did to you?"

"How many times do I need to say he raped me when I turned twelve?"

"This is the last time thank you."

"You told your mother on the night of the shooting. How did she react?"

"Not good."

"Can you elaborate?"

"She cried."

"So she believed you immediately?"

"Yes."

"Why do you think that was?"

"Because she had called him a sicko before because of his weird behavior around my girlfriends."

"And what was that behavior?"

"Saying sexual things to them …"

Once Brittany stepped down, Rosetta was called to the stand by the defense attorney who had prepared her to testify. After explaining her involvement in the case and giving insightful information as to the turn of events, she stood to leave the stand. But before stepping down, she stared at the jury and then at the judge and asked if she could say one last thing. The judge nodded and she addressed the jury: "*Please,*" she said, eyes begging. "Try to imagine a beautiful young girl in your life. Can you picture her in your mind? Gentle, innocent, the love of your life. She has an angelic smile until one day it disappears. It's gone day after day, week after week, month after month and year after year," she said, tears forming, hand trembling. "You ask over and over to see that smiling face once again. *It never happens.* You ask her why. She shrugs and won't look at you. She can't say. Then one day, she breaks down and tells you that she has been *repeatedly violated day after day for years.* You confront the monster that has done these horrible things. The monster roars and slaps you around. Your rage turns into *insanity* for the moment. You flee and return to confront the fiend. He has to be stopped before he totally destroys her. *No one can stop him but you.* And that is exactly what Mrs. Engel did to protect her daughter. Now," Rosetta whimpered, tears streaking her face and then taking a deep breath. "Now, imagine that girl –" she faltered. "That beautiful young girl – was *your mom while growing up.*" Some jurors gasped, others were teary-eyed and some cringed as Rosetta pleaded once again, "*Your mother.* Think about it."

"Objection," the prosecutor spat.

"That's all I have to say," Rosetta cried. "I'm done. He was a monster," she said stepping down, gazing at the jurors.

By the time the court day was done, Brittany and her mother were exhausted. The big day for the jury was to happen the next day to decide on the mother's innocence or guilt of second-degree murder.

The next day, everyone in the courtroom was teeter-tottering between anxiety and suspense. The community sentiment was for the mother. The prosecution gave their final argument. "… and there is only one possible verdict," the prosecutor emphasized. "Mrs. Engel admitted that she pulled the trigger that ended her husband's life... You have no choice, but to convict …"

When the defense presented its final argument, the attorney sighed, and said, "All the facts have been presented. Yes, an enraged mother, out of her mind, totally insane for the moment, pulled the trigger that ended the monsters life. *Why*? Her daughter so vividly recounted the long agonizing horror she experienced the past five years of her young life. That is why! We are talking about the life of a good decent woman who saw a monster in front of her. Yes, a depraved raving maniac ready to attack, confronted by a mother protecting a child. In her mind, it was them or the monster. It is no different than if a rabid, crazed beast attacked you. Do you stand helpless and permit it to devour you? *Or do you take a stand and fight for your life*? That is what Mrs. Engel did for her and her daughter. She was a weak helpless victim facing an insurmountable force and she prevailed like David over Goliath. If your conscience prevails, there can only be one verdict. *Not guilty*. I rest my case."

The jury convened to the chamber. Returning in less than an hour, all eyes in the courtroom were surprised by their quick return. Once seated, the judge called the court to order. "Have you reached a verdict?" the judge asked.

"Yes we have your honor," the jury foreman responded and handed the judge an envelope.

Opening the envelope, the judge looked at the serious eyes eager to hear the verdict and then addressed the accused. "… For the crime of second-degree murder, *not guilty*," he announced to the delight of the crowd. While Brittany and the mother hugged, Rosetta hurried to them giving both a squeeze. Once the crowd dispersed, Brittany and her mother were ushered away from the press. Rosetta stood looking at the courthouse breathing a sigh of relief. This was a victory for her and all the victims awaiting trials across the country. The national news had followed this case and played it for all they could get out of it. For Brittany and her mom, it was a chance for a new beginning.

Later in the week, Rosetta and Mike returned from a date and went to his house for the first time. Giving a tour of the cozy two-bedroom home, he delighted in saving a special room for last. Going down the basement steps, Mike led the way to a recreation room with a pool table and stopped in front of a bookcase.

"I like this," Rosetta said.

"What do you think of the bookcase?"

"It could use a few more books on it."

"Normal looking? Anything unusual?"

"Hum, I would say pretty normal looking."

"Great, that's just what I wanted to hear," he said, pulling the hinged bookcase away from the wall, revealing a hidden room.

"*Wow*, I would have never guessed. That's neat. What's behind the door?"

"I don't want you to be shocked."

"Let me guess. A trunk full of gold."

"I wish."

"Alright, don't tell me. You got something weird like a mummy or a, oh no, you don't keep a maniac locked-up down here do you?"

"You're getting close," he said, pushing the door open, flipping a light switch, and then inviting Rosetta in.

"Holy cow," she said, eyes brightening. "Don't tell me you're really an ax murderer."

"Don't be like that. What do you think?"

"Well, at least I don't see any blood on them. They look really old."

"They are very old. Some," he said, reaching up, and removing a sword from the wall, "are hundreds of years old. Some are from the American Revolution. Some are Civil War swords. This is a rapier that dates to the late fifteen hundreds. See the unicorn mark on the blade? It was Clemons Horn's mark." A master swords maker."

"Wow, it's long."

"The blade is forty-six inches long. It's worth a lot. Want to hold it?"

"Sure," she said, taking it from him. "It's like Zorro's sword. How many do you have?"

"Thirty-seven. I've collected them since I was around twelve. But the one in your hand is my best and most expensive one."

"How did you get into collecting?"

"They're all antiques. I followed my mom and sister around when I was young when they went antique shopping. What's a boy going to get into at shops like that? Well, I started seeing a sword now and then and would ask for one for a birthday or Christmas present. That's how it all got started."

"They gotta be worth a lot of money."

"That's why they're hidden back here."

"Touché," she said, holding the sword like a fencer.

"So do you like?"

"Yeah, cool."

"So now you know my big secret."

"I've got some antiques in my house."

"I noticed. Some look expensive. Oh by the way. What's the deal with you having such a great house at your age?"

"It's a secret."

"Come on."

"What are these?" she asked changing the subject. "They look new."

Grabbing the pair of foils, Mike handed her one, saying, "En garde. These are for fencing."

"I've never known anyone that fenced," she said, holding the blade up. "Touché," she smiled.

"Do you want to learn?"

"Yeah, sure."

"Here," he said, handing over a fencing mask and a padded vested. "Let's play."

Both slipped on a vest and helmet. "This is how you stand," Mike said. She bent her knees getting into the stance that he demonstrated. "Now, try to jab me." Lunging forward with the blade, he blocked the plunge and tapped Rosetta's butt with the end of it. "How did that feel?"

"Getting fresh are you?" she said, putting the end of the blade above his crotch.

"You missed. It's a little lower."

"Ha, ha, I meant to get you higher. I'm not the fresh type."

"Okay, whatever you say."

"So who do you fence with?"

"Just people I like."

"So what number am I on the list?"

"You're the first."

"I doubt it. How many girls have you showed your hideout to?"

"You're the first."

"Give me a break."

"I'm serious."

"You going to tell me you haven't shown off your collection down here to anyone else?"

"Just some of my buds from work," he said, moving closer, setting his hand on her shoulder.

"Watch it bud," she said backing up, leaning the blade against his chest. "I know how to use this. I had a good teacher. Don't you think it's getting a little stuffy down here? Maybe we should go upstairs."

Looking down, he sighed, smile sucked in fearing to rush things. "Sure."

After taking their equipment off, setting their fencing foils down, Mike shut the room's door and placed the bookcase in front of it. Rosetta led the way up the stairs, and Mike followed.

Once upstairs, Mike turned some music on. "I didn't know you liked this band?" Rosetta said.

Looking frustrated, he said, "You mean because I'm a cop?"

"Hey, are you upset with me?"

"No, not at all."

"Then smile," she said, giving him a kiss. He responded, hugging her, still trying not to rush things. Sitting down on the sofa, they cuddled and fell back holding and kissing. "Slow down," she said, pushing him away.

"I'm only in first gear. It's just that you drive me crazy."

"I think you better shift into reverse. I don't want to rush things. I've got a lot of baggage."

"I know."

"Are you angry?"

"No, just, I don't know. I mean –"

"You've really been patient and understanding."

"Just my good old Catholic upbringing I guess."

"I've never heard of you going to church."

"I haven't since getting out of high school. I guess I've become kind of an agnostic."

"So you don't believe in God?"

"I don't know what I believe. Maybe there is and maybe there isn't one. I just don't know."

"I understand," she said, dejected. "It's hard to believe when you've been through hell. I mean –"

"Don't fret, I understand."

"Do you really?"

"You can't do this work for close to eight years without feeling all the pain that you've come across."

"Yeah, I guess not."

"Right out of college, I jumped into this garbage can called Copland. It'll drive you crazy if you let it. Murders, rapes, abuse, I mean, the pain goes along with the badge. If you want to carry one, you better get used to it. You know what I mean?"

"What do you think about all of these terrible cop abuses all over the news?"

"The news media and people are quick to judge without a complete investigation, but there are bad cops out there. I will not deny it. They give us all a bad name."

"It's bad out there. You're a special guy," she said hugging and kissing him. "I'm still dealing with a lot of anger. I don't ever want to take it out on you."

"I've learned to be patient."

"Good because it will take a special person to deal with my mood swings. I'm still fighting the past."

"You're not alone. I'm here for you. I mean it."

"You're not the typical cop type."

"Not like the movies, huh?"

"You're tough like the movie cops but gentle like a teddy bear."

"I don't know what to say. It sounds kind of nerdish."

"Oh no, not you. Can we lay here and just hug all night?"

"All weekend if you want."

Cuddling together, they hugged and kissed leaving their concerns and frustrations for another day.

Chastity continued to work behind the scenes, preparing and attending to the strippers needs while discovering a world of drugs that she could not resist. Ecstasy became Chastity's favorite drug of choice and liked smoking pot while using it. Sitting at a dressing table, Candy bent forward, put some powder to her nose, and snorted it. Chastity stood behind rubbing her shoulders.

"Your turn," Candy said.

Bending down, Chastity snorted the powder. "This coke is great. So much better than the stuff we use to get at the home. I wish my boyfriend could get this stuff."

"I think this batch has something else mixed with it."

"Whatever it is, I love it. It makes me feel sexy. It makes me want to be a star like you."

"You might get your chance. Have you thought about Big Jake's offer to go to China?"

"My boyfriend don't like the idea. So I don't really know what to think."

"Screw the bum."

"I don't know. I kind of like him."

"Yeah, I know his type. He sounds like a dork from what you've said about him. Dump the bum."

"You think so?"

"Hell yes. You want to be able to show off that body of yours and be a *star* then listen to me."

"Well, he is pretty damn possessive and jealous."

"Dump him. He's holding you back."

"I don't see why I can't do it here?" she said, unbuttoning her blouse and pulling it off her shoulder.

"Jake's paranoid. People would like to bust his ass. You're underage."

"I got my papers saying I'm legal."

"He's afraid there's a loophole. He don't want to do something stupid and end up in the can."

"But getting back to my guy. If I left him," she said dreamy-eyed. "I'd be taken care of, right?"

"You'll be taken good care of sweetie."

"God this stuff makes me feel good. You think I got a good enough body to show off?"

"You're hot baby."

"I don't know."

"I've got eyes and you have what it takes."

"You really think so? Do you care if I try a costume on?"

"Here, try this on," another stripper said, listening in the background. "This looks like your size."

Chastity grabbed the costume, took it to a private room, and put it on. "Oh, wow, this is neat," she said looking in the mirror admiring how her cleavage popped up. Wiggling around, acting as if she was stripping, Candy walked in.

"What did I say about you looking hot?"

"Think so?"

"I know so."

"If I went out there wearing one of those masks no one would know who I was. Would they?"

"You don't want to piss Big Jake off. Abandon the thought."

"He wouldn't need to know now would he?"

"Believe me, sweetie. You couldn't keep a secret like that for long. You don't want to mess with Big Jake. You hear me?"

"Yeah, I hear ya. Hey, tell me if mine are good enough," she said, wiggling her breasts. "They're natural you know."

"They're perfect."

"You haven't seen me nude."

"I see enough. You're a knockout. You don't have anything to worry about. I'm telling you, you'd be a hit in China or Timbuktu. Then when you're old enough you can come back here and be a star."

"I have a lot to think about."

"You're up Candy," a voice called.

"Hey, that's my cue. You hear them clapping? They all want a piece of Candy," she said, flowing out of the room, arms extended gliding onto the stage.

"I want to be a star," Chastity said, still in costume, moving like a butterfly, pretending she was going out on the stage.

Big Jake, comfortable that Chastity was not a police plant decided to proceed with sending her to China. Chastity's boyfriend was the biggest obstacle. Uncertain if she was going to drop him, he sent two of his men out one evening to visit the guy. Knocking on the door of the low rent apartment in the rat-infested neighborhood, the men teetered from toe to heal, waiting for the door to open.

"Yeah who's there?" a voice said.

"Your grandmother," one of the men named Charley said.

"What do you want?" he said, putting out his pot pipe.

"To give you some money."

"For what?"

"We can't talk out here, open the door."

"Who are you?"

"It's about your girlfriend Chastity."

Cracking the door open, he whined, "I don't know you."

Angered by the delay, the wiry man, Billy, shoved the door open knocking the young man back. The two men walked in. "Hey dickhead, I'm Charley and this is Billy. We don't got time for your bullshit. We're here to make a deal with you. We want you to tell your girlfriend how you're moving on 'cause you got another chic you wanna be with."

"What?" he cringed.

194

"You're dumping Chastity," Charlie said, handing the young man an envelope. "Open it."

Opening the envelope, he pulled out twenty hundred dollar bills and a bag full of ecstasy. "This is for me? What the hell's going on? Who are you? You're not cops are you?"

"We're not cops. Don't matter who we are. Just don't want to mess with us. The money's good. The ecstasy is worth a few thousand on the streets. You can take every pill or sell 'em. Your choice."

"What do I have to do?"

"Just break up with Chastity."

"Why? What if I don't want to?"

"Are you stupid?" Charlie snorted, grabbing his shirt. "This ain't a request ding dong. It's an ultimatum if you want to continue breathing?"

"Yes," he said, quivering.

"Smart kid. Why don't you try one of those pills, then we'll take you down to the club to announce your breakup? We want to see it happen."

"Yeah, I'll do it. She's not worth the hassle. And I get to keep the money and the ecstasy?"

"That's the deal. Of course, breathing is important too."

"Well yeah, that's for sure. I want to keep doing that. I hear you," he ranted. "Very important."

"Shut up," Billy said, "that's enough. Come with us now. Tell her not to come back to your place and make it convincing. Understood? If she has stuff, get 'er altogether. Got me?"

"Yeah sure. She don't have much, but I'll get it packed."

"She better never show back up at your place," Charley said, pulling out a pistol resting it against his chest. "Slap the bitch around. Make her hate you. Understand what we're saying? Alright, get her stuff."

Once they were on their way, the young man, seated in the back seat, drifted off enjoying the ecstasy. "You think," he said, "I could get a quickie before I tell her?"

"Don't be a dumbass," Charlie growled.

"But this shit you gave me is really good."

"Just shut the *flying f* up and do as you're told."

Reaching the club, the car pulled up to the rear entrance. "Alright," Billy said, "just go on in the back door and pull Miss Hot pants out here and lay it on her. We'll be here with the windows down listening."

"I hear you," he replied.

"Go to it boy," Charlie commanded. "It's unlocked asshole."

Exiting with a bag of belongings, he went to the dimly lit doorway, set it down and entered. Five and then ten minutes passed. "What the hell is he doing?" Billy said. "I seen him go in."

"I don't know, but if he ain't out soon, we better check."

A minute passed and both men exited the car and went to the back entrance. With his hand on the door, Charlie stopped. "You hear something?"

Listening, they heard moaning and groaning as if someone was enjoying himself. "That stupid prick," Billy said. "I think he's getting a piece of ass before he breaks up."

Charlie's fist clenched, "I'll kill him," he said, pulling the door open.

Chastity and her boyfriend, sweat rolling off their faces looked at the men entering. In anger, Charlie slammed it shut, which snapped the young man out of his drug-induced passion. "What was that about?" Chastity asked.

"Oh shit, I'll be right back," he said, pulling up his pants, rushing out the back door.

"Hey guys," I was just trying to tell her.

Grabbing him by the neck, Charlie exploded, "You stupid squirrelly dumbass. I said no quickie."

"It's the drug. I couldn't help myself."

"Get her butt out here right now." Pushing the man to the ground, Charlie shoved his shoe into his groin. "One minute or you won't have to worry about your pecker again. Got me?"

"I'll – I'll get her now," he whined with Charlie stomping his groin. "Please, I promise."

Removing his foot, he said, "Don't screw up this time. You should be too sore to screw-up. Right?"

Struggling up, he hobbled back in while they returned to the car. Thirty seconds later, the young man drug Chastity out by the arm. "*Get out here*," he wailed.

"What are you doing?" she whined.

"I just wanted to tell you I'm through with you. Don't come back to the apartment. Another babe moved in. I got all your stuff packed here."

"I don't understand. What was all the huffing and puffing all about? Are you crazy?"

Shoving her backward, he said, "Yeah, I'm crazy so just stay away."

"You're a bastard. I was about ready to dump your ass anyway. Just go."

"I'm out of here," he said, turning and fleeing down the alley.

After crying for a few minutes, Chastity pulled herself together, grabbed the bag of belongings and went inside. When Candy was done with the performance, she returned to Chastity who was crying and swearing at the same time. "I hate him," she bellowed. "My boyfriend dumped me. I'm out on the streets now."

"Girl, suck it up. You can stay at my place. It'll be okay."

"You'll let me stay at your place?" she said wiping away tears.

"If you don't mind a couple of kids around?"

"I like kids. You have kids?"

"Two adorable rug rats."

Chapter 16

After getting the boys settled in bed for the evening, Tom asked another worker to watch over the unit while he attended to other business, indicating he could be reached on his cell phone. Leaving, he made his way to the records room and looked over his shoulder all the way there. Earlier in the day, he had checked the room to see if there was more information on Aaron. A large file existed, but paranoia kept him from reading it then as the room was next to the director's office. While the secretary was out to lunch, he confiscated a spare key to the room, planning to go through the file after first shift left. Standing in front of the door, he checked in all directions, unlocked it, entered, relocked it, and then turned the light switch on, revealing a dozen file cases. Finding the folder, he set it on a table in the room and began thumbing through it. On hearing footsteps, he gasped, glancing back and forth between the door and the paperwork, as the room was off limits after regular business hours. Holding his breath, the footsteps passed and he resumed searching for anything to confirm that Aaron was Rosetta's child. A minute later, he beamed seeing a paragraph describing Aaron's delivery as being traumatic due to the father's insistence on the mother giving birth in the traditional Indian fashion. When he read the following sentence, he had the confirmation he sought after: "Forced by the father to a remote wooded area, the mother was left alone to give birth to Aaron... The father was shot that evening and died ..."

"Oh yes," he said to himself. "This is it. Can't be two situations like that in this town or any town." Taking the page, he left the room just long enough to copy it in the room next door. Returning the page to the file, he went back upstairs. Although he felt as if something was accomplished, he now worried about what to do with the information. After calling Amy it was decided to discuss the matter at home. Sitting back, feet on the desk, Tom's eyes closed. While he drifted in thought, one of the boys sneaked out of the unit planning a runaway scheme for him and his girlfriend on

Amy's floor. The plan included pulling the fire alarm which hadn't been done in some time. The fire chief threatened to have the home closed down after the last incident, which had followed two other false alarms in a week period. The boy had no concern about the consequences, as he placed his hand on the alarm only thinking about him and his girlfriend spending the night together. The plan was to stuff their beds with pillows giving the appearance of someone in bed and to sneak back early in the morning hoping not to have been missed. Looking around, he pulled it and hid waiting for everyone to start exiting.

"Oh, shit," Tom hissed distressing over the blaring noise. Springing to his feet, he hurried to get everyone up and out, even though he suspected a false alarm. *"Let's go, let's go,"* he shouted down the hallway. Kids moaned and groaned, lethargically moving out of the building as the fire engines arrived. The boys and girls stood shivering while the firefighters made their inspection and reported that all was clear.

Approaching Tom, the fire chief grumbled, and then exploded. "I'm sick of the nitwits here. It does no good to chew them out. They're a bunch of retards."

"I'm very sorry," Tom said. "We'll deal with them, I promise you."

"Bullshit! I've heard it before. There's no dealing with these screwball delinquents. Just do whatever you can. I've had it ..."

After work, Tom and Amy reflected on the alarm going off and the new information he uncovered. "You know," Tom said. "Dealing with that irate fire chief was easier than trying to decide whether to tell Rosetta about Aaron or not."

"It's probably a matter of the right time to tell her," Amy said.

"And how do you define the right time?"

"I don't know right now, but when it's time we'll know. Until then we should sit on it. Okay?"

"Yeah, I guess so. I have enough to worry about."

"You're going to get an ulcer."

"I know. I need to control my anger. Maybe I should write. It helps you know. Just getting it all out. But this madness I'm feeling needs to be controlled when I write."

"That's for sure because what you wrote the other night really pissed me off. I don't like it when you write about us arguing. What I read the other night was pure bullshit."

"I took the scene out of the story."

"I hope so. Why do you have to write about us anyway?"

"We're part of the story."

"Well, if we broke up are you going to write about that?"

"Break up," he said, eyes squinting. "Please, calm down."

"Just go write. You drive me insane."

"Alright, alright."

Sitting at his desk, he began typing at his computer:

Sweat rolled off my brow, waiting for the axe to drop as I imagined my head rolling down a gutter. An anxious person by nature, I believed a conspiracy existed to throw me out the door the first opportunity that came along. The boss gave me a funny look earlier in the day and I knew people were talking about me behind my back. Losing my mind and job ate away at me, toying with my ability to reason. They were waiting for me to make a mistake. Looking over one shoulder, and then another kept me on my toes, but I was tiring and asked myself if I should throw in the towel before the axe finally came down. Yes, I was paranoid. I had reason to be with Rob breathing down my neck. He told me I was a marked man. I may as well have painted a bull's eye on my chest....

Pushing away from the computer, he sighed, feeling more stress than relief from working on the scene. "This is ridiculous," he told himself, looking at the screen. "Wait a second. Did I spell axe right or is it ax? Shit. There's got to be a better way to get rid of my stress." After crushing a scrap piece of paper, he turned the computer off and went to the bedroom, where Amy was reading a book. "I need to run my butt off," he said.

"You choose the craziest times to jog. Besides, you jogged before work today."

"I'm sorry writing isn't settling me down. It's exercise, drugs or insanity."

"You're already insane so just go run. Don't forget your phone."

Changing his clothes, he put sweats on for the chilly spring evening. "I'll be back in an hour," he said. "Hey, do you spell axe with or without an e at the end?"

"Without."

"Are you sure?"

"That's my free answer. If you want the correct answer, I charge ten dollars."

"Ha, ha," from Tom.

"Oh, by the way, Brenda and I are going out this weekend when you're at Jerry's bachelor party. I bet you guys are going to a strip club? Aren't you?"

"I don't know."

"You mean yes don't you?"

"Hey, Marty's picking me up. I'll be going wherever he takes me."

"Brenda's picking me up. *I'll* be going wherever she takes me."

"Come on, it's a bachelor party."

"I didn't say anything."

"It's the tone of your voice."

"*Tone of my voice?*"

"Just forget it. I'm taking off. See you later."

"Yeah, later. Don't get soaked."

"Soaked?"

"The news said rain tonight."

"Which means it won't. Right?"

"I don't know about that," she said looking out the window.

"I'll beat the rain," he said, leaving.

An hour later, Tom returned, knocking at the door shaking as Amy opened it.

"Take your clothes off right there," she insisted.

"I'm freezing," he shivered.

"I warned you."

"Ten more minutes, I would have beaten it."

"It's pouring and you're soaked."

"I'm freezing," he said, dropping his clothes, standing naked. "Come here." Grabbing Amy's shoulder, she pushed away.

"I don't want to feel your freezing body."

"Come on, warm me up." Trying to grab her once again, she ran to the stairway with him following.

"Get away," she yelled, running up the stairs, into the bedroom and locking the door.

Heading to the bathroom, he said, "You're no fun." After the shower went on, Amy came out and set pajamas in the bathroom for him.

With the passing of time, Andre and Windy's anxiety quelled since the stranger had not returned to the shelter. They hoped he had nothing to do with Big Jake or at least that Windy was believable enough that no one would be back asking questions. A week had passed, and normalcy had returned as much as it could for them. On occasion, they stared out the window, seeing people standing across the street or strolling by glancing in, but convinced their selves not to overreact. Andre, for the most part, kept away from the window and out of sight so he wouldn't have to speculate. On this day, a young woman walked in carrying a duffle bag.

"Can I help you?" Windy asked.

"This is a runaway shelter isn't it?"

"Yes. Are you a runaway?"

"That's me," she said peering past Amy at the surroundings.

"Did you want to enter our program?"

"I just might want to," she said.

"What's your name and where are you from?" Amy asked, feeling uneasiness about the girl's demeanor.

"Jenny, I'm from Illinois."

"Really?" she said being from Illinois. "Where at?"

"Chicago."

"Me too. What part?"

"Well," she hesitated looking away. "You know, a –
Chicago's Westside."

"Oh yeah, huh. So right near Lake Michigan?" she asked,
knowing the lake was on the east side of town.

"Yeah," she muttered, looking down. "Right on the lake."

Andre opened the office door, stepped out, looking at Windy
and the girl, and then walked in the opposite direction.

"Hey," the girl said, "I desperately need to take a leak. Can I do
that before we finish talking?"

"Well, yeah sure. It's down at the other end."

"I see it," she said, hurrying off. Nearing Andre, she said,
"Andre."

He turned, looking at her, "Did you need me?"

"No, I'm headed to the bathroom."

"Oh, okay," he said as she passed.

Continuing down the hall, he stopped to talk to some kids.

The girl came out of the restroom, returning to Windy.

"You ready to continue?" Windy asked.

"You know what, I think I'm going to go back to my boyfriend
and try to straighten things out before I decide to stay here or not."

"It's your choice. We're open around the clock if you change
your mind."

"Okay, got you."

Watching the girl walk up the street, Windy couldn't help think
something strange, questioning why she was confused about the
Chicago directions, but then shrugged it off. Returning to the
office, Andre came in asking where the girl had gone.

"She decided to try to work things out with her boyfriend for
now. She might come back."

"What did you talk about?"

"The usual. You know. Where she was from … Then she had to
go to the bathroom real bad."

"How did my name come up?"

"It didn't."

"How did she know my name?"

"I don't know, I didn't mention it."

"As she came up behind me she said, *Andre.*"

"Are you sure?"

"*Dead sure.* I even turned and looked when she said my name."

"I don't know what to think. She seemed to be confused about knowing where she lived in Chicago."

"I don't like how this is sounding."

"Do you think – *he* sent her here?"

"Maybe, I don't know. You're sure you didn't mention my name?"

"*Positive.* Our conversation wasn't that long. You know what?" she paused reflecting. "She suddenly wanted to use the bathroom after you came out of the office."

Looking down, hand on chin, he drifted off.

"Hey," Windy said, looking at the office desk, "maybe she saw your nameplate?"

Andre's eyes shifted from the floor to the desk, looking at the plaque saying Andre. "You would have to really be looking to notice it from out there. I don't know it's all too weird."

"I had a funny feeling about her."

"Hey, all we can do is keep our eyes open like we've been doing."

"'You're right. We're probably overreacting."

One of the boys came up to them and said, "Is something wrong?"

"Don't worry about it," Andre said. "We got it covered. We're the professional worrywarts."

"Whatever you say," he replied, walking away.

"Let me ask you this?" said Windy. "If he was really looking for you what would he want?"

"To get even. He's not the type to forget. I really pissed him off. And we both know what he is capable of. He's powerful and controls a lot of people."

"Do you think he's mafia?"

"He's a big time asshole. He's a cancer. I mean, I can still see him and his jackals that night hauling you away at gunpoint. I felt so helpless. He cornered us and I made a deal with the devil saying I would get him, girls. Fleeing was our only way out. That's been close to five years ago."

"You didn't really make a deal with him. You just told him what he wanted to hear."

"I screwed him and he probably wants blood now. Then I stood up to him right in his own club here in town. God, he must want me dead."

"If he finds out we have this shelter don't you think he'll try to pull the same shit he tried back in Springfield? You know the runaways we have here would be perfect for him to traffic. They could disappear for good."

"Anything's possible with him," Andre said pacing. "I hate to even think about it."

"We can't let him ruin our lives again."

"I'm done running. If all this paranoia is real then I'll do whatever it takes to fight him."

"We need to settle down. Nothing's for certain. We're probably reading into it. Don't you think?"

"Thinking is the problem," Andre said noticing the kids watching him pace. "Let's get back to work. We have an arrival coming in soon. I have a lot of paperwork and phone calls to make."

"Alright, let's get to work."

Big Jake received a phone call and boarded a plane to Los Angeles the next day. Greeted by a limousine at LAX, he arrived at his club an hour later. Several men welcomed him when he entered the club and after a drink at the bar, they went to a conference room. Six of them sat around a table carrying on while being served dinner.

"You want to hear all the updates now?" a man asked.

"What's wrong with you Louie?" Big Jake said. "You know I don't want to talk business while eating. How many times has my stomach got upset and churned when I had to hear a bunch of crap? You sitting on your brains again or are you getting senile on me?"

"No, no, no. It's just the way you hurried out here. I thought you might not be able to wait."

"Well, you're wrong. I'm hungry and want my food to digest. Just 'cause you got good news to tell me don't mean you ain't going to piss me off about something else. So shut up and eat, you knucklehead."

"Cheers," another man said, holding up a glass of wine. "To Louie keeping his big mouth shut."

"Salute," Big Jake said. "My ass is the only thing bigger than Louie's mouth." Louie leaned back smiling delighted by the analogy. Once dinner was over, they attended to business.

"Alright," said Big Jake. "Let me hear the bullshit first."

Louie nodded, saying, "Chen is supposedly tied up for a week so there's no progress on getting your girl to China. They might be playing us for fools. I can't figure it out if we're being fed baloney or what."

"Great, just keep it coming," Big Jake motioned with his hands. "What else sucks?"

Another man spoke up, "We're having big problems getting the drugs through the border with the government and cartel war going on down there. It's a bloody mess and screwing things up. I know it's not shut down, but getting what we want is very slow right now."

Shaking his head, Big Jake said, "Come on ass-wipes keep the bullshit coming so I can hear the good news."

"I hope you're ready for this?" another man said. "Some of the boys had to knock off a low life junkie caught stealing from us."

"*What?*" Big Jake wailed.

"It couldn't be helped. The guy –"

"Shut up!" Big Jake blasted. "I don't want to hear the *damn* whys. There better be no trace to us."

"Everything is covered. The body will never be found."

"Shit," he frowned. "Just make me smile once you nitwits."

"Cory's getting hitched," Louie said holding back a grin.

"Now that is bullshit," Big Jake said, patting Cory on the back. "The poor lady's going to be sorry."

"She's no lady," Louie said. "She's one of the strippers."

"Oh yeah, which one?" Big Jake asked. "It better not be my favorite squeeze-box."

Louie added, "If you're thinking big milk shakes you're on target."

"*Sally*," Big Jake said, looking at Cory smiling. "Just don't expect her to retire." Cory frowned as Big Jake squeezed his bicep. "Hear me?"

"Come on boss, she'll be my wife."

"We'll see," he replied.

Louie interjected, "Of course you're here 'cause of the good news."

"Damn right I am. Just make me smile."

"He's working at a runaway shelter downtown."

"You're certain?"

"The guy fits the description and his name is Andre. One of our girls was nose to nose with him at the place. I mean how may Andre's are there? Especially that fit the description and work with kids."

"Sounds like the jackpot to me. Good work."

"So what do we do?" Louie asked. "You want us to grab him?"

Pondering, he said, "He screwed me in Illinois. He screwed me here. My ass is sore as hell from this fucker. I need to think. If we had some leverage, we might have a gold mine with these runaways. I don't know what's up with this idiot. He ran the last time I tried to squeeze him."

"Dead men don't run," Louie blurted and then sneezed repeatedly.

"Damn you, damn you, damn you," Big Jake chirped. "Turn your head you nitwit. At any rate dumbass, we can always put him six feet under, but I'm always thinking bucks. If we could control him, he's in the perfect position to get us untraceable runaways. You know one's that won't cause a big media blitz. If he's still with that woman, we could force his hand if we snatch her. The key would be not to return her until he has actually given us a kid or two."

"Good plan boss," Louie said with a slight smile. "I get it. His chic's the bait and once he's hooked – you know actually dirtying his hands. He's all ours."

"I don't know," Big Jake reflected, "it sounds too simple."

"What'll keep him from going to the cops?" another man asked. "You know, once we snatch the girl?"

"He does have balls," said Big Jake. "Just keep a close eye on the place while I sort it all out. You know, we snatched that bitch of his once before and thought we had him by the balls then. Then they just disappeared for years until now. Don't want no screw-ups this time. Watch the shelter and follow him home so we know where he lives. You hear me? Louie, you're in charge of carrying it out."

"Got you boss."

"Good. Now let's go raise some hell and watch Cory's hot mamma put on a show for us."

Cory snickered, "Just screw with my head guys. Thanks a lot."

With a playful slap to the face, Big Jake said, "Hey you numskull, you're going to need my blessing so don't get smart. Now let's go out and watch her show."

"But she's not working now," Cory said.

"I saw her here," Big Jake said standing. "She'll work if I tell her to."

"Come on," Cory pleaded.

Smiling, Big Jake led the way into the club with the boys following him. Going up to Sally, Big Jake patted her bottom. "Hey sweetie, whaddya say you put on a show for us right now?"

Looking at Cory, she said, "Well, as long as Cory don't mind."

"Mind, hell, he suggested it. Didn't you?" Big Jake said, eyeing Cory.

Forcing a smile, he said, "Just do it."

Going up to Cory, Sally said, "Anything you want baby face." Giving him a kiss, she headed backstage.

"Baby face," roared the group, patting him on the back.

"Come on," Big Jake insisted, "let's sit along the stage."

They sat and soon Sally's music blared, followed by an introduction by the announcer. "All right gang. One of our hottest draws is here to delight you. Welcome, our own Amazon Queen that we just call long tall Sally. Come on boys and ladies give her a big, big hand." Cory sat back humiliated but took the slap on the face knowing they were trying to give him a hard time.

"Cheer up," Big Jake said, squeezing Cory's shoulder.

Frowning, he replied, "Boss, you're just having way too much fun with this. Aren't you?"

Rosetta hurried to an art class across the college quad one day with the latest class assignment, a small portrait that she carried in a cloth bag. The task was to create a painted image of someone not seen in years showing how they imagined that person looked and why they chose to portray them as they did. While waiting her turn in class, Rosetta kept the portrait in the bag, and hands clamped to it. One student after another went to the front of the room to have their painting interpreted by the class. Rosetta's mind drifted during the discussion, thinking about the painting and what she would say about it. When it was her turn to present, she froze up for a moment.

"Rosetta," the professor said. "Rosetta, back to earth. It's your turn."

The comment drew laughter from the students.

Standing, she went to the front and pulled out the painting, revealing a young child who had the body of a four or five-year-old, sprouting wings but had the face of an infant baby.

"Of course," said the professor. "Rosetta is determined to paint in the Sistine Chapel. This is interesting. I won't say anymore. Class, what is your interpretation?"

"Torn between two worlds," a female student said. "Growing up but wanting to remain a baby so they can be held and cuddled."

"A very happy but frustrated baby," said a male student. "I think he's constipated."

The students laughed.

"No, no," another male said, "I see sad eyes. I think the kid's in a time warp."

A female student said, "I've got it. Remember, this is someone you haven't seen in a long time. Obviously, this was a baby when last seen who has grown older. The memory is as you last saw the child, but acknowledging that they are older and different now. The wings express the angelic angel remembered, but the sad eyes and body show that a change has taken place. I think the child is sad because so many years have passed. You know, since they've seen the artist. That's how I see it."

"Interesting ideas," said the professor. "Traditionally, a baby with wings represents a child that has died and gone to heaven. But let's hear from the artist herself."

Rosetta was speechless; a tear formed in her eye, trying to speak, she sighed, "I don't feel so good. Please excuse me. I really need to leave." Picking up her belongings, she left the classroom and wandered thinking of her child and then found a secluded area to sit under a tree.

Chapter 17

It was a Saturday evening when Marty picked Tom up for Jerry's bachelor party. Jerry, a co-worker, was at the mercy of his friends for the planned night out. Marty picked another person up and then Jerry who had suspicions of where they were headed. Another group of friends was to meet them at the designated location. As they headed out of town, the destination came into focus, causing Jerry to squirm. One nightclub was on the road ahead and it was Springfield's sole striptease club. Pulling into the parking lot, the neon light flashed *The Lost Souls Club*.

"I should have known," Jerry said. "You guys are bad."

"You're going to be chained up after tonight," Marty said. "This is your last night of freedom."

"Just rub it in."

The group got out of the car, strolled into the club and met up with the others who had a table near the stage. Beer and laughter kicked the celebration off while an exotic dancer's introduction song got their fingers tapping to the beat and their heels bouncing to the rhythm of the music. Soon the dancer had them captivated, causing their eyes to dilate, begging to see more. When the performance was over, Burt Crebo ordered a round of tequila shots and stood, gawking at the group.

"To Jerry," Burt toasted. "May he come to his senses before it's too late?" Everyone downed the shot.

"Hey Burt," Tom said, pointing to the restroom. "I just wanted to let you know where it's at."

Burt looked at the restroom, smiled and said, "But your cup's closer Tom."

"Good thinking," he replied still envisioning Burt peeing down his stairway.

Jerry soon was the center of attention as two ladies came to the table and pulled him up to the stage. The group cheered while Jerry sat big-eyed on a chair in the middle of the stage. The girls danced around him, shedding their skimpy outfits and rubbing their bodies against him. The group continued to cheer. When one naked stripper wrapped her legs around Jerry and fell back as if sliding down a pole, the group of men stood, yelling and cheering him on. The commotion got Chastity peeking through the curtain to see what the hoopla was all about. When she saw Jerry on the stage her mouth dropped, but a big smile erupted on seeing Tom with the rowdy group of men at the table. Rushing back to Candy who was snorting cocaine, she paused until she was done.

"Here, take a snort," Candy said, and then lit up a one-hitter pot pipe.

Chastity eager to talk held off as she put her nose in the powder and snorted it. Taking the one-hitter from Candy, she sucked on it with eyes lighting up and blew the smoke into the exhaust fan. "This is great," she sighed, drifting off glassy-eyed. "There was something I wanted to say," she said laughing. "I think there was at least."

"Your eyes say it all baby," Candy replied.

"God, what was it?"

"Don't think about it and it'll come to you."

"Guess it was nothing. Oh, well," she giggled. Once again, there was an explosion of yelling and cheering in the nightclub. "That's it," she said, going to the curtain and peeking out at the crowd. "*Bingo*," she cheered. "I remember. It's Tom Paradisio. That ass wipe is out there and oh boy would I love to mess with him big time. Oh yeah, baby. Oh yeah."

"Who?" Candy asked.

"This jerk that worked at the home I was at. He loved throwing me into the lock-up room. His wife was in charge of our unit and she was a real bitch. I'd like to screw with him and get her all pissed off. Will you help me?"

"Sure, but how?"

"What did you say goes on in the V.I.P. room in back?"

"Oh, a lot of things. It's for our special customers. You know, ones with bucks to spend. Why? What's on your mind?"

212

"Sweet, sweet, revenge. Oh yes, please Candy help me screw with this dude. I'd get a hell of a charge in seeing him squirm. They loved to see me squirm. It's my turn. Whataya say?"

"Sure, why not. You want to get him real fucked up?"

"You got that right."

"Well, if we take some of this powder and some of this and slip it into his drink, I think you'll get what you want. Better yet, one of the girls has a hit of GHB. You know. The date rape drug."

"I don't want to rape the dork."

"It will knock him silly. That's what you want. Right?"

"Yes, knock him on his ass."

"If you point him out I'll go get it. Then I'll stroll about and drop it in his drink."

"Come on," she said, leading the way to the curtain and pointing him out. "You think we could do something to him once he's all fucked up? I have an idea."

"Save it, let me slip him the treat first."

"Go for it."

Candy left, found the friend and then headed in Tom's direction. Strolling around the audience, playful with several customers, she came up behind Tom laughing with the group still watching Jerry girl handled on stage. In a flash, she plopped on Tom's lap causing him to gasp in surprise. "How you doing big boy?" she said, dropping the pill in his beer while shoving her chest in his face. All eyes at the table were still on the stage performance until Marty looked over.

"Hey there," Marty said. "He's a married man."

Scooting off Tom's lap, she sat on Marty's lap. "How's this?" she said, pushing his face into her cleavage."

"Wonderful."

"Hey," Tom said, smiling. "He's a married man."

"Oh my," she said, getting up. "I'm at the wrong table." Wandering off, Tom and Marty's eyes followed her until she disappeared.

"A toast," Marty said, "to cleavage."

Tom held up the remainder of his drink and downed it.

Back in the dressing room, Candy and Chastity talked over a plan. "I want to be in one of the photos with him," Chastity insisted.

"We got to get him in the V.I.P. room," Candy said. "He's going to be really messed up so it shouldn't be too hard. We just got to get him away from that table."

"He'll have to go to the John won't he?"

"Let's give them a couple of free pitchers of beer. He'll be taking a leak real soon. I'll go tell the girls in back and get my camera phone ready. I better get the beer to them first."

"This is great," Chastity said.

"I'll be back to get you when everything is done."

"I'm going to put one of the costumes on, okay?"

Candy smiled, nodding her head and left the room. Chastity watched from behind the curtain. Before long, she saw Candy setting two pitchers of beer on the table and then poured herself and Tom a glassful. Pulling up a chair next to Tom, she sat while the others at the table drooled looking her over. Tom and Candy toasted their mugs and flooded their mouths, racing to be the first one done. Tom won, but Candy was satisfied knowing his bladder would need relief soon.

"*Damn*. That went straight to my head," Tom said, and then belched.

Candy's foot shot up, dropping in Tom's crotch. "Hey, big boy," she whispered in his ear. "Don't pee your pants. Why you're sweating up a storm."

"Oh, Jesus," Tom squirmed sweat streaking his face. "Gonna explode. Too much beer and tequila."

"I guess so. Later big boy," she said and left for the V.I.P. room. Five minutes later, she came out looking for Tom at the table, but he was gone. Peering about, she saw him stumbling around toward the restroom. Hurrying backstage, she led Chastity through the club to the V.I.P. room, which was empty other than for three dancers. Chastity stayed put with two of them while Candy left with another girl to the restroom entrance. Standing there until Tom staggered out; they wrapped their arms around him and escorted him to the private room.

"You going to make it?" Candy asked, opening the V.I.P. room door.

"I feel great," he muttered, eyes closed, and smiling. "Tired but great. What is this place?"

"It's Heaven, don't you think?"

With arms over both girls' shoulders, he glanced at them. "It sure ain't Hell," he chuckled.

"That's what you think," Candy said under her breath as they helped him over to a sofa where he flopped down seeing double vision.

From around the corner, Chastity stepped out in a skimpy costume, sat next to Tom on the sofa, and then curled her legs up while wrapping her arms around him. Tom's eyes opened as she nibbled and sucked on his neck until a hickey sprouted. Candy snapped photos as Chastity continued in different poses, which included kissing him and placing the side of his face against her cleavage. Tom drifted in and out, opening his eyes and closing them.

"What's going on?" he slurred.

"Amy's going to love these photos. Don't you think?" Chastity said, unbuttoning his shirt revealing his bare chest. The two other girls joined in for the photo shoot, dropping their tops and cuddled up to Tom who had a hard time keeping his eyes open.

"This guy's in another zone," one of the girls said to Candy still snapping pictures.

"I think we got plenty," Candy said. "We better get him back to his friends."

"Hold on," Chastity said, pulling his pants and shirt off. "Let's get one of him in his birthday suit with all of us all over him. Maybe I should leave his underpants on."

"Last photos," the girl with the camera said. The half-naked girls swarmed all over Tom. Unlike the other girls, Chastity kept her top on while pulling his eyelids open for the camera to begin clicking.

Once Chastity was satisfied, they got him dressed, and lifted him to his feet. Candy and another girl helped him back to the table. "Your friend is loaded," Candy said to the group of men. He passed out in the restroom. Don't give him any more to drink." Setting him down on the chair, he collapsed back and then slouched to one side struggling to keep his eyes open.

"Tom," Marty said prodding him. "Wake up. The night is young."

"Where are we?" Tom mumbled.

"It's Jerry's bachelor party. Come on. Let's get rowdy man," he said, pulling Tom forward who plopped his chest and head on the table.

"He is messed up," Jerry said. "Maybe we better get him home."

Springing up, Tom said, "No I'm fine. Look at that."

"What?" said Marty.

"I don't care. Whatever," he slurred.

"Just go to sleep," Marty said and returned to the party.

Two hours later, they decided to call it an evening. Two men helped Tom stand with a man on each side of him keeping him upright and taking him to the car. On returning him home, Marty and Tom stumbled about with Marty dragging Tom to the front door. Marty stood ringing the bell. "I'm coming, I'm coming," Amy repeated opening the door.

"He's messed up," Marty said as they helped him up the steps, into the house, and to the sofa.

"How much did he drink?" she asked.

"A lot," he chuckled.

"Maybe you better spend the night here," Amy said. "We can call Patsy and tell her."

"No I'm fine," he insisted.

"Sit down and let me call Patsy."

Being too inebriated to fight her demand, he sat in a recliner, laughing to himself.

After getting a hold of Patsy, she said she would pick him up. Once Marty was gone, Amy threw a cover over Tom who was sound asleep. She went to bed half-frustrated, but happy they had made it back to the house in one piece.

Mike sat at his office desk texting Rosetta while awaiting his old grade school friend Jack to show up. A moment later, Rosetta texted him back, "See you tonight." Starting to text her again, he stopped when his office phone rang. Jack had arrived, but before going to him, he finished his text message. Once back in the office, they reminisced about old times and then started on business.

"So what's the good word?" Mike said, sitting behind his desk.

"Word is Big Jake is squeaky-clean."

"Oh yeah? Do you believe it?"

"You know, what's to believe? What's not to believe? What exactly are you looking for?"

"Hey Jack, did you shower in Jack Daniels this morning?"

"Oh, yeah, it was a long night. I didn't have time to change and make it here on time."

"A long night, huh. Who did you talk to?"

"What do you mean?"

"What do I mean? Where did you get your info? Did you talk to the big guy himself?"

"You want me to talk to him?"

"Talk to him. I want you to sleep with him."

"Yeah," he chuckled. "Maybe he'll give me a job again. You know I'm out of work."

"Well if that happened you could be my eyes and ears there."

"So what exactly are you looking for?"

"Anything he wouldn't want a cop to know."

"Why are you wanting to nail the dude?"

Standing, he walked over to Jack, rested his hand on his shoulder, bent down and whispered, "Because I think he might be a maniac *fairy*."

"What?" he said and looked up confused.

"Just keep your ears open, okay buddy?"

"Well, yeah. I just thought I could be looking for something in particular."

"Now this is just between you and me, okay?"

"My lips are sealed."

"A couple of guys have been viciously raped near his club. That's all I can tell you right now."

"Huh, well, whatever you say. You're bullshitting me aren't you?"

"See if he'll give you a job. How are you getting by anyway? Boozing isn't cheap. Did he give you money?"

"No, man. Come on," he said, squinting, looking away with a shuffle. "What's a guy suppose to do? The economy sucks. I've been without work for over a year. My unemployment ran out. I've been doing some yard work to pick up a few bucks."

"Where are you staying?"

With frustration, he said, "You know times are rough. I'm at my parent's house."

"Give me their phone number."

"You're not going to call them are you?"

"Why would I do that?"

"You want their number."

"You spacing out on me," he said squeezing his arm. "Since you don't have a cell phone how am I supposed to get a hold of you?"

"Oh yeah, no."

"I think you had a little too much last night. Who did you say gave you some money?"

"No, no," he blurted, looking down. "No one gave me money. I didn't say that. You know, I've got a buck or two saved. That's all I can tell you now. What's with all the questions?"

"Okay buddy, I'll let you off the hook. You hear anything let me know. So where are you off to now?"

"Same thing I do every day. Look for a job."

"Alright then. I'll be in touch."

When Rosetta and Mike met up that evening, she was eager to hear about his meeting with Jack but held off popping the question, as he seemed irritated about something. Letting out a sigh, he paced around the living room, stopped to look at one of Rosetta's paintings on the wall and then smiled.

"What's up?" she asked.

"The sky, the ceiling, and my frustration I guess. Heck if I know."

Moving closer to him, she grabbed his hand. "Let's sit down." Side by side on the sofa, staring at one another, Rosetta said, "Is it work or is it me?"

"Oh, I don't know. It's nothing."

"It's me then."

Looking into her eyes, they kissed. "It's me. It's just that I'm uptight sometimes when we get close. I want to be a, well, a bad boy, but I can't."

"Oh yeah. And why's that?"

"You're special. Everything you went through and all, I mean, I can't do anything to hurt you."

"You're really different. You remind me so much of Tom."

"Your former foster dad?" he said with a frown. "So I'm a father figure to you?"

Chuckling, head shaking, she said, "Don't be silly. You guys are about the same age."

"I'm almost eight years older than you. I don't know, I'm confused."

"First of all, I've always had a crush on Tom. He's good looking just like you. He's Italian just like you."

"Oh great, now I'm a substitute for him."

"Knock it off," she said kissing him. "What I was trying to say is that you're no father figure. I was a teen with a crush on a guy being a dad to me. That's all. He was a very young good-looking dad. That's what he'll always be to me. Tom and Amy are my best friends. They helped me a lot. They saved my life. In fact, I'm thinking about doing social work when I graduate. So are we squared away on this issue?"

"I guess so."

"Don't guess. Say yes."

"Yes, yes. We're squared away Miss Social Worker."

"Good. Now back to you being a bad boy."

Looking down and away, he said, "I'm crazy about you."

"I agree you're crazy."

"I'm glad we agree on something."

"My past bothers you?"

"What you had to go through."

"You don't know the half of it."

"I know enough."

"Maybe, maybe not. Don't feel sorry for me."

"I hate thinking of what you went through."

"I still have nightmares. I have anger in me. Can you deal with all my baggage? Can you deal with me wanting to take it out on Big Jake? My dad should be out of prison by now. I have a lot of issues. Can you handle me?"

"Every bit of you."

"Even being a good boy?"

"Yeah," he garbled. "Even that."

Putting a hand to her ear, she said, "Can you speak up a little?"

"The problem is that I'm not a kid."

"Which means you have more self-control? Is that what you're trying to say?"

"Yeah, well, if you put it that way."

"Well, well, maybe there is a future for us."

"But you make me feel like a kid."

"A big tough cop like you. What would the guys at work think?"

"They would say I'm, well this is what *they* would say –"

"Go ahead spit it out. I know how they talk."

Chuckling, he whispered, "They would say I'm pussy whipped."

Blushing, looking down, she said, "Are you?"

"We've already established that I'm crazy," he sighed. "I guess I am."

"I don't know if I can give you what you need."

"You give me a lot."

"But can the bad boy in you wait?"

"It won't be easy, but you're worth it."

"Aren't you sweet? So what do we do now?"

"How about taking a cold shower with me?"

"I think that's just what you need."

"Alright, let's go grab a bite to eat."

"We can do that."

Driving to a restaurant, letting their emotions calm down, Rosetta wanted to pursue the Jack issue, but hesitated, and was relieved when Mike brought it up. "You know I spoke to my old friend Jack today about Big Jake."

"Oh yeah, how did that go?"

"I don't know if I can trust him. Right now, I'm feeding him B.S. while I sort things out. He's jobless, a drunk and vulnerable to being bought."

"And he's your friend?"

"Well let's see, gee," he said. "Thinking back to Big Jake and the kid he killed."

"Gomez."

"Yeah, Gomez. To use your analogy. A friend isn't the right word. Let's just say I use to know him."

Snapping without thought, she roared, *"Does that mean he drugged and raped you?"*

Speechless, he gazed at her. "I'm sorry, I didn't mean –"

Putting her hand over his mouth, she said, "No I'm sorry. You don't have to say anything. I mean it."

With a quizzical look, he nodded his head and continued to the restaurant. "Mexican okay?"

"Sounds great. You okay?"

"I'm fine. Are you okay?"

"I told you there is a lot you don't know."

"I don't want the past to come between us," he said parking the car. "The past is past. Okay?"

"Sure," she said, kissing him.

Big Jake returned from Los Angeles to Springfield due to his insecurity about the police asking questions and the fact that Jack had been looking for him. In fact, on this evening, he waited for Jack's arrival. When he arrived, they went into his backroom office.

"Before we talk," Big Jake said, "give me your phone number and address in case I need to get a hold of you.... Alright now let's get down to business. So you talked to this dago cop and what did you learn?"

"He wants to nail your ass for some reason."

"I want more," he said, rolling his fingers.

"Have you heard about some rapes around here?"

"What the hell are you talking about?"

"Well, you know, a," he stammered, "a, has anyone been raped near the club?"

"*What*? Not the hell that I know of. What's that got to do with me?"

"I don't even, shit, know exactly how to say this."

Slamming his fist on the bar, Big Jake yelled, "*What the fuck you trying to say*? Out with it."

"Do you want me to use his exact words?"

"I want you to tell me what this numskull said."

"Could I have a shot?"

Big Jake grabbed the whiskey bottle and poured a drink. "Drink the damn thing and speak to me."

Downing it, Jack said with confidence, "Now remember, this is what *he* said."

"Spit it out shit head."

"He said he thinks you're a, a maniac fairy."

"A what?"

"A, a, a maniac – a, a manic fairy's what he said."

Grabbing Jack by the throat, "What kind of crazy bullshit is this?"

"He said it," Jack pleaded. "I swear that's what he said."

Letting loose of his neck, Big Jake paced and then exploded. "*What the hell is that suppose to mean*? Come on, what else did he say?"

"Just that there had been a couple guys raped near your club."

Growling, Big Jake grabbed Jack by the hair saying, "*What kind of bullshit is this?*"

"Please, that's all I know. That's exactly what he said. I swear it."

"He needs a bullet in his head," he said letting loose of Jack. "Listen to me you son-of-bitch. I don't ever want to hear you repeat what you told me to anybody. Do you understand me? Or I'll be putting a bullet in your head. This dago is crazy. So what's going through that infantile mind of yours?"

"Nothing."

"You don't think I'm a queer do you?"

"No," he whimpered.

"Are you a queer?"

"Oh no."

"I don't like queers. Why the hell did he say that?"

"I don't know."

Pacing, wiping the perspiration from his forehead, he poured himself a glass of whiskey and downed it. "This is insanity. What's this dago after?"

"It doesn't make sense," Jack said. "That's what I thought."

"If you had any idea what I went through when I was a kid, I'd have to cut your nuts off and shove them down your throat."

"I don't want to know," Jack said, cringing. "What do you want me to do?"

"So you working for me now?"

"Oh yeah, I want to work for you."

"You're on the payroll then."

"Great. What do you want me to do?"

"Put a bullet through that son-of-bitches head to start with."

"Now wait a second, you know I don't kill people."

Walking up to Jack, he grabbed his earlobe, squeezed it and said, "I'm just screwing with you. I mean *messing* with you. You understand, messing with you."

"Yeah, yeah, sure."

"Just keep talking to the guy. Feed him some bullshit. I want to know what's going on."

"Yeah, yeah, okay, but I was really hoping to work in the club?"

"Not now. I want to know what's going on with this guy."

Jack nodded, "Got it."

"Follow him without being seen?"

"I can do that."

"Good. Do it and report to me where he goes during his workday. I want to see if he's on to anything concerning me. You got me? Am I clear?"

"Follow him. Take notes, right?"

"Take notes. Hell, get in bed with him."

"Damn, that's weird. That's what he told me to do to you."

"What's that?" he said, head flinching.

"He told me to get in bed with you."

"That rotten dago," he hissed. "I'm no *queer*."

"Oh no, he just said the same thing. You didn't literally want me to get in bed with him. Well, he didn't either. Right?"

Pacing, lip twitching; Big Jake said to himself, "This whole thing bugs the shit out of me. There's no way he could know what happened to me as a kid. I didn't report it. What's going on with this guy? Is he messing with me? I don't like to be messed with. Yeah, messed with. Gotta square things up with that priest. I've buried it way too long. That perverted priest ruined my life. Now I got this crazy cop wanting to screw me."

"Should I go?" Jack asked watching Big Jake pace.

"What?"

"Are you done with me? Should I go?"

"Yeah, get the hell out of here. No! Hold on. Get your ass over here. Here, have another drink," Big Jake said, pouring two shots of whiskey and making a toast. "Cheers. To you getting in bed with this dago." Jack came over with a smile and downed the whiskey. Then Big Jake grabbed the front of his shirt. "You better not be playing me for a fool. You hear me? You want to work for me? Well, my secrets become your secrets. *Understood?*"

"Please let go," Jake begged. "I understand."

"You're going down the shitter if you're messing with me. You hear me? You screwed up when you worked for me before. Do it again. You'll wish you never came back here. Got me?"

"I got you," he said, quivering. "No screw ups."

Jack left and Big Jake continued pacing. "What in the hell's going on?" he asked himself. "This bullshit and that photo bullshit. I'm going nuts. Don't like feeling like this. Need to calm down. Maybe I need to see a doctor? Something to calm me down. Either that or someone's going to get killed. I don't want to make any mistakes if they're watching me. Everything sucks when you're not in control."

Going out in the club, Big Jake went up to Lee, the club manager. "What's up boss?" said Lee.

"You know that guy that just left?"

"Yeah ."

"Here," he said handing him an address. "Have one of the boys tail him for awhile. I don't know if I can trust him."

"Sure thing. Got it covered."

Chapter 18

Los Angeles was sweltering from a heat wave while the faltering economy had a stranglehold on the city causing layoffs and many city cutbacks. The state itself was no better off and budget cuts were affecting social service programs across California. Andre and Windy sat in their office at the shelter reading a letter from the state.

"This is terrible news," Windy stressed.

"They're cutting half our budget now," Andre said, "and more could be coming. How did those idiots get us in the mess we're in? What do we do?"

"All these poor kids. It makes me sick. We can't turn kids away."

"We won't. We'll cut services as much as we can. I'll look over the books and decide where to cut. There probably won't be money to send kids back home. I don't know. I'll do my best."

At the end of the day, relief staff took over and they left the building. "Do you see that guy over there?" Andre said.

"The guy with the ball cap?"

"Yeah. I saw him two other times today standing across the street."

"Don't start being paranoid again."

"Let's eat at the old Irish pub. We'll see if he follows us."

"Well, let's go. It's like an oven out here."

With the sun pounding against their faces, they rushed to the comfort of the air-conditioned pub. Seated at a table, Andre was satisfied that he did not see the man with the baseball cap. A peaceful dinner followed, but concern about the budget cuts frustrated them. "What do you say we have one drink?" Andre said.

"I don't know."

"Just a shot to calm the nerves. No whiskey or scotch. None of our past poisons. Let's try the tequila like last time."

"One shot," she said.

"Just one."

Once they had their shot of tequila, Andre tapped Windy's glass. "To a return to sanity."

"Cheers," from Windy.

Downing the shots, they seemed to be relaxed for a moment until Andre focused on the man in the baseball cap across the street.

"You got the tequila sweats or what?" Windy said.

"Don't turn around, but it's that guy again."

"With the ball cap?"

"Oh yeah."

"Stop it. Just stop it. *I mean it*. No one is watching us. No one is following us. Do you hear me?"

"Everything is just getting under my damn skin. But like you said – you can't live in fear."

"Good it's settled. He probably lives around here. Okay?"

"Right. You're right. You ready to get the hell out of here?"

"Settle your butt down. Come on," she said, leading the way out the door.

Five minutes later, they drove off toward their home. Looking through the rearview mirror, Andre said, "For the past five minutes I've noticed a car keeping its distance, but staying behind us."

"Don't do this to yourself and don't do it to me. I'm serious."

"I know, I know."

After a thirty-five minutes trip, Andre pulled into their driveway and then into the garage. Looking into the rearview mirror while the garage door was shutting, a car crept by catching Andre's eye, but he didn't say anything not wishing to overreact. With the garage door down, the car turned around and drove back past the house with the driver looking at the address and writing it down.

At home one evening, Big Jake sprawled out on the bed after dinner watching the national news. Headlines were of terrorist attacks and of the Catholic Churches cover-up of child molestation scandals in Europe and other parts of the world. Hypnotized on the screen, he flashed back trying to fight off thoughts of his altar boy days. Father Murphy's image kept appearing, as he remembered lying down and the priest's hands undoing his pants and exploring his body. Sweat trickled down his face as his whining son, David, entered the bedroom.

"*I hate you*," he snapped. "No one wants to be friends with me anymore. I know it's because of you. I've heard things. None of my close friends will come around me anymore."

"Shut up," said Big Jake, eyes still on the television screen. "Look at this shit. And you want to become a priest?"

"You're ruining my life."

Face flush, he shouted, "*Get out of my sight.*"

David stormed out of the room and Big Jake sprung up, turning the television off and headed to a private room where he sat in front of a computer and began typing:

I am a disgrace. I am a pervert. I like little boys. I do not deserve to live. I've done terrible things throughout my life. If there is a heaven, I will never find it. If there is a hell, I am on my way there now. I confess my sins before I leave this world …

Continuing to type, he struggled with every word until the letter was completed. Then, he printed it; folded it; stuck it in his pocket, and left the house for the garage. On finding a rope, he grabbed it and left in his car. An hour later, he pulled in front of a church with a rectory next to it, parked across the street, and waited to observe for fifteen minutes. Lightening filled the sky on this evening. A sudden downpour made it hard to see, but a flash from the rectory to the church caught Big Jake's eye. The rainstorm let up and Big Jake grabbed the rope, hurried to the churches entrance, and entered. Walking up the aisle, he glanced about and saw the choir loft above. Moving to a stairway, he went up, tied the rope to a pew, dropped it over the balcony and then returned below, where he grabbed a folding chair, made a noose, placing the chair under it. Standing on it, testing the loop, he was satisfied. After moving up the aisle, he looked back at the chair and rope before heading to the front of the church. Once on the altar, he crept to a door, stopped and listened to the dead silence. "He must have left," he told himself. "Must be back in the rectory." On opening the door, no one was in the room. Looking out a window at the rectory, he saw a figure sitting at a table. As he clasped his hands watching, he didn't see anyone else. Leaving out a side exit, he went to the parish house door and knocked.

An older priest opened the door. "Can I help you?" he said.

"Father," Big Jake said. "There is something you need to see over in the church."

"I just checked on a leak problem we have had when it pours down rain. Is that it?"

"That and something else."

The priest and Big Jake went into the church. The priest headed to the leaky area and looked up. "No leak so far," he said. "Oh my, it's starting to pour down again."

"Just follow me."

Big Jake led the way, up the aisle toward the church entrance. "What is this?" the priest said.

"Destiny," Big Jake said.

"Destiny, I don't understand?" he said, eyeing the chair and rope.

"Watch me," Big Jake said, standing on the chair and placing the noose around his neck.

"Please," the priest begged, "get down from there." Taking out the letter he had typed, he handed it to the priest. "What is this?"

"Read it. Read it out loud," he said as a drop of water splashed down on the foot of the chair from above. When he looked up; a drop of water, flashed by his face, causing him to jerk back.

Opening the letter, the priest began reading aloud: "*I am a disgrace. I am a pervert …,*" he read trembling. "*I confess my sins before I leave this world …* Please don't do it."

"*You're right,*" Big Jake jubilated, taking the noose off and stepping down. "*I've seen the light.*"

"Thank God Almighty," he said. "For heaven sakes, you scared the heck out of me."

"Father Murphy, don't you remember me?"

"You know me?"

"Know you – I've lived with you all my stinking life."

"I'm sorry. Refresh my memory. I'm getting old. The mind doesn't work like it use to."

"It's been close to thirty years ago. I was your favorite altar boy. Remember me? Little Jake you use to call me. You were at St. Patrick's parish then. You would say I looked tense. Then you would massage my neck. Is it coming back?" he said with unforgiving eyes.

"It's been so long ago." Father Murphy stood trembling.

"How have you gotten away with it all these years?"

"I don't understand?"

With thunder exploding and rain pounding against the church, Big Jake's hands opened and lip twitched three times. *"This is your letter Father,"* he said. "You ready to face the world? You wanting me to open a can of worms?"

He stood speechless, shaking and then pleaded, *"Please,* I am so sorry. I've prayed for forgiveness."

"I'm glad you remember now because I can't bury it any longer."

Looking down, Father Murphy fell to his knees praying. "What now? I am sorry. Will you forgive me?"

"I am sorry too. You took my childhood away from me. How many little Jake's were there?"

"Please pray with me."

"The letter tells you what you must do."

"What?" he shuddered?

"I heard you say, 'I confess my sins before I leave this world.'"

"Oh no. Please," Father Murphy begged. "There's got to be another way?"

"Not unless you are willing to confess to the world. Can I call the press? Will you tell them what you did to me? Can you handle that?"

"Please have mercy," he said, voice wavering, feeling a splash of water on his forehead. "There must be another way." The water kept dripping against his face. He noticed Big Jake open up his lightweight jacket, revealing a pistol stuck in his pants.

"After what you put me through," he said, hand on the pistol grip. "I would hope you wouldn't want to make me a murderer. *You* made me a sick person. *You* ruined my life in this world. Are *you* going to make me forfeit my life in the next world? Don't make me do it. You don't deserve mercy."

Water dripping, streaking his face, Father Murphy said looking up, "He's so sad. You're right I must pay for my sins. I can't condemn you to Hell. But he will forgive me and you must too."

"You sent me to Hell. Vengeance will be mine saith the Lord. Right!"

"God will deal with me," he whined. "Not you but God."

"Then let it be," Big Jake said, hand on the pistol.

Setting the letter down on the wooden bench, Father Murphy stepped up on the chair, placed the noose around his neck while wavering and praying. "Please forgive me ..."

Pulling out his cell phone, Big Jake said, "The number for your local TV news is ready for me to call. Should I do it?" Looking up, Father Murphy's face was washed with a steady stream of rain water as he shook, causing the chair to move back and forth. Big Jake watched his teetering feet and then saw Father Murphy either lose his balance on the chair or kick it away. Big Jake couldn't tell for sure but was hypnotized on the dangling body as Father Murphy grabbed the rope, struggling to no avail. More thunder and the pounding rain came with the leak spreading toward Big Jake who moved from its path. "Judge, jury and executioner," Big Jake thought to himself. "I couldn't have planned it better."

Having recovered from the bachelor party, Tom had no recollection of the evening and assumed he had drunk too much. One day after arriving at work, Tom and Amy checked their mailboxes on the main floor before going upstairs to begin their shift. After thumbing through the in-house mail, a large postmarked envelope caught Amy's attention that she looked at with interest.

"What do you have there?" asked Tom.

"I don't know. There's no return address."

"Well open it. I'm curious."

"Alright, I am too." Pulling out large computer printout photos, Amy's jaw dropped seeing Tom and Chastity together half-nude. Tom looked over her shoulder causing his eyes to spring open like a jack in the box. Flipping through all the images left both of them speechless for a short moment.

"*With Chastity?*" Amy hissed. "And all those other girls?"

"I – I don't know a thing about it," Tom shuddered. "I don't have a clue."

"*You're obviously at the strip club,*" Amy snapped.

"I don't remember a thing. I wouldn't have done that. I'm serious. I blacked out."

"*How convenient,*" she growled, shoving the photos back in the envelope, cringed and stomped away.

"*Amy,*" Tom pleaded. "You have got to believe me."

Walking up the hall, she ignored his pleas, refused to turn around and flipped him the finger, which to him was like receiving a nail in the coffin while clawing to get out. Uncertain of what to do, he meandered upstairs to prepare for the on-slot of kids returning from school. Overwhelmed, he stressed trying to remember something about that night, but it was useless. When he got to the unit desk, he picked up the phone and called Marty at his new job. Marty told Tom as much as he could remember, but it was of little help. The more he thought, a theory formed and once convinced of it, he called Amy.

"*I don't want to talk to you,*" she barked.

"Please listen. Only one thing makes sense. Just hear me out, okay?"

"This ought to be good."

"If Chastity was there?"

"What do you mean *if*? It sounds like B.S. already."

"Let me finish."

"Hurry up I got to go."

"You remember the prank Chastity pulled here at the home with me? Remember the video they tried putting on the internet?"

"Hell yes, I remember. I guess it confirms you really were messing with her."

"No," he spat. "Damn it, shit. It confirms just the opposite."

"How do you reason that?"

"She was trying to get me in trouble then and I think that's what happened down at the club."

"I've heard some bullshit stories before, but that takes 'em all. You think I'm an idiot?"

"I'm serious."

"So am I. There's no way she could have set you up there. Why would a fifteen-year-old have been there in the first place? Like I said, I'm no idiot. If that's the best you can do just forget it. Goodbye, I've got to go," she said slamming the phone down.

Tom being unable to concentrate the rest of the evening became apparent to staff and kids. Over in the corner of the room, Tommy Wizel and a boy named Joey were causing a ruckus arguing. Tom stared at them, but may as well have been staring at the wall. Another worker went over and broke up the argument. Tommy slammed his fist against a table as he watched Tom from a distance, surprised that he just sat emotionless. Hurrying over to Tom, he said, "What's wrong? Are you spaced out on drugs or what?"

"What?" he said. "Drugs? No, no, just an overdose of life."

"Maybe you could use some real drugs then. Remember what Professor Frantic said in his book?"

"Hard telling, I can't remember much."

"He said there is a drug for every disaster and a disaster from every drug."

"That sounds about right. So what's the point?"

"Don't you get it?"

"It's as clear as mud."

"You're damned if you do and damned if you don't. So I would say pop a pill or two and join the *cuckoo-cuckoo club*."

"That's about right. What kind of pills are we talking about?"

"They're a real treat," he said reaching into his pocket. "They made me take them. Go ahead. Try one."

"I don't think so. What are they?"

"It's the new drug they put me on at school," he said smiling.

"So you've found a way to make them think you're taking it? Right?"

"Right on," he said with pride. "They're a bunch of fools. They don't know up from down. Try a couple of them. Who knows? They might solve your problem. Just because it made me feel like a zombie, doesn't mean it'll do the same to you."

"Since I already feel like one, I better pass."

"Good going, Tom. You're smarter than you look."

Nodding, Tom said, "I really needed that. Guess it's time to come back to earth."

"I'll tell you what, I think if you go smack Joey around you'll feel better. He's a real dork."

"Joey?"

"Yeah, the dork with a smirk on his face over there that you're going to smack around."

"Thanks for the advice, but I'm only half-brain dead today. Good try, though."

"I have a thought," Tommy said, looking off like a message was being relayed to him by a higher power. "It's coming. It's coming. *I got it.*"

"This ought to be good."

Bending forward, he whispered in Tom's ear, "Bang, bang, ya need to bang your banger. You like the sound of that? Bang, bang, ya need to bang your banger." Tom stared off, thinking the words had a nice rhythm to them, but refocused on seeing a girl enter through the unit door. "Alright," Tommy said, seeing the girl approaching. "Bang, bang," he repeated, causing the girl to frown.

"Your wife," said the girl, handing Tom a letter, "asked me to give this to you."

"Thanks, I think," he said, watching the girl walk away.

"Open it," Tommy said.

Looking at the sealed envelope, Tom's hand trembled. "I'll wait."

Grabbing the envelope from Tom's hand, Tommy said, "I'll open it."

"*No*," Tom exploded, grabbing the envelope back.

"Cool it man. Don't you want to know what's in it?"

"I don't know right now."

"Something's up man, isn't it? You're sweating."

"I think I'm coming down with something."

"Go in the other room and bang your banger."

"What?"

"You're no fun tonight," he said, walking away.

Gripping the envelope, Tom held it up to the ceiling light hoping to catch a glimpse of the intent of the letter, which was useless. Fearing the contents, he set it aside for a minute, but could not resist. Picking at the seal, it opened and he read:

Tom,

I need time to think. Please find somewhere else to stay tonight. I've arranged to get a ride home. Don't try calling or seeing me tonight.

Amy

"Shit almighty," he said to himself. "I knew I didn't wanna open it. I don't believe this is happening. This is insane. What do I do? Where do I go tonight? I got to talk to her. This is ridiculous. I couldn't have done what those photos show. But they show it. How do you explain it? ..."

Up on the third floor, Amy and Brenda sat talking at the desk in the recreation room while the girls were busy with activities. Pulling out the envelope of photos, Amy handed them to Brenda. "Just take a quick look," she said, "I don't want anybody to see them."

Brenda's eyes flickered as she thumbed through the photos, "Wow," she blurted. "Tom and these hot looking babes. *Chastity?* Where did you get these? Are you okay? I wondered what was wrong."

"Is it obvious?"

"Hell yes."

"While we were out this was what Tom was doing. Now that video incident at the home makes sense. He must have really been messing around with her."

"What did he say?"

"Doesn't remember a thing if you can believe that. He said he thinks he was set up by Chastity. *Shit, shit, shit*, I don't know what to believe. What do you think? "

"He looks really spaced out in the photos. I've never seen him with his pants down."

"I told him to find somewhere else to stay tonight. Will you give me a ride home?"

"Of course. How did you get the photos?"

"They were here in the office mail box."

"Well then, I would think Chastity had to have sent them."

"I guess so."

"Why would she send them? It makes me suspicious."

"What do you mean?"

"If something was going on between them why would she want you to know? Think about it."

"It's hard to think clearly."

"Maybe she did set him up."

"Why would she be at the club and how would she know he would be there? It doesn't make sense. I don't see it," Amy said, hiding the envelope. "Here comes the girls. Can we talk more after work?"

"Of course."

With most of the boys out of sight, Tom was still in a daze, and unaware of what was going on in a back bedroom. The other male staff was preoccupied playing pool with Tommy who did not mingle well with the other kids and preferred to hang out with staff. With the bang of a cue ball, Tom snapped out of his stupor, redirected his thoughts wondering why it was so quiet, and wandered down the hallway. Discovering all the bedroom doors shut, he began opening them. No one was in the first two rooms, which concerned him. Instead of opening the next, he put his ear against it, heard nothing, and went to the next door. Listening again, this time he heard faint laughter and the chatter of voices. Uncertain of what to expect, he tried opening the door, but something was holding it shut. Shuffling footsteps and whining voices caused him to push with a Herculean thrust and it opened enough for him to step in. Flicking the overhead light on, Tom yelled, "Busted!" Kids tossed their cigarettes out the window, another stomped on a joint, and another hid two pints of liquor under a pillow. Scooting out the window, two girls hurried up the fire escape back to their unit. "You guys are bad," Tom said, looking up at the disconnected smoke alarm. "Come on," he said, nodding his head. "I want cigarette packs, the pot and whatever else you have?"

"That's it," said a boy, handing over the remainder of the joint while two more boys each gave him a pack of cigarettes.

"Larry," said Tom, "I smell booze. "What are you hiding under the pillow?"

"Shoot," Larry said, uncovering two pints of alcohol.

"Come on," he said motioning with his hand. Larry handed over the bottles to Tom, who looked at the labels shaking his head. "Just what you guys need, gin and tequila. Everyone in their own rooms and leave the doors open."

"What's going to happen?" the group whined.

"You're going to Hell, the whole lot of you. But for now, you're confined to your bedroom until I can figure out which circle of Hell to put you in."

Tommy and the other staff walked in the room, "He's talking about Dante's Hell, you hell-raisers," Tommy snickered at the mystified kids. "Haven't you ever played Dante's Inferno? It's a great video game you chumps."

Once all was quiet, Tom called Amy upstairs. "I told you not to call," she complained.

"I just busted a pot and booze party in one of the rooms and a couple of your darlings scrambled up the fire escape. Just thought you might want to know. It looked like Wild Willa and that cutie face Tamra. That's it," he said and hung up. Staring at the bottles of alcohol, he opened the desk drawer to set them in it, looked about, saw no one, and then placed them in a briefcase. Sitting back in the desk chair, he watched the clock tick, waiting for the shift to end, and then propped his feet on the desk with eyes closed, trying to remember what happened the night of the bachelor party.

Chapter 19

Back at the Springfield club, Big Jake was relieved and satisfied that he had put closure to his childhood secret, but could not get Father Murphy's dangling body out of his head. The thought was pleasing and painful at times. Despite the distress he had endured all those years, he was now in awe believing his actions condemned him to Hell. "I mean he was a priest," he battled over in his mind, sitting in his office alone. "But a bad priest. Besides, you didn't lay a hand on him. You just made him see the light." Sitting back, feet on the desk, he grabbed his gin and tonic while recognizing the music in the background as Candy's introduction song. Tapping his fingers to the tune, he tried to divert his thoughts, but Father Murphy's image reappeared. "He got what he deserved. He for sure won't mess with any more boys. I did the world a service. Besides, I've already sealed my fate with the devil. If anything, this might give me a reprieve. That's right. I've done something good for a change. I can't figure it out, I mean his feet were shaking but did he step off or fall off? He grabbed the rope struggling like he didn't like how the noose felt. It was great seeing him squirm. He made me squirm. Come here Little Jake he would say with those squinty beady eyes. Let me massage your neck. Neck my ass. I mean, hell, if it were just my ass that wouldn't have been so bad. But my ass was on the ground when he rubbed those grubby, filthy hands all over me. Then he would say open your mouth," he thought, lip twitching as he spat on the floor with a scowling expression. Gulping his drink, he mellowed and moved his fingers to the cadence of the music. "The Father Murphy shuffle," he rejoiced, smiling. "Halleluiah," he thought. "The wicked priest is dead." Taking another swig, he let the alcohol settle in his mouth, swished it around, and then gargled. Swallowing it, he jabbered, "Yes, yes, it's time to celebrate. Lord Almighty, I did a good deed. I'm a do-gooder. Just call me a damn social worker." Springing to his feet, he left his office and entered the club feeling jovial.

With second shift over, Tom gazed out the window watching Amy and Brenda leave together. Feeling sick to his stomach, he swallowed hard, and then pulled himself together and left. Unsure of where to go, he drove to the park where he and the boys had jogged at on many occasions. Parking, he tried reliving the night at The Lost Souls Club, but downing a mug of beer was the last thing he remembered. Shudder curtailed, he opened his briefcase and pulled out the tequila, took a swig, and then another before putting the bottle away. Mind swelling, sweat trickled down his forehead on this warm spring evening. Taking deep breaths, he tried to stop hyperventilating which happened after a couple of minutes. The fire from the tequila was kicking in and he seemed to have a burst of energy. "One for the road," he told himself, pulling out the bottle and took another swig. Determined to unravel what had happened that night, he headed to the club to get answers.

Amy and Brenda, out on the town for the evening, went to Burt Crebo's favorite hangout, the Crazy Horse Bar, and Restaurant, hoping he might shed some light on Tom's behavior on the night of the bachelor party. Sure enough, Burt was there. The three met up and sat at a table together.

"Where's Tom?" Burt asked. "What are you drinking? I'm buying." He left and returned with two beers. "Where did you say Tom was?"

"He's busy," Brenda said.

"What happened the night of the bachelor party?" Amy interjected.

"Just a bunch of guys raising hell. You know, naked girls," he smiled, "and a lot of booze."

"What happened to Tom?"

"I think he got plastered," Burt said chuckling.

"Did he leave you guys?"

"What do you mean leave? What's going on?"

"Do you remember Chastity?"

"Remember her. I got kicked in the nuts by her."

"Did you see her at the club?"

"Nope, I would remember that. What's with the thousand questions?"

"Do you remember Tom leaving you guys for awhile?"

"I guess. He went to take a piss. He didn't want to do it in the cup like I suggested."

"And?" Amy persisted.

"It seemed like he was gone for awhile, but boy oh boy when he returned he couldn't stand. He was wasted."

"How much did he drink?"

"A lot, I guess."

"Enough to pass out?"

"I never saw him do that before. Maybe someone slipped him a Mickey," he chuckled.

"Are you serious?"

"I'm just talking. I'm not used to being interrogated. No, I'm not serious about anything right now ..."

Stepping out of the car, Tom focused on the flashing light, *The Lost Souls Club*. His memory of the nightclub entrance was from years earlier when Gomez was shot rather than the night of the bachelor party. In awe, he went into the club, peered about trying to reconnect his lost memory. Being a weeknight the club was not busy. Strolling like he was lost, he tried remembering the faces in the photo and eyeballed the waitresses and girls performing. While ordering a drink, he said to the bartender, "Does a girl named Chastity work here?"

Looking at Big Jake, standing nearby, he said, "Speak up, who did you say?"

"Chastity," he said raising his voice, which caught Big Jake's attention.

Big Jake shook his head and the bartender said, "No one here by that name."

"Are you sure? Do you know any Chastity that hangs around here?"

"No," he replied.

"What's the problem here?" Big Jake said to Tom.

"There's no problem," Tom said.

"Good, I don't like problems in my club."

"You familiar with a young girl named Chastity that hangs around here?"

"No young girls hang around here. What's your problem?"

"No problem," Tom said, walking away, going to a table and sitting down. He could feel the man's intense stare but ignored it and then examined the girl's faces as they walked by or tried to entice him to buy a lap dance.

"You look lonely," said a stripper, "you could use a lap dance?"

"No thanks. Hey, do you know a girl named Chastity?"

"Who's asking?" she said with an evasive smile.

"An old friend," he said, thinking this girl looked familiar.

"No, I don't know any Chastity. Gotta get going if you don't want a lap dance."

"Hold on," he said, "how much for a dance?"

"Now you're talking," she said with a smile, grabbing his hand. "Come on follow me."

"The price?"

"Not much, come on. We'll talk about it."

Standing, Tom followed her to a sofa in a dark corner where he plopped down and she sat on his lap. Before she got in motion, Tom grabbed her shoulders, saying, "Listen to me."

"No touching," she insisted. "Those are the rules."

"Just hold up, I recognize you, don't I? Don't you recognize me?"

"You do look familiar."

"Would you remember me better with my pants pulled down?"

"It's you," she said stunned.

"You remember, don't you?"

"How could you remember?"

"Because you just told me so," he said gripping her arms. "What did you do to me that night?"

"Please let go of me. I don't know what you're talking about."

"*Not until you tell me.*"

Big Jake, who was watching Tom since he mentioned Chastity, hurried over to the commotion, yelling, "What's going on?"

"He won't leave me alone," the girl whined.

Big Jake called out for help; two men rushed over and pulled the girl loose while grabbing Tom by the neck. "Let go of me," Tom roared, struggling to get loose, which he did due to his strength and wrestling abilities, having been an all-state high school champion. Soon three other men assisted in holding him down.

"I ought to call the cops," Big Jake said, grabbing his jaw.

"I know who you are," Tom spat.

"Oh yeah."

"You killed Gomez, didn't you? Now I guess you're trying to blackmail me with those bullshit photos."

"What the hell are you talking about?"

"Ask her if you *really* don't know."

"Hey, ass-wipe. Did you have something to do with that photo of me being scalped by that crazy kid?"

"I don't know what you're talking about."

"Get this asshole out of here."

The group of men held on to Tom until they got to the door and then shoved him out causing him to tumble to the ground.

"I'm pissed," he said under his breath, stood and returned to his car. Undecided where to go, he drove by his house, saw all the lights off and wanted to stop, but held back. Instead, he went to a bar, sat at a table and ordered a beer. A few tables away were a group of young women drinking and celebrating a birthday. Three beers later, Tom drowned in sorrow, picked up when the girls at the table started making comments about him being a hunk.

"Hey cutie," one of the girls yelled at him. "Why don't you join us?"

Smiling, Tom pointed at himself. "She talking to me?" he asked himself.

"Yeah you," she said.

"Come over and join us," said two other girls.

Shrugging his shoulders, he half-staggered to their table. "Hey," he said, "you're all having a great time aren't you?"

"Sit down," said a girl, making room for him to pull up a chair.

"What's the celebration?" he asked, sitting down.

"It's my birthday," said the girl.

"What are you drinking? The next round's on me."

"Whatever you're drinking," the birthday girl said.

"Well, I've been drinking beer and tequila tonight."

"I'll do tequila," she said.

Half the girls ordered a beer and half tequila. Tom switched back to tequila. After an hour of partying, Tom put his anguish aside. Before long, a young man walked through the front door towards the group at the table. Ten feet away, he froze, glancing at the group and then focused on Tom and the birthday girl who were talking. When Tom saw the man's harsh eyes on him, he looked away for a second. Then, from the corner of his eye, he noticed that the man was approaching. "Now what?" he thought."

Bending down into Tom's face, the man roared, *"That's my wife you're talking to."*

"Oh," he replied, "I didn't know."

"You better get your *ass up* and away from here."

Tom stared into the angry eyes, puckered, holding his tongue, grunted, and then moved away to the bar. Grumbling in an undertone, he glanced at the man through the bar mirror and noticed the man gazing at him, eyes full of rage, looking like he was ready to explode. Tom turned and stared back. It became a stare down with the stranger's teeth clenching and saliva dripping out of his mouth. Sweat trickled down Tom's forehead into his eyes. Brushing the sweat away with fingertips, he was able to focus again and saw the man wasn't letting up. Tom's face contorted and the man exploded, grabbing a full-size stool, throwing it close to twenty feet at him. Tom's hand shot up to block the flying object. Somehow; a minor miracle, the leg landed perfectly in his hand, which surprised him and angered the man even more. Standing, holding the stool in his hand, shocked by the perfect catch, he saw the man's face ignite and in a flash the man was on top of him crashing his fist against Tom's nose. With good reflexes, Tom's head jerked back enough to soften the blow, but not enough to keep from getting a bloody nose. Dazed, Tom didn't need to react, as the huge athletic bartender grabbed the man and then was assisted by two other workers. Another person called the police while they held the irate man down. Tom stood looking in disbelief. The police showed up in minutes to Tom's surprise and handcuffed the man.

Pulling Tom aside, the officer took his statement and then asked, "Are you going to be okay? Do you want to press charges?"

Feeling guilty for having been at the bar with a group of women, Tom said, "No, just forget it. I don't want to press charges." The officer proceeded to the angry man while Tom made his exit.

Walking out the door, a man said to Tom, "I wouldn't mess around with that dude. He's been in prison for stabbing someone. No one to mess with." Tom nodded his head and walked out to the parking lot. Another police car pulled up. On feeling his stomach marching up his throat, Tom hurried to the side of the building and barfed. Feeling better, he headed to his car but was uncomfortable with the police around to drive away. Sitting in the car for awhile, he tried calling Amy but she wouldn't answer. Talking to himself, trying to figure out whom to call to pick him up, he hesitated, but then called Rosetta.

"Hello," said Rosetta, trying to wake up.

"I'm sorry," Tom slurred.

"Tom," she said. "Is this Tom?"

"Yes, I'm sorry to wake you."

"That's okay, I was awake. What's going on?" she said with concern.

"You won't believe it."

"What?"

"Amy kicked me out of the house tonight and I got, well, I had a little too much to drink. There's cops all around 'cause of the fight. I don't think it's a good idea to drive. I hate asking this —"

"That's okay," she interrupted. "Where are you at, I'll pick you up?"

"The Poison Apple."

"I'll be there soon."

"Thanks," he said, and then heard dead silence. "Hello, hello. Did you hang up? I guess you hung up." After closing the phone, he talked to himself. "I guess she's coming. Holy shit I don't believe I called her. What did I say? She's never seen me drunk. I'm an idiot. What will she think? What should I do?"

Fifteen minutes later, Rosetta arrived searching for Tom. When she found him half-conscious, she tapped on the car window saying, "Tom, it's me."

Eyes cracking open, Tom muddled, "Rosetta? Is that you? What are you doing here?"

"Come on," she said, "you're going with me."

"Where we going?"

"Come on. Get out and lock it up."

"Oh yeah, yeah," he stammered, getting out. "All locked up. All locked up. Where we going?"

"You're staying the night at my place."

"Take me home."

"You said Amy kicked you out."

"Oh shit, you're right. Just drive by there. Okay?"

"I can do that. What the heck happened?"

After getting in the car, Tom told her everything that had happened, including having gone down to Big Jake's club that night. Rosetta boiled and then said, "That no good creep needs another scalping."

"Hey, it's funny you said that. He asked me something really weird. He accused me of sending him photos of him being scalped. Do you believe that?"

Half-delighted, she said, "He seemed uptight about it, huh?"

"He's nuts. Everything is insane. I don't know what to do about Amy." When they neared the house, Tom said, "Slow down. Stop. Look at the cars in the drive." Rosetta did as asked. "Whose cars?" he grumbled. "I'm going to go look."

"I don't think that's a good idea."

"I'll be right back," he said, exiting and crossing the street. Going up to the cars, he jabbered, "Brenda's car and shit, Burt's car." Moving up to the house, he peaked in the window, saw Brenda in a chair and Amy and Burt on the sofa talking. Face pressed against the glass, he started seething and imagined Burt taking his place. Walking around the house, he looked in another window.

Rosetta, out of concern, stepped out of the car and hurried to Tom. Reaching him, she whispered, "Tom, let's go."

"Look," he insisted.

With a quick glance, she said, "They're just talking. Come on let's go."

"Something's going on."

"No, it isn't."

"I better go in don't you think?"

"Listen, you'll make things worse," she said, grabbing his bicep. "Trust me."

"I don't know. I think something's going on with Amy and Burt. Look at them, they're drinking."

"Please," she insisted, trying to pull him away.

"Alright, alright."

"You're being too loud."

Leading him away, he stopped and looked in another window, but this time, he started tapping on it. Rosetta pulled him away. "Listen to me. You don't want the cops called out here, do you? We have to go. Talk to her tomorrow. From what you told me about the lap dance girl, I think she'll believe you. Don't make things worse. Please come on."

"Alright," he conceded and managed to leave without Amy knowing he had been there.

When they returned to the car, Tom stood at the door. Rosetta opened it for him, but he didn't get in. "Come on, get in."

"I should go back."

"No!"

"I feel like a screw-up," he said, looking off in a daze and started pouting.

"It'll be okay," she said, giving him a hug and helping him into the car.

On arriving at Rosetta's, she kept a watchful eye on him leading the way to the door. Once inside, the dog started barking at Tom. "Leonardo, it's okay. You know Tom."

"It's me," he said, getting on his knees. "Come here boy." Leonardo went up to him and licked his face. "That's right, that's right," Tom said falling over backward with the dog all over him.

"That's enough," Rosetta said, pulling the dog back. "You okay?"

Struggling up, he said, "I'm fine."

"Come on I'll take you to your bedroom."

Tom followed through the hallway, using the wall for support and when he grabbed a door handle, it opened with him stumbling into a room. Flicking the light on, he murmured, "Don't see no bed."

"No Tom," she said, "wrong room."

"Wow," he said, seeing all the paintings. "This is great. You're the real Leonardo, not the pooch."

"You've seen them before," she said.

"I see new ones. Right?"

"There's always new ones."

"Since you're in here, you mentioned something earlier," she hesitated. "Come here." He followed her to a back corner where she pulled a painting out into the light.

"Holy shit!" he exclaimed. "Man oh man, alive. There's that asshole getting what he deserved. That's great. I mean, it's a little eerie, but great. I love it. This could be my book cover. Don't you think?"

"It would be perfect if you're putting that horrible scene of Gomez in your story. Are you?"

"Hell, I'll write the story around the painting. I'll have no choice but to use it. How do you do it? I'm getting the shivers just looking at it. It's so real. If Big Jake could only see it."

"Tom, think what you told me earlier."

"What's that? Let me see. You mean the photo? Is this what he was talking about?"

"You better believe it."

"I don't understand. He accused me of sending him a scalping photo. That's a painting."

"You've had way, way too much to drink."

"I'm sorry you never should have seen me like this. I should be ashamed. Trying to guide you all those years ago and look at me. But hold on now. What's the deal with the painting? Explain?"

"I've taken photos of the painting and anonymously sent them to that shit head."

"That's great," he said snickering. "I mean why? I'm confused. You mean 'cause he killed Gomez?"

"I found out that he was the person responsible for getting my dad to sell me. I just thought I would try tormenting him some. I still have a lot of anger in me I guess."

"It apparently worked. He was livid about the photo."

"That's great to know. Come on, you need to sleep."

"You're right, let's go. Hold on, who's the baby in that painting?" he asked, pointing at it.

"Just how I remembered my little one. A sweet angel."

"Well, he's not so little and definitely no angel anymore."

"What?" she said, squeezing his arm.

"Oh, nothing, I'm just messed up. Don't know what the hell I'm talking about. Really, really I don't know. Shit almighty," he grumbled, eyes closed, shaking his head.

"You know something? *Don't you*? Please tell me. I mean it."

"Aw shit, I opened my mouth. I know something. Can't think right now. Ask me in the morning."

"You better believe I will," she said, leading the way. After getting him settled down on the bed, he closed his eyes and was out like a smoldering-flame drenched in a downpour.

Chapter 20

The next morning came earlier for Rosetta than for Tom who snored while she attended to daily chores. With her final exams completed a week earlier, she was preparing for graduation in two weeks. Looking at the clock, she realized it was two hours earlier in California and hoped she wasn't waking Andre and Windy when she called their phone number. She fidgeted while the phone rang until Andre answered it. Quick to unload her concerns about Tom and Amy, she then mentioned the Big Jake and Tom ordeal, which caused Andre to sit up in bed quivering. Once finished talking, Andre rubbed his temples feeling a headache coming on, and then bombarded Windy with the details.

"There's just no end to this maniac and his stranglehold on the world," Andre carried on. "I feel like I need to do, shit, something. You know?"

"Calm down," Windy insisted. "You're so stressed about him you're going to have a heart attack."

"I was trying to put him out of my mind and now *this*. Damn, my head hurts."

"Tom can take care of himself. He's too smart to let Big Jake screw with him. I'm sure they'll work things out. If they don't, there's nothing you can do about it anyway."

"But he's screwing with them like he's screwing with us. He could end up breaking them up."

"Don't forget, Rosetta's been telling us for a long time things haven't been good between them."

"I know, but Big Jake's a blood sucking leech. He just wants to suck the life out of everyone."

"We at least know he ain't here bothering us."

"There's gotta be something we can do?"

"There's no arguing with you. Just do it."

"Do what?"

"Whatever you're going to do."

"He needs to be locked up like the ape he is. You know I've got enough shit on him in my head to do it."

"Without incriminating yourself?"

"No, I didn't say that."

"Well, you're not doing it. Thinking about it is insane. *Do you hear me?*"

"Yeah, I hear you."

"You're blowing this whole thing out of proportion. It sounds like Big Jake may not have even been behind Tom's problem. And every shadow you see is Big Jake. You're going to be flipping out on me if you don't get control of yourself. *Do you hear me?*"

"Alright, why don't we do this? We're going to Rosetta's graduation anyway, so why don't we take an extended trip to visit and see if we can help. It'll be like a vacation. Right?"

"Don't sound like a vacation, but let's do it. Rosetta keeps asking us to come to visit."

"We won't stay with her since she has this cop boyfriend and all."

"That's fine. We'll just have to cover all our bases here before we go."

"It won't be a problem. We'll do it. I got to get rid of this headache."

"Then it's settled. At work today, we'll make all the arrangements. Come on, we're running late. And please take something for your headache. Do you hear me?"

Getting out of bed, he said, "I'm up. Yeah, I'm up alright, up to my head in shit."

That morning, Big Jake received a phone call at his Springfield Hilton Hotel room waking him. His wife was crying. "It's David," she said. "He's threatening to *kill himself* if you don't let him see his boyfriend. His friends are afraid to talk to him because of you. Please change your mind. I'm scared he'll do something to himself."

"Calm down I'll take care of it."

"Can you come home?"

251

"Is he home?"

"He's in his room."

"Just let me talk to him."

"I'll get him," she said, going up to his room. "David, your dad's on the phone and wants to talk to you."

"I won't talk to him."

"Please."

"No."

Picking up the phone in his room, she said, "He won't talk to you."

"I'll be home tomorrow. I have loose ends to deal with here."

"But I'm afraid."

"Tell him when I see him tomorrow that we'll talk about me changing my mind."

"Do you mean it?"

"Just tell it to him. Okay? I've got to go."

"Okay."

Getting out of bed, Big Jake's head throbbed. Taking painkillers, he ate breakfast at the hotel and left. While driving to the club, he saw a sign flashing – *Gypsy Rose Lee's Fortune Telling*, as he had every time he left the hotel en-route to his club. Feeling like he was coming unraveled, on impulse, he turned into the parking lot and sat staring at the sign for a moment. Getting out of the car, he went up to the door, and a smiling plump, thirty-year-old woman greeted him. "Please come in," she said.

Looking her over, Big Jake said, "Now this isn't a bunch of bullshit is it?"

"Oh no," she replied.

"It better not be."

"Here's our services and prices," she said pointing to a wall poster.

"I don't care about the price. Just tell me something about my future."

"Follow me," she said, leading him to another room. "Have a seat." She grabbed his hand and looked at the lines in the palm. "Oh, my."

"What?" he said.

"You have very strong lines and your life line is long. You have a long life ahead of you."

"That's good. What else?"

"I see problems in this wavy line."

"Yeah," he blurted.

"You're very stressed. You have big responsibilities. Yes indeed. I can feel it and I'm seeing a picture."

"What?"

"Something bad could happen if you don't slow down. You're rushing to make decisions. You need to back off."

"What specifically do you see?"

"It's fuzzy, but," she said, noticing his wedding ring, "your wife is involved."

"*And?*" he raved, seeing someone from the corner of his eye, peeking from behind a curtain.

"I see kids."

"Oh yeah," he said, frowning. "It's my daughter, right?"

"Definitely."

"You lying piece of shit," he seethed, grabbing her arm. "I don't have no daughter."

A young man sprang from behind the curtain yelling, "*Get your hands off of her.*" When he grabbed Big Jake, Big Jake pounded his fist against the man's face, knocking him down. He then stomped on his head and pulled him to his feet by the hair. "Don't," the man pleaded.

"Don't my ass," Big Jake said, ramming his fist into the man's face knocking him out. Seeing the woman making a phone call, he leaped, grabbed her hair and flung her across the room. "You lousy bitch." As she moaned, he crushed her cell phone with his foot, picked it up and threw it against the wall. "You don't fuck with me," he yelled, backing toward the door and then slammed it behind him.

Speeding off, he cussed all the way to his club. Making sure Chastity and Candy were there for him, he had one of his men pick them up. When he arrived, they were waiting outback smoking cigarettes. After going to his office, he waited for them. Showing up with suppressed smiles, they knocked on his door. On opening it, he stared at them in disgust. "We're here," Candy said.

"Both of you. S*it down*," he ordered.

Looking frightened, they did as they were told. "Something wrong?" Candy asked.

"We had this tough guy asking about Chastity last night. He accused me of trying to blackmail him with a photo. You know what I'm talking about *don't you*?"

Chastity looked on speechless and Candy said, "I'm not sure."

"Should I refresh your memory? Cherry told me a little tale last night since this knucklehead recognized her from a photo supposedly taken here. Can you imagine that?"

"Well," Candy paused while Chastity held back a smile.

"*Well, my ass*. What's the story? And I don't want to hear no bullshit."

"It's like this," Candy said. "We were just having some fun." While she explained what happened and what they did, Big Jake paced, listening and nodding with an occasional grunt.

"I don't need people snooping around asking questions. You just opened the door for that. *Damn it anyhow*. I don't need this shit. Do you hear me?"

"Yes," said Candy.

"I want to hear from you," he said to Chastity.

"Yeah, sure. Whatever you say."

"So you ready to go down across the border? I'll make arrangements."

"Where's that?"

"Mexico. The land of the Tequila sun."

"You were talking about China before."

"They're dragging their feet. You've forced my hand with this bullshit you've created. I can't take it. You need to disappear. Vamoose. Comprende that?"

"Can't I just stay here?"

"*Hell no*. You want to work or not. Or I can put you out on the street."

254

"Well yeah, but Mexico. I know the dope is good, but aren't there bad things going on?"

"It's just like the states. Don't worry about it."

"Can one of the girls go with me?"

"I'm in no mood for hassles. Understand?"

"I guess," Chastity said.

"That's a yes, right?"

"Yes."

"Good. No more shit from either of you. Am I clear?" As they nodded, he said, "Get out of here."

While Tom continued to sleep, Rosetta drove over to talk to Amy who was surprised to hear Tom had spent the night at her place. "I want you to know, Tom talked to a girl at that club last night who practically admitted he was set-up."

"Can he prove it?" she asked. "I mean he said, she said, can only go so far. The photos say a lot more than words. "See for yourself." Grabbing an envelope, she handed it to Rosetta who examined the photos. "Like they say, a picture's worth a thousand words. Especially with no proof."

"I think he looks drugged. And you know my experience with drugs."

"I know, but –"

"*Chastity has pulled shit before.* Do you put it past her to do something like this?"

"No, but I don't know what to believe. If there was proof, I'd feel better. Plus, I think you know things haven't been all that great between Tom and me."

"I know, but don't use this as an excuse to end things. Want proof. I'll get proof."

"How?"

"I just have an idea. Let me take one of the photos with everyone in it. Which one's Chastity?"

"Now don't do anything stupid. Hear me?"

"I don't do stupid things anymore. I have a cop boyfriend. I'll show it to him."

"So what are you thinking of doing?"

"You know what they say. Where there is a will, there is a way."

"I don't know what you're thinking, but *he* needs to prove it to me."

"While we're trying to sort things out can he come home?"

"He infuriates me."

"Give him the benefit of the doubt. Something will break to prove it. That is unless you're looking for an excuse to break up?"

"I'm not. Just tell him to come home for now."

"Thanks, Amy. Please work things out. I mean it."

"We'll see."

When Rosetta returned home, she found Tom up, looking like he had taken a beating, but smiled on seeing her. "I'm sorry about last night," he said. "I should have never called."

"You did the right thing."

"I know but –"

"*But nothing.* I just spoke to Amy. It's okay to go home."

"What did you say? What did she say?"

"I told her about the proof."

"You didn't say anything about the lap dance?"

"Of course not and it shouldn't matter considering everything."

"I just don't want to fuel her fire. But what did she say?"

"I'll be honest. She doesn't want to accept that as proof. You know, *he said, she said* doesn't cut it with her."

"Do I need to go grab this rotten girl and take her to Amy?"

"Don't do that. I'll get Mike to help out. I've got one of the photos. Here," she said, holding it and showing it to him. "Point out the girl you talked to. Amy already pointed out Chastity to me."

"For Christ sake," he said, looking at the photo. "My pants are down."

"I didn't look," she said, trying to keep from smiling. "So which one is she?"

Tom pointed her out and said, "Is Mike going to talk to her?"

"Probably, but we'll take care of it. Hear me?"

"I need a shower and a change of clothes."

"Shower here."

"That's okay, if I can go home, I'll shower and change there. I guess I better go."

"Not until you tell me about my little baby."

"What?" he said perplexed.

"You said something about my little boy last night. You've seen him haven't you?"

"I was drunk."

"Don't lie to me Tom. Tell me the truth."

"Holy shit. Alright. I can't lie. Your little boy," he paused. "He's living at the children's home. Unbelievable, huh?"

"What?" she said stunned. "I don't understand. Why?"

"You're not going to like this. All the documentation's there. It's him. I don't know what to say, but –"

"You've got to tell me. Please."

"It's not pleasant."

"I don't care."

"His adoptive parents gave him up when he was a year and a half old. They said he was – well, out of control. They couldn't handle him. He's been in many foster homes, but no one could deal with his behaviors."

"Have you seen him?"

"Yes, I was there when he was admitted."

"What does he look like? How's he doing? I want to see him."

"Do you really want to do this to yourself?"

"Tell me."

"He looks a lot like you with the dark hair."

"Does he have blue eyes like me? They were blue when he was born."

"He has dark eyes like Gomez's. Baby's eyes can change you know."

"I know. Where's he at?"

"You know the large, old, brick building where I work."

"Yeah."

257

"There's a smaller building behind it. That's where he's at."

"I want to see him," she said. "Maybe from a distance at least. Can I see him today?"

"If you're there at three o'clock, you'll see him dropped off from his therapy session at the front of the back building. He has serious problems."

"It's all my fault giving him up. Are you sure it's him?"

"Yes. Don't do this to yourself. Come on now. I mean it. I don't have to leave yet. Do you want to talk?"

"I'm fine. Go home."

After Tom left, she was in great awe thinking about seeing her son but knew she had to do it.

Greeted with coldness when he returned home, Tom cleaned up and prepared for work. Fearing to say anything, he hoped the chill from Amy would thaw, but prepared for a heat wave of torment. When he saw her sitting, nose in a book reading and ignoring him, he went to his computer and clicked on the new novel file. Once it opened, his fingers were like dancing elves working there magic, as sentence after sentence rolled off heartfelt emotions and uncontrollable rage.

Big Jake returned home to deal with his son. Before getting out of the car, he finished a phone conversation making what he considered appropriate arrangements to resolve David's issues. His wife, Gail, cornered him when he walked in the door. "I've been a nervous wreck," she said. "I don't know if he's serious about his threats, but he scares me. He won't unlock his door. He says you're a maniac and he has nothing to live for."

"I'm dealing with it. He'll be leaving with me soon."

"For where?"

"For therapy. I made an appointment for him with one of the best nut doctor's around."

"Really?"

"You bet. So he's locked himself in his room?"

"Yes," she said surprised by his actions.

"Don't worry about it," he said going up the steps. "Just stay down here while I talk to him."

Going up to his son's room, he turned the door handle to no avail. "David," Big Jake said.

"I don't want to talk to you."

"Come on, open up."

"No."

"I'm having a change of heart about things. Don't you want to talk about it?"

"You mean I can see him?"

"Maybe, but there's something you need to do first."

"What?"

"Let me in and we'll talk."

Standing, waiting, the door unlocked and David opened it. "You better not be lying," he said. "So what do I have to do?"

"Just come with me. You're going to see a therapist. She's great. Believe me, you won't be sorry."

"Then you'll let me be myself?"

"Then you can be super stud or whatever the hell you want."

"You want me to come now?"

"You have an appointment right now. So let's go."

A half-hour later, Big Jake pulled up in a BMW at an old two-story building, located in a rundown neighborhood. Getting out of the car, David's eyes wandered with a concerned look but followed his dad up a flight of wooden stairs. Knocking at the door, an attractive young woman in a suit opened it. "You must be David," she said. He smiled. "Big Jake why don't you come back in an hour."

"You're in good hands," he said, patting him on the shoulder. "I'll be back."

"Follow me, David," she said, "I'm Doctor Cynthia." He followed her into another room where a sofa sat. "Come on, sit down," she said, sitting herself down on the sofa. He stood petrified, unable to move until she grabbed his arm pulling him down. "I want you to relax. I'm here to help you. You've been having some problems I understand."

"Yeah, with my dad. Otherwise, I'm fine."

"Come closer," she said, "you need to loosen up." Moving next to him, she put her hands on his shoulders and began massaging them. "How does that feel?"

"I don't know," he said, shaking, surprised to see a tattoo on the back of her neck as she bent forword. Nothing was adding up in his mind, but David went along, too fearful to resist.

"Turn around so I can work those muscles loose." He did as requested. "So I hear you got a boyfriend?"

"Yes and my dad don't understand."

"So you don't like girls?"

"No, I like my boyfriend."

"I bet you've never been with a girl have you?" she said. "Come on, follow me." Leading him into another room, she said, "Lay down on the therapy table."

"Therapy table," he said, noticing the table with sheets and the stand next to it with a vase of artificial flowers in it.

"I understand your problem. I want to help."

"Yeah but I thought we were going to talk?"

"We are talking. Go ahead lay down. I'll be back in a minute. Just close your eyes and relax. I'll be right back. Don't open them, okay? Think pleasant thoughts. It's part of the therapy."

He did as asked, while she went to another room. When she returned, she said, "Keep your eyes closed and give me your hand." Taking his hand, she pressed it against her bare chest. What do you feel?"

Shaking, he said, "I don't know. I'm afraid."

"You can open your eyes."

On opening them, his heart fluttered, as she stood there naked. Jerking his hand away from her breast, she straddled him causing him to feel like he was suffocating. "We're going to turn you straight," she said, lying on top of him, unzipping his pants as he shook like a mouse smothered by a cat's paw.

An hour later, Big Jake returned with a big smile on his face. Opening the door, he stopped to listen and was surprised to hear weeping. Moving to the back room, where the sound came from, he stood alarmed, eyes on his crying son, standing over the lifeless body of the girl bleeding from the head. A trail of blood flowed from her head to a smashed vase ten feet away.

"What the *hell* have you done? Shit almighty!" he screamed, taking out his phone and making a call. "We need a cleanup crew right away. Bring a complete set of clothes for my son, including shoes ..." David dropped to his knees and buried his head weeping. "Listen to me. Nothing happened. Do you hear me?"

Chapter 21

Andre and Windy sat waiting for the long flight to the Midwest, which included a stopover in Dallas in-route to Springfield, Illinois. While reading the newspaper, Andre could not help looking over his shoulder from time to time, wondering if Big Jake's creeps were on his trail. Taking a moment to smile at Windy was short lived when his phone rang, causing his heart to flutter as he grabbed his phone, saying, "Hello."

"Have you left yet?"

"Just waiting to board the plane," he said, taking in a deep breath. "What's going on?"

"Andre," said Rosetta, "you won't believe what Tom told me today."

"Oh?"

"My baby's at the home he works at. The adoptive parents gave him up ... *I'm going to go see him,*" she said, excited. "You know, I need to do it. But I'll do it from a distance. Don't you think that's the best way? Or should I go up and talk to him. *I don't know what to do?*"

"Calm down. Take it slow. There is plenty of time to sort everything out. Where do you want to go with this? "

"What do you mean?"

"First of all, can you handle it?"

"I don't know. That's what I'm going to find out."

"Be careful because I can tell you're very emotional about this right now."

"I just want to see him."

"I know. I wouldn't try talking to him now. Think about it. What would you say? You can't just go up and start talking. You need to go through proper channels. Do you hear me?"

"I guess," she said, then pouted.

"I mean it. Don't act impulsively. In fact, I don't think you should even try seeing him until you've had time to think about it."

"That's all I've done. I don't know if I can help myself."

"Talk it over with Tom and Amy."

"I don't know. Things are so messed up with them right now. Tom got plastered last night, stayed the night at my place. They're really struggling to deal with this mess."

"Just hold off a day. We'll be there tonight. We can talk about it later. There's no rush. You hear me?"

"I hear you but my heart's pounding away. You know what I mean?"

"I know you're going to do it. Just don't try talking to him. Okay?"

"Okay," she sighed. "I better let you go. See you tonight. Call me when you get in. I mean it ..."

After hanging up, Windy questioned Andre about the call, and he gave a detailed account of Rosetta's emotional state. "The poor girl," Windy said. "She's torn. I know what she's going through. I still think about my kids being taken away from me. I was a bad mother then. I guess that's why I'm doing what I am now. I'm trying to make up for my past mistakes. It's hard. She's really stressed over it. I know she is. She'll go there today. You know she will."

"I know. I just hope she can deal with it."

"She can't. That's why she called."

"That's not all that's an issue. Tom and Amy are really struggling. He got drunk last night ..."

At 2:45 PM, Rosetta pulled into the children's home drive and followed it past the main building. When the small brick structure came into view, her foot slid off the accelerator letting the sports car creep to a halt twenty feet from the entrance. Gazing at the doorway, phone in hand; she opened and closed it unable to focus, but managed to send Mike a text message. Nibbling on a fingernail, wondering what he would look like, she remembered his birth: Out in the woods alone; terrified, excruciating labor pains, unknown creatures lurking about as she pushed to free him. "The Indian way," she thought, thinking of being kidnapped from the hospital by a mentally deranged Gomez, obsessed with an imagined Indian heritage, and then dumped in secluded woods to deliver the baby. Snapping back to the present, eyes opening, she pulled on the door handle but froze unable to move. Eyes on the clock, it was minutes away until he was to arrive. Swallowing hard, labored breathing, a bead of sweat trickled down her face, to upper lip, and was then stopped by a restless tongue, absorbing the salty drip. After several deep breaths, she gained control but stayed seated. Watching the clock, 3:00 PM came and then 3:05 PM crept up. Unable to sit still, she pushed the door open, stepped out in a hypnotic state drawn toward the building. A minute later, a car came up from behind passing and stopping ten feet away. A woman got out, opened the passenger door and out stepped a young boy. Paralyzed, Rosetta noticed his dark wavy hair and large dark eyes that flashed up staring at her. Unable to breathe, she watched the boy break free from the worker. Within seconds, he grabbed her leg, squeezing as if magnetized to it.

"I'm sorry, I'm sorry," the worker repeated.

"That's okay," Rosetta said, touching the boy's shoulders, as the woman pulled him away. "It's okay," she repeated, feeling the small hands pull away. "What's your name?" she blurted.

"Aaron," he said. "I like you. I know who you are. I like you."

"Stop it," said the woman. "I'm sorry." Dragging the boy away, Rosetta looked on, mouth open like a Venus fly trap, as the door shut with them disappearing. Weeping, she hurried to the car, got in, unable to control herself, and drove dazed with tears running down her face. Too emotional to drive, she stopped in front of the main building of the children's home, parked and drifted away rethinking what had just happened. Opening the door, she was drawn into the building, asked for a job application, and returned to the car.

Tommy Wizel sneaked up on Tom who sat at the front desk staring out the window not realizing Rosetta had just parked nearby. "What's up beside the sky?" Tommy whispered in his ear.

"Huh?" said Tom.

"I think we need to have a therapy session."

"It's that noticeable?" said Tom.

"What do you mean?"

"You think I need therapy?"

"No, I need therapy."

"Oh, yeah sure. Well, let's go to my office," he said, noticing that things were calm and that other staff were around. Leading the way to the office, Tom shut the door and they began. "So what's on your mind besides the sky?"

"I was reading a passage by Professor Frantic last night that got me thinking about you," he said, holding onto the book. "You know, you seem to be in a daze a lot lately like you're worrying."

"Well, I don't know, but what's the passage?"

"I'll read it, okay?"

"Go for it."

"It's wild," he said, opening the book and began reading out loud:

The problem with worrying is that it usually leads to mind-boggling disasters. And since you are a reader of this book, I suspect your thoughts are creeping up to remind you of your dreaded fears. If that is the case: Your paranoia is real. The sky is falling. There is no way out. People are conspiring against you. People are talking about you behind your back. Murphy's Law is reality. The men in the white coats are really coming to take you away. However, you do have a choice – to worry or not to worry. I think not to worry is the wise choice. Please, do not worry about this or else you have missed the point and are doomed to the schizophrenic mumble jumble, which means they are coming to take you away, ha, ha.

"That is wild," said Tom. "Were you really thinking about me when you read that? You know, the way I've been lately, I can't blame you. Sometimes I feel like the sky is falling."

Rereading the last lines to himself, Tommy said, "You've missed the point."

"I can't argue with that. I've missed a lot of points."

"Stop worrying about it because when you do, the schizoid mumble jumble takes over your mind. You look like a zombie 'cause you keep worrying about it."

"So who's giving the therapy here? You or me?"

"Why you are."

"How do you figure?"

"Because I'm worrying about it means that I'm screwed up. So I need help. You get what I mean?"

"We all need help, but let's not worry about it. Do you follow me?"

"Thanks, I needed your insight."

Smiling, Tom said, "You're trying to push me over the edge aren't you?"

"You're on the edge too?"

"Forget it Tommy, you're driving me *insane*."

"How do you think I feel?"

"Tell me."

"Sometimes I feel like the men in the white coats are *really* going to take me away."

"Why's that?"

"'Cause people are always talking behind my back."

"Oh yeah?"

"Kids and staff think I'm nuts, don't they? Don't lie."

"Not true. You want nuts. I'll give you nuts," he said springing up. "I won't lie. The secret behind a lie is when no one knows the truth the lie becomes the truth, which means the lie is no longer a lie and becomes fact. So let it be said that I do not lie about the truth unless the truth is a lie. Need I say more? I rest my case."

"*Bravo, bravo*," Tommy gleamed, shuffling his feet. "Professor Frantic couldn't have said it better. I'm a believer. If what you just said is a lie, then I give up and don't give a flying rat's ass out of hell. Thanks. I mean it. You really helped to screw my head on right today. You're really good Tom."

"Think so?"

"*Hot damn*," Tommy said, giving him a high five. "*You're the man.*"

"Alright then, let's not think about it. You ready to get out of here? It's getting stuffy."

"Let's do it."

Returning to the unit, Tom went to the window staring out thinking about what had just been said. Noticing the parked sports car, he looked closer and realized it was Rosettas. Glancing at his watch, he knew that she had come to see Aaron. When he noticed someone was in the car, he rushed out of the building. Reaching the car, he tapped on the window as Rosetta was looking over the home's job application. She jumped, turned the application over hiding it from Tom and then rolled down the window.

"So did you see him?"

"Yes," she said with a nervous smile.

"Are you okay?"

"Yeah."

"You can't lie to me. I know better."

"Is it that obvious?"

"Yes, it is."

"I'll be okay. It was just a shock. I don't know what to do. "

"How close did you get?"

"He ran up to me and grabbed my leg."

"And?"

"I froze."

"I know it's hard, but the boy has major problems. Believe me."

"Like Gomez and –," she stammered. "And like me, huh?"

"You're doing great. You were a wreck when you came to us. Remember?"

"Sometimes you don't want to remember. But you know what, you're right. I was a mess. I had major problems. Didn't I?"

"That's right."

"That's what you just said about my little boy. If I am so much better, I guess he can get there too."

"Of course he can. I didn't mean it was hopeless. I don't know what you're thinking, but leave it to the professionals to deal with him."

"Yeah, you're right," she said with cynicism. "An institution makes a fine parent."

"You're right, it doesn't. I don't know what to tell you."

"There's nothing you can say. Forget about me, I'm concerned about you and Amy."

"I know we need to work things out. Don't worry about us. Hear me? Hey, you have a big day coming up. You're a college graduate and I'm really proud of you."

"You'll be at my graduation won't you?"

"Wouldn't miss it for anything."

"Thanks. I better go. Please work things out with Amy."

"Grabbing Chastity and making her tell Amy the truth is the only thing left. I'd probably end up in jail."

"Back off from Chastity, I've got an idea."

"What's that?"

"If she told me the truth," Rosetta said, "Amy would believe me wouldn't she?"

"And why would she tell you?"

"Just wait and see."

"I don't know what you're thinking. Just don't mess around with Big Jake. Got me? I mean it now."

"Don't worry about me. Just work things out with Amy. Oh, Andre and Windy are coming into town."

"When?"

"Flying in tonight. We'll all have to get together. Talk to you later."

Nodding his head, Tom watched Rosetta back the car up and leave. As Rosetta drove home, she received a phone call from Mike who explained that he was tied up on a new investigation and that he would call later. "My head's ready to explode," she thought, "I can't think about my boy right now. I've got to help Tom. All I have is jeans and lady type dresses. Need to stop and find a sexy dress. Yeah, that's what I'll do. They want to play games, I'll play. I'll play to win. I hate the thought of dressing like that. You can do it. It's for Tom and Amy. I can't sit back any longer. Big Jake you've ruined too many lives. I'll get the proof. So help me, I will."

Stopping at a department store, Rosetta searched the young ladies section for a seductive, revealing dress, but could not find the right one. On a whim, she grabbed the closest dress to her wants and got it in a size smaller. In the dressing room, she slipped into the tight-knit red dress revealing a good amount of cleavage and a lot of legs. At last satisfied, she purchased it, went home, fitted into the tight dress and caked make-up on. "You look like a whore," she told herself. "What would Mike think if he saw you? What would he do if he knew what I was planning? He wouldn't let me so it's good that he don't know. It's best no one knows." Looking herself over in the mirror, brought back unpleasant memories of drug addiction, coerced prostitution and of a past she had hoped not to revisit. "You have no choice," she assured herself. "You're going to help Tom and Amy and if you're lucky you might be able to bring that lousy creep down to size. Jake the snake you've met your match. I'm not afraid of you. I've dealt with snakes like you before. I was a mess back then and still crushed another creepy snake. Yeah, my pimp boyfriend needed to be stopped too." Staring off thinking, she flashed back to the other creepy snake from years earlier:

"I see you," she screamed, hallucinating in her drug induced mind, watching her boyfriend's pet snake escape from its cage and slither across the floor. Rushing to it, seeing its eyes change to an indigo blue, resembling her boyfriend's, she stomped on its head until it was lifeless. With glazed eyes, she poured a shot of Southern Comfort Whiskey and downed it. After pouring another one, she picked up a number of unsorted pills, pushed them in her mouth, and flushed them down. Walking a straight line to the bathroom, she got a needle and a magic marker, disrobed and printed the word damned around her belly button. Then with the needle, she jabbed around to make sure the red ink was thoroughly absorbed. Satisfied with the acupuncture, she began to trace a line down to her crotch when unexpectedly she heard someone at the door trying to unlock it. Anticipating Stretch walking in, she grabbed the snake, staggered toward the door, robe half-open and enraged. Awaiting his entrance, she flung the snake backward holding on to it like a bat, and in a cocked position, she clobbered Stretch, lashing at him over and over as if the snake were a whip. Backing up with each blow, he retreated, but Rosetta kept coming at him whipping away as he backed down the hallway and out of the building.

"Please Rosetta," Stretch pleaded, "calm down."

"What kind of boyfriend are you pimping me out you sicko freak?" she bellowed, with onlookers, gawking at them. "I thought I just got through stomping all over your head, you blue eyed rotten snake."

Shouting obscenities, grabbing hold of the snake, he tried yanking it, but her will and out of control body resisted.

Screaming, "You're dead!" Rosetta pushed, causing Stretch to back up into the street with her charging like a bull. Traffic stopped as they were in the middle of the street. Arguing and screaming at each other, onlookers stood watching while a person in their car called the police. Hearing sirens and seeing flashing lights rushing towards them, Stretch took off running. Rosetta stood in the middle of the street holding the dead snake, wearing an open robe revealing her nude body. As cars honked at Rosetta to move, she whipped the car in front of her with the snake. By the time the police arrived, Rosetta, exhausted, sat in the middle of the road crying still holding onto the dead snake.

Snapping out of the hypnotic state, panting, Rosetta gazed in the mirror at the trickling sweat across her forehead. "And then I was taken into custody," she told herself, "which eventually led me to Tom and Amy. Some things need forgetting. But look at you. Déjà vu. Just like the whore you were back then. All for that bastard Stretch. I don't need these memories. I don't know if I can do it. Just maybe you can help everybody by doing it. Even yourself if you can stick your foot up Big Jake's ass. I don't know. If I do it, I need to concentrate on helping Tom and Amy right now. You can't get sidetracked by your own demons. And then there's my son. Oh shit, it's more than I can handle right now.

Sorry baby but you're going to have to wait for now. But I won't forget you. Just go out and do what you have to do. They helped you get your head on straight. Now I'll help them."

Gail paced waiting for Big Jake to come home from one of his Chicago clubs. After glancing at the clock for the third time, she called him and learned that he was on his way. Returning upstairs, she went into David's room. Lying on the bed covered up, he whined and refused to go to school. "At least talk to me," she said. Grabbing and yanking at the cover, he held onto it. "I called your dad. Just tell me what's wrong?"

"Life," he blurted.

"I thought your dad worked things out for you?"

"He's made me crazy. I hate him."

"What happened?"

"Nothing will be the same. I should have killed myself when I had the chance. Then it wouldn't have happened."

"*What in the world happened?*"

"I became like him. A monster. My life's over."

"Please don't talk like that."

"Tell me what happened?" she said as the downstairs front door opened.

"There's nothing to tell. Dad turned me into a heterosexual. That's all. I like girls now. I just don't want to get out of bed."

"Well, your dad just walked in the door. You can tell it to him."

Stomping up the stairs, Big Jake grumbled under his breath. When he entered the room, he motioned for Gail to leave. Shutting the door, he went to David's side and yanked the covers off him. "I told you not to think about it. It didn't happen. Do you understand me? *It did not happen.*"

Looking up at his dad, he said, "Yes, it didn't happen."

"So why no school today?"

"You know why."

"No, I don't."

"Because of what happened."

Grabbing David's shoulders, he exploded, "*God bless it, David, nothing happened.*"

"Yeah right, nothing happened."

"So why no school today?"

"They had church and I didn't want to go."

"You like church."

"Not today. They were going to have us go to confession."

"So?"

"You know what I have to confess."

Letting loose of David, he pushed him down. "No David I don't know what you have to confess. Is there something you have to confess?"

With a blank stare, he said, "No, there's nothing to confess."

"Listen, you're sick today so just stay home. Is this *issue* settled?"

Nodding, he closed his eyes and covered his head.

Leaving the room, Big Jake went downstairs and confronted Gail. "Just leave him alone. He'll be okay."

"No he won't," said another son from the living room.

"*Don't bother him,*" Big Jake yelled. "I mean it."

"Did something happen?" whispered Gail. "He said you made him a heterosexual."

Whispering back, he said, "He always was, he was just confused. Everything's okay now."

"He's not okay," said the whispering voice of his son in the other room. "He's a *fairy.*"

Angered, Big Jake stormed into the living room raving, "Shut your mouth."

"I'm leaving, I'm leaving," he said, walking toward the front door.

Gail hurried to Big Jake, grabbing his arm. "Let him go," she said.

"He's not too big to put over my knee. Get out," he growled watching his son leave. Turning to his wife, he said, "I'm taking a plane to Springfield."

"Why?"

"Something's come up I need to deal with down there. I should be back in a couple of days."

"What about David?"

"He's okay. You hear me. He's okay. He just doesn't feel good today. "

Chapter 22

It was late afternoon when Rosetta crept into the garage, stood trembling with hand on the car door handle, but willed herself to open it and got in. The post office was the first place she stopped, dropping off the children's home application. With apprehension put in perspective, she was determined not to let it interfere with the mission at hand. As she pulled into The Lost Souls Club parking lot, a new sense of concern arose knowing there could be a danger. Being early, there were but a half-dozen parked cars and trucks. Looking in the rearview mirror, she cringed at the caked makeup and then turned the anguish off. On opening the car door, a foot at a time slid to the ground, as she stood, revealing well-proportioned legs in the short red dress. With the voluptuousness of Marilyn Monroe, she was dressed to kill, carrying a small purse while strutting in high heels toward the entrance. A man getting out of a car stopped dead, watching, enchanted by Rosetta's knockout appearance. She was putting on a show but had to do it. Walking toward the entrance; heart pounding, she wondered if the man she detested almost as much as her father would be present. Despite hating the facade, she kept control, determined to help Tom and Amy no matter what. At the entrance, stood a large man whose eyes feasted on every move she made. She smiled at him but avoided eye contact.

"Hello there," said the goggle-eyed man. "Never seen you before. But hot damn baby, hopefully, you're here looking for a job because I'd like to see more of you?"

"Maybe," she replied.

"Talk to Lee," he said opening the door.

Walking into the club, she scoped the place out and noticed a girl on the main stage performing. Despite the crimson atmosphere, heads were turning in her direction. Hungry eyes were all over her body, which made her want to turn around and run, but she was determined and stayed on course. It didn't take long for Lee, the club manager, to approach her.

"Hopefully you're looking for a job?" Lee said.

"You the manager?"

"That's me. My name's Lee."

"I thought someone named Big Jake was the boss here?"

"He's the owner. He'll be in later. But he has clubs around the country and is here just once in awhile. So I'm the man you need to deal with. More importantly, who are you?"

"I just might be looking for a job."

"Oh yes," he nodded with a big grin. "Come on. Let's go to my office and talk."

"Lead the way."

Walking by a room, Lee said, "That's Big Jake's office and here's mine. Come on," he said entering the room. He stood delighted as he looked Rosetta up and down. "Where have you been all my life?"

"So you like what you see?" she said.

"Oh yeah, baby. Why don't you show me more?"

"Oh, no," she said smiling.

"Thought you wanted a job?"

"Maybe, but I want to see your layout and meet your girls first."

"Well," he hesitated.

"Don't you think I'm worth pleasing?" she whispered, licking lips with hand on hip flaunting the curvature of her body.

"Well, I won't argue with you there," he said, eyes flickering in delight. "Aw, come on, I'll show you the layout and let you meet people." Leading the way, Rosetta followed. "How old are you anyway."

"Old enough."

"Perfect."

"It's a big club. Just lead the way."

"Sure thing. Come on."

At the children's home, things were quiet and Tom was desperate to unburden himself to Amy. Telling the other worker that he needed to go upstairs for awhile, he hurried there until near the entrance and then stopped to ask himself what he was going to say.

"I've got to make her believe me," he told himself. "I still love her. I think she loves me. But I'm not sure anymore. God bless it. What am I going to say? Maybe she doesn't want to know the truth. What if she just wants to break up? Get control of yourself." Moving through the entrance, he saw Amy talking to one of the girls up the hallway. Standing, waiting, he stuck his hands in his pockets, took them out and put them back in thinking of his next move. "Stay calm," he told himself. "Let her finish."

The girl talking to Amy noticed Tom and said, "Hey, your hubby's here."

"What?" from Amy.

"Tom's standing over there."

Amy looked and said, "Well, if we're done, I better see what he wants."

"Yeah, we're done."

Amy walked toward Tom who tried assessing her demeanor. "Smug looking," he thought. Prepared for the worse, he needed to air out his feelings. "We need to talk," he said.

"This isn't the time or place."

"Come on," he insisted grabbing her wrist. "Let's talk out in the hallway."

"Alright," she said, jerking away.

Once in the hallway, Tom stared into cold, unreceptive eyes. "Please listen to me. I think you know I was set up don't you?"

Head shaking she said, "I don't need this now."

"Do you even care about the truth?"

"Of course I do."

"You don't act like it."

"How am I supposed to act?" she sneered. "You practically had your mouth on her breast not to mention the other girls."

Stepping back, he said, "I don't believe you. You know there's no way I would mess with Chastity. She's a kid. A messed up kid. Give me a break. I'm not an idiot or some pervert. I wouldn't do that."

"But you'd have no problem messing with those other floozies in the picture now would you?"

"That's not what I said."

"Listen, I don't want to discuss it right now. We're getting too loud. I need time to think."

"Think about what? Burt?"

"What's that mean?"

"He was over at the house the night you kicked me out."

"So now you're spying on me," she hissed. *"Just get away from me."*

"No," he snapped back.

"Now look," she said seeing two girls walking their way. "Go."

Seeing the approaching girls, Tom sighed, turned and walked away.

Lee led the way, having given Rosetta a tour of the public part of the club. Entering the dressing rooms, he showed her the costumes, and then entered the room where Chastity sat talking to one of the girls. Rosetta recognized Chastity from the photo but acted indifferently. "This is Ginger and Chastity," he said.

"You both performers?" said Rosetta.

"I am," said Ginger. "I'm up next."

"I work back here," said Chastity.

"Yeah, and we're going to miss her," Ginger added.

"Oh?" from Rosetta.

Smiling, Chastity said, "I'll be going to Mexico real soon to become a star."

"Enough," said Lee. "She's not interested in your aspirations."

"Sure I am."

"Well, enough has been said," said Lee, leading the way out. "So what do you think?"

"If you don't mind, I'd like to hang around and just get a feel for things?"

"Drinks are on the house. Let me know what you want to do."

"Good. I'll let you know."

Lee walked away and Rosetta moved to a corner trying to be inconspicuous as she waited for Ginger to start her performance. When Ginger stepped out on the stage, the girl leaving the stage went out into the audience to congregate rather than going backstage. Inspecting the club, Rosetta hurried along the wall toward the backstage entrance, as the patrons were eyeing the dancer. Sneaking to the back, she peeked around a corner to make sure Chastity was alone and entered the room.

Chastity smiled on seeing her. "So you working here now?"

"Yeah," Rosetta said. "Where does that door go to?"

"To the back parking lot."

"Can you do me a favor and let me borrow one of your cigarettes."

"Sure."

"Come on show me out back and I'll light up."

"I can use a smoke too," she said, leading the way.

Once outside, Rosetta and Chastity lit their cigarettes. Rosetta, a nonsmoker, faked smoking and began talking. "I heard you like to have a good time around here. One of the girls told me about a prank you pulled on a guy the other night. Do you do stuff like that a lot around here?"

"You talking about the *photos*?"

"Yeah."

"Oh no, Big Jake blew a fizzy when he heard about it. He scares me sometimes."

"So why do you want to go to Mexico?"

"I can break in as a stripper down there. You know I'm only fifteen, but I am an emancipated minor. It's just that he wants me to break in at a club down there. I don't get it, but it's a chance to see another country."

"Listen girl. You don't have any idea what you're getting yourself into. What you need to do is leave with me before it's too late."

"Whataya mean?"

"He traffics teens to other countries to make prostitutes out of them."

"How do you know that?"

"Because years ago he bought me when I was your age and tried sending me to another country to be a prostitute."

"Why are you telling me this?"

"Because I want to ring your neck on one hand, but don't want to see your life flushed down the toilet. Just come with me. I'll get you away from this mess. You can stay at my place for now."

"But I love this business and I want to become a star."

"Staying alive is more important don't you think?"

"Why should I believe you?"

"Because I went down the road you're headed."

"I don't know what to think. You said you work here now."

Stomping out the cigarette, Rosetta said, "Believe me, I'm trying to help you."

"Let me think about it."

"I give up. Don't believe me," Rosetta said. "It's your life. Walk away from me and you may never be heard from again."

"No, I better stay. I think you're wrong. Besides, I don't even know you."

"*Fine,* but you are going to do one thing for me."

"What?"

Pulling out a cell phone, Rosetta entered a number, and then grabbed Chastity's wrist. "I'm calling Amy Paradisio right now and you are going to tell her the truth of what happened to Tom."

"*No way.* How do you know their names?"

With a tightening grip, Rosetta said, "You don't want to mess with me. I will put you down on the ground and hurt you if you don't."

Resisting, trying to pull away, Rosetta grabbed the back of her hair, clamping down hard. "Okay, okay," she squirmed. "I'll do it."

Rosetta called Amy at the children's home saying that she was with Chastity who wanted to explain what had happened to Tom. Struggling to get all the details out, Rosetta kept a tight grip until she had told the entire truth including having drugged Tom. After hanging up, they both returned inside the building.

"I don't get it," Chastity said. "If you're working here why do you want me to leave?"

"I'm not working here. I wanted to spare you from a lot of misery. You change your mind, get a hold of Amy and she'll contact me. Don't wait until it's too late." Two of the showgirls walked in the room and Rosetta nodded saying, "I'm leaving, take me serious." Walking out of the room, she returned to the club. Satisfied with her accomplishment, she still wanted to find something incriminating on Big Jake. Seeing Lee preoccupied on the other side of the club, moving like a sly fox along the wall toward the backroom offices, she ducked into the dark hallway and found Big Jake's office locked. However, Lee's office was unlocked. Going in, she shut the door, turned on the light and searched through the desk drawers. Looking at the door, she saw keys hanging next to it and went to them and discovered that they were labeled. Big Jake's office and desk key were there and she grabbed them. Going into his office, she locked the door, flicked the light on and began searching. In a closet, she found clothes hanging, but was soon looking through a large desk. A smile erupted on finding the photo she sent to him. Pulling it out of the drawer, she set it on the desk staring at it. Disappointed in not finding anything else, Rosetta sat on the desk chair thinking. Hearing a noise in the next room, she locked the desk, scrambled to turn the light off and then hid in the closet. Shaking, she took slow deep breaths. Fifteen minutes passed and she could still hear voices next door, but couldn't make anything out. On hearing the office door open, her heart thumped like a startled beaver slapping its tail against the water.

"Finish the arrangements," Big Jake said to Lee.

"Everything is under control. I'll get back with you when all the details are finalized."

Big Jake closed the door and before he could sit down, his cell phone rang. "Yeah," he said … "Alright, alright, I'll talk to him. He's not going to kill himself. Do you hear me? Put him on."

"Dad," David whined after his mom left, "I want to turn myself in. I killed her."

"David you listen to me," he said pacing. "You didn't kill her. It was an accident."

"No, I don't think so. She put her hands on my thing. I told her to stop but she wouldn't. I pleaded and pleaded. She said she had to do it. I couldn't take it. I grabbed the vase and made her stop. Blood was everywhere. I can't get it out of my head. It wasn't an accident. I knew that tattoo on her neck was a bad sign. She wasn't no doctor."

"You're right. Knock the crap off. She was just a whore. You make me sick David. You're my son and you act like shit almighty, I don't want to even think of it. You understand? She didn't exist. She's ten feet under never to be found again. There never was a woman. Put it out of your mind for good."

"I need to see my friend. He'll understand."

"Don't push things right now. Your little faggot friend is the reason all this happened. Stop scaring your mom with your talk. We'll talk about your friend when I get home. Okay?"

"I hate you."

"Get your mom and put her back on the phone."

David yelled for his mom to get the phone. A moment later, Gail said, "Please come home."

"If he continues to act up, I want you to call Lonnie. He'll deal with David. I'll talk to Lonnie."

"Alright," she said frustrated, hanging up.

With a grumbling sigh, he plopped down in his desk chair. Sitting back he closed his eyes. On opening them, he saw the photo of his scalping setting out causing him to jerk back. "What the shit?" he growled. "Why is it out? Or is it a new one?" Opening the desk drawer, he realized it was not there. "What the hell is going on? Did I leave it out? So much shit has gone on I guess I could have. Am I losing my mind? I can't take it …" Lost in thought, Big Jake jumped on hearing the sound of a phone ringing. "What?" he blurted. Rosetta scrambled to turn the phone off, but several rings had Big Jake looking around his office and opening the closet. "*Who in the hell are you?*" he said as she pulled the phone out of a small purse.

In awe, she stood facing Big Jake for the very first time. "I'm a, I'm hiding."

"I see that. How did you get in here?"

"The door was open."

"So what the hell are you hiding from?"

"A guy was chasing me through the club. I ducked back here and hid."

"This is crazy. I don't know what to believe. Stay put," he said making a phone call. "Get back to my office right now." Hanging up, he said, "Something is screwy here."

Thinking he had called Lee, she said, "I was here looking for a job. This guy wouldn't leave me alone so I ran back here and hid."

Walking in, Lee said, "So you met our future star."

"What the hell is the deal with her?"

"She said she might want to work here so I showed her around."

"Why in the flying shit was she hiding in my office?"

"You didn't let her in?"

"Hell no. She said she ran from some guy and hid in the closet. Was my office unlocked?"

"No, no way."

"Check on your wall for the master key."

Lee left and Rosetta stayed calm. "I'll get out of here," she said bold-faced. "The guy's probably gone now."

"Just hold on."

Lee returned and said, "The key to your office and desk are missing."

"Give me your purse," he commanded and she handed it to him. "Empty." Walking up to Rosetta, he started patting her down. "I'll give you this, you're one dressed to kill bitch. No pockets, huh? Let's see what's down the front of your dress," he said, reaching for it. Backing away, hands up, she blocked his advance. "Cooperate or I'll pull your dress off." Grabbing the dress at the waist, he pulled her close to him and she pushed away. "Stop it," she whined as he put his hand down the front of the dress.

"What do I have here?" he said pulling out keys. "So who the *fuck* are you?"

"I was looking for work and," she hesitated.

"*And my ass,*" he said, grabbing her neck. "The bullshit is over. The truth. And give me your phone."

282

"Okay, okay," she said handing it to him and watched him put it in his pants pocket. Eyeing the photo on his desk, she cracked a smile. "It's all about a scalping. Isn't it?"

Letting loose of Rosetta, Big Jake looked down at the photo with frustration. "Lee, get out of here. I'll deal with this." Lee left and Big Jake picked up the photo. "Did you have something to do with this?"

"Yeah, you bet I did. I'm your damn conscience."

"*What do you mean?*" he roared.

"You think you're unstoppable? Who do you think you are? God?"

"Who the hell are you?"

"Just one of a list of people you've tried to destroy."

"Screw you because I'm not done yet."

"Maybe not, but you are stoppable. Gomez came close to stomping you out. Didn't he?"

"Did you send this to me?" he said, frowning as he picked up the photo.

"We all sent it to you."

"*We?*" he said, eyes ready to burst.

"Everyone that you've stuck your fangs into."

"You're a real smartass aren't you?"

"Smart enough to finally face fear in the eye. I've had nightmares about you–you beady-eyed creepy snake. I even stomped all over your head in my dreams. So how's that grab you?"

"Beady-eyed my ass. You sure have a lot of balls for a girl. I'll give you that much."

"You even got your fangs into your son's life, don't you?"

"Shut up!"

"Don't like hearing the truth?"

"I want to know who you are?" he said in desperation. "Who sent you?"

"I already told you. Everybody you've walked all over."

Angered, he grabbed her throat. "Where did the *photo* come from?" Squirming, gagging, trying to get loose, he pushed her away. "You're a real looker. Dressed to kill, huh. You a killer? You want to kill me?"

"I sent it because you like to hurt kids and good decent people. Apparently even your own son, right? You made a killer out of him. You just like hurting people don't you?"

"I don't know who the hell you are or why you're here, but you know way too much for your own good."

"You don't know the half of it. But your days are numbered."

"I'll tell you what. That mouth of yours has sealed your fate. Too bad, you would have been a star here with that body and face of yours."

"Well, that photo has sealed your fate. You're on canvass for life. You'll never be free. Your scalping will dictate the rest of your life."

Baffled, he stared, shaking, wanting more answers. "Sit down," he commanded. She sat and he paced. "So you think I'm a beast?"

"I know it."

"You don't know anything about me."

"I know enough."

"Enough my ass. I'm a human being too, but you know what? We reap what we sow."

"What's that suppose to mean?"

"I plant the seed of fear and I am rewarded for it. I've got everything I want. *Money. Power. Control.* What more could you ask for?"

"How about dignity, self-respect, self-esteem or happiness to start with."

"Don't preach to me."

"I'm not preaching. I'm calling it as I see it. You definitely don't have *control.*"

"You're really something else."

"Don't like facing the truth? Don't like being stood up to?"

"The truth? You're not going to like where you're going. You're not standing up to me," he chuckled. "You're sitting down. And that's where you're staying. *Down.*"

"Think you're funny, huh? You might keep me down, but you can't keep the truth down."

"What do you know about truth? *Huh?* Tell me? Just tell me how you would have liked being raped as a kid?" he ranted, lip twitching. "Tell me?" he said, licking his lips, grabbing a Kleenex and spitting into it. "Come on tell me."

"I wouldn't have," she said red-faced.

"What would have you done to have stopped that raping monster from destroying your life?"

"Nothing."

"What could have I done as a terrified kid to stop him?"

"Hid. Cried. Repressed the horror."

"Smartass! You think you know what I went through. You don't know shit."

"Oh, I know shit all too well."

"You can't walk in my shoes."

"You're wrong. If what you're telling me is true, I'm walking in your shoes."

"There is a price for pain and I'm dishing it out."

"I guess you are. Does that make you happy?"

"What does happiness have to do with it?"

"Everything if you want to be free of pain."

"I have money, power and –"

"Can't say *control* anymore can you?"

"I'll show you control," he said, making a phone call. "We have one damn hot bitch back here that will be leaving with you and Chastity. Send a couple of the boys back to my office."

"You only think you have control. Your fate is sealed in the portrait. It happened and you'll never forget it. Will you? I'm walking out of here. Don't try to stop me." Moving toward the door, Big Jake grabbed her arm and she kneed him in the groin, causing him to let loose.

"*Shit almighty*," he yelled as she fled out the doorway.

Two men hurried up the hallway and saw Rosetta scrambling toward them. "Grab her!" Big Jake shouted, rushing out the door. When he saw that they had stopped her, he sighed in relief. "Take her out the back door. Don't let loose. She's not going willingly as Chastity. I'll get with you in a bit."

Leading a resistant Rosetta away, she shouted, *"This won't heal the wounds."*

"It might," he snapped back.

"It won't," she said being herded away. "You say you faced a monster as a kid. Well, you're the monster now."

Sitting down at his desk, he buried his face in his hands. "I am out of control," he told himself. "What's wrong with you? Telling her the shit you did. You losing your mind?" With the photo under his nose staring at him, he quietly seethed. "I can't get the image out of my head," he thought. "The pain that kid put me through. She's right. It'll always be with me. I'm trapped forever in a portrait. Did she put me there? I can feel his knife slicing, pulling at my skull. She can't be right. Can she? ... Why is all this shit happening? Then there's David. He's driving me crazy too. My head feels like it's going to burst," he said, touching the back of his head where he had been scalped. "I guess the ongoing headaches will always be a reminder of that crazy kid cutting my head open and then when I think about it – oh my God just thinking about it makes my head hurt." Opening a bottle of pain medication, he took two pills, chewed them and downed a shot of whiskey.

Chapter 23

Big Jake sat alone in his office drinking gin and tonic for two hours after Rosetta was shanghaied. Glass in hand; he squeezed it hard while glaring back and forth between it and the scalping photo. Building up a sweat, he cussed and swore at himself that the girl was wrong and didn't know what the hell she was talking about. Head pounding, he looked at the new bottle of pain medication that said may cause drowsiness ... do not drink alcohol ... Swearing in an undertone, he took two more capsules with the gin and tonic, pulled a cell phone out of his pocket and phoned his wife who didn't answer. "Damn her," he grumbled. "Answer the damn phone." After hanging up and punching redial two times, Gail answered the phone.

"I don't know who the hell this is," she ranted, "but you better stop calling."

"Gail," Big Jake said. "What the hell's wrong with you?"

"Jake?" she said.

"Who the shit did you think it was?"

"I didn't recognize the phone number."

"What do you mean?"

"Never mind, I'm glad you called because I had to call Lonnie to come over to deal with David. He's talking to him right now."

"Good. That's what I told you to do. I just wondered if he settled down."

"I hope so."

"Lonnie will take care of it. You hear? He has a way with David. David likes him. Okay?"

"I guess ..."

It was going on 8:00 PM when Andre and Windy's plane arrived at Springfield's Abraham Lincoln Airport. After renting a car, they checked into the Springfield Hilton Hotel. Once settled, they called

Rosetta as promised, but the phone rang half-dozen times with no answer.

"Maybe she's out with her boyfriend," Windy said.

"Maybe," replied Andre. "She was adamant about us calling as soon as we got in. This Tom and Amy deal really has her upset." Unwilling to give up calling, he hit redial. This time it was answered.

"Yeah, yeah, who the hell is this?" a muddled male voice said. "This better be good."

Andre paused believing he recognized the voice. "Is Rosetta there?"

This time Big Jake paused thinking he recognized the voice. "Who is this?" he asked not aware that he was using Rosetta's phone.

Heart stopping, Andre reflected, unable to speak fearing he knew the voice. "I –" he paused and then hung up. "I don't know if I called the right number, but if I didn't I swear that was Big Jake's voice on the other end."

"What?"

"I know it's crazy," he said sober-faced, "but God I froze. I don't know."

"Let me see the number you called." After looking at it, she said, "You did it right. Maybe you should call Tom."

"Maybe, but I wish we had her boyfriends number. What's his name? Mike?"

"I bet Tom has it."

"Probably, I don't want to be overreacting, but, shit it couldn't have been him. Why would it be? It doesn't make sense."

"Call Tom and settle yourself down. I'm sure there is a logical explanation."

"Yeah, you're right. I just feel uneasy calling there with what's going on between them."

"Do it."

"Alright. I need to use the bathroom first."

Tom and Amy were cruising along in their car headed home from work. Silence prevailed until Amy spoke up. "Well," she said, half-reluctant, "I guess I owe you an apology."

"Oh," from Tom.

"Rosetta called from that strip club and put Chastity on the line who said she drugged and set you up."

"*Damn it.* I told her not to go there, but at least you found out the truth. I didn't have a clue how I got in those photos. But you wanted to believe the worst. Didn't you?"

"Turn the tables around," she said. "Imagine me in those photos half-naked with a bunch of guys. How would you react?" As he paused in thought, jaw-dropping, she said, "It's not so easy to think nothing was going on? You would have been a raving maniac calling me a whore and every name in the book."

"No I wouldn't have, I mean, I would have believed you if –"

"If I what? Can't even say it because it's BS. Right?"

"I mean, I don't know. I would have trusted you."

"Give me a break. You're always suspicious about guys."

"No, I'm not."

"What about Burt?"

"Yeah, well, I swear I heard him say I want to go to bed with you the night he pissed down the stairs."

"And I said you were crazy. You were drunk."

"Just forget it. You know the truth now. Right?"

"I guess."

"Can't you just say yes?"

"I'm sorry. It's just those damn photos seem so real."

"I was drugged," he said. "Aren't you going to let this go?"

"I'm honestly trying. I'm sorry. I get it. I really do."

"That's better. I mean, I guess I can see your point about how you think I would have reacted if the tables were turned."

"Thank you."

"So where do we go from here?"

"Home to start with," she said with an evasive smile.

"Good 'cause we're almost there."

Rosetta, Chastity, and two men were on the highway headed south towards Texas in a sports utility vehicle. Chastity and Rosetta were in the back with Rosetta's wrists bound with masking tape. Both girls tried to sleep as Billy and Charley, the two men who had roughed up Chastity's boyfriend, drank coffee, listened to music and carried on about getting down to the club on the other side of the border. Jeans, a blouse, and sandals had been given to Rosetta to change into for the trip.

Unable to reach Rosetta by phone, Mike stopped by her house and became concerned when she wouldn't answer the door. Peeking in the windows, no one appeared to be home. Going to the garage door window, he confirmed that the car was gone. Once again he tried calling but no one answered. Texting resulted in no response. Unsure of what to do next, he sat in the car waiting and thinking. He remembered she had a spare key to the house hidden under a rock in a plastic container but decided not to look for it. Thinking about their earlier, but brief phone conversation did not help resolve anything. Her text message was not helpful, but he remembered that Andre and Windy were arriving tonight. Believing she might have gone to meet them eased his concern, but he was troubled that she wouldn't answer the phone. He decided to sit and wait in his car.

Billy and Charley listened and sang to a song on the radio. Rosetta, who was never sound asleep, sat up and leaned forward between the two men and spoke. "I've got to go to the bathroom."

"What?" the front seat passenger Billy said.

"I've got to go to the bathroom," she said. "Like real soon and please undo my hands."

"You say you want to give me a big kiss," Billy said, lips puckering up.

"You're a real funny guy. I could just pee here on the seat. Maybe you like the smell of pee."

Charley chuckled, "Don't do that, I'll find a place to pull over off the highway."

"Good," she said. "You won't regret it. How about the hands?"

"Don't worry," Charley replied, "I'll wipe for you."

"You're not funny," she said.

"Charley's a gas," Billy said. "But I won't let him touch you. I'll personally take care of your problem."

"Shut up ass-wipe," Charley said. "You're not my boss."

"Come on guys," Chastity said, "don't be jerks. Let her go to the bathroom without your bullshit."

"You feeling neglected?" Billy said. "I can help you go to the bathroom too."

"Hey," Chastity said. "I work for Big Jake just like you guys."

Charley started laughing. "Chastity you really are going to be a working girl for Big Jake. I definitely want to try you out myself."

"What do you mean?" Chastity said.

"Don't pay any attention to him," Billy said, and then lit up a pot pipe, sucking on the stem and handed it to Chastity. "Take a hit and calm down. I'll take good care of you. I won't let this fool mess with you."

"I really need to go," Rosetta interrupted.

"There's an exit up here I'll get off," Charley said.

"Thank you," she replied.

Once off the exit, a dark side road was taken and the vehicle stopped. Everyone got out and stretched. "I'll go behind those bushes," Rosetta said.

"Let's go," Charley said, waving a napkin. "You're going to need this."

"I need to do this alone."

"I've seen too many movies where the chic says that and the next thing you know she's escaped."

"I won't."

"I know you won't," he said leading the way behind a tree.

"You're really going to watch?"

"Just do it. It's dark there's nothing to see."

"The hands?"

"Give them here," he said cutting the tape with a pocket knife. "Don't try anything stupid."

After taking the napkin from him, she unfastened her pants and dropped them down. "Please don't watch," she said.

"Jesus, you sound like a horse. You really had to go."

"Take my word next time," she said, struggling to pull the pants up.

"Come on, let's go."

Back at the vehicle, Charley took out the masking tape. "Please don't tape my hands," she whined.

"I have to," he said. "I'm no dumbass."

"Hey guys," Chastity said, "you will stop at a restroom later for me won't you?"

"When we gotta go," Billy said, "you can go."

All got into the vehicle and drove off. "You know this is all going to end badly for you don't you?" said Rosetta.

"For us?" Charley laughed. "I ain't no genius, but who's tied up?"

"My boyfriend's a cop and he'll get you. That's a promise."

"You're in no position to make promises," he replied.

"You'd be much better off letting me go and saying I escaped."

"Where ya get that confidence from?" Billy asked.

"I've been around the block a few times and always see your type end up behind bars."

"What the hell you mean our type?" Charley said.

"You know," Rosetta said, "the type who is led by a crazy man."

"You mean Big Jake?" Billy said.

"It's pretty obvious he's not dealing with a full deck isn't it?"

"How's that?" said Billy.

"'Cause part of his deck got sliced off at the top of his skull didn't it."

"How did you know that?" Charley said.

"Because I'm psychic. So listen to me before it's too late."

"What are you all talking about?" asked Chastity.

"Tell her boys," said Rosetta, "how Big Jake lost part of his mind when he got scalped."

"Scalped?" Chastity blurted.

"You boys want to be scalped too?" Rosetta said.

"Just shut up," Charley said. "You don't know what the hell you're talking about."

"Oh but Billy knows," said Rosetta. "Don't you Billy?"

"I don't know shit," he said. "Do as Charley said and be quiet."

"Sure thing, don't say I didn't warn you."

Mike had waited long enough and decided to drive by Tom and Amy's. Knowing Rosetta had been concerned about them, he hoped to find her there. On approaching the house, he saw lights on but did not see Rosetta's car. Calling the police station, he got Tom and Amy's phone number and contacted them. After learning they were both worried about Rosetta, he said he would be right over as he was in the area. Turning around, he drove right back to their house. Once inside, he learned that Andre and Windy were on their way over because of the same concern. Ten minutes later, Andre and Windy arrived. After all compared notes, it was apparent that Rosetta could be in trouble. Her calling from the nightclub and having Chastity talk to Amy was the clincher that resulted in all of them rearing to go to the club. When the five of them arrived there in Mike's unmarked car, they drove around searching for her car in the parking lot.

"There," Andre said, recognizing his old car. "That's it."

Mike stopped, got out and looked the car over. "Okay," he said returning. "I'm going in." Andre and Tom said they were going in too. "Tom," said Mike, "they know you inside. It might be better for you to wait out here. No sense tipping anyone off."

"Yeah," Tom said, "I guess you're right."

"All of you keep your eyes open while we're in there."

Mike and Andre went into the club after paying the admission fee and wandered around, seeking a clue, but came up empty handed. It was time to ask questions and Mike grabbed a waitress's arm. "Who's the boss around here?"

"What do you need good looking?"

"The boss."

"Well, the manager will be back in a bit. The owner is here in his office. Tell me what you need maybe I can help."

"You know a girl named Chastity?"

Big-eyed and head shaking she said, "No, don't know her."

"Right," he said nodding and glancing at Andre.

Walking away, Andre said, "She's lying."

"Definitely. She said the owner is in his office."

"That would be Big Jake," Andre said. "Let's check it out."

Searching for an office, they noticed a hallway exit ahead and made their way to it. No one appeared to be watching them and they scrambled through the closed curtain. An exit sign glowed at the end of the hallway. Creeping to a door where a light was on, they stopped and listened to a voice on the other side. The dialogue seemed incoherent and more of a rambling than a conversation. "I think that's him," Andre said. "He sounds drunk."

"Let me handle him," Mike said, hand on the doorknob and pushing the door open. Big Jake looked up but was slow to react. "Hello butthead," Mike said, "just keep your ass down."

"Who the hell are you?" he mumbled, eyes cracking open.

"I'm the man who's going to throw your butt in jail," he said showing him his badge, "if you don't start talking."

"What's this?" he slurred.

"Where's the girl?"

On seeing Andre, he said, "*You.*"

Trying to stand up, Mike pushed him back in his seat. "The girl."

"What the fuck are you talking about?"

"I'll tell you what the fuck I'm talking about," he said, taking out his phone and calling Rosetta's number. The phone setting on Big Jake's desk started ringing. "*That girl,*" he said, grabbing Big Jake by the shirt.

"What the hell does that mean?" Big Jake said, looking at the phone. "So you called my number?"

Mike grabbed the phone, shut it off and said, "What's your phone number?" When he gave it to him, Mike called it. When it rang, Big Jake looked down toward his pants pocket. "Get it out and answer it."

Pulling the phone out of his pocket, he answered it. "Yeah, what's the deal?"

"*The deal!*" Mike shouted into the phone causing Big Jake to hang up.

"I don't understand? What the hell's going on?"

"You stupid son-of-a-bitch," Andre snapped, pushing Rosetta's phone in his face. "*This is her phone.* Don't even try to deny you don't know who she is."

Mike grabbed Big Jake's hair. "*Alright,*" Big Jake squirmed, "some whore. Why do you care?"

"Whore my ass," Mike said, grip tightening. "Where is she?"

"I don't know, I guess she left her phone here. She wanted a job. I told her to hit the road."

"You're lying," Mike growled.

"Take it easy."

"I've had enough of your lying shit," said Mike, pulling out his gun and handcuffs. "Stand up and put these on." Pushing Big Jake forward, he directed him toward the side exit of the building. Big Jake stumbled around, moaning that his head hurt and said he needed to go back and get his pills. Once outside, they lead him to Rosetta's car. "This is her car. Where is she?"

"Hell by now," he stammered falling to the ground.

"Wake up," Mike said shaking him, but it was of no use. "He's passed out. Come on. Help me get him to the car." Andre and Mike carried him to the car where everyone got out on seeing them holding the man. "Are you with me on getting him to talk?" Mike shouted at the group.

"You're the cop," Tom said.

"There isn't time for police action here. She could be dead if we follow the book. Do you hear me?"

"You're right," Andre said with the rest agreeing that they were with him.

"Let's take him to my place until he wakes up," Mike said. Loading him into the car, everyone squeezed into it for the ride to Mike's house.

Rosetta's captors were seven hours on the road and determined to drive straight through to Mexico. Billy and the girls were asleep when Charley pulled off into a highway rest area. After eyeing everyone, he saw no reason to wake Billy. He went straight to the restroom and then stopped at the coffee machine. Soon after he left, Rosetta's eyes cracked open, having heard the door open and shut. Looking up, she saw the rest area building and noticed Chastity and Billy were asleep. With breath held, she inched her way toward the door and pulled on the door lever. It opened and she looked back fearing the noise might have awakened someone, but it hadn't. Convinced this was an opportunity to escape, she pushed the door open and one foot at a time crept out. Looking at the building, she spotted Charley at the coffee machine and a man and a woman walking in. Breathing heavily, she moved away from the vehicle with wrist taped together and headed toward the wooded area. Adrenaline kicking in, she accelerated, but didn't see the curbside and tripped tumbling to the ground. She fell hard which shook her up for a moment. Struggling up, she hurried toward the side of the building. Charley wasn't standing by the coffee machine and was nowhere in sight. Heading around the structure into the dark, she slowed down searching for the best way to go. The moonlit revealed a tree line thirty feet ahead. Dashing towards the woods, she was blindsided by Charley and hit the ground with him landing on top. "Surprise," he said. "I just knew you wanted to be alone with me."

"I was going to use the woods to go to the bathroom," she said, pleading for him to get off.

"If that's the case I'll just give a helping hand," he said trying to unbuckle her pants.

"*Get away*," she screamed, kicking him in the groin.

"*Shit*," he moaned. "Shut up."

"Stop it or someone will hear me scream."

"Alright," he said putting his hand over her mouth which she bit. "*Damn you.*"

"Are you going to leave me alone?"

"Holy crap almighty! Just get your butt up and shut up," he said grabbing her arm.

"Take it easy I'm coming."

Once at the vehicle, he shoved her in and they drove off.

At Mike's home, Big Jake snored, stretched out on the floor with Mike, Andre, Windy, Tom, and Amy seated around him. "This really sucks," Tom said. "He's passed out and we don't know what the hell happened to Rosetta. "I can't just sit here. I'll tell you what I'm going to do. I'm going back to that club and see if Chastity or someone else knows something."

"I feel the same way," Mike said. "It's just that I've got to try something else to get his ass woke up."

"Yeah sure," Tom said, "work on him. I'll see what I can dig up."

"I'll go with you," Andre said. "The three of you can handle him can't you?"

"Yeah go," Mike said. "Maybe we can try throwing him in the shower."

"Go for it," Tom said. "We'll hurry our butts too. Let's go. Shit! I don't have my car."

Mike threw him his car keys. "Take my personal car. It's next to the car we came in."

Tom and Andre took off and sped away. When they arrived at the club, Tom said, "Let me take the lead. I know which girls to talk to."

"Sure thing."

Relieved that the attendant didn't know that Tom had been thrown out of the club days earlier, they paid and entered. Even though it was early in the morning, there was still a small crowd. Tom led the way searching for one of the girls from the photo. The only girl's face he recognized was on the stage revealing more than a smile. "We'll have to wait until she's done," said Tom.

"I don't think so," Andre replied. "See that guy at the bar talking to the bartender?"

"Yeah."

"That's Lee, don't you remember him working at Prism at the group home. He then became an agency social worker."

"Oh, yeah. He quit suddenly didn't he?"

"You got that right. He went to work for Big Jake because he is what I would call an educated low life and it appears it's still true. I say we grab his ass."

"Let's do it."

"Wait a minute, let's make sure and ask a waitress if he works here." Going to a waitress, they learned that he was the club manager. "How does this look," Andre said, grabbing a towel off the bar and putting his hand under it with his finger straight-out.

"Is it supposed to be a gun?"

"We don't have time to mess with him. Do you think it'll work?"

"Give it a shot," Tom said.

Going up to Lee, Andre looked him in the eye. "Hello Lee, remember me?"

"Well yeah," he said baffled. "Andre?"

"I think we need to talk."

"I don't have anything to say to you."

Jamming his finger in Lee's side, he said, "Take a look."

"Why do you have your finger covered and stuck in my gut? You want to feel a real gun in your gut?"

Andre looked at Tom who went up to Lee and grabbed his groin, saying, "You remember me?"

"*Oh shit*," he moaned. "Oh God, please it hurts. What do you want?"

"To talk, okay? In private."

"Okay," he said squirming. "Let's go to the back office."

Lee led the way with Tom's hand clamped to his bicep. Entering the office, Andre shut the door. "What's this about?" Lee asked.

"First of all," Tom said, "where's Chastity?"

"She's not around here anymore."

"Why's that?"

"Too much trouble as you should know."

"I'm cutting to the chase," Andre said. "The beautiful dark haired girl who was here earlier is missing. Where is she?"

"I don't know what you're talking about."

Once again, Tom grabbed Lee's groin causing him to say, "Oh shit, please let go."

"Not until you tell us the truth. We know she was here and spoke to Chastity. Her car and cell phone were left here."

"Okay," he squirmed. "They went to Mexico."

"Who and how," Tom said continuing to squeeze. "The dark haired girl, Chastity and a couple of the boys."

"*Why*?"

"Let go," he pleaded. "A trip to the beaches."

"*Beaches my ass*," Tom said clasping and yanking as hard as possible.

"To a bordello to put them to work," he said ready to pass out.

"Where?"

"I don't know the details. Big Jake does. I swear. All I know is they drove."

Tom let go and looked at Andre. "I'd say he's telling the truth," Andre said.

"Yeah, let's go."

Big Jake sprawled out in a bathtub with shoes and suit intact while Mike, Amy, and Windy looked on. "You ready?" Mike asked.

"Ready," Amy said.

"Let him have it."

Amy turned the cold shower on causing Big Jake to moan and grumble. "Stop it," he yelled. "Leave me alone. I'm tired." Never opening his eyes, he continued to babble, but the cold water only served to let them know he was still alive. After a few minutes, Mike shut the shower off.

"I hope the boys had better luck," Mike said, clenching his fist. "Just leave him in there. This is going to be a long night."

Ten minutes later, Tom and Andre arrived at Mike's. Walking in, they saw the group sitting around with long faces. Mike stood, eyes begging for answers. "Tell me you got something," he said.

"We got something," Andre said.

"Oh, yeah?" Mike said with all eyes on Andre.

"They're on their way to Mexico."

"*What*?" Mike roared.

"But only Big Jackass knows the details."

"Who's they?" asked Mike, stepping toward Andre.

"Rosetta, Chastity and a couple of Big Jake's boys. They're sending them to a bordello."

"The no-good *asshole*," Mike raved rushing to the bathroom, grabbing Big Jake by the front of the shirt with one hand and slapping him with the other. "*Wake up you stupid bastard.*"

"Aw," Big Jake moaned, but didn't snap out of his stupor.

Returning to the group, Mike growled, "How did they go?"

"Driving," Tom sighed. "That's what he said."

"Ten to one they're not entering the country legally. They're going down a back alley you can bet on it. It would be impossible to track them without assholes help in there. If they make it across the border, we got one hell of a job ahead of us. I might have to pull some strings. Shit almighty. I can't believe this is happening."

"I'm going too," Andre said.

"And me," Tom said, pacing.

"Someone's going to need to stay with him," Mike said. "We'll hold him until she's found. He's our leverage. It's not legal, but it's too risky to have the law do this. We could lose her for good. He'd have his attorney and time would be against us. I want you to know what you're up against. You don't have to be a part of this. Do you hear me?"

"We are a part of it," Tom said. "I'm with you."

"Definitely," from Andre.

"Screw the law," Windy interjected.

Amy grinned and shrugged. "I don't know what to do," she said. "I guess I'm with you. Everything's happening so quickly."

"Timeout everyone," said Mike. "Take a breather because nothing's happening until he wakes up."

Chapter 24

Just beyond El Paso, Texas and the Rio Grande lies a hidden tunnel that stretches between the Mexico and the New Mexico border. The man made tunnel had served human trafficking and drug smuggling for years. The entrance on the New Mexico side was concealed by a warehouse that was owned by Big Jake. The tunnel led to another of Big Jake's warehouses on the Mexico side that was a half-hour away from Ciudad Juarez, a border city across from El Paso, which was plagued with corruption, gang warfare, murders, and prostitution. Big Jake owned a well-known bordello there that catered to an upper-class clientele and to those with authority, money, and power. The drive between Springfield and the warehouse was close to twenty hours, but Charlie and Billy were ahead of schedule making it in eighteen hours. On arrival, a large overhead door opened up and the vehicle pulled in. After getting the girls out, a man greeted them saying, "I'll take these sweeties off your hands."

"They're all yours," said Charley grabbing Rosetta's arm. "Watch out for this looker, she's a wild one."

"A wild one for the wild lands," said the man.

"We need to rest up," Billy said.

"You know the routine. Come on girls, you're going with me." Leading the way, the girls followed the man into another room where they took stairs down to a lower level and were greeted by three men. Pulling a wall panel open revealed the entrance to a tunnel. "Let's go girls."

"Why are we going in there?" Chastity asked.

"It's the easiest way into Mexico. Just follow me." He led the way with the girls behind and the other men behind them. The tunnel was close to five feet high and four feet wide and lighted.

"It's creepy," Rosetta said.

Chuckling, the man said, "Don't worry the real creeps are on the other side of the tunnel."

"That's good to know," Rosetta said.

"It's close to two home runs long," the man said. "The Jose Alberto Pujols type. So don't hold your breath thinking we'll be through in a minute. Expect ten or fifteen minutes. You hear me?"

"Yeah, sure," said Chastity.

Once they were through, they came out into a lower level of a warehouse and were greeted by some Mexican men. "Bonanza," the head Mexican said on seeing the girls. "These are real hot tamales. Business will boom with these lookers."

Rosetta leaned toward Chastity's ear and whispered, "You have aids."

"What?" Chastity whispered back."

"Aids," she said, being pulled away from her.

"No secrets," the Mexican said, holding onto Rosetta's arm. "We take you to Juarez now. No more talk. You understand?"

The girls nodded, looking at one another uncertain of their fate.

At Mike's everyone camped out in the living room on sofas and chairs, realizing there was nothing they could do until Big Jake woke up. Being a Saturday morning, everyone was off work for the weekend. Mike tossed and turned and would check on Big Jake who remained asleep in the bathtub. As mid-morning passed, the sunlight awoke everyone but Big Jake.

"You ready to try the shower on him again?" said Mike.

"Let's go for it," said Tom with the others agreeing.

All crowded into the bathroom and Mike jerked the shower handle on. The floodgate opened on Big Jake who began moaning, eyes cracking open, as he raved, "Turn that damn freezing water off." Pushing himself up in a sitting position, Big Jake's droopy face contorted on seeing the group of people gathered around him. "What the hell is this? *You*," he blurted on seeing Andre. "

"Yeah," Andre sighed. "It's time to give that tumor between your shoulders a dose of chemotherapy."

"What is this bullshit?" he said.

"Why don't we just call it," said Mike, flicking on a handheld tape recorder and set it on a table, "this is your life down the drain. We don't have time to waste. Get your ass up."

"And who are you?"

"The man who's going to bust your ass and throw your butt in jail if you don't cooperate." Mike flashed his badge and revealed a gun on his waist. "We've been waiting the whole damn night to tear into your ugly mug. So stand up."

"I'm soaked. Where am I and what do you want from me?"

"*Answers*," Mike wailed smacking his head.

"Oh no, my head is killing me. Don't touch my head again."

"*You sent two girls down to Mexico*," Tom roared, "and you are going to tell us where."

"Get out of my face assholes. You're full of shit. Don't know what you're talking about."

Once again Mike smacked Big Jake along the side of the head. "If you think that hurts just keep lying."

Waving his hands in front of him, he said, "Hold on. I'm freezing in these wet clothes. If you want to talk let me get into something dry."

"You'll change when we've heard the truth," Andre said.

"And you," flared Big Jake, "I should have taken your head off when I had the chance. I see you got your pretty little woman with you. We know where you live in LA."

Andre exploded, grabbing his hair saying, "You're in no position to be threatening anyone you disgusting scumball."

"Alright, alright, my head for Christ sake."

"No more bullshit," Andre said. "The girls."

"We've already been told," said Tom. "That your boys drove off to Mexico with the girls to work them in a whore house."

"This is no time for games," Mike added. "We'll get the truth out of you if it kills you."

"I want my lawyer," Big Jake said. "You're a cop and I demand my lawyer."

"You want a lawyer," Mike said, gripping his hair and yanking him toward the toilet bowl. Holding his face over the bowl, he said, "I think your ears need to be flushed out."

"You can't do this. *I know my rights.*"

"*What about the rights of those girls?*" Mike shouted shoving his face in the commode and flushed it over and over. "Hey piss head? You had enough?"

"Okay!" he screamed. "My head's ready to explode. I'll tell you just let me up."

Pulling his head out, Mike let go of him. "Stand up and talk."

Clasping his head, moaning, Big Jake mumbled, "Juarez."

"What?" said Mike.

"Ciudad Juarez. Across from El Paso."

"*That's where the cartel's at war with the police,*" Mike gasped. "*It's all over the news.* It's a damn bloodbath down there you rotten jerk."

"They'll be in a safe place. I have a nice layout there for a good clientele. No one bothers us."

"How are they crossing the border?" Mike demanded.

"Is this legal?"

"Listen you piece of shit. I don't care about your operation. I want the girls back. Then you're a free man to carry on with your bullshit. I'm not acting as a cop. If you want me to act like a cop I'll arrest your ass now for kidnapping. You want to walk down that path or do you want to give me the girls and be off the hook?"

"So you leave me and my operation out of this for the girls?"

"That's the deal," said Mike.

"I wish my head didn't hurt so much so I could think clearly." Mike jerked his open hand up as if to smack Big Jake. "No, I mean yeah it's a deal. You get the girls and you're out of my life. I'm on board. How do I know I can trust you not to bring up charges?"

"Because I'm not acting as a cop. Everything would be thrown out of court."

"*Damn it,*" Andre said, "we just want the girls back."

"Then I can fuck with you later?" Big Jake said to Andre.

Andre cringed and churned, saying, "I want you to leave every one of us alone."

"Alright, alright, it's a deal. I'll get the girls back."

"Do it now," Mike insisted.

"Okay," he said reaching for his cell phone and opening it. "Shit, it's all wet and not working."

"Use my phone," Mike said.

"You don't understand – my phone contacts were in my phone. We'll have to go back to my office to find the numbers. I can get into some dry clothes then too and I need my headache pills."

"Let me see," said Mike, grabbing the phone. "*Shit*. Come on I'll take you. We'll use the back entrance. You don't talk to anyone or try anything foolish. Understood?"

Juan Miguel and another man carted the girls over rough terrain from the secluded warehouse to Ciudad Juarez. The girls were enthralled during the journey unfamiliar with the dry desert like setting. Juan eyed the girls from his rearview mirror and said, "You two look like fine young ladies. You will do well at the hacienda. Business will boom with you lovely girls. I know. I've done this all my life."

"The hacienda," Chastity said. "Is it like Big Jake's club back home?"

"Very nice hacienda," Juan said. "You know, I American Mexican now. I got my papers. But Juarez like the Wild West. You stay at the house for safety. Many bad men out on the streets. I take good care of you."

"But the hacienda," Chastity said, "is a big nightclub, right?"

"It's a nice club. Good people there."

"I wanted to strip back home, but Big Jake said this was better."

"Oh yes, much better than striptease. You don't want to do that down here. Too dangerous."

"What do you mean?" she said.

"He means," said Rosetta, "that you're not going to be at a strip club."

"What's the house then?" she asked confused.

"Hey Juan," said Rosetta. "You want to tell her about the house? Chastity really wants to become a striptease star."

"Oh sweetie," said Juan. "You will be *stripping* and you will be a *star*. That I promise you."

"I don't understand."

"Just wait and see," Juan said. "We make you a big star. Both of you will be stars."

"Good," said Chastity. "Because someday I want to be like Candy. She's a big star back home."

"You will be," said Juan. "We're entering the city now. We don't have far. We're on the outer edge about ten minutes away."

As they headed down a narrow street, the girl's eyes were mesmerized on rundown buildings and shacks along the way. Two men were fighting along the street and girls were displaying their assets trying to lure men to pay for a good time. Frightened by what they saw, they remained quiet as a little boy and girl came up to the car at a stop sign begging for money.

"Can't we give the poor baby's some money?" Rosetta asked.

"No dinero," said the passenger. "Just little ladron."

"What's he mean," said Chastity.

Juan smiled, turning to the girls, "They little thieves. Survival makes the little ones steal from a starving baby and even scavenger dogs. They bite the hand that feeds them. They're all over the city. Stay away from them. Comprende?"

"It's sad," said Rosetta.

"They know how to survive," said Juan. "Don't worry, they be okay."

"And I thought I had it bad at the children's home," Chastity said.

"Very bad area. See billboard," he said. "Says, '*Be careful – watch for your life.*' They all over the city."

"Sounds like a great town," said Rosetta.

"Much violence in Juarez. It gets better near hacienda."

"Whatever you say," said Rosetta.

"That's what I say," Juan said.

"*What's that?*" Chastity shrieked.

"Don't look," said Juan, speeding up.

"What was it?" Rosetta fretted.

"Don't need to know," from Juan.

"What terrible thing was it?" Rosetta insisted.

"If you must know, then I tell you. A dead baby being buried in the dumpster."

"Sick," said Chastity.

"Why?" said Rosetta.

"Baby burned up in trash fill. No money to bury baby proper in casket. You put baby in hole in the ground and the animals dig it up and feast on it."

"I'm going to be sick," Rosetta said.

"Me too," said Chastity.

"Enough of sickness. Nice place where we going. You like it. Nice place," he repeated. "Sometimes you have to go through hell to get to heaven. We're getting there. You'll see. You'll like."

"There's a church," Rosetta said.

"Some people still go to church," Miguel said. "Nice padre there."

"Maybe," said the passenger, "he come and visit you girls at the house and hear your confession." The man chuckled to himself. "Yes, the old padre."

"Does he speak English?" Rosetta asked.

"Yes, he do," Miguel said. "I know the padre. We're right on the Mexican border. Many speak English here."

As they approached the outskirts of town, a big house was seen in the distance a half-mile away. "Is that it?" Chastity said.

"That's it," Juan said.

On arriving at the large two-story, white stucco house with a terra cotta tiled roof that overlooked a rundown neighborhood in the far distance; Chastity seemed excited while Rosetta was cautious, anticipating the worst. Walking along the terraced path with a splash of fuchsia lining its border, they approached the rustic door entrance and entered a large room with a bar and sofas where several Hispanic girls lounged waiting for customers. The girls and men were greeted by another Hispanic American who welcomed the group.

"I am Bono," he said. "We welcome you to your new home. American girls do well here. We have a room for each of you upstairs. This is a large house. A dozen girls work here. Nighttime is our busy time."

"Where's the stage?" Chastity asked. "I want to become a star."

"You have star status already. Important people know of your arrival and wish to meet you today. Police, army officers and high officials are coming to see both of you."

Chastity cast a quizzical look at Rosetta. "You know I'm only fifteen," she said.

"We have other fourteen and fifteen-year-olds working here. Young is good for business. In your rooms is a wardrobe of comfortable clothes for you to change into. Follow me," Bono said leading the way up the stairs. "Rosetta this is your bedroom and Chastity this is yours," he said pointing at the rooms next to each other. "Go on in and get comfortable. Each of you has important guest on their way here. You are both very popular. A police captain and very rich business man on their way here right now. Go on in and get ready."

"For what?" Chastity said, sensing that things were not as she expected. "I'm supposed to become a stripper."

"You will be stripping," Bono said. "A private show is how you break in."

"You think that's easier than in front of a large crowd? Is that what you mean?"

"Much easier."

"But I loved the sound of the crowd back home."

"You will love our way here. You will be the star. I promise. Now go change. I'll wait here to see how you look. Now go."

"What if I *refuse* to do this?" asked Rosetta.

"No such word here. You do it. If you think differently you will pay an unpleasant price. Do you understand me? I want each of you in at least garter belts and hosiery. Don't overdress," he chuckled.

"I understand," Rosetta said, looking at Chastity who showed fright in her eyes for the first time. Chastity walked by Rosetta who whispered, "Aids. You got aids." Chastity looked at her in bewilderment and each went to their room and closed the doors.

What each girl found were skimpy, revealing clothes with garter belts and fishnet hosiery. Each dressed in the attire and stood by the door not wishing to exit the rooms.

"You done?" Bono shouted knocking at their doors. "Come on." Within seconds of each other, the girls opened their doors. "Yes, yes, you are both stars," he said grabbing each of their buttocks and squeezing. "Don't back away. Maybe I should break each of you in before they come."

"That's alright," Rosetta said, "I don't think your guest would like to know that they had sloppy seconds to you now would they?"

"Okay smart-aleck lady," he said, "we'll do it your way for now. Just go to your rooms and wait for your visitor. You do good or else I will break you in and break you like you've never been broken before. I'm a real stallion senoritas. So do your job good. Real good."

"Back home, I was getting ready to be a cop or do social work," Rosetta said. "And you're the epitome of everything I despise and have prepared to combat with my new life. You're scum –"

"Enough said," he hissed. "Little Miss Social Worker, I'd say you're dressed to kill now aren't you? You'll be one killer cop with those double barrel thirty-sixes under your top. So we'll see who has the last laugh. But for sure you're going to be one naked social worker real soon," he chuckled.

"Back where I come from," she said bold-faced, "a naked social worker means going into places unarmed, unprotected using your wits to deal with people regardless of the risk. And so here I am standing almost naked, but armed with the knowledge that I won't be beaten by your type again. I'm a fighter and you won't want to try to be a stallion with me. That I promise you."

"Get out of my sight. Both of you work your butts off in there. Now go."

Rosetta smiled without another word said and both girls went into their rooms waiting for their visitors. Rosetta looked out the bedroom window seeing traffic in the distance, but no cars were approaching in their direction. Squinting, into the blinding sun, she

310

noticed the church steeple they had passed on the way in. Planning ahead, she looked around the room searching for anything that might help in her defense. There was nothing of use. On impulse, she grabbed a glass vase wanting to smash it, but stopped, realizing that breaking a piece off could be used as a knife. Wrapping the vase in a large towel from the adjoining bathroom, she set it by the foot of the bed, lifted the bed leg up and dropped it three times until it broke. A six-inch piece was perfect. Putting a washcloth around half of it enabled it to be gripped like a knife. She was satisfied, cleaned up the remainder of the broken glass and hid the homemade knife under the pillow. Meanwhile, Chastity paced, realizing what was happening, unsure of what to do, but to sit by the window staring out awaiting her fate.

With two important men en route to the bordello, Bono stepped outside to wait for them when his phone rang. He nodded after being briefed by Big Jake about the girls needing to be returned to him and that he was making arrangements for it to happen. "I understand," he said to Big Jake. "The girls will be returned," he hesitated, "but you must know our protection, the police captain, and our top business associate are right now having their way with the girls. As soon as they are done they will be returned."

Big Jake was silent for a moment and said, "Good they are safe with you. I want them sent back *ASAP*. *Got me*." Hanging up the office phone, he said to Mike, "It's done. So now what?"

Grabbing hold of the pistol from his holster, Mike said, "Now you're coming with me and we'll make arrangements to go get the girls."

"What do you mean *we*?"

"You're not out of my sight until the girls are safely back. So let's go. No tricks you hear? Let's quietly get out of here."

After the men returned to Mike's house, Tom and Andre insisted on going down to the Mexican border with them. Windy and Amy argued that they wanted to go, but were convinced not to. Amy agreed to tell Tom's work that he had an emergency and would hopefully be back to work on Tuesday. Mike got personal time off and told the women about Rosetta's hidden house key so they could care for the pets. Although Big Jake complained, he was persuaded to rent a van for their journey to pick the girls up. Not wasting any time, the group was off within an hour headed south.

At the hacienda, Rosetta and Chastity were in their rooms with the expected visitors; Chastity was to entertain the business associate and Rosetta the police captain. The business associate was well dressed and spoke perfect English despite being a native to Mexico. "Your youthful beauty has lived up to its billing," he said.

"I'm fifteen, but I'm an emancipated minor."

"What does that mean?"

"It means I can do whatever I want. I am free to be my own person."

"Very good."

"I was told I could be a big star down here as a stripper."

"You wish to strip for me?"

"I want to strip for a big audience like they do back home."

"I can arrange for that."

"You can?"

"Of course. I'm a powerful man in town. There's a club in town that would be perfect for you to perform at. In fact, I own it."

"You do?"

"Turn around slowly," he said. "Oh yes, you would be an instant star."

"Really?"

"But you must pay the price for such fame."

"How?" she said, wide-eyed.

Putting his arm around her, his hand moved to the lacy panties covering her buttocks.

In Rosetta's room, the police captain set his gun and holster on the armchair and then undressed down to his underpants. "You are the most beautiful girl I have ever seen. Your long dark hair is like silk and those ocean blue eyes of yours are so inviting."

"Are you a poet?" she asked.

312

"Very much so. I am a police captain on the streets but very much a poet in the bedroom."

"You speak very good English."

"I went to the university in your country. I come from a good family. You are special. I want to take you with me. You don't need to be here. I will arrange for you to leave with me. How does that sound?"

"You sound like a man who gets what he wants."

"Oh yes and I want you," he said, embracing and pulling her down on the bed. While on top of her, panting, hands roaming at will, Rosetta's hand felt under the pillow while his hand crept to her panties. "Are you ready my sweet?"

"I wouldn't go down any further if I were you," she said, clasping his neck with one hand, and pressing the glass knife to his throat.

"You're right," he said removing his hand. "Bono was right that you are a wild one. Now, what?"

"Slowly get up," she said keeping the pointed glass pressed to his neck. As they crept toward the chair, Rosetta's hand reached out grabbing his pistol and pulled the hammer back.

"You seem to know how to use that."

"My boyfriend is a real cop and he taught me well. Don't think for a minute that I won't use it."

"You are convincing."

"Good because it would be a mistake to think otherwise. Face the door, don't look back and get dressed," she said holding the gun to him and then backed away to where her clothes were at. Gun in hand; she dressed at the same time. Once both were ready, Rosetta peeked out the door.

Chastity at the mercy of the businessman was under him as he kissed her neck and whose passion was boiling. "I will make you a star," he whispered.

"Please stop," Chastity blurted out. "There's something you need to know."

"I know all I need to know."

"No you don't," she said looking away. "I, a, have aids."

Muscles twitching, frown erupting, he said, "*What?*"

"I have aids, but I feel okay."

Backing off of her, he trembled. "Do they know downstairs?"

"No I couldn't tell 'em 'cause I wanna become a star."

"And you let me touch you?" he said quivering.

"But I stopped you before you could get it didn't I?"

"*I should beat you,*" he cringed and then started dressing. "I'm very upset. You will be punished."

"I didn't do anything," she said, frightened, rambling and putting on her clothes. "You don't have it. You're okay. I told you before it was too late. Don't hurt me."

Finished dressing, he said, "Someone's going to pay." She backed up as he approached, grabbing and then clamped his hand around her throat.

"*I lied,*" she struggled to say fighting off his stranglehold.

Opening his hand, he said, "What?"

"I don't have aids. I said it to make you stop."

"I don't know what to believe you little bitch."

"Well believe this," Rosetta hissed, pushing open the door with the captain in front of her and the gun pointed at the business man.

"Be careful," he whined.

"Finish dressing," Rosetta said to Chastity. "Both of you jerks stand together."

Once Chastity was ready, she moved toward Rosetta. "Now what?" she said.

"Captain," Rosetta demanded. "Throw your handcuffs and the key to Chastity." He complied. "Both of you go to the bed." They did as told. "Captain lay on the bed." He did as told. "Chastity throw him the handcuffs. Now cuff your wrist and put it under the bedrail and you cuff your wrist," she told the other man. "Good, I don't think you're going anywhere soon," she said, satisfied that they were securely cuffed under the metal bed rail together. "Give me your car keys," she said to the businessman aiming the gun at him.

"Here," he said tossing her the keys. "Don't think you're going to get away with this?"

"That's right," said the captain. "You're making a big mistake. You have nowhere to go. Just let us go and we'll forget everything. Do you want the police and cartel after your butts?"

"Shut up," said Rosetta. "I'm not stupid."

"What you're doing isn't smart," he replied. "You won't get away."

"Hope not to see you, boys, again," she said opening the door directing Chastity out. Descending the flight of stairs, the working girls gazed, and Bono's jaw dropped on seeing the gun in Rosetta's hand.

"What are you doing?" Bono said.

"*Getting the hell out of here*," Rosetta snapped.

"What have you done?" he said. "You know who those men are?"

"Not very happy," she said.

"Roberto," he said referring to the businessman "is with the cartel. *What have you done to them?*"

"Don't worry," said Rosetta, "they're alive and we're out of here."

"Listen to me. Big Jake called and said both of you are to be sent back to your home. They are on their way right now to pick you up."

"We're not stupid," said Rosetta.

"No, we're not," added Chastity. "You wanted to make me a whore, not a star. I'm not stupid."

"Believe me. You're to be sent back today. Don't leave," he said moving toward her.

"Stop!" she screamed and pulled the trigger aiming at the ceiling causing him to freeze. "I don't believe you," she said backing out the door. "Don't come out or I will shoot."

"*Shit almighty*," Bono raved, watching the girls go to the car and drive away. Panicking, he rushed upstairs to the handcuffed men who swore and cussed at him. "I'll get you free. I'll be back." Hurrying away, he mumbled, "Do I call Big Jake or what? No," he

315

told himself, "we'll find them and get them back. He don't need to know."

On entering the town, Rosetta slowed down to a creeping pace. "We need help," Rosetta said. "Look at that billboard. It looks like the one Juan said meant, '*Be careful – watch for your life.*' Do you believe that?"

"What are we going to do?" Chastity said. "This place scares me."

"I don't know what way the border is but we'll need help getting across. They're all in this together. The cops won't let us cross. People sneak across the border all the time. We'll need help."

"Maybe we could call someone," Chastity said.

"We need a phone. It won't be long before they're looking for this car. We're going to have to dump it. I've had my eye on that church steeple up ahead since we got here. Maybe the priest will help us."

"Good idea."

"We really need to drive a mile or so away and dump the car to try to throw them off track and then head back to the church."

"Go for it."

Driving off they stopped after five minutes, parked the car behind a building and took off walking. Rosetta stuck the gun in the front of her jeans and pulled her blouse out to cover it. The radiating sun pounded down, causing them to squint as they moved along the side of the road. The church steeple in the distance guided them. Staying off the main drag, they weaved back and forth taking side streets. While passing a cantina named, Desperados, they glanced in and many hungry eyes feasted on them. A moment later several men were in pursuit like a wild pack of dogs.

"They're following us," Chastity said, glancing back.

"Stay calm."

"I don't like the looks of those suckers."

"Just keep walking."

"They're getting closer."

"Chicas calientes," the voice's yelled out with their feet stomping like a wild herd.

"We're going to stop now," Rosetta said, reaching under her blouse, grabbing the pistol. Turning, she aimed the gun at the men whose feet screeched to a halt against the hot tarred gravel like pavement. Ten feet away, the three men stood smiling, hands raised, and heads shaking while grumbling unknown words to the girls. When Rosetta cocked the hammer, the men backed away and hurried in the opposite direction.

"You're good with that gun," Chastity said.

"I've been taught well. Come on, let's go."

As they rushed along the side street, eyes followed, voices whispered and wandering kids and dogs came up to them, but they had nothing to offer but a stare of desperation. "I don't think we'll get out of here," Chastity whined.

"We will. Come on keep up. Look," she said pointing at the church. "Just a few blocks away."

"It's hot," Chastity said. "I'm very tired."

"We'll rest in the church."

Approaching the church, the girls were relieved but checked all around before entering. People were walking by and Rosetta held Chastity back. "Wait until they pass. It's best if no one sees us go in." Waiting until no one was visible; they then entered the front door and found no one inside. Making their way up a stairway into a choir loft, they explored and found folded up canvas cots in a storage room, which they opened and made use of. "I could sleep until tomorrow," Chastity said, plummeting on the cot. "Aren't you exhausted?"

"We'll take a little nap and then go look for the priest. There's a house behind the church. It must be where the priest lives."

"At least we're out of the sun. It was making me sick. But it is warm in here."

On their backs looking up, towering above them was a stunning six by twelve-foot cross done in stained glass and lead that hung from the ceiling above the choir loft so the entire congregation could see its glowing beauty above them as the sun shined through it. "I feel safe now," said Rosetta gazing at the cross shining above them.

"That's a nice cross," Chastity said.

"It's a masterpiece. What a great artist. When we get back home, I need to do a painting of the cross. I must remember it in every detail," Rosetta said, eyelids fighting to stay open. "Every detail."

The girls closed their eyes and fell into a deep sleep being exhausted from the trip from home and all that had occurred since. The afternoon faded and nightfall came. With the evening cooling down the church, the girls were even more comfortable and continued to sleep throughout the night. As sunrise broke, a priest prepared for an early mass and his ramblings caused Rosetta's eyes to open. Noticing the sun rising from the window in the distance, she realized they had slept the entire night. Tapping Chastity, she whispered, "Wake up."

"What?"

"We slept the entire night. It's morning. I hear noises down below."

Sitting up, the girls looked over the choir balcony and saw the priest in the distance doing something on the altar.

"Should we go to him?" asked Chastity.

"Yeah, I think we should. Come on."

Together they made their way down the stairs and walked up to the altar. The priest turned around half-startled, "*Oh mi Dios*," he shrieked.

"Father," said Rosetta. "We were told that you speak English."

"Why yes, I'm sorry you came up so quiet I wasn't expecting to see anyone."

"We need help," said Rosetta.

"What can I do? I'm Father Serrano."

"It's a long story. Do you have time to listen?"

"I'm getting ready for mass, but if you can wait until it's over."

"We can wait, but really don't want anyone to see us. That's why we need to talk to you. Is there somewhere we can wait?" she said staring at the stained glass cross.

"In the rectory."

"That cross radiates hope, doesn't it? Who did it? It's a treasure."

"An American from your country. Theodore Hile stayed here with me at one time doing odd jobs. I discovered he was a great artist with wonderful displays of his works in public places in Chicago. I believe he said they were at the Navy Pier. He did the entire cross from broken bottles that he found along the railroad tracks and donations by all church members. Yes, it is an achievement that we cherish dearly. May his soul rest in peace. We remember you, Teddy. Come," he said, leading the way to the rectory. Once inside, Father Serrano said, "There's the kitchen. Fix yourself something to eat while I'm saying Mass. I'll be back."

"Thanks," Rosetta said.

"Yeah thanks," Chastity added.

An hour later, Father Serrano returned. "Did you eat?" he asked.

"Yes," the girls responded.

"Alright, I'm ready to listen. Now, what can I do for you?"

"We need help," said Rosetta.

"People want to hurt us," said Chastity."

"That's what I thought. News travels fast. Please tell me what's happened to you?"

"This is the deal," said Rosetta who went on to explain all the details of their predicament.

"That is quite a story," said Father Serrano. "Of course I will help you. Word is already out on the streets about you girls. In fact, there is a reward for turning you in. We are a very poor parish here. Some of our people cross the border for work to feed their families. Maybe I can connect you with those folks and they could get you back to the states. It has to be someone I can trust because that reward will be tempting for some. Do you know that you have angered the police and the cartel? I must think what to do. You're

319

probably not even safe here. They're looking for you everywhere. I knew when I saw you who you were. This is a very rough city with the highest murder rate in the world. Hundreds of young girls have been assaulted and murdered here …"

"Can we use a phone?" Rosetta asked.

"That I can help you with."

Chapter 25

Four stiff tired bodies stretched as they exited the van after having driven straight through to Big Jake's warehouse on the other side of El Paso, Texas. Big Jake sighed, thinking he was about to be set free from his captors and made a phone call to a man on the inside of the building. Anxiety heightened for the others while a huge grin erupted on Big Jake's face.

"Remember," Mike said, grabbing Big Jakes arm. "Don't screw with us. I have a file of incriminating evidence on you with a cop friend ready to fry your ass if we don't return. I even have your voice taped admitting to what you have done."

"I get it. I don't want to have to see your ugly face again. I don't want any more trouble."

The side door opened and a man came out to greet them. "Mr. Big Jake," the man said holding out his hand to shake.

Big Jake waved his hands, saying, "I'm in no mood for shaking. Just get the girls out here."

"They're not here."

"Why?"

"Bono said there is a problem and that you need to call him when you got in."

"If there was a problem why didn't he call me?" The other men hearing the news frowned casting angry eyes at Big Jake who was quick to growl. "There was no problem when I called telling him to get the girls back here."

"He just said he was hoping to resolve it before you got here."

"The damn idiot," he said pulling out his phone.

"Yeah," Bono said answering the call.

"Hey you numskull, what the hell is going on?"

"Big Jake. I've got bad news," he said, explaining what had happened. Big Jake's face reddened, which caused Mike to grab his arm. "I'll get back with you. Let me know if anything develops."

"What?" Mike said, holding onto his bicep.

"Leave us alone," he said to his employee causing the man to return inside the building. "You're not going to like this 'cause I don't. The girls escaped and haven't been found."

"*What?*" from Mike.

"It sounds like B.S. to me," Tom added.

"*Don't mess with us,*" Andre said.

Holding up his hands to shield their anger, he said, "I swear I'm not lying. I just want them out of my hair and in your hands. I agreed to the deal. This is no bullshit. Listen, we can all go over and try to find them if you want or we can wait while my men search."

"*We're going,*" said Mike. "How do we get into the country? Do we do it legally or what?"

Big Jake grunted, saying, "Do you want to take the time to go through legal channels?"

"*Hell no,*" Tom flared with the others agreeing.

"You have to swear what I'll show you will not be revealed to anyone. Do I have your word?"

"You got it," Mike said with the others in agreement.

"Alright," said Big Jake, "follow me." Leading the way, he took them to the tunnel entrance. One of Big Jake's men opened the wall panel revealing the passage. "Lead the way," Big Jake ordered his man while another man closed the entrance behind them.

While the men were below ground, Rosetta made a phone call to Mike, but there was no connection due to their location. She next tried Tom and then Andre's phones, but had the same results. "Darn it," she said frustrated. "It won't go through." Next, she tried Amy's phone who answered. Learning that her friends were at the border was relieving news.

"I just spoke to Tom fifteen minutes ago when they arrived. I'll try to get a hold of them. I'll let them know where you're at. You said you're at the Guadalupe Mission Church in Juarez near the hacienda … Give me your phone number there."

Exiting the tunnel into the warehouse in Mexico, the men were greeted by more of Big Jake's men who were pleased to see him, as his visits were few. Juan Miguel said, "I will drive you to the hacienda. You are armed, right?" he asked.

"Actually," said Big Jake, looking at his captor companions. "We're not, except for him," he said looking at Mike."

"Get them guns," Miguel said. "Much violence going on in Juarez. The cartels are at each other's throats."

"Yeah," said Big Jake. "What the hell's going on down here? I heard on the news about a blood bath for Christ sake. You can't tell the good guys from the bad guys anymore."

"There many atrocities in Juarez," Miguel said.

"I'm thinking of the line up like the Saint Valentine massacre of the Capone days."

"That was a bloodbath," he replied. "Also many men have been found beheaded. You take guns. All of you."

"You hear him?" Big Jake said looking at Mike.

"Yeah," Mike said. "Everyone take a gun."

All the men were handed a pistol. Putting the weapon in the front of his pants, Tom thought to himself, "This is totally unreal. It's unbelievable. I've never carried a gun. At least you know how to use one. What if I have to use it on someone while we're here? This is totally insane. Feel like I'm going into a war zone."

Juan Miguel got everyone in the vehicle and they drove off. Mike stuck his pistol in Big Jake's side, pointed at the pistol stuffed in his pants and motioned for him to hand it over, which he did with a frown. While on their way, Big Jake made a phone call trying to connect with Bono at the hacienda. No one answered. "Come on pick up," Big Jake said. "What's wrong with you Bono? Someone pick up. Why's no one picking up Juan?"

"I don't know boss," he replied.

Twenty minutes later, on the final stretch, Juan, and the group saw two cars coming toward them which were halfway between the hacienda and the town's edge. On passing each other, the men in all three cars looked at one another as they passed. Arriving at their destination, Juan led the group up to the front door, opened it and stopped at the entrance.

"What's wrong?" said Big Jake.

"Heaven almighty have mercy on us," Juan said walking in the house with the others following. All the men reached for their pistol handles as their eyes widened and their brows arched.

Father Serrano led the way into the church with the two girls following him. "I will lock the front door for now. We need time to plan for you, girls."

"Just look at it," Rosetta said, hypnotized by the glass cross radiating colors on the church floor.

"It's neat," Chastity said.

"The Lord is shining brightly for us today. He will guide us. He tells me to lock the church up." While Father Serrano was locking the front door, he saw two cars pull up in front of the church. "Hurry upstairs," he told the girls. "Men are coming. I'll lock the back door and will be right up."

At the hacienda, blood, guts, and butchered bodies paved the entrance. A deep sickening feeling left the entire group of men in awe. "Why?" Big Jake roared. "I don't understand." Four dead girls were scattered throughout the room. Bono's lifeless body stretched out at the top of the stairway. All the men followed Big Jake as he led the way up the stairs. Stopping at Bono's facedown body, he turned him over and saw his throat had been slit open. Continuing to the second floor more bodies were discovered. Mike, being a cop, was familiar with dead bodies. Andre had seen action in the service and saw guts and blood. Although he would never admit to it, Big Jake was familiar with dead bodies as was Juan. Tom, on the other hand, had only seen a dead person at a funeral home.

"I'm getting very sick," Tom said.

Looking in every bedroom, a girl and a man were found sprayed with bullets as they engaged in intercourse. In the bedroom, Andre looked out the window and saw the church tower in the distance as if it were the only safe place in the city of fear that surrounded it. "That's where they would have gone," he muttered. "The girls were in this house, *right*?"

"Yes," Miguel said. "I dropped them off right here."

"Would they have been upstairs?"

"I'm sure they were," he replied.

"Look," Andre said pointing out the window. Everyone looked. "What do you see?"

"A big old violent town," Miguel said.

"The church," Big Jake said. "That's what I see."

"Definitely," from Tom.

"What's your point?" Mike asked.

"Wouldn't that be the place to go for salvation?" Andre said. "If the girls planned their escape from this house don't you think they saw the church like most of us?"

"It's worth checking out," Tom said, looking very pale.

"What are we going to do with this mess?" Big Jake said. "Christ almighty."

"Call the cops," Mike said.

"They were supposed to protect us," Big Jake said. "But I'll call them. I hate to say this, but Bono told me over the phone that the cartel was looking for the girls. The girls stole one of the big shots cars when they escaped."

"You don't think they figured out the church sanctuary idea do you?" Mike said. "Come on let's go check it out."

All the men left the horror behind them and drove toward the church. While on their way, Tom's phone rang. Amy told him Rosetta called and where they were at. "We're on our way," he said hanging up. "Rosetta called Amy and said they are at the church."

"The one up ahead?" Mike said.

"The one near the hacienda she said. It's called the Guadalupe Mission Church. It's got to be it."

On arriving there, the front sign said Guadalupe Mission Church. All got out of the vehicle and went to the front door, which was locked. Mike spoke up. "Tom and Andre go to the left and we'll go to the right." Making their way along the side of the church, their scurrying eyes peeked in the windows. While scoping the empty church, all eyes were drawn to the stained glass cross. "Heaven help us," Mike said, swallowing hard. "You don't think your hacienda visitors have already been here, do you?"

With Mike reaching for his pistol, Big Jake said, "I don't know. Be ready for anything. But could I have my gun back? At least for awhile."

"I feel my gut churning," Mike said. "Here," he said handing him the pistol.

"The rectory is in back," Juan said.

All moved with caution towards the back. When they reached it, Tom and Andre were at the door looking in. Mike joined them while Big Jake and Miguel looked in a side window of the house. Rosetta, Chastity, and Father Serrano were in another room still as mannequins, realizing people were outside the home. Rosetta peeked around a corner and her heart stopped when she saw Big Jake's face by the window. Backing away, she shook.

"I saw her," Big Jake yelled. "They're in there hiding."

"It's Big Jake," she said. "I think he saw me."

Mike hurried to the window where Big Jake was at. "Where?" he said. "Was she okay?"

"I think they're just hiding," Big Jake said.

Mike looked in the window, started pounding, yelling, "Rosetta, Rosetta. Come on it's me. It's me. Look at me." Tom and Andre had gone down to the next window and tapped away seeing the girls. When Rosetta saw them, she gleamed in relief and then looked around the corner and saw Mike at the other window.

"*It's all my friends,*" she shouted. "I must have hallucinated seeing Big Jake," she carried on running to the front door with Chastity and the priest behind her. On opening it, she gave Tom a big hug. Andre stepped in relieved to see Rosetta while Mike rushed in grabbing, lifting and kissing her with overwhelming elation. Once all the embracing was over, Rosetta noticed Big Jake standing nearby. "Him," she blurted. "Why's he here?"

"He saw the light," Mike said. "He's our passage out of this place."

Father Serrano, spoke up, "Men were here not long ago looking around the church. It's not safe here."

"We'll be happy to take the girls off your hand's padre," Mike said.

"I'm just blessed that you got here before something terrible happened. The cartel is looking for the girls. Get out of this city."

"We're ready," Mike said, looking at everybody who nodded in agreement.

Chastity gave Tom a half-smile and he smiled back, saying, "You okay?"

"I guess. I want you to know I'm sorry."

"Oh?" he said.

"I mean it."

"Okay, I believe you."

"Do you hear that?" Mike said. "Sounds like pounding on windows."

"Those men may have returned," Father Serrano said. "I think they're pounding on the church windows. They might be coming back here. Everybody in the backroom, I'll talk to them. Hurry, I see two men coming."

All moved to the backroom while Father Serrano went to the door. "I'm going out the back door," Mike said as the other men and Rosetta pulled out their guns. "I'll come up behind them in case there's a problem." A loud banging at the door caused everyone to tense up. Spanish voices could be heard speaking and then arguing. The sound of someone being smacked around left all fearing for Father Serrano who fell to the floor. "Alright drop your guns," Mike yelled out causing Tom to peak around the corner. The men yelled back in Spanish and Tom saw that they hadn't dropped their guns but were pointing them at Mike. It was a Mexican standoff and all the men were screaming at each other, which set Tom in motion barreling at the men who had their backs to him. With a Herculean leap, he took them by surprise knocking both men standing side by side to the floor, embracing one man in a bear hug making him helpless while Mike put his pistol to the other man's head. Big Jake and Juan hurried into the room with their guns pointed at the men. Father Serrano got up off the floor and the girls rushed to him.

"I'm sorry," Rosetta said to the priest. "We've created a mess for you. You won't be safe now."

"Yeah he will," Big Jake said. "We'll tie these bastards up, put them in the trunk of their car and take them with us to the warehouse. The padre will be off the hook and I'll get myself some information from these two jackals. Is that alright with everyone?"

"They're yours," Mike said.

"Yeah, take them," Rosetta said.

"Miguel," Big Jake said. "Pull the car around back and someone bring the van back here. And Father, do you have some masking tape?"

"Sure," the priest replied. "I'll get it."

The two men were carried and loaded into the trunk of the car. Juan got behind the wheel of the car and Big Jake told the others to get in the van. The girls hugged and thanked Father Serrano. With everyone inside the van, Big Jake drove off. The girls looked back at the priest and waved. Although there was a great sigh of relief by all in the van, they kept alert, hoping to avoid problems. A half-hour later, they had reached the warehouse and were on their way through the tunnel back to the United States. Once on the other side of the tunnel, they knew they had made it. The van they had arrived in was waiting for them.

"I can't leave here now," said Big Jake. "There's unanswered blood to deal with. Take the van back and return it to the rental agency."

"That's fine with us," Mike said.

"Let me ask you?" said Andre. "Are you going to leave me and the rest of us here alone? I want to bury the hatchet with you but you've got to promise to stay out of our business."

"Yeah, yeah, I got bigger problems. You leave me alone and I leave you alone. That means no more scalping photos too," he said looking at Rosetta.

"I hear you," Rosetta said, "but you'll never forget."

"I'm not going back to the club," Chastity said.

"Of course you're not. I'm done with the lot of you. Just be on your way."

The men and girls headed back home with the men taking shifts driving while the others slept once dusk arrived. With much time to think, Tom wondered what Chastity's plans were since she had severed her relationship with Big Jake. Debating whether to say something or not caused him to fidget. On one hand, he was still angry that she had put him and Amy through so much turmoil, but sympathized with what she had just gone through. Deciding the debate was over, he spoke up. "Chastity," he said. "Can I ask you something?"

"Yeah," she said with a puzzled look.

"What are your plans when we get back?"

"What do you mean?"

"Where are you going to stay? How are you going to live?"

"I don't know, but don't *even think* of me going back to the home. You know I'm emancipated."

"I forgot. And what does that mean?"

"It means I can do whatever I want."

"What is that you want to do?"

"To be free of people telling me what to do."

"There will always be someone telling you what to do. A boss for one. Law's and cops for another. A boyfriend or husband and on and on I could go. There really is a price for freedom."

"Oh yeah, what's that?"

"To have a roof over your head, put food in your mouth, have clothes on your back. You know the basics. Do you want to surrender your freedom to some pimp or a bad relationship to have it?"

"*Not me.* I'll get by."

"At what expense?"

"What's your point?"

"You're fifteen with no job, nowhere to live and no money. I know. You're going to get by on your charm? Am I right?"

Smiling she said, "Now you're making sense."

"I knew I would eventually say something to trip your trigger. Now I may be off my rocker for even thinking this, but I don't remember charm as being one of your better strengths."

"Oh yeah," she half-smiled. "I think you're still mad at me and just want to see me get pissed off."

"I'm honestly over my anger with you. If you don't let it go it'll destroy you."

"I don't know."

"And if you let it eat away at you, you'll go out of your mind."

"I can relate to that. I can get damn angry," she said. "I guess that's why I tried to screw your life up."

"We all get angry. I get so pissed off sometimes I swear the anger controls me, but controlling *it* can make you stronger and smarter. It's time to make some good decisions. You need to make up your own mind what's best for you. Just think about it. The home isn't so bad compared to some things."

"What I need is a life," she blurted. "I think I'll just take a nap right now."

"Believe me. You have a life. Just take control of it. Be smart. That's all I have to say."

Rosetta nudged Chastity and whispered, "He makes sense you know?"

"I don't know," she said, closing her eyes and cuddling up trying not to think.

Close to fifteen hours later, the group arrived in Springfield near dinner time. Everyone was exhausted. Rosetta invited Chastity to stay the night until she could figure out what she was going to do. Tom headed home being too tired to go into work which he had already missed the first few hours of his shift. Amy told him over the phone that she explained to the home's director what had happened. Andre met up with Windy at the hotel they were staying at. Mike went with Rosetta and Chastity. When they arrived at Rosetta's house, Chastity went to bed in a spare bedroom. Rosetta told Mike to spend the night, which surprised him. "I just want to hug you all night," she said to him. "You know what I mean?"

"I know," he said. "I don't want to let go either. You know what I mean?"

"I know."

Late the next morning, Tom and Amy sat talking in bed about all that had happened in Mexico. Tom couldn't get the bloody massacre out of his mind which caused Amy to tremor just hearing the story. She initiated a hug, thinking that he could have been killed. It was the most compassionate they had been to each other in months. "I think," Tom said, "I'm going to need to write about this trip in my new novel."

"How do you fit that bloody gore into it?"

"I don't know. All I know is I'll have to do it someway. I can't get it out of my head."

"Let's change the subject. You know I can't believe you were actually nice to Chastity after everything. You even implied that she should come back to the home. I guess you are pretty shook up."

"She's just a kid. She just went through hell and maybe she can change. Don't you believe in people changing?"

"Can you change? Things have been pretty bad between us. We have a lot of issues to resolve."

"We can work things out. Don't you think?"

"Let's take it slow."

"Sure, whatever it takes. I feel totally beat-up right now. I mean mentally and physically. Can you promise me an easy day at work?"

"I wish I could promise both of us an easy day at work."

"But they understood why I wasn't there? Didn't they?"

"Well, the staff sure did. The ladies were calling you a real stud for going after her."

"Yeah, right."

"I mean it."

"What about Rob?"

"No, the director didn't call you a stud."

"You know what I mean. Did he seem understanding?"

"You know it's hard to read him."

"I don't like the sound of that."

"Don't read into it. Don't worry about it."

"You know what? My mind's fried. Hell, after what I went through this weekend nothing should bother me. I really feared the worst for Rosetta and then what I saw down there. I mean, screw the home."

"Tommy was acting out last night and the staff suspect it was because you weren't there."

"He likes order and whenever anything is a little off track for him he freaks out."

"That's what he did last night."

"I'll settle him down …"

Mike went out to get breakfast for him and the girls. While they waited, Chastity was compelled to get Rosetta's opinion about her options. "Being out on your own," said Rosetta, "is not a good thing. You're at everyone's mercy because you can't support yourself. That is not freedom Chastity. You got to earn freedom."

"How?"

"By straightening your life out first of all. Getting away from drugs. Don't tell me you're not using. I've been there. I know. You're not prepared for the world."

"How do you know that?"

"Once again. You're at everyone's mercy to take care of you. At least at the home, you didn't have to worry about food, shelter or clothes."

"You sound like Tom."

"That's because he's right. I made a lot of stupid mistakes when I was younger, but taking Tom's advice wasn't one of them."

"So you think I should go back to the home?"

"That would be a good start."

"*But I fought so hard to be emancipated.* I would be a joke to everyone there."

"You could be an inspiration for others not to do what you did." Grabbing her shoulders, she said, "Trust me. I know what I'm talking about."

"You know what?"

"What?"

"I actually think I might believe you."

"Believe me and then believe in yourself."

"Only one thing."

"Yeah."

"Remember when you said for me to say that I had *aids*."

"I didn't think you understood me. I thought you were too doped up to get it. Did it work?"

"Well, I was high and it did take awhile to sink in. But my point is you weren't quite right about it."

"How's that?"

"Well yeah, he didn't want to have sex with me, but he wanted to kill me instead. Hearing I had aids really pissed him off. So maybe you're not right about everything."

"I would never say I'm right about everything. I've been a screw-up. It's not fun."

"So did you tell that Bozo or should I say your John that you had aids?"

"I was a little more subtle."

"Oh yeah?"

"I put a jagged broken bottle to his throat."

"Are you serious?"

"I told you I've been around the block. I was ready for him. But hear me out one last time. You don't have to go down my road."

"Well, I'll say this. Aids wasn't such a bad idea. So I won't beat you over the head about it. You seem to have your head on straight. Yeah, maybe I should listen to you."

"Trust your gut feeling and go with it," Rosetta said. "Don't be in the position to look back and say if I could only do it over."

"But I had wanted to be a star so bad," she whined.

"You can be."

"Yeah right."

"Listen to me. Don't be afraid to go back. If you face your fear you'll never fear it again. My motto is to do what you fear the most and you will have kicked fear where it hurts the most."

"You mean right between the balls?"

"You said it baby. Not me."

"I'm not afraid to go back to that home."

"But can you go back and be a fifteen-year-old, not fifteen going on thirty?"

"I don't know."

"Can you try?"

"I guess."

"When you succeed. *Do you hear me?* When you succeed you will *illuminate* that home and you will be a *true star*. So are you with me on this?"

"Like I said," she said smiling, "I won't hold the aids thing against you."

"I'm glad to hear that."

Chapter 26

Bursts of lightning streaked the sky and rain clouds loomed overhead while Tom and Amy walked up the concrete steps to the brick children's home entrance. In a daze, reflecting on the past days and wondering what to expect, Tom looked up and shivered seeing the spine-chilling lightning, followed by a rumbling. Walking in the door, Tommy Wizel greeted them. "Why aren't you in school?" Tom asked.

"If you can play hooky, I can too."

"I'm going on upstairs," Amy said.

"See you later." Looking at Tommy, he said, "I didn't play hooky, I had an emergency to attend to."

"I don't like it when you're not here."

"I'm not here a lot of the time."

"But I know when you're not here. You were supposed to be here yesterday."

As they moved up the hallway, Rob, the home's director, stepped out of his office and stopped Tom. "Tom," the director said, "I need to speak to you now. Tommy go on back to the unit."

"Can't you talk to him later?" Tommy said.

"No, I can't. Go on back."

"Cripes," he spat, tromping away.

Tom looked on in dismay, wondering what was up, but figured it was about taking the day off. "So what's up Rob?"

"I need to talk to you right now," he commanded, leading the way into his office. "Have a seat," he said with a disdain expression, which caused Tom to squint as he sat down. "You know Tom we've talked before about your poor performance here and how you should be looking for other work."

"What poor performance?" he said. "I mean –"

"Enough, I don't want to hear it. You were supposed to be at work yesterday and you didn't call in."

"Amy explained things to you."

"It wasn't sufficient."

"It was an emergency."

"It wasn't a family emergency. I'm sorry, but I'm going to have to fire you for an unexcused absence."

"*What?*" Tom said, shocked. "Amy said she explained everything. I have vacation and sick time coming that can be used. Please don't fire me for this."

"I told you before, one screw-up and you were gone."

"You're serious?"

"It will be the best thing for you. You have no future here. There's nothing I can do. You fucked-up Tom. Go do your real estate."

"I told you it isn't working out because of the economy."

"I'm sorry there's nothing I can do. Go to your office and pack up your belongings and be out of here. I'll give you ten minutes. If that's not enough time Amy can gather the remainder of your belongings."

"Can't you give me a month so I can see if I can find another job?"

"You should have been doing that all along. You will get unemployment, we won't contest it."

"How about two weeks? I have a mortgage to pay."

"No. It's final. You're done here. Just go home and have a beer. You're burnt out. There's no future for you here. Plus I think you're clinically depressed. You and Amy need to see a counselor."

"I know things between Amy and me haven't been good. But this will make things worse."

"Like I said there's nothing I can do. You've been repeatedly warned. You're done. You and Amy have worked together too long. I don't know how you two have stood it? I know I couldn't work at the same place with my wife. Besides, it's only a job. People lose jobs every day … You have ten minutes."

Sitting, looking down reflecting, he was speechless. "A, a, I mean," he stammered. "Can I, a, at least say goodbye to the kids?"

"*No.* I'll go down with you to your office," he said standing. "Let's go."

Leading the way, Tom followed looking like he was being led to a firing squad. His eyes roamed, looking at things in a new light, realizing this would be the last time to see the hallway and everything else he was so familiar with. Going in his office, he found empty boxes sitting on the floor next to a dolly. "Hurry up," the director said, "I'll wait right here." After gathering his belongings, the director escorted Tom out of the building. Standing at his car, Tom gazed at the mighty brick fortress feeling like his life had just ended. As he drove home, it poured down rain. Fumbling with his phone, shaking, he called Amy and told her what had happened. She was shocked and angry. Once he got home, he took the director's advice and opened a can of beer. One beer led to another as he replayed in his mind what had happened. Thinking of what Rob had said and what he had said to him, he drifted back to standing in front of the home watching his security fade away. Eyes closed, every sound amplified in his head. The clock ticking paralleled his head pounding causing him to open his eyes seeking relief in a swallow of beer. He turned the television on, staring at it and turned it off. Nothing seemed real. Anxious for Amy to return home from work, he kept looking at the clock hand which ticked like it was covered in molasses. At one point, he read through the want ads but found nothing of interest. Pacing, he seemed lost in his own home. The clock was moving way too slow, but he couldn't help watching it wanting to push the hand forward. Picking up the phone, he called Marty who had gone through the same thing months earlier. The conversation was comforting as Marty told him he would find a better job. At last, the clock was on his side. He stood by the window looking out. "Amy should be home any time now," he told himself. "I've got so much on my mind. What is she going to say? Nothing seems real. It's like a bad dream. What am I going to do? There's nothing in the paper that I qualify for. Come on Amy where are you?" Moving to the door, he stood with his hand on the doorknob. "By the time I count to one hundred," he assured himself, "you will be pulling into the drive." Staring out the door window, he began counting. When he got to ninety, he slowed down. At ninety-five, he stammered repeating himself. All he knew was that he could not get to one hundred without her pulling into the drive. Eyes closed, slurring ninety-eight repeatedly until a flash of light shined through his closed eyelids. He was relieved, opening his eyes; Amy was pulling into the drive. "One hundred," he blurted with joy. "At least something's gone right for me today," he thought. Turning the doorknob, he paused, backed away to the sofa, sat down, grabbed the television remote control and clicked it on.

Amy walked in looking sad. "So how are you doing?" she asked.

"I'm doing pretty good," he said looking up from the sofa.

"Everyone at work's upset."

"Who?" he said.

"No one can believe you got fired for helping Rosetta and Chastity. In fact, they thought it ironic that you would help Chastity after everything that had happened and this is how you get rewarded for it."

"What did Jerry say?" he asked, referring to the staff whose bachelor party he had attended.

"He talked about sabotaging the place. He was furious."

"Really," he said half-delighted.

"What about all the other staff?"

"They're all angry and up in arms. You sure you're okay?"

"I think I'm in a state of shock. I don't think it's hit me yet. It felt so weird being here alone. How did the kids take my firing?"

"They were all upset."

"And Tommy?"

"He was screaming, cursing, and swearing at Rob," she said. "He had to be restrained ... What have you been doing all evening?"

"I was on the phone with Marty for awhile. I've had a couple of beers."

"A bunch of workers are getting together for a drink or two. Do you feel like meeting up with them?"

"Sure. Where at?"

"The Eagle's Nest."

338

Fifteen minutes later, Tom and Amy walked into the neighborhood bar greeted by half-dozen somber faces. They welcomed Tom with open arms patting him on the back expressing their anger and sorrow and one worker shouted, "Rob can stick his head where the sun don't shine …" All the workers joined in unison repeating the phrase. Putting his unhappiness aside, he drank and was merry for the moment.

"Let me tell you something," said a young man. "You're free of that prison."

"No more putting up with bullshit at the home," Brenda yelled.

"I am a lucky man," Tom boasted. "I am free."

"That's right," Brenda said. "We're all stuck in that shitty place but you're free of it."

"Tomorrow I'll start looking for a sane job. I know there's got to be one out there. A sane job," he stammered. As the night dragged on, the beers kept coming and Tom kept drinking them. With the evening coming to a close, Tom stumbled out of the bar with Amy's arm wrapped around him to keep his balance. "I am free," he mumbled with a sorrowful look. After driving home, Amy helped Tom up the steps to the front door. "Hold on," he slurred. "I want to make an announcement." Looking up at the dark sky, he roared, "I am free," and then danced, clapping his hands. Lightning and thunder followed, causing him to howl with the sky lighting up as raindrops trickled down muffling the sound.

"Come on," Amy laughed. "Neighbors will hear you."

"Okay," he snickered, looking up. "Raindrops keep falling on my face," he began singing.

"Don't you mean falling on my head? Silly. Come on, we're going to get soaked."

"It feels good," he said closing his eyes as they both got drenched. "Raindrops keep falling on my –"

"Come on, "she said, dragging him into the house. "Take your clothes off here," she insisted standing on the carpet right before reaching the hardwood oak floor. They both stripped near the doorway with Amy helping Tom to the living room. "Come on let's get to bed." Gripping the stairway rail, Tom pulled himself up to the bedroom with Amy behind him. Plopping on the bed, they got under the cover. Tom embraced Amy, kissing and hugging and she returned the affection. Love making commenced, but fizzled as the alcohol suppressed Tom's stamina causing him to drift into dreamland.

Arranging for Chastity's return to the children's home took a lot of coordination on Rosetta's part. The home was willing to take Chastity back only if the court were to rescind the emancipation. The bottom line for the children's home was receiving money for readmission. The entire process was frustrating to Rosetta, which was accomplished with the state social services intervening on Chastity's behalf. An emergency court hearing cleared the way for Chastity's return to the home, but when Rosetta and Chastity learned what had happened to Tom, they were enraged with Chastity swearing not to return unless they let Tom return to the home. When Tom heard what was going on, he told Rosetta that he was on his way over to talk to both of them. On arriving at Rosetta's, he found two sad-faced girls. Rosetta hugged Tom and Chastity wanted too but stood back. "Those people at that home are idiots," Chastity said.

"I won't argue with you about some, but you know most of them aren't."

"What about Dickhead?" Chastity said.

"Dick Muster's out of there."

"Thanks to you from what I heard," Chastity said.

"And that's why you were fired," Rosetta said. "We all know the story."

"Well," he sighed. "I pissed them off for going to the paper."

"Because they wouldn't do anything," said Rosetta.

"You got that right. Now listen to me," Tom said to Chastity. "Rosetta told me you had made up your mind to go back. It was a great decision. I know Rosetta worked her buns off to resolve things so you could return. What's happened to me has nothing to do with you going or not going back."

"They just *piss* me off," said Chastity.

340

"I understand how she feels," Rosetta added. "I mean," she hesitated. "Well, I was actually thinking of working there."

"What?" Tom said surprised.

"It was all going to be a surprise," she said, frowning. "I put in an application and yesterday I was asked to come in for an interview, which I did and was offered a job."

"That's great," Tom said.

"It was before I knew what happened to you. I mean now I don't want to take it."

"What did you tell them?" asked Tom.

"Well, I said yes but that was before I knew they had railroaded you."

"And I'm telling you," Tom insisted, "the same thing I just told Chastity. I'm not in the equation. *You hear me?* Both of you. Rosetta, I'm proud of you when I think back to where you were at a few years ago. I mean it. So proud of you. Your graduation is this Friday evening. You have a professional job and you are going to take it. *Do you hear me?*"

"I don't know," she said.

"I didn't know you were going to work there," said Chastity.

"I was going to surprise you. But they want me for the young boys' unit."

"Really," Tom said in amazement. "Then that means," he paused in thought. "Hold on let me call Amy." Making the call, she answered. "Hey, did someone from the young boys' unit just take my job? Oh, yeah. Alright," he said hanging up.

"Now it's even worse," Rosetta fumed. "I'm getting a job because they fired you."

"Don't go there," Tom stressed. "It's okay."

"Well," spat Chastity. "I'm not going back if she won't take the job now."

"Rosetta," Tom reflected, "I know why you applied. Go through with it. It's eating away at you. Just do it."

"I'm just frustrated," she said.

"Alright Chastity," said Tom. "If Rosetta goes to work there will you return?"

"I don't know, I guess."

"Yes or no?"

"Alright, yes."

"Rosetta," Tom said, squeezing her shoulder. "Please take the job."

"Well, gee, you sure make things difficult."

"No, I don't. You've worked your butt off to turn your life around. Now put all that learning to good use and make the right decision."

"You're mean," Rosetta said with a half-smile.

"No, I'm right and you know it."

Looking at Chastity, Rosetta said, "Well girl, I guess we're both going to the home. You don't know this, but I've lived in homes like this myself."

"Really," she said.

"Yeah, really," said Rosetta. "Before I went to Tom and Amy's foster home."

"Then it's settled," Tom said, smiling.

"But what about you?" Rosetta said, eyes pleading and body wavering.

"I'll be okay. Hey, I'll be getting unemployment until I find another job. You know what they say about a crisis don't you?"

"What's that?" from Rosetta.

"With every crisis, there is an opportunity to better yourself."

"Why is that?" said Chastity.

"Because it forces you to make changes and you are in the driver's seat to face a new challenge. Yeah, I fear the unknown right now. I won't lie. But there is something better for me out there and I'll find it."

"Now," said Rosetta, "you sound like the Tom I remember as my foster dad."

"Hopefully that's good."

"Believe me," she said hugging him, "it is."

"So when do they want you to start?" he asked.

"This coming Monday."

"You graduate on Friday and start on Monday. That's great," Tom said, nodding. "So we're squared away here, right?"

"I guess," Rosetta said.

"Chastity?" said Tom.

"I'm on board too, I guess."

"Good. I guess it's settled," he said smiling. "I've got things to take care of so I'll see you Friday night at graduation."

Chastity returned to the children's home and tried to look at things in a new light, but faced great pressure from the other residents who expected her to live up to the former firecracker reputation she had established. Amy's presence on the unit was a reminder of all she had been through, which helped her to remain focused and have a positive attitude. While Chastity got settled into the home's routines, Rosetta was preparing to graduate from college. Friday evening came and Rosetta walked down the aisle in a graduation robe with Mike, Tom, Amy, Andre and Windy in the audience. When it was her turn to receive the graduation certificate, the presenter said, "Rosetta Meady and I am proud to announce that Rosetta is the recipient of this year's Leonardo Da Vinci Award for the most accomplished, imaginative artist at our university this year."

Rosetta gleamed walking up to the front of the auditorium. The audience stood and applauded. On being handed the award, she held onto it with both hands. A tear formed in her eye which she tried to hold back, but it streaked down her face. Looking at the audience, she hesitated and then said, "Thank you. I'm speechless."

When the ceremony was over Rosetta congregated with all her friends, giving everyone a hug and kiss. The group gathered for dinner at a classy restaurant. A non-alcoholic bottle of sparkling champagne was served out of respect to Rosetta's sobriety for many years. Andre stood and proposed a toast. "To Rosetta, a living example of what we all hope to be someday." Rosetta squirmed, looking at Andre with anticipation. "That is admired by all for being an inspiration to others."

"Oh come on," she blushed.

"Oh no, it's true," everyone said and took a sip of their drink.

"And a special toast," Andre continued, "for putting Big Jake in his place."

"Yes, yes," came the response from the others.

"You're all so kind," Rosetta said. "And I propose a toast to all of you for helping me accomplish what I have so far. I've faced fear in the eye and overcome it thanks to all of you. I mean it sincerely. Thank you guys," she said, touching Mike's shoulder. Mike stood and gave her a kiss. "And one more toast," she said, "to becoming a real social worker like all of you guys." Looking at Mike, she continued, "And I know you don't consider yourself a social worker Mike, but we know you're out there every day serving people. You're just an armed social worker because some people don't appreciate the job you do."

"Well," said Mike, "you got a point there, but heaven forbid the person who doesn't appreciate you helping them because we all know you don't need a gun to get the job done."

"Well let's hope not," she said, hugging him.

"You may be unarmed," Tom said, "but you're definitely not defenseless. You have the wit, the perseverance, and the courage to accomplish any challenge. You really have graduated. You're light years ahead of all those other graduates."

"And let's not forget," Amy added, "what a great artist Rosetta is."

"I second that," Windy said. "You have so much going for you. I don't know how you paint what you do, but it's incredible. Don't ever stop."

"Enough is enough guys. I appreciate everything, but you're really giving me a big head and I need to come back to earth because that's where I belong. You hear me? I mean it knock it off." Smiling, she looked up at the restaurant window, noticed a man peeking in, and shuddered believing he was watching her. Not wishing to look at the man, wanting to gain control, she stood, "I'll be back. I need to go to the restroom." Walking away, she passed a large wall mirror, glanced at it catching a glimpse of the man's face, which caused her to hurry into the restroom. In desperation, she took deep breaths and thought about all that had been said on this evening. "You've got to face fear in the eye," she told herself. Gaining courage, she walked out of the restroom and told the group as she passed by them that she would be right back. Going out of the restaurant door, she headed to the man by the window. "You want to see me?" she ranted. "Well, here I am." Reaching the man, she stood stupefied.

"I'm sorry," the man said. "Do I know you?"

"Oh no, I'm sorry. I just thought you were someone else. My mistake."

Returning to the group, she smiled, shaking her head. "Who was that?" Mike asked.

"You know what guys. I still have a long ways to go. I thought that was my dad looking in the window. I wish it was because I was ready to give him a piece of my mind."

"There you go," said Andre. "You're already there for real. He just wasn't there. That's all. You went to face him. You're there."

"I don't know," she said. "But you know what? I think I want to face him and get it out of my system."

"You sure you're ready for that?" asked Mike.

"I'm dead serious. I mean it, but enough of my issues for tonight. Let's just enjoy the rest of the night. Okay?"

The rest of the night was enjoyed by all, even Tom who put his anxiety aside for the evening. When the celebration came to an end, Rosetta thanked everyone and gave Andre and Windy a hug as they were headed back to Los Angeles the next day. She then pulled Amy aside, asked about Chastity and then asked Tom how he was holding up.

"I'm fine," he said. "This job thing's no big deal."

"But with the economy like it is and the high unemployment," Rosetta said, "I'm concerned for you."

"I'll bounce back. I'm just happy for you. Mike's a great guy."

"I think so too."

"Alright," he said giving her a hug and kiss on the cheek. "Just be careful about working with Aaron. The boy has some major issues. Try not to make it personal. You hear?"

"Oh, I hear. Don't worry. I'll do what is right. We'll talk to you later."

At last Rosetta and Mike were left alone together. "You have a great group of friends," Mike said.

"They're the best."

"So what do you want to do now?"

"Well, I was thinking. Since I'm so much into facing my fears tonight, how about us going to your place?"

"What do you mean facing your fears? You don't fear me do you?"

"Of course not. So are we going to your place?"

"Sure, let's go."

On reaching Mike's house, they got cozy on the sofa hugging and kissing like on many previous occasions. Mike, as usual, restrained his passions due to his respect for Rosetta and all the baggage she was carrying. "I have something for you," Mike said.

"A graduation present?" she said.

"Yes, if you want it?" he said pulling a tiny wrapped gift out of his pocket. In great awe, he handed it over.

She smiled and opened it. "Oh my," she said, seeing the diamond engagement ring.

Mike held his breath uncertain of what to expect. "Well?" he said.

"I want you to know that I had a baby because of Gomez and I gave the boy up."

"You told me about it before."

"I wasn't sure if you were listening."

"Believe me. I'm okay with everything."

"And my dad?"

"I said everything."

Taking the ring out of the box, she put it on and then hugged and kissed Mike saying, "I love you."

"I love you," he said relieved. "So you accept it?"

"Of course I do." More hugging, kissing and fondling followed on the sofa. Both of their passions were boiling. Rosetta, stood, pulling Mike up. "I think it's time that I see your bedroom."

"Really," he said surprised.

"Yes, really," she said, hugging him. "Lead the way."

Entering the room, hands as one, they moved to the bed and sat together on the edge and let their emotions go. Before long, they were undressed making mad passionate love. It was the first time in over five years that Rosetta had a sexual relationship. The last time was at the forceful hand of Gomez and the drug induced delusion he put them through. Aaron was the result, but Mike was all that she cared about at the moment.

Chapter 27

It was only a job. People lose jobs every day. But I wasn't burnt-out like the director said. I had been betrayed for doing the right thing. Just say it like it is. I felt like my life was over. You know kind of like floating in the middle of the ocean with a life jacket keeping you afloat with sharks swarming all around ready to devour you. The job was me. It was who I was. But it was only a job. That's what he said to me. Maybe he was right? I only felt dead. Death is mutilated bodies, a carpet of blood, retched dry heaves and a stench that was enough to kill you. That was death. I was just a damn naive social worker, walking into a carnage that will be stamped in my brain forever. That's what I saw and here I am complaining, feeling like I am dead. What's wrong with you? Are you a man or are you a whining baby? You're breathing. They were breathless. Their demise was so horrifying that it makes a person in a casket look like they are happy. I can't get those faces out of my mind. You know what? He was right. It was only a job. There are other jobs and you'll find one. You still have your real estate. I only wish it was a real job. Maybe the economy will turn around and business will blossom. But in the meantime, you get off your butt and you find something. At least you have unemployment insurance for awhile. You're not dead. You just feel like it. Those agonizing faces and lifeless bodies I can't get out of my mind confirm that. It was unreal. I feel sick.

Pushing himself away from the computer, Tom took a deep breath and then hit save on the screen before shutting it down. For a Saturday morning, Tom was sparking with energy while Amy slept. In fact, the sun had not even risen. Looking out at the darkness, he wondered if every morning would be like this – writing, working on a novel with no outlined plot, but waiting for the plot to develop as he lived one day to the next. This was no way to write a novel he thought and yet knew it was the only way for now. He believed his life was the novel and he had to see where it was taking him. It was a madness that had to be controlled, but he felt out of control. Standing, he paced for five minutes and plopped on the sofa, covered his head with a pillow and tried to go to sleep, but tossed and turned. Three hours later, Amy got up and saw Tom sleeping on the sofa. "Hey," she said, shaking him. "We need to be at the real estate office in less than an hour."

"What?" he said, burying his head under the pillow.

"It's time to get up."

"Oh yeah, do you think it's even worth going?"

"It's a meeting. We're supposed to be there. So get up."

"Alright, I'm up," he said still motionless.

"I mean it."

"Okay," he said forcing himself up.

"Why were you down here?"

"Couldn't sleep. I came down to write. I was writing like a mad man until I felt sick to my stomach."

Walking to and opening the front door, Amy returned with the newspaper. "Here," she said handing him the job ads. "Finding a job will make you feel better. You can look at it while I drive us to the office."

"Yeah right. There was nothing in it yesterday."

"Today is a new day."

"Alright, don't get bitchy."

"*Bitchy*," she flared. "I'm trying to help."

"Okay, okay. Sorry, I'm just on edge. I'm up. I'll get dressed."

"I'll fix us something to eat."

"Go ahead. I'm not hungry."

"You sure?"

"I'm sure."

Rosetta and Mike left town in guarded eagerness to visit her dad in Joliet, a three-hour drive of flat farmland and blue skies. The last time she saw him they were in a courtroom. Her testimony sent him to prison. Rosetta convinced Mike that she needed to confront him to try to put the past behind. After contacting the police department that morning, Mike got the needed information to locate him as he had a parole officer to report to. On arriving in Joliet, they found the one room efficiency apartment where he lived. It was early afternoon and they hoped he was there. Mike looked at Rosetta, and they hugged before getting out of the car. Walking up to the apartment, she trembled, clenched her fist and then pounded on the door, imagining it was her dad's face with every blow, but no one responded. "Where is he?" she said pounding once again.

A man came out of the next door apartment, "He's probably over at Joe's Tap. He usually is."

"Where would that be?" Mike asked, thinking he was violating his parole being in a tavern.

Pointing, the man said, "Right up the street. See it? About a half a block away."

"Yeah, I see it," said Mike. "Thanks."

Getting in the car, they drove to Joe's Tap. "It figures he would be drinking. That's how I remember him. A drunken maniac."

"Maybe I should go in and check things out first?"

"No, I'm fine. I need to see this through."

"What are you going to say to him?"

"I don't know. We'll find out."

Mike entered the tavern with Rosetta following him. As they looked about Mike let Rosetta step in front of him. Rosetta's ears perked recognizing her dad's voice in the distance. At the end of the bar, he sat on a stool half-slumped over blabbing away to the bartender. "You're full of shit," she heard the bartender say. Moving forward, wavering, she inched toward him.

"You can do it," Mike whispered.

"He's more than full of shit," she sighed squeezing Mike's arm. "I know, I'll do it."

Within a body length of him, she froze listening to his ranting voice. "I don't give a damn what that prick says, he's a nut case, a real screwball. He don't know who the hell he's dealing with. He don't know who I am."

"*Well I do,*" Rosetta spat moving right in his face.

"What?" he said half-shocked, gazing with a blank stare.

"You're more than full of shit you know. You're rotten to the core."

"Who are you?" he said dumbfounded.

"What do you mean who am I?"

"What's your problem?" he slurred. "You got a problem?"

Looking him square in the eye, she said, "You know *damn well* who I am. I am finally facing you. You're through ruining my life. Do you hear me?"

"What lunatic farm did they let you out of? You're crazy. I don't know who the hell you are."

"Go to hell," she said.

"Who are you?" he said again, looking perplexed, and then nodded his head.

"You know what? If you don't know then you are dead and out of my life for good."

"Maybe I don't want to remember. You're a crazy bitch," he said laughing. "Just like your mom."

"You're disgusting," she snarled and slapped him. "She died after an argument with you. I was only one, but I know the truth. You're dead as far as I'm concerned. You're not going to haunt me anymore."

"Her death was an accident, but you putting me in jail wasn't. What more do you want?"

"You put me through hell and I'm getting out. What I want is to know that I looked you square in the eye for the first time in my life. I don't ever want to have to face my fear of you again. I don't think that's too much to ask. The only decent thing you did for me was to kick me in the stomach causing me to miscarriage your baby. What I want is my nightmare of you to end."

"Leave me alone," he whined.

"Those are the same words I said *over* and *over* to you. *Leave me alone. Leave me alone.* You never listened to me. Did you? I would say you got off easy. I bet you never had a nightmare about me, did you? You were a slobbering drunk back then and you still are. I guess I'm done. Just don't say another word." Turning to Mike, she said, "Let's get out of here."

Driving home Rosetta and Mike were quiet in thought when Mike said, "Are you okay?"

"Part of me is and part of me isn't."

"I'm proud of you. It took a lot of guts to face him."

"That's the good part of all of this. The bad part is wondering what you're thinking?"

"I just told you what I was thinking."

"You don't have any questions?"

"Well, actually," he said, "I was kind of wondering –"

"I knew it," she said, hands clamped together.

"Knew what?"

"Just say it."

"I was wondering if I should have said something to him. I just wasn't sure. I didn't want to jump into stuff that wasn't my business. You know what I mean?"

"That's what's bothering you?"

"Well, yeah, kind of."

"I thought," she hesitated. "I really thought it had something to do with what I told him. You know, what I hadn't told you about."

"Listen," he smiled, wrapping his arm around her, "the past is past. I already accepted it. What you went through is enough for anyone. I don't want to make it worse. If you want to talk about it that's fine and if you don't I understand."

"Are you for real?" she said, cuddling next to him.

"All that matters is that I love you. You hear me?"

"Yeah. I hear you. Well, you may as well know one other thing. This is something fairly new that has developed." Smiling, she hesitated, "It has to do with my new job at the children's home."

"And here I thought you were going to become a cop. Actually, I'm glad you're not. So what's the big news? "

"You know how I gave up my baby to an adoptive home, right?"

"Right."

"Well, Tom discovered something recently at the home. It's totally unreal. A boy almost five years old was placed there," she paused. "It's hard to believe, but he's my son."

"*What*? How? I mean he was adopted."

"The people couldn't handle him and gave him up."

"Wow that's strange isn't it?"

"There are a lot of failed adoptions from what I've found out."

"And you're going to be working with him? So that's why you applied there. Does anyone at the home know about it?"

"Just Amy. So how does that grab you?"

"It makes me wonder what's going on inside of that beautiful mind of yours."

"It's complicated. I guess I don't know yet. I'll have to figure it out."

"I know you." Cocking his head, he said, "You're plotting something aren't you?"

"I just want to get to know him."

"And then?"

"Let's just start with that."

"It all sounds so complicated. You did give him up and for good reason. You were young and, gee I don't know what to say. He was adopted and now he's in a children's home. I'm not sure where all of this is going, but if you are asking me does this scare me? The answer is," he hesitated. "The answer is no."

"You hesitated."

"Somehow the picture of us suddenly included a boy. Just a thought, but there's no way I'm scared off. Do you believe me?"

"We'll see."

"I mean it."

"Alright, I believe you I guess."

"Good. Are there any other curve balls you want to pitch to me?"

"So," she smiled, "I'm throwing curve balls, huh?"

"You know what I mean. Nothing's going to scare me off. You're my extraordinary, beautiful, and very talented fiancée."

"You're very persuasive," she said kissing his cheek.

After their arrival at LAX in Los Angeles, Andre and Windy wasted no time in catching a taxi and returning to the shelter. The disaster in the California economy with the state being unable to pay its bills meant major cuts in social service programs. Holding a letter in his hand, Andre read with great concern and set it down on the desk. Windy was in another room admitting a new runaway. When she was done, Andre broke the news. "It is finally official. All of our state funding has been cut effective next month. I guess, shit, I mean," he stammered, "I guess we're out of business."

"Oh no," she said. "But these kids? We've got a lot of money. We can just use our money."

"We'll hang on as long as we can. But I don't know if we can last forever using our own money – there's rent, food, utilities, transporting kids and on and on. But more importantly, I don't know what this will mean for our license with the state as a provider. I mean we have to provide services. I don't know, I'm just shocked and yet I knew it was coming. It's ironic, isn't it? We finally get Big Jake off our backs and now this."

"Are you sure about Big Jake?"

"What do you mean?"

"There's a guy across the street that I remember seeing before. We thought he was watching us. He has a baseball cap on."

"Where?" Andre asked, looking about as Windy pointed through the window. Gazing at the man, Andre seethed, clenched his fist and stormed out of the building toward him. The man saw Andre coming and headed up the street. Andre pursued picking up the pace. Glancing back, the man sped up and turned the corner. Andre exploded into a run and was on top of the man before he knew he was caught. Grabbing him, Andre shouted, "So what's the deal?"

"What do you want?" the man pleaded.

"Why are you watching us?"

"I wasn't."

"*Liar, I've had it,*" he yelled, grabbing the back of the man's hair.

"Alright! Alright!"

"Haven't you talked to Big Jake?" he said, yanking the man's head back. "We're to be left alone. Do you understand? Give him a call now."

"Okay," he moaned. "I'll do it. Don't have his number with me, but I'll call him. Just let go."

"You do it and hear directly from him that we're not to be bothered anymore. Do you understand?"

"I hear you. I don't know much. I'm just a runner."

"Well," Andre said letting loose, "you run your butt off and find out the latest information."

"I got you."

"Here," he said, pulling out a card from his wallet. "Ask Big Jake to call me."

"I hear you. We'll work it all out. I'm out of your hair man."

Pushing the man away, he said, "Go."

Andre returned to the shelter, told Windy what had happened, and then attended to business. Later in the day, Andre received a call from Big Jake telling him that he was still down in Juarez dealing with many problems, but had told his people to leave them alone. Andre and Windy were relieved on one hand but disheartened on the other having to direct their attention to money issues.

David had calmed down but was far from resolving his problem. Although feeling like the nightmare would not end, he had stopped threatening suicide. At school one day, an announcement was made that a priest would be hearing confessions at the nearby church for interested students. David was compelled to go when the final bell rang dismissing classes. Walking to the church, he noticed his friend Ben approaching and turned toward him, saying, "I don't feel like talking."

"What is wrong with you?"

"Just leave me alone."

"You're going to church? You must be off your rocker. *Shit,*" he laughed. "Why would you be going to confession? What did you do that you're acting so weird?"

"Just leave me alone."

"Whatever," he said, stopping and watched David walk away. Once he was out of sight, Ben hurried to the church, entered and saw his friend kneeling near the confessional, waiting his turn. Observing David make the sign of the cross, cover his face and pray out loud made Ben more curious as he waited in the distance concealed from sight. When a girl left, David went into the confessional, knelt down and could barely open his mouth, but did after the priest spoke up telling him to begin.

"Bless me father for I have sinned," David said, as Ben sneaked up to the confessional to listen. "It has been six months since my last confession."

"Oh my," said the priest. "Six months is way too long my son. We encourage everyone to go at least once a month."

"I know, I know," he repeated. "Everything is insane. I feel like I'm in a dream. I didn't want to do it. It just happened."

"Slow down my son. Please start from the beginning."

"I don't know where to start."

"The beginning is a good place."

"Which beginning is what I mean?"

"I'll leave that up to you."

"My dad was all freaked out because I'm different. Do you understand?"

"No, explain."

"You know I'm like you guys. I like boys."

"Please do not judge me by misguided priests."

"Whatever you say. It don't matter. What matters is what my dad put me through."

"And what is that?"

"He wanted me to like girls. Do you understand?"

"Yes, go on."

"He said he was taking me to a therapist. What he did was take me to a girl, left me with her and she said she was a therapist. I believed both of them. I should have known better the way the place looked. She had me lay down on a table. My eyes were closed. The next thing I knew she's naked forcing my hand against her breast. She said she was going to make me straight. I couldn't take it. I grabbed the vase and made her stop. Do you understand?"

"Please slow down. I don't understand what happened."

"I smashed the vase over her head. Blood was everywhere. Now do you understand?"

"Oh my, yes. Was she okay?"

"She wouldn't move. She was *dead*. My dad came back and called for a cleanup crew and said it didn't happen. He took me away."

"It didn't happen?" the priest said confused. "I don't understand?"

"It was like I was dreaming and none of it was real."

"I'm very confused. Was it a dream?"

"I don't think so. Even my bloody clothes disappeared."

"I don't know what to say," the priest stammered. "Don't know what to say."

"Aren't you going to tell me what my penitence is Father? I'll say a thousand Hail Mary's or whatever you tell me to do. I've never committed a really bad sin like this before. Will God forgive me? … Or was it all a bad dream? …"

While David continued to ramble, Ben was in awe unsure of what to do but decided he better leave before he was spotted. Hesitating, he then scrambled away to a side door on hearing the front door of the church open.

Chapter 28

With the summer heat nearing record temperatures, Amy's demeanor swayed between a sizzling fuse and fizzled out one as she walked by Tom who sat at his desk typing. Noticing Amy's tight jaw and arched eyebrows, he froze, squinted with a sigh, detecting smoldering eyes peeking at him.

"I give up," he snarled. "I think you're pissed, but you're smiling?"

"*Smiling?*" she sneered, fuse reignited.

"I know things suck right now, but I'll find a job."

"You're not looking very hard."

"For Christ sakes, I just lost my job."

"Yeah, but you were told months ago by Rob to find another job."

"So you're sticking up for him now?"

"No, but I'm frustrated with a lot of things. I think we need to see a marriage counselor."

"What?" he cringed as if he had just been punched in the face.

"You heard me."

"Things will get better."

"I'm dead serious about it."

Looking down, shoulders shrugging, he said, "If that's what you want I don't care."

"Well, you need to care."

"Do you have someone in mind?"

"I guess we should go through the Human Service Center. They charge based on income."

"Alright, make an appointment," he said dejected.

"I'll do it now. Okay?"

"Fine," he pouted, stood and went upstairs. Grabbing weathered jogging clothes off of a closet hook, he fumed, thinking, "I can't take it," as he dressed.

Rosetta had started her first day of work at the children's home. Feeling fortunate to get first shift, she spent the first two hours filling out forms, being explained work policy procedures and given a tour of the home. When it was time to go to the young boys' unit, Rob, the director, escorted her to the small building behind the home. "The first week," Rob said, "there will always be someone with you while you are learning the ins and outs of the job."

"That sounds fair," she said as they entered the building.

"I'll be leaving you with your supervisor John Sanders and he'll go over everything." While led to an office, Rosetta noticed two boys watching television and a staff sitting at a desk near them. She thought the one boy was Aaron but was uncertain since his back was turned. Knocking on the door, a voice said come in. "John," Rob said, "I have your new worker here. This is Rosetta."

"Nice meeting you," he said holding out his hand which she shook.

"I'll leave you two alone."

Rosetta and John discussed what was expected of her and the general routine for first shift. Next, he described the five children she would be working with and explained each one's treatment plan. When he was done, he asked if she had any questions, which she did and could not help asking specific questions about Aaron. "Why do you feel that Aaron's problems stem from fetal alcohol syndrome?"

"His behavior points to it. All the signs are there. The mom was obviously a drinker. He definitely has a detachment disorder."

"I think there could be other reasons," she said on edge.

"Why is that?"

"Because," she said searching for an explanation. "Because everything that I have studied says there are many factors for his type of behavior."

"Well, it will be interesting for you to enlighten me someday, but for now the issue is the behaviors and dealing with them which will be quite challenging. Personally, I think the boy is bipolar, but it's hard to diagnose at such a young age. You have your work cut out for you with him and the other boys. Why don't I introduce you to him? He and Michael are watching television. Are you ready to mingle with them?"

"Oh definitely, I'm ready."

John led the way and Rosetta followed. As they approached the boys, Rosetta's eyes brightened, but her body quivered. Pulling herself together, she bent down by the two boys whose eyes protruded like ball bearings magnetized to the screen. "High there," she said.

Michael turned and looked. "Hi," he said, and then refocused on the television. Aaron never turned to look as he was captivated by the cartoon.

"Aaron," John said, touching his shoulder, "don't you want to meet the new worker?"

"Huh?" he said, looking at John. "I want you to meet Rosetta."

Aaron turned, eyes lit up and was drawn like a hungry baby to a nipple, hugging away saying, "Mommy, mommy."

Rosetta bent down hugging back, struggling to hold back tears. "Baby," she whimpered.

"Oh mommy," he repeated.

"That's enough," said John, "Rosetta's the new worker. He likes to call a lot of women mommy."

"*No mommy*," Aaron said hanging on.

"That's enough. This is Rosetta."

Rosetta's clock had been turned back. She wanted to say yes I'm mommy but regained control seeing John staring. "I'm, I'm Rosetta. You have," she hesitated, wanting to say wild eyes, but said, "big bright eyes."

"I love you, mommy," he whined.

"Stop it," John said. "Let go of her before she has second thoughts about working here."

"Oh no, it's fine," she said standing up. "He's a real cutie. We're going to get along fine. Aren't we?"

"Oh yes mommy," he said holding onto her leg.

"Calm down," John said. "I have to show Rosetta around the building. Come on Rosetta."

"Don't leave me, mommy," he cried not wanting to let loose.

"I'll be back," Rosetta said.

"Do you promise?"

"I promise."

"Okay," he conceded, big-eyed, as they walked away.

Rosetta turned, half-smiling, half-fretting and said, "I'll be back."

Shaking his head, John said, "I've never seen him act like that before."

"I thought you said he calls a lot of women mommy?"

"Well, yeah, but not to this extreme and all the hugging and holding on aren't in character. You definitely made an impression."

"I don't know what to say."

"Don't worry about it. Before long I am sure you'll wish that's how he behaved all of the time. I mean with all I've told you about his bizarre behaviors."

"Well yeah, we'll see, but he seems like a little sweetheart to me."

"Good. Keep thinking that. Maybe you can reach him. No one else has been able to."

"I'll give him a lot of love."

"Believe me it's going to take more than love. You should know that. Right?"

"I know. He just seems so love deprived. Don't worry. I understand behavior modification and all of the psychological principles."

"Well, I would hope so."

"What do you know about his mom?"

"Really nothing. He was adopted at birth. The adoptive parents gave him up at around a year and a half because they couldn't deal with his behavior. Can you imagine that? Only a year and a half and the kid was bouncing off the walls. He hasn't been here that long, but he's been a handful. He sees a therapist. I hope he isn't scaring you off already."

"Of course not. Why would you say that?"

"The guy that you're replacing could not handle the boy. He couldn't wait to get out of here."

"Are you saying he's the worst kid here?"

"They all have problems. Aaron's just a little bit bizarre at times. His parents must have been something else."

"Yeah," she whispered looking down. "Especially his dad."

"What did you say?"

"You know," she said. "The dad must have been the problem. He says mommy all of the time."

Andre carried a sign to the front of the shelter and taped it on the window. Returning to a boy sitting at a computer, he told the boy to come to his office where Andre made a phone call to his parents. A half-hour later, the boy walked out of the office smiling. Andre sat back looking as if he had won a chess match. Before long, his jovial expression changed. "What's wrong?" he said to Windy who entered the office.

"I was just talking to a girl who was looking at the sign you put on the window."

"A girl?" he said puzzled.

"A sad-looking girl was standing outside the building and I went out and spoke to her. That's all."

"And why do you look sad?"

"It's just the sign and what the girl said."

"What did she say?"

"She goes by here every day. We helped her friend and she thought we might be able to help her someday. But that nasty sign you put out told her we wouldn't be here anymore. Her friend said she could trust us."

"We're still here."

"She said she wasn't quite ready."

"What's her problem?"

"She wouldn't say. All she said was that we came highly recommended. Then she walked away."

"Believe me," he said, "it was hard putting the sign-up."

"I know. We made our decision."

"The state made our decision."

"Well yeah."

"You know we've tried everywhere to get backing. Everyone is out of money."

"I just hope we have better luck back in Illinois. Getting funding is supposed to be bad everywhere."

"We'll work something out back home. We only left because of Big Jake and he's off our backs now. It feels good to be free once again. I do have a political contact back home that might be able to help us out with support for a shelter."

"But we wouldn't be high-tailing it out of here if we hadn't lost our funding."

"I know. It's sad leaving everything behind. Unfortunately, there's always going to be a need for a shelter. It would have been nice if we were going out of business because there were no more runaways or destitute kids needing our help. Right?"

"Well yeah, but it'll never happen. The world's a rotten place for a lot of kids. They're going to show up at any door we open up to them."

"You got that right."

As the evening came to an end for Andre and Windy at the shelter, their replacement staff stopped at the front entrance, looked at the sign in the window and came in with sad eyes. "It's so sad," she said.

"I know," Windy said.

"It was really hard putting the sign out there," Andre added.

"I can't even think," the female staff said. "What is it two, three weeks left?"

"Two and a half weeks," Andre said. "I'm sure you'll find another job. I've given you a great reference. I'm confident you'll land on your feet."

"Oh, I appreciate that. It's just there aren't any jobs. I've been looking, but it's the kids I'm sad for. You two go on. I'm okay."

"We'll see you in the morning," Andre said.

Andre and Windy left out the front door, stopped to look at the kids inside carrying on as if nothing was changing. Looking at the sign, Windy read, "*No money. No shelter. Closing at end of month.*"

"The challenges will be tougher," he said, "but we'll be up for it. It means we'll get tougher. Right?"

"Yeah, right," she said punching his arm. "We won't let those idiot politicians get us down."

"We both know you either pay now or pay later. If you don't help people who really, really, need it, you eventually build more prisons to house them after they commit crimes to survive."

"Just like our kids here. Some are a step away from jail. You know, you're smarter than you look."

"I took my smart pill today."

"It's about time. I can remember when you weren't so smart. Remember your crazy infatuation with that Nietzsche guy. You use to drive me crazy spouting off statements of his. Especially when you were drunk. But there was one interesting thing you use to say – what was it? Something about standing and walking before flying."

"I'm surprised you remember that from all those years ago. You're referring to Nietzsche's character Zarathustra who was his mouthpiece. I remember it. Let's see what was it? I know – 'he who would learn to fly one day must first learn to stand and walk and run and climb and dance: one cannot fly into flying ...' You mean, I actually taught you something?"

"It was one of the few things I remember you quoting from him that kind of made sense."

"He had a lot of great thoughts. Let me think there was –"

"That's okay. Quit while you're ahead."

Smiling, looking at the sign, he said, "Well, we definitely will not be walking, running, climbing or dancing back to Illinois."

"But are we flying into flying like he says? I'm serious. Are we moving too fast into everything?"

"All I know is that I feel free of Big Jake and we can go back home. I'm just trying to create some sanity out of this whole insane ordeal."

"I guess I can buy into that."

364

"Like you said – sometimes I'm smart."

When Big Jake returned from Mexico his wife smiled giving him a big hug. "What did you buy?" he said.

"Nothing, but that don't sound like a bad idea."

"Why the pleasant mood?"

"David just seems in a better mood which makes me feel better. It's strange, but I swear I've been hearing him pray out loud."

"Praying? I think I'll go talk to him."

"He actually has his door open."

"Well that's good, I think." Walking up the stairs, Big Jake had a baffled look on his face. "There you are," he said walking into David's bedroom and closing the door. "Has something good happened?"

"Oh yeah."

"Well, what the hell happened?"

"I said a thousand Hail Mary's."

"For what? What did you do?"

"What do you think?"

"I'm not in no mood for games. I've had a very bad week. *So spit it out.*"

"I went to confession."

"And you told the priest what?"

"That's between me, the priest and God."

"Damn it, David," he said grabbing his arm.

"That hurts. Alright! I told him what I did."

"What did you do?" he said letting loose of him.

"You know."

"I don't know."

"The dead girl."

"I told you there was no dead girl," he said, face flushed. "Do you understand? It was a bad dream."

"I don't know but I feel better."

"*So who did you tell?*" he said half-frantic.

"Just the two of them."

"Two!"

"The priest and God."

"Alright, what did the priest say?"

"He thought a thousand Hail Mary's would be a good start."

"And then what?"

"God didn't say anything to me."

"*Shit Almighty.* You're going to drive me insane. I don't want to hear another word about this. You got me?"

"Whatever."

Grabbing his arm again, he blasted out, "Don't you get smart with me."

"*I'm not.* Alright, I understand."

"That's better," he said, shaking his head and walked out of the room.

Later in the day, Big Jake heard a knock on the door and answered it. To his surprise, two detectives held out their badges. "We're with the Evanston Police Department and need to speak to David," said the middle-aged lead detective.

"For what?" Big Jake roared.

"That's between him and us. We've received some information and need to speak to him in private."

"Well, he's not here."

"Who's that?" a detective asked, pointing to a boy standing nearby. "Hey," he said, "are you, David?"

"He's upstairs," the boy replied.

"Are you the father of David?"

"Yes."

"Get your son now."

"I don't think so."

"If you interfere I'll have to arrest you."

"Arrest me. I think I better call my attorney."

"It's like this," said the lead detective, "you either cooperate or else we'll have to take your son into protective custody and call DCFS."

"What's that mean?"

"We have cause to believe that he might be at risk of harm from you."

"That's a bunch of bull. You have no right to see him. Turn your butts around and leave."

"Sir, you are under arrest," he said. "You have the right to remain silent ... Now put your arms behind your back." The detective handcuffed Big Jake and told his partner to take him to the car while he spoke to the son. The lead detective went upstairs and saw a boy sitting at his computer. "Are you David?"

David looked up and said, "Yes, who are you?"

"I'm Detective Snyder. I need to talk to you."

Fifteen minutes later, the detective came out of the house, opened the backseat of the car and had Big Jake get out. Removing the handcuffs from him, he said, "Charges are being dropped. You're free to go."

Returning inside the house, Big Jake went to David's room, perspiring and looking pale. "What in the hell was that about?"

"One of my friends said they heard me in confession and were going to tell the cops if I didn't tell him what had happened. I told him it was none of his business. Someone made an anonymous phone call to the cops. It had to have been him."

"*So what did you say?*"

"The truth."

"What do you mean?"

"I told him it was all a bad dream."

"That's right. It was all a bad dream. Don't ever forget it. A bad dream."

"Sure, just a head splitting bad dream," he said, making the sign of the cross and then began praying. "Hail Mary full of grace, the Lord is with thee ..."

Big Jake's eyes closed, head shook, hands clasped the back of his head, feeling a slicing pain, envisioning Rosetta's painting of him being scalped. "I know all about bad dreams," he toiled in thought. "She was right. I can't get it out of my head for Christ sake ..."

With head pounding, Big Jake's thoughts were drowned out by David's prayers. "Our father who art in heaven ..."

After Rosetta's first day of work, she returned home and finished the painting she was working on. An hour later, Mike showed up as planned and was shown the masterpiece. "Fantastic," he said. "Our visit to Juarez will always be remembered. I'm surprised you want to remember it."

"I'm just into facing my fears. I do see hope in this. That's you, there's Tom, that's Andre."

"And I bet that's Big Jake and Juan?"

"That's right and there's Father Serrano."

"And there's you and Chastity. It looks like you're looking in the church window. We're all there, but it's that stained glass cross that's so amazing. It's shining down casting its colors on you and me. It's such a neat effect. It's like saying we were meant to be together."

"Think so?"

"I know so."

"Maybe, but there's something else on my mind."

"Let me guess. Your new job? How did everything go?"

"Great, really great. You wouldn't believe what Aaron did?"

"Oh?"

"He grabbed a hold of me and wouldn't let go and kept calling me mommy. I didn't know what to do. I was in shock."

"Are you serious?"

"It was unbelievable."

"That is freaky."

"I think he knows."

"How?"

"I don't know."

"What are you going to do?"

"This may sound off the wall, but I wonder if," she hesitated, "if I could get him back somehow? You know adopt him or something?"

"Are you serious?"

"You think it's possible?"

"I don't know, but you need to slow down. You're very emotional right now. You need to think rationally. Put the emotions aside and give yourself time."

"I know I'm overreacting, but he seemed to need me."

"Please, take it slow."

"Yeah, you're right. Take it a day at a time. Get to know him."

"You heard Tom say he had major behavior problems. Is he right?"

"Who wouldn't after what he went through? It's all my fault for giving him up in the first place."

"Don't beat yourself up. You did what you had to."

"There's something about his eyes," she said.

"Like what?"

"They're like looking into a mirror of the past. He has his dad's eyes. Gomez is someone I would sooner forget. I guess my baby represents the best and worst of times in my mind. Maybe that's why I let him go? I needed to bury those bad memories of Gomez. I think he's more like me than Gomez, but I don't know what to think or what to do."

"Like I said," Mike said hugging her, "take it slow."

"I guess," she sighed, and then focused on the painting. "You didn't look inside the church."

"What?" he said confused.

"The *painting*. Remember me and Chastity were looking inside the church window."

"Oh," he said going up to it, looking inside the window. "Huh, how about that? A baby is lying on the altar. What does it mean?"

"I'm not sure. I just put him there before you got here."

Examining the image, Mike said, "The stained glass is reflecting on the baby too."

"That must be good," she said. "Don't you think?"

"I would imagine so."

"I think it's good."

"Then it is good. He's safe, he's protected and he has you as his creator. Rosetta the artist and Rosetta the mother. Everything will come together. Just give it time."

"Do you think he really knows who I am?"

"I don't know how unless you said something?"

"No, no, not at all."

"Maybe he calls all women mommy."

"That's what John my supervisor said."

"Well, there you go."

"He also said he never saw him act like he did holding on to me calling me mommy over and over."

"Maybe you should be working somewhere else at the home."

"Oh no. You know how I faced my dad?"

"Well, yeah."

"I have to face this like all of my fears so I can move on. You're right I created him in the painting and in life. I don't want to fear him. I want to be at peace. Am I insane to think I could adopt my own son?"

"You're not insane, but I'm totally *crazy, crazy, crazy* about you. So is it settled who's insane?"

"You mean I'm not crazy, but you are?"

"That's right," he said.

"Okay, I'll go along with that."

Lifting Rosetta up, Mike swirled like a merry-go-round saying, "I'm nothing without you." She giggled, head free falling and long dark hair flowing wild as if caught in a whirlwind.

"It's a good thing you're crazy," she yelled, "'cause this is driving me wacky. Please put me down." Both were laughing and dizzy as he set her down. On the verge of falling over, Mike grabbed Rosetta's wobbly body just in time. Together they plopped back on the sofa, and after regaining their bearings focused on the painting in front of them.

"I really like the effect of that cross," Mike said.

"I like how it shines on the baby, you and me," she said with a cheerful smile. It makes me feel like we're just a couple American kids like John Cougar Mellencamp sang in "Jack and Diane." Do you know the song? It's before both of our times."

"I love the song. Does that mean we have to stay sixteen?" he said with a smile.

"Wow," Rosetta said with a gleam in her eye, "you do know the song."

"Yes, I do," he said hugging her, whispering in her ear lines from the song that made Rosetta gleam with an ocean-wide smile.

"Just keep whispering sweet nothings," Rosetta said, "and you'll have my ear forever."

Amy had made an appointment with a marriage counselor and she and Tom sat in a room, looking like they were waiting to be scolded by a principal. Neither one of them would look at the other. Each could only anticipate what the other was going to say. When they entered the therapist's office, they greeted him with fallen faces. Seated next to each other, Tom and Amy's defeated look evolved into a quarrelsome bout. By the time they were done with round one, they left with battered egos. Driving home, Amy broke the silence. "I can't believe it," she snapped. "You were so damn different talking with the therapist. You made me seem like an idiot. Like I didn't know what I was talking about."

"I was just being myself."

"*Bullshit.*"

"I was."

"You acted like I was the one with the problem. I'm sick of everything. Then you brought up Burt ..." As they approached their house, Amy said, "I'm dropping you off, I'm meeting Brenda for lunch and then I'm going into work."

Once Amy was at work, she soon forgot about her frustration with Tom after Chastity and another girl were horsing around causing a disruption in the recreation room.

"Give it back to me," a girl yelled.

"Take it from me," Chastity screamed as the girl playfully tried to grab the opened condom from her.

Amy stormed into the room, "Both of you knock it off," she shouted.

"We're just goofing around," Chastity snickered.

"Give that to me," Amy demanded. Giggling, Chastity pulled back on the condom as if it were a rubber band and snapped it against Amy's butt. *"I've had it with you,"* Amy roared.

"Aren't you glad I'm back?" Chastity said giving her the finger and then ran to the tall support pole, climbed up it and slid halfway down, hanging upside down as if a stripper.

Swearing under her breath, head shaking, Amy stormed off up the hallway to pull herself together. At the end of the shift, she was headed out of the building, when Tommy Wizel yelled, "Hey, can you do me a favor?"

Turning to him, she said, "What Tommy? I'm just leaving for the evening."

"Here," he said, the wrapped gift in hand. "Could you give this to Tom for me?"

"Yes, I can do that," she said taking the gift and walked away.

When Amy arrived home and walked in the front door, Tom was sitting at the computer typing and said, "Hey."

"Hey," she replied, handing him the gift. "It's from Tommy."

"No kidding. That was nice of him." Amy walked away and he stared at the gift for a moment in wonderment and then opened it. "Huh," he chuckled, looking at the book – '*The Mumble Jumble Schizophrenic Chronicles*' by Professor Frantic.

Amy returned saying, "So what did he give you?" Smiling, Tom held up the book for her to see. "Well, he must have been listening to our therapy session."

"Ha, ha," from Tom.

"You know you really pissed me off. Oh, by the way, your girlfriend Chastity was being a real ass today."

"Don't start up a bunch of garbage. I'm not in the mood."

"The only garbage was you with the therapist. I can't wait until our next session. That's all I have to say," she said walking away.

Having read the book before, Tom opened it to the last page and read the last line. 'There is hope. There is always hope. I hope.' "I certainly hope so," he said in frustration.

A week later, Tom and Amy were seated in the therapist's office. The therapist looked at both of them and said, "What do you want from each other? Who would like to go first?"

Tom and Amy glanced at one another with Tom speaking up first. "I'm tired of the belittling. I want to see some real feelings for me. She's so self-absorbed with her girlfriends I feel like an outsider. I want the thoughtful, compassionate Amy that I married not the smart-aleck Amy who makes me half-sick sometimes ..."

"It's Amy's turn to express her feelings," said the therapist. "What do you want from Tom?"

Amy churned inside and then exploded, "I want to have a baby. I'm going to have a baby in one year *with* or *without him* ..."

"You're not leaving Tom," interjected the therapist, "much elbow room. You've painted a totally black and white picture ..."

Casting a hard cold look at Amy, Tom flared, "Isn't that what I said was the core of our problem when we were here last week? You denied that it was the problem ..."

"I'm not sure having a baby," said the therapist, "should be the basis for working out your problems. You both need to want a child and it needs to be based on love and affection for one another ..." Looking at his wristwatch, he said, "Well, it's that time again. Let me ask this. Do you two want to try to stick it out, separate or divorce?"

Tom and Amy eyed one another and in unison said, "Stick it out."

When the weekend approached, Tom and Amy drove to the real estate office for a meeting. The owner of the real estate company painted a doom and gloom picture to his employees about the current market. With that said, he said he understood if anyone wanted to leave the field and pursue other opportunities. Once he was done, all of the agents paired up in cars to take a look at the new houses listed by the agency. Tom and Amy went with an agent named Fernando who drove the three of them around. Fernando was quite jovial and loved to talk and sing while he drove. "*You know*," Fernando sang, "*love is better the second time around* ..." Tom and Amy sat back pondering his lyrics as they looked straight ahead. "Did you know I'm getting married in a month?"

"No, that's great," Tom said.

"I was married for twenty-three years. But do you know what?"

Amy and Tom gave him a puzzled look. "What?" Tom said.

"Love," he sang, *"is better the second time around* ..." Tom and Amy smiled, looking at one another. "How old do you think I am?"

Pondering, Tom said, "I'd say you're about forty."

"What do you think Amy?" asked Fernando.

"I would guess you're –"

"Be kind," he said.

"I agree with Tom. I'm thinking late thirties."

Chuckling, he said, "I have grandkids and I'll be fifty-two."

"Boy," said Tom, "that's hard to believe."

"But I feel twenty-five," he said and began singing again. *"Love is better the second time around* ..."

Tom and Amy glanced at one another with quizzical looks, but as the car turned the corner a blinding sun caused them to squint, wiping away the reflective moment.

Made in the USA
San Bernardino, CA
12 February 2017

SAM ON BACK DECK AT HOME, EAST PEORIA, IL